Thanks for Support!

Drug Revenge

By

Joseph J Landers

Joseph J Landers
6/21/2012

Acknowledgements

First of all, I would like to thank God, for without him, nothing would be possible.

A special thanks to my family for their patients and support. I would especially like to thank my wife who helped with phrasing and finishing of the first draft.

Also would like to thank our friend, Sharon Wouters, who tirelessly proofread and helped me better develop my characters.

Chapter 1

Stake outs have never been my favorite part of the job, but with a limited budget and an officer off with the flu, I'm designated to pull a long night of watching endless chatter as Gloria Curry converses, with every member of her church, while she stands in the church yard.

I'm Sam James, Chief of Police for Thorton, Alabama. I have the responsibility of keeping the budget for the police department while keeping the citizens of Thorton safe. That's why I'm parked at Bud's Bargain Bazaar in my newly acquired 1996 Mazda MPV, watching the congregation of Friendship Fellowship Church as they discuss the blessings they've received through the night's service.

As I said before, I have the boring task of watching Gloria Curry in hope that she'll lead us to her son, Rodney Curry, who was charged with drug possession with intent to distribute. He failed to appear in court for his hearing and as far as we can tell, dropped off the face of the earth, but we suspect Gloria has been in contact with him and knows where he's staying.

Drug traffic has gradually increased in Thorton over the last few months with a drastic increase in cocaine and methamphetamine use. Meth labs seem to pop up in any abandoned building around town and the area hospitals have reported an increase in overdoses, almost one daily.

Drug activity has become a major problem in Thorton and we have made it a major priority to remove these drug dealers from the streets. Rodney Curry is known to be one of the major players in the drug trade and must be taken off the street.

As I watched, Gloria Curry walked up to Reverend Marvin Cox, wrapped her arms around his neck and gave him a hug. He hugged her back and rubbed her left shoulder. She laughed as she stepped back and they began talking.

I looked at my watch which indicated they had been standing in the church yard and talking for thirty minutes. So, I took a deep breath, picked my thermos up from the passenger side floor and poured only a half a cup of coffee, didn't want to lose the opportunity to catch Rodney Curry because I had to stop and find a bathroom.

I took a sip, put my cup in the cup holder and watched as Gloria walked to her car. I cranked the van and slowly pulled away from the two Ford E350 Super Duty XLT vans I was using to hide between, and drove to the end of the parking lot to wait for Gloria.

Gloria got in her crystal white Lexus RX 350 and sat to wait for everyone else to leave. As the parking lot cleared, she cranked her car and slowly drove toward the exit. When she reached the street, she turned right and carefully drove toward her house.

I let her pass, then pulled in behind her and followed slowly.

She stopped at each stop sign and waited the appropriate amount of time, before proceeding. She stopped at the traffic lights when they were on yellow and drove the speed limit. I was thinking, she obeys the traffic laws better than I do, but does she respect the law when it pertains to her son.

I stayed at least three car lengths behind and slowed at each stop to avoid being seen if she looked in her rearview mirror. As we neared her house, I turned into Bee Boys Drug Store and parked next to the building. I angled my car so I was facing the front yard of Gloria Curry's house and turned the engine off.

She slowly pulled into her driveway and parked in front of her garage. After a few minutes, Gloria got out of her car and looked around as if she was looking for someone. Then she reached in the back seat, pulled a light brown purse out and draped it over her shoulder. After one last look, she quickly walked to her front door with her keys in her hand. She inserted the key, unlocked the door and rushed inside.

I watched, as she walked through the house closing all the shades to the windows when she passed and turning the lights on in every room. The last light turned on was up stairs, which I assume to be her bedroom.

I looked back at her car in the driveway and wondered way she hadn't parked it inside the garage. A Lexus RX 350 should always be parked inside a garage, unless there's not one available, but then she probably uses her garage as a storage building like most everyone else does.

As I watched, the lights slowly began to be turned off, from the ground floor leading up to the top, until all were turned off. I tensed as a Cadillac STS turned down the street and slowly drove toward Gloria's house. It seemed to slow a little when it reached her driveway, but slowly drove passed and turned into the next driveway. The Cadillac stopped outside the garage, waited until the garage door opened and then drove inside.

After the garage door closed, I turned my attention back to Gloria's house and watched for anything unusual. Three hours of staring at a dark house was all I could stand, so I cranked up and drove home.

Chapter 2

The next morning I assigned Richard to watch Gloria's house while I went to talk to some of the area drug abusers to see if they might be willing to talk.

I turned left on 10th Avenue and 23rd Street and pulled into the parking lot of Franks Tire and Lube. I sat and scanned some of the abandoned buildings across the street to see if anyone was awake.

The shadows of two figures standing in the doorway of what use to be Jill's Dry Cleaning darkened the sidewalk announcing their presence. It was known in the area to be a good place for homeless people to get shelter from the weather. So, I got out of my car and walked across the street.

I walked away from the two figures, crossed the street, then doubled back and approached them from the side of the building. I skirted along the edge of the building, staying out of their view, until I was within a few feet. Stepping out I said, "Hello ladies, I need to talk to you a second."

They jumped and began tossing things on the ground.

I looked at a wadded up paper bag lying in the corner that had recently been thrown down then turned to a dried up red head with pock marks along the side of her face from her Methamphetamine use and asked, "What's in the bag?"

"What bag?" she asked defiantly.

"The bag you just threw in the corner," I said.

"I didn't throw anything down," she said and glanced at the bag. "Why are you out here picking on us?"

"I need to ask you a few questions," I said. "If you give me the right answers, I might forget to look in that bag."

"What'd you want to know?" she asked suspiciously.

"What's your name?"

"Danielle Watts," she said incredulously. "Friends call me Dannie."

"Who's your friend?" I asked and looked at the other lady who looked to be in her mid-forties, with jet black hair and the same pock marks on her face.

"My name is Kim Black," the other girl said. "Friends call me Blackie."

"Alright Dannie," I said, as I turned back to the red head. "Do you know where Rodney Curry is hiding?"

"Who's Rodney Curry?" Dannie asked, as she looked at Kim.

Kim began to get agitated and started breathing fast. She looked across the street and asked, "Did anyone follow you?"

"I don't think so," I said, as I looked behind me and followed Kim's stare. "Why?"

"They'll kill you," Kim said and moved further back in the doorway.

"Who'll kill me?"

"The dealers," Kim said. "You mess with Rodney and they'll kill you."

"Do you know where he is?" I asked.

"They'll kill us too," Kim said. "I don't want to die," as she sat down on the concrete and covered her head.

"Are you trying to get us killed?" Dannie demanded.

"I'm trying to help save your life by getting him off the street."

"We can't talk out here," Dannie said, as she turned away. "We can't talk out in the open."

"I can arrest you and take you back to the station," I said. "We can talk in my office."

"I ain't done anything wrong," Dannie demanded.

"Yes, I want you to arrest us and take us to jail," Kim nervously announced, as she raised her head.

"What?" Dannie asked, as she looked at Kim. "I don't want to be arrested."

"If he don't take us with him, we'll be killed after he leaves," Kim said with concern in her voice. "They saw him talking to us and probably think we're his informants."

"What about our stuff?" Dannie asked and looked at the paper bag on the ground.

"I didn't think that was your bag," I said and smiled. "If that's your bag and it contains drugs, I'll have to destroy whatever's in the bag and charge you with possession."

"That's not our bag," Kim insisted, as she started shaking her head. "Let's just go with him and leave everything behind."

"We can drive around for a while and talk, then I'll drop you off somewhere else or I can take you to the station and lock you up for a few days," I said. "But if I drop you off, you won't need to come back in this neighborhood."

"Let us think about it while we talk," Kim said, as she stood up.

"I'll cuff you, to make it look real," I said, as I put handcuffs on Kim and then handcuffed Dannie. "Walk in front of me as we go to my car."

They walked side by side to my car. I walked behind them, with my hand on each girl's arm, so it appeared that I had them restrained. When we got to my car, I put them in the back seat and drove away.

After driving a couple of blocks and making sure I wasn't being followed, I pulled into Jed's Pawn Shop's parking lot and took the handcuffs off of Kim and Dannie.

"Do you want something to eat while we talk?" I asked.

"Can we eat while you drive?" Kim asked, as she nervously looked around.

"Sure, I'll go through a drive thru and get us some sandwiches," I said, as I pulled into Joe's Sandwich Shop's parking lot and got in line at the drive-thru.

I ordered three sandwiches with bacon, ham and cheese and an order of curly fries. After taking my sandwich and a bag of curly fries out and laying them on my seat, I passed the bag to the back. Then I slowly drove out of the parking lot and drove toward the police station.

"Alright, do you know where Rodney Curry is hiding?" I asked.

"I've heard he's been moving every few days to a different place," Kim said. "Some of his friends stay in the apartments across the street from where we were today but I hadn't seen him with them."

"That's why we didn't want to talk to you in the open," Dannie said and giggled as she wiped mayonnaise off the side of her mouth. "They were probably watching us from their apartment window."

"Have you ever bought drugs from him?"

"He don't sell drugs," Kim said. "He has people sell drugs for him."

"What drugs are you on?" I asked, as I looked at Kim.

"I take whatever I can get," she said defiantly. "I snorted cocaine for a while, but it got too expensive, so now I'm using smack when I can get it and sometimes I use a little crank."

"What about you Dannie," I said. "What are you taking?"

"We usually share the cost and do the same drugs," Dannie said. "I prefer crystal over crank cause I don't like needles."

"Have you tried to quit using?"

"I've quit twice," Dannie said triumphantly. "Once I started back because my mom died and I needed a way to deal with her death, and the other time a friend slipped some Ecstasy in my drink, which got me hooked again."

"It's hard to stop using when our friends are using," Kim said defensively.

"Maybe you need new friends," I said, as I looked in my rearview mirror.

"That's easy for you to say," Kim said. "You're not a user."

"Your right, I don't know what you're going through because I don't have an addiction to drugs, but I know it's hard to stop doing anything if you're around people that are using," I said. "It would be hard to stop smoking if you are around people that smoke and hard to stop drinking if you're around people that drink."

"What are you saying?" Kim asked.

"In order to stop your addictive behavior you need to avoid the temptation which means you need to stay away from people using drugs," I said.

"I still want to use drugs even when I'm alone," Kim mumbled, as she lowered her head.

"That's when you need to pray to God for strength to help you through the urge," I said.

"God won't listen to me," Kim said. "I haven't prayed in years."

"You might want to start by asking God for forgiveness," I said. "You could start going to church and reading God's word."

"I don't have a Bible."

"Would you read it if you had one?"

"He don't care about us," Dannie interrupted. "He's just trying to get us to help him find Rodney."

"You're wrong," I said. "I do care but unless you really want to stop taking drugs, I can't help you."

"Yes," Kim whispered.

"Yes, what?" I asked.

"I would read the Bible if I had one," Kim said with sudden assurance.

"Dannie, what about you?" I asked. "Would you read the Bible, if you had one?"

"I don't know," she said, as her voice faded away and she dropped her head.

"I tell you what I'm going to do," I said. "I have a friend that runs a home for recovering addicts and if you really want to stop using drugs I'll call her and see if you can stay there."

"What would we have to do?" Kim asked suspiciously.

"She requires everyone to go to church on Sunday and have devotions every Wednesday," I said. "She also requires a drug screen every week to make sure you're staying clean."

"That sounds like we'd be in jail," Dannie said.

"You'd have the freedom to go anywhere you want to go, but you'd be monitored to make sure you're not using," I said. "You'd also have people around to give you support."

"I'm willing to try," Kim said emphatically.

"You'd need to avoid anyone using drugs," I said.

"I can do that," Kim said with determination.

"What about you Dannie, are you willing to follow the rules in hopes of getting off drugs?" I asked.

"I'm not real comfortable in church, but I really do want to get off drugs" she said, as she looked at Km and continued, "I'll try."

"I thought you picked us up to help you find Rodney Curry," Kim said.

"I did, but maybe God sent me to help change your life," I said.

"Do you believe that?" Kim questioned.

"With all my heart," I said with confidence.

"What's the name of this place?" Dannie asked, as she looked out the window.

"Lighthouse Miracle Works," I said. "It's an old Victorian home that was converted into a house for women recovering from drug and alcohol addiction."

"What's your friend's name?" Dannie asked.

"Rose Franks," I said. "I go to church with her and the house is partially supported by the church."

"So, this don't cost anything," Dannie said.

"Rose has a bakery business in the basement of the house and everyone that lives at Lighthouse works at the bakery," I said. "She'll pay you for the work you do, but a small portion will be taken out of your check for your room and board."

"Is this her way to get cheap labor?" Dannie asked.

"Just talk to her," I said. "I think she pays a fair wage especially since you have a place to live."

I turned right on 6th Street and looked in my rearview mirror. No one was in sight, so I turned right on 9th and continued driving toward Rose's house.

"Do either of you know if Rodney has a girl friend?" I asked.

"I really don't know anything about him," Dannie said. "He stays behind the scenes and lets his goons sell the drugs."

"I don't know either," Kim said. "You might want to ask Daisy Mayfield."

"Daisy Mayfield," I said. "Where would I find her?"

"She hangs out on the street corner of 18th Street and 7th Avenue," Kim said. "She used to be really involved with Butch Frost when he sold drugs on that corner."

"What happened to him?" I asked.

"Disappeared," Kim responded matter-of-factly.

I slowed and pulled to the side of the street in front of a large white colonial house with a wrap- around porch. I turned the engine off and announced, "Here we are."

"This is it?" Dannie asked with a frown. "There's no sign."

"They don't like to advertise the house since some of the residents might be hiding from their husbands," I said. "When we walk in let me talk to Rose for a minute."

"No problem," Dannie said.

We got out of my car and walked to the door. They stood behind me as I knocked on the door. After a few seconds, a lady in her early twenties opened the door and asked, "Can I help you?"

"I need to speak to Rose for a minute," I said and smiled.

She looked at me, then looked behind me and tilted her head. "She's in the kitchen," she said and opened the door.

We walked inside and were immediately standing in the living room. Dannie and Kim sat on the couch and I walked in the kitchen. Rose was standing over a bowl of cake batter instructing one of the residents on the importance of blending the ingredients together.

"Sam, what are you doing here?" Rose asked when she realized I was standing at the door.

"I brought two ladies that need your help," I said. "They're interested in getting off drugs."

"Where did you find them?" she asked reluctantly.

"They were on the street," I said. "I told them about you and the Lighthouse and they said they would like to get off drugs."

"I'm a little concerned about you talking to them instead of them talking to you," she said. "If they don't really want to get off drugs, then I can't help them."

"Why don't you talk to them anyway and see what you think?" I asked with a pleading look on my face.

"Alright," she said looking at me with cautious optimism, "I'll talk to each one separately," and we walked into the living room.

When we entered the living room, Dannie and Kim stood up simultaneously. I stepped around Rose and said, “Rose, this is Danielle Watts and Kim Black.”

Rose looked at both ladies and smiled.

“I need to talk to each of you individually before I’ll know if I can help you,” she said. “Danielle follow me and I’ll talk to you first,” and she walked across the living room to an office in the back.

After they left, Kim looked at me and asked, “Did she say she might not help us?”

“She has to determine if you’re willing to stop taking drugs,” I said. “If you’re not determined to stop then you might bring drugs into her house and she’ll not allow that to happen.”

“I want to quit,” she said. “I’m tired of being a slave to drugs.”

“She’s ready to see you,” Danielle said, as she walked in the living room. “It’s the first door on your right.”

“What did she say,” Kim asked.

“She didn’t say anything, just ask a few questions,” Danielle said and sat down on the couch.

Kim slowly walked out of the living room.

“She has to be careful who she brings into this environment,” I said. “She’s trying to protect the other ladies.”

“I don’t know if I can do this,” Danielle admitted.

“You can with God’s help,” I said.

Danielle turned away and didn’t say anything.

After about five minutes, Rose and Kim walked in the room. Danielle stood up when they entered and waited as Kim moved beside her.

"What do you think?" I asked, as I stood up and stepped toward Rose.

"It may be a long shot, but I think with God's help these ladies can be drug free," Rose said as she opened a drawer, took out two compact Bibles and handed one to each lady. "This is probably one of your greatest weapons against drug abuse."

"How can this be a weapon?" Kim asked, as she took the Bible.

"God's word can give you comfort and strength during any time of weakness and believe me you'll have times when you doubt what you're doing," she said. "The devil will put doubt and conflict in front of you, but if you turn to God you'll make it through."

"What about our clothes?" Kim asked.

"Where do you live?" I asked.

"In the back of Jill's Dry Cleaning," Kim said and looked away. "The building was empty so we thought we would use it until someone else rented it."

"Do you want me to go by and get your clothes?" I asked.

"That would be great if you would," Dannie said. "There should be two large black garbage bags filled with clothes."

"They'll be fine until you get back with their clothes," Rose said with enthusiasm. "I have a storage room filled with clothes and I'm sure they'll find something they can wear."

"I don't want to impose," Kim said quietly. "My clothes will be fine."

"You'll learn fast that we're one big happy family and are willing to share when we have extra," Rose said. "But, I do understand that you want your own clothes."

"I'll bring your things to you this evening," I said and walked to the door.

"Thanks for your help," Kim said.

“Yeah, thanks for your help,” Dannie said.

“No problem, just let Rose help you break this habit,” I said and walked out the door.

Chapter 3

I went by the police station to change my clothes before going to find Daisy Mayfield. I keep a set of street clothes, which consist of a pair of blue jeans, plaid long sleeve shirt and an old pair of tennis shoes, in the closet for this purpose.

After changing clothes, I got the keys to the Mazda MPV out of my desk and walked into the squad room. The room seemed extremely quiet from lack of activity. Johnny Pew's desk was empty because he still had the flu. Richard Johnson, who was sitting at his desk had turned and was staring at me with a smile.

"Doing a little undercover work?" he asked.

"I need to talk to a prostitute and I didn't think she'd be very receptive with me in uniform." I said. "And it could get her killed."

"She'd run before you got out of the car."

"Yes, I know and it would be a wasted trip."

"Where are you going?"

"Corner of 7th Avenue and 18th Street."

"Do you want backup?"

"I think it would be good if you were within a few blocks of where I am," I said. "Why don't you setup on 16th Street and 5th Avenue and be ready in case I need you."

"Do you think it's dangerous?"

"I don't know, but I'd rather be prepared."

"I'll be ready in a minute," Richard said, as he got up. "I need to put my vest on," and he walked to the back.

"Are you about to go out?" Rachel Clark, our day shift dispatcher asked, as she walked in the room.

"Yes, I'm trying to get a lead of Rodney Curry and I talked to a couple ladies this morning that gave me the name of a person that might know where he is or at least might know someone who knows where he is staying."

"And this particular person works on the street."

"Of course," I said. "She has to get money to buy her drugs and that's the easiest and fastest way to make money."

"I wouldn't say that's the easiest way," Rachel said sarcastically. "It would have to be very degrading to sell your body."

"Maybe that's why most prostitutes use drugs."

"I think most people turn to prostitution because they use drugs," Rachel said. "I knew some people that started using drugs and before long they were selling themselves to support their habit."

"Are they on the street?"

"For all I know they could be dead," she said. "I haven't seen them in years."

"That's probably a good thing," I said. "At least they're not stealing from you."

"Drugs can cause people to do unspeakable things when they need a fix," Rachel said. "You remember Heather Welch's son threatened to kill her and burnt her house down because she refused to give him money for drugs."

"He doesn't remember what he did, because he was so strung out on drugs," I said. "Maybe the five years in prison he got will help him remember."

"I heard he was up for parole in a few weeks."

"He has two months before his parole hearing."

"So, how long has he been in prison?"

"About two years."

"He was sentenced five years and he's up for parole after only serving two years?" Rachel said. "That doesn't sound like a long time."

"It's not, but our prisons are full and he's really not a danger when he's not on drugs."

"Is he clean?"

"He's been in a recovery program in prison," I said. "The last I heard he's been clean for six months."

"Do you think he's safe to let out on the street?"

"I think he is as long as he stays off drugs," I said. "It's hard to tell what he'll do once he gets on the street."

"Will he be allowed to see his mom?"

"That will be up to her."

"That would be a hard decision to make," Rachel said and she walked to her office.

I watched Rachel leave, then raised my leg and strapped a small compact .22 revolver to my right calf. I stuck a Beretta M9 revolver in my waist band and covered it with my black leather jacket.

"Alright, I'm ready," Richard said as he walked in the room. He took his jacket off the back of his chair and slipped it on.

"I'll follow you to 16th and then drive the rest of the way," I said and walked to the door.

I opened the door and walked outside.

Richard followed and closed the door.

"Do you think she'll be on the street corner?" Richard asked, as we walked to our cars.

"I'm not sure, but I was told she's there almost every day," I said, as I opened my car door and got in.

Richard got in his patrol car and slowly drove out of the station parking lot.

I followed.

Chapter 4

Richard pulled into the parking lot of Mike's Convenient Store and parked beside an old pay phone booth. I pulled beside him and stopped.

"I'll call you on your cell phone if I need you," I said after I rolled my window down.

"That's fine," Richard said. "I'll keep the car running just in case I need to get there in a hurry."

"When all is clear I'll call to let you know," I said and rolled my window up.

I pulled out of the parking lot, turned right on 16th Street and slowly drove toward the corner of 18th Street and 7th Avenue.

When I reached the stop sign on 7th, I spotted two women standing on the street corner talking to a man wearing a pullover shirt with a hood over his head. I pulled to the side of the street and watched them as they talked.

He seemed to be animated with his conversation. Pointing his finger in the women's face and occasionally bumping up against them as he talked. He raised his right hand and slapped one of the women.

She turned away and stepped a couple of steps back.

The other woman stepped between them as the man moved forward.

I put the Mazda MPV in gear and drove to the corner where the women were standing. When I stopped, the man stopped talking and looked toward me. We stared at each other for several seconds before I got out of my van and walked toward the women.

"You might want to get back in your van," he said threateningly, as I stepped on the sidewalk.

I glanced at both women as they looked away. The one that had been slapped had blood slowly running out of the left side of her nose.

"You might want to leave these ladies alone," I said.

He looked around and laughed. "What ladies?" he asked. "I don't see anybody but these whores."

"You need to leave," I said.

"You need to make me," he demanded, as he got in my face.

"It's alright, we were just talking," one of the women said.

"I saw how he was talking and that's not how you talk to a woman," I said.

"You were warned to leave, but you wouldn't listen," he said with a smirk on his face. "Now I'm going to have to teach you a lesson," then I heard a click.

I glanced toward the sound and found the source of the click. He had a switch blade firmly grasped in his right hand, which he held beside his leg.

He brought his right hand toward my face as I stepped back and dodged to his left.

He looked puzzled when he didn't connect with the knife.

"I'll give you one more chance to leave," I said, as I repositioned my legs to be ready for another attack.

He brought the knife up to my face. "I'll slit your throat before I'm done," he said and swiped the blade toward my throat.

I moved to his right and hit him in the nose with the palm of my hand.

Blood instantly started running down his face.

He lunged toward me with the knife.

I hit his wrist with my right forearm and knocked the knife to the ground. Then I brought my elbow across the side of his face, which knocked him to the ground.

He jumped up and charged toward me.

I stepped aside and slammed his head into the side of the van.

His knees buckled when he hit and he fell backward, landing on the ground.

"He'll kill you!" one of the women screamed.

"Who is he?" I asked, as I watched him lying on the ground to make sure he didn't move.

"His name is Avery Moore," one of the women said. "He runs this part of town."

"What's your name?" I asked.

She looked at Avery, who was still unconscious and lying on the ground. "Ruby Marks," she said.

Ruby looked to be in her early twenties, but she was wearing enough makeup to disguise her age. Her hair was cut short and colored neon red. She was wearing a short maroon dress with matching shoes.

"How old are you?"

"I'm whatever age you want me to be," she said and smiled.

Her teeth were brown and beginning to rot from methamphetamine use.

"And what is your name," I asked as I looked at the other lady, who was in her mid-thirties with shoulder length brown hair. She was wearing a thick coat of makeup with blood running from the left side of her nose that was slowly eroding a trail beside her mouth. She had on a bright red long sleeve dress that draped across her thighs and a pair of black boots.

"Daisy Mayfield," she said, as she tried to wipe the blood off her face. "Who are you?"

"My name is Sam James," I said. "I'm the police chief for Thorton."

She moved back and looked across the street. "I can't talk to you," she said, as her eyes widened with fear. "If anybody sees me talking to the cops, they'll kill me."

"How will they know I'm a cop?" I asked, as I pointed at the clothes I was wearing. "As far as anyone can tell, I'm just a man looking to pick up a girl."

"You didn't fight like someone just looking for a girl," Ruby said. "You fought like someone with training."

"That don't mean I'm a cop."

"Why are you here," she asked.

"I'm looking for Rodney Curry."

"You really are trying to get us killed," Daisy said. "If I knew where he was hiding, I wouldn't tell you."

"Could you give me an idea of where he might be staying?"

"I wouldn't know."

"For goodness sakes, tell him where Rodney is staying," Ruby said. "After all, he did save you from a beating from Avery."

"He just postponed it," Daisy retorted. "He didn't stop anything."

Daisy raised one of her sleeves up which revealed a long line of track marks, and scratched her arm.

"What are you going to do with him?" Ruby asked, as she looked toward the man lying on the ground.

"I'm going to take him to jail for assaulting a police officer," I said.

"Then they'll know you're a cop," Daisy said and began to shake.

"I don't think he'll remember when this happened, let alone that you were here."

"But you can't guarantee that," she said with certainty.

"No, I can't guarantee what he'll remember but I can assure you that I'll do the best I can to protect you," I said with confidence.

Daisy and Ruby stood quietly looking at each other.

"We can't stand out here all day," I said. "I need to know are you going to help me or not."

"Alright, Rodney has been staying in the abandoned warehouse on Wilsonville Street," Daisy said.

"The old shirt factory?" I asked.

"No, the warehouse beside the factory," she said. "I think it's called the Millwood Fabric Warehouse."

"Yes, I think you're right," Ruby agreed.

"They used to store rolls of cloth for the factory to use when they were making shirts and dresses, but when the factory closed down the warehouse closed too," Daisy said.

"How does he get inside?" I asked. "That place has been boarded up for years and it has a security guard on duty at all times."

"His uncle, Matt Curry, guards during the day and he lets him inside to hide," Daisy said. "And the night shift guards don't walk through the building."

"Do you think he's there now?"

"I wouldn't know cause he moves around from place to place, but he mostly stays at the warehouse."

"Thanks for the information."

"Just leave," she said. "You're interfering with our business."

"You ladies need to leave this corner or I'll have to arrest you," I said. "My officer will be here soon to pick up this scum bag."

"After we helped you, you're going to arrest us?" Daisy asked indignantly.

"No, but I don't want anyone seeing you here when a cop car drives up," I said. "It could look like you're an informant and that could get you killed."

"We're leaving," Daisy said and started walking toward the buildings. "Come on, Ruby."

I watched as the ladies walked toward a building with its windows broken and the door pulled off its hinges. The sign above the entrance indicated it used to be Paul's Fine Jewelry, but now it was nothing more than a pile of rubble. I opened my phone, when I saw them disappear through the open doorway, and called Richard.

Within three minutes, I saw him turn down 18th street. He pulled in behind my van and got out.

"What's going on?" he asked.

"We need to load this guy up and take him to jail."

"It looks like he ran into the van," Richard said, as he pointed to a large bent in the side door.

"Yes, he was trying to teach me a lesson and he tripped," I said, as I grinned.

"It's bad when you lose your balance," Richard said and laughed.

"It was bad for him," I said, as I reached down and grabbed his arm.

"Alright buddy, let's get in the car," Richard said, as he grabbed his other arm and we lifted him on his feet.

We held him up for a few seconds, but his legs continued to buckle so we carried him to the car and carefully helped him into the back seat. As we loaded him, his head accidentally hit the door frame.

"Ouch, that will leave another bruise," Richard said and laughed. "He's going to feel like a truck ran over him when he wakes up."

"Maybe that will teach him to be careful who he threatens," I said.

"He'll probably just make sure he has backup before he threatens anyone," Richard said, as he made sure the prisoner was securely positioned in the back seat and closed the door.

"I have something to do before I go back to the station, so just lock him up and I'll book him when I get there," I said, as I reached in the van and got a towel from under the front seat. I picked the switchblade up with the towel, securely wrapped it around the knife and handed it to Richard. "Put this in a plastic bag when you get to the station and leave it on my desk."

"Was he going to use that to teach you a lesson?"

"He thought he was."

"It's against the law to carry one of those."

"It's also against the law to assault a police officer and he did both."

"He may get to spend some time in jail."

"I bet if we look, he already has a warrant or two for his arrest," I said. "If everything works out right, he might go to prison for a long time."

"Or at least a couple of years," Richard said, as he got in his car. "I'll see you later," and he drove away.

I looked back at the building, then got in my MPV and drove toward what used to be Jill's Dry Cleaning.

At Jill's Dry Cleaning I parked in the back, got out and walked to the door which was off the hinges and leaning against the door frame. I stepped inside and began looking for two large garbage bags filled with clothes.

The first room was empty, so I continued looking. After searching three more rooms, I found the one with the bags of clothes.

I carefully walked through the door, trying to avoid needles lying on the floor. The garbage bags were sitting side by side in the back of the room. Dodging debris as I approached, I saw what looked like a rolled up sleeping bag lying against the wall. When I got closer, I realized it was a person curled up in the fetal position, so I got my gun out of my waist band and walked over. I pushed against their shoulder with my foot and asked, "Are you alright?"

After no response, I pushed a little harder. She still didn't respond, so I bent down and checked for a pulse. The pulse was faint, but present, so I called 911. I rolled the body onto its back and realized it was the body of Kim Black. I looked to see if her chest was rising to make sure she was breathing and it was, so I looked for wounds.

It didn't take long for me to find the source of the problem. When I looked at her right arm, I saw a syringe sticking out of the vein, with blood beginning to ooze around the needle.

I didn't touch anything else, I just stood back to wait on the ambulance.

As I waited, she began to move around and moan. She moved her head from side to side.

"I thought you were at Lighthouse Miracle Works," I said.

She turned her head toward me, blinked her eyes, but didn't say anything. She moaned again then closed her eyes.

I turned as I heard the paramedics coming through the back door. "Alright move aside," they said, as they entered.

I stepped over to the bags of clothes.

"What happened here," one of the paramedics asked, as he opened up her blouse and began placing leads on her chest.

"I think she overdosed," I said.

"Sam, is that you?" One of the paramedics asked, as he started to work. "I didn't recognize you when we came in."

"Oh Chuck, I didn't recognize you either," I said. "I was trying to get out of the way."

"How did you end up here?" Chuck asked.

"I was getting clothes for someone that I took to Lighthouse Miracle this morning."

"Too bad you didn't take her with you," he said and shook his head.

"I did," I said. "I guess she didn't have the desire to quit."

"If you took her this morning, she couldn't have been craving the drugs that bad," he said. "She just didn't want to quit."

"I know," I said. "She seemed fine when I dropped her off this morning."

I watched as Chuck checked her vital signs, which indicated her heart rate was 69, her blood pressure was 79/49 and her oxygen saturation was 86%. The other paramedic put a heart monitor on her, placed a mask over her nose and mouth and started her oxygen at 100%. Chuck removed the needle from her arm, started an IV and began normal saline.

After they made sure she was stable, they loaded her on the stretcher and rolled her out of the building toward the ambulance. "We'll take her to Walker," Chuck said and they slid her inside the ambulance.

Chuck jumped in the back with Kim and the other paramedic got in the driver's side and quickly drove toward the hospital.

I decided not to get Danielle's clothes, even if I could determine which bag was hers. Instead, I got in my van and drove toward Roses.

Chapter 5

I walked up the steps of Lighthouse Miracle Works and knocked on the door. The door was opened by the same lady that had opened it earlier, but this time she just opened it wide and mumbled, "Come in."

When I walked in, I saw Danielle Watts sitting on the couch watching television.

"Where's my clothes?" she questions, when she noticed me standing at the door.

"I don't have them," I said. "When I went to get them, I found Kim lying on the floor with a needle sticking out of her arm."

"What has that got to do with my clothes?" she asked, with no concern in her voice.

"Did you not understand what I said?" I asked, as I stepped toward her. "Your best friend overdosed and might die."

Danielle looked at me for several seconds then smiled and said, "You really don't understand the life of a user," and she sat up and continued, "When you're on the street you don't have a best friend. You take from whoever you can to get by. I used Kim just like she used me. We shared drugs and food but I didn't care for her any more than she cared for me."

"So, it doesn't sadden you to hear that she overdosed?"

"Honestly, I could care less," she admitted. "I just need my clothes," she added assuredly.

"I didn't know which bag was yours and which one was hers so I decided to leave both."

"Then what will I wear?" she asked, as she stood up.

"I have some clothes you can wear," Rose said, as she walked in the room. Then she turned to me and asked, "What did you say about Kim?"

"She overdosed a little while ago," I said and looked at Danielle. "She's on her way to the hospital."

Danielle didn't react.

"Danielle, did you know she was gone?" Rose asked.

"I didn't know she went to shoot up," Danielle defensively said. "She said she needed to get some fresh air."

I looked at Rose and said, "I'm sorry. I thought bringing her here would encourage her to quit."

"Even if Kim recovers from the overdose, she won't be welcome back here until she can prove that she can stop using," Rose said. "I can't allow that influence in my house."

"I understand," I said.

"These ladies have enough temptation without having it in their face," Rose said and looked at Danielle.

"How are you doing Danielle?" I asked.

"I'm alright at the moment, but it's only been a few hours since I used," she said.

"The real challenge will be in a couple of days when the craving gets intense," Rose said. "But we're here to give you support and to help you through the cravings."

"I really want to stop using drugs," Danielle said with exuberance.

"Then pray for strength and guidance from God and you'll make it through," Rose said. "Everyone that lives at Lighthouse has been an addict at one time, but by the grace of God we all beat the habit."

"Even you Mrs. Rose," Danielle said.

"Yes, I was addicted to alcohol," she said. "But by the grace of God I've been sober twenty years."

"God can help us through all our tough times if we allow him to," I said.

"What kind of clothes do you have for me to wear?" Danielle asked, as she stepped up beside Rose.

"I have a storeroom filled with clothes, that people donate and you can choose whatever you want to wear," Rose said. "Karen show Danielle where the clothes are and let her pick something out."

The lady that opened the door, stood up and said, "Follow me," and started walking across the room.

Danielle followed.

"I'm just glad Kim didn't bring drugs into this house," Rose said.

"Me too," I said. "What do you think about Danielle?"

"It's going to be a rough couple of days, but if she can get through it, she'll be fine."

"When will she start working in the bakery?"

"I'll let her start next week after some of the withdrawal systems have subsided."

"Don't you think that could help her keep her mind off the drugs?"

"It might, but I don't want to train someone and have them leave."

"What will she do during her withdrawals?"

"We have a lot of activities to help keep her mind off her addiction, but the desire will still be on her mind no matter what she's doing," she said. "That's when she needs to read the Bible and ask God for strength."

"Will someone be with her during this time?"

"Yes, I will be some of the time and when I'm not, someone else will be beside her," she said. "We've done this before."

"I'm sorry, I didn't mean to imply that you didn't know what you were doing," I said. "I'm a little concerned because I brought her here."

"With all addictions, the major reason people don't recover is their lack of desire to quit and not enough support," she said. "We'll give her the support, but the desire has to come from her."

"This is going to be a rough week for her."

"Yes, it is and it's not going to be pleasant for us either."

"I'll pray that God gives you and her the strength and wisdom to make it through the week without failing."

"We'll need all the prayers we can get."

"Thanks for giving her some clothes," I said, as I stood up. "I didn't know which bag was hers and I wasn't sure what was in the bags."

"I think we're better off leaving everything behind, including her clothes."

"Call me if you need me," I said and opened the door.

"I'll let you know how things are going," she said and she gave me a hug.

"I'll see you at church," I said and walked out the door.

Chapter 6

"Your prisoner has been threatening to kill you," Richard said when I walked in the police station.

"So, he finely woke up," I said. "Did he remember what happened?"

"I'm not sure," Richard said. "All he has said is, he wants to kill you."

"Did you read him his rights?"

"I thought I'd leave that up to you."

"What did you do with the knife?"

"I put it in a plastic bag and laid it on your desk."

"I'll need to lock it up in the evidence room, but I think I'll talk to him first."

"He's been quiet for about ten minutes," Richard said. "I bet that will change when you go back there."

"Well, let's go meet this man and read him his rights," I said, as I started walking to the back.

"He might get violent."

I stopped and looked at Richard. "I'm going to stay outside the cell," I said. "I don't want to have to fight him again," then I took another step toward the back.

"Probably a good idea," Richard said, as I turned my back and walked toward the hall.

I walked down the hall and stopped outside the second cell. Avery Moore was lying on the bunk with his back toward me. He rolled over as I wiggled the door and sat up on the side of the bunk.

"You have the right to remain silent," I said.

"You don't have to read that junk to me!" he yelled, as he stood up. "I know my rights."

I continued reading him his rights, even though he protested. After I finished, I asked, "Do you want an attorney?"

"I don't need an attorney!" he screamed. "I didn't do anything wrong!"

"You attacked me with a switchblade."

"I was trying to protect my girls," he said. "I didn't know who you were. I thought you were trying to hurt them."

"By punching one of them in the face."

"I didn't hit anybody," he said. "Just ask my girls."

"Your girls ran as soon as we started fighting."

"See, they were afraid of you."

"You still attacked a police officer and tried to stab him," I said. "And you will be charged with assault with a deadly weapon."

"You will regret hitting me," he said and smiled.

"Be careful what you say," I said.

"What are you going to do about it?" he asked.

"I'll charge you with threatening a police officer," I said, then turned and walked into the squad room.

I went in my office and got the switchblade. I carried it to the evidence locker and locked it up.

"Did he want a lawyer?' Richard asked when I got back in the squad room.

"He said he didn't do anything wrong and didn't need a lawyer," I said.

"Did he know you were a police officer?"

"He does now, but he still don't think he did anything wrong," I said as I walked to the coffee pot. I poured a cup of coffee and asked, "Did you run his name through the system to see if he has any outstanding warrants?"

"There's no warrant out on him, but he is still on probation for carrying a concealed weapon," he said. "That switchblade should send him back to jail."

"I need to fill out the paperwork and get him sent to the county jail," I said and walked into my office.

After I finished with the paperwork, I faxed it to Sherry Howard, the County District Attorney, and put the original in my filing cabinet.

"Sam, I think you need to come out here a minute!" Richard yelled.

I closed the cabinet and walked into the squad room, to find a man wearing a canary yellow shirt, with a baby blue tie hanging from his neck, leaning against the counter. He straightened up when I walked into the room and stepped toward me.

"Can I help you with anything?" I asked.

"I understand you have my client locked in your jail."

"Who are you?"

"My name is Phillip Mays," he said and he handed me his card. "I represent Avery Moore and I understand he's locked in your jail."

"He didn't request any representation," I said. "How did you learn of him being here?"

"That's not relevant," he said. "The point is that I'm here to represent him and you have to make him accessible to me."

"I don't have to do anything," I said. "But, I will ask him if he would like to see you."

"I need to see him and you can't keep a prisoner from seeing his lawyer," he said, as he raised his right arm to reveal a sparking gold bracelet dangling from his wrist. "I'm not trying to challenge your authority, but it's the law."

"The law requires me to offer him a lawyer, but I can't make him take one," I said. "Let me tell him you're here, but I can't make him talk to you," and I walked to the back of the police station.

I saw Avery standing beside the door of his cell when I entered the room. "What's going on out there?" he asked as I got near him.

"A man claiming to be your lawyer is here."

"I don't have a lawyer, but my boss may have sent his over," he said. "What's his name?"

"Phillip Mays."

"I guess I can talk to him for a minute," he said hesitantly.

"You don't have to talk to him if you don't want too," I said.

"I know, but I don't want to make my boss mad."

"Alright, I'll send him back," I said and I walked back in the squad room.

"What did he say?" Phillip asked.

"He'll talk to you," I said. "Just go down that hall and he's in the second cell."

"Thanks," he said, as he started walking toward the hall. Within seconds he was nowhere to be seen.

"Who do you think sent this guy?" Richard asked.

"I don't know, but whoever did, probably has a lot of money," I said. "He's part of the law firm of Richardson, Mays and Dixon."

"That don't impress me," Richard said.

"They represent some of the biggest names in town and are known to win most of their cases," I said. "They have a long list of clientele, which includes the Mayor and city council members."

"That's not saying much," Richard said and laughed. "You know Thorton is a small town."

"I know, but they also represent some of the State Representatives and have worked with Jefferson County on some of their financial issues."

"Did they solve them?"

"No, they just gave them advice."

Phillip Mays walked back in the squad room and demanded, "I need bail for my client."

"Not tonight," I said. "I've sent the paperwork to the District Attorney's office and you can have your day in court tomorrow or the next day."

"With the jails being over capacity wouldn't it be better to circumvent the court system and set bail tonight," Phillip said.

"He broke his probation and tried to kill me, so I think he should stay in jail and I'm sure they can find a small cell for him to stay at the county jail."

"I don't see the benefit of us arguing, so I'll see you tomorrow in court," Phillip said and walked out the door.

"Are you not going to let me go?" Avery yelled from his cell.

"I'll let you go to the county jail tomorrow," I yelled.

"I want to see my lawyer!" Avery yelled.

"He'll see you tomorrow," I yelled. "Now go to sleep."

"It's not time to sleep."

"Then be quiet," I said. "I'd hate to add disturbing the peace to your charges."

"Very funny," he said then all went quiet.

"Do you think they'll set bail for him?" Richard asked.

"Probably, because the jails are overcrowded and they try to let as many people out on bail as possible."

"But he tried to kill you!"

"I know, but that's the system we have and until we can do something about the overcrowded prisons, we have to let people out," I said then added, "Even if they keep committing crimes."

"The system needs to be fixed," Richard said, as he looked toward the back. "This guy doesn't need to be let out on the street."

"I agree."

"What are we going to do tonight?"

"Since we have a prisoner, I want you to stay here until Franklin comes in and tell him to stay in the squad room unless he gets a call," I said. "If he leaves, he needs to lock the door."

"Do you think we might have trouble tonight?" Richard asked.

"I don't know, but I'd rather be safe," I said. "Tony Ford should come in tonight to work with Franklin."

"It's nice having another officer."

"I know," I said. "I'm thankful they increased our budget so we could hire another officer for the night shift."

"What do you think of Tony?"

"He seems a little brutish, but he'll learn the ropes and I think he'll make a fine officer."

"I like him too."

"It's been a long day," I said as I stretched to relieve some tension in my back. "I think I'm going home," and I walked to the door.

"See you tomorrow," Rachel said, as she stuck her head out her door.

"Good night," I said, as I walked out the door.

Chapter 7

When I pulled into my driveway, I saw Jenna, my beautiful wife, standing in the yard watching Seth, my son, and Jenny, my daughter, as they played on their bicycles. She turned, as I got out of my car and smiled.

"It's good to have you home this early for a change," she said and she gave me a hug.

"I hope to make this a habit," I said. "If we can keep crime down, I won't have to spend as much time at work."

"Lord knows, you put a lot of time in when you were trying to solve those murders," she said. "I pray no one else will be killed."

"Me too."

When Jenny saw me, she jumped off her bike, ran and jumped in my arms. Seth followed, but he stopped and gave me a hug.

"Dad, I'm so glad you're home," Jenny said and she kissed me on the cheek.

"This is great," Seth said. "You can see how good we can ride our bikes," and he ran back to his bicycle.

Jenny jumped down, got on her bike and followed Seth as he rode around the house. They screamed in delight, as they jumped hills and circled bushes at high speeds.

"They're really good with their bikes," I said. "I've missed a lot."

"Yes you have, but I know you have to work and sometimes that means long hours," Jenna said. "They're happy your home."

"I am too," I said.

"What do you want for supper?"

"I've been craving fried boloney sandwiches."

"You come home early and all you want is fried boloney sandwiches."

"Yes, that's what I want."

"I'll fix that after the kids have some time to play."

"That sounds good," I said. "I'd like to watch them for a while," and I sat down on the steps and watched as they circled the house.

Jenna sat beside me and leaned her head on my shoulder. "We truly are blessed," she said.

"God has blessed us greatly," I said.

"How did your day go?" she asked, with her head still leaning on my shoulder.

"Well, I took two ladies to Lighthouse Miracle Works earlier today," I said.

"That's great," she said. "Where did you find them?"

"I stopped to question them about Rodney Curry," I said. "They were afraid to talk to me on the street, so I picked them up and bought them something to eat."

"Did they tell your where Rodney is staying?"

"No, but they gave me a name of someone that might know," I said.

"How did they end up at Lighthouse Miracle Works?" she asked with a puzzled look on her face.

"Oh, they were afraid to go back to where they were staying and they said they wanted to stop using drugs, so I took them there," I said.

"You sound a little sad," she said, as she raised her head off my shoulder and looked at my face.

"One of them left and overdosed on drugs before I could get back with their clothes," I said.

"It must be hard to get off drugs."

"I'm not sure that she was ready to quit."

"It's impossible to stop anything, if you're not determined to stop, because the temptation will always be around."

"Especially if you hang around people that are doing what you are trying to quit," I said. "If you're trying to quit smoking, drinking or using drugs, you must disassociate yourself with people that are doing those activities."

"Sometimes, that means changing friends," Jenna said.

"Most of the time that means changing friends," I said.

"How is the girl that overdosed?"

"I don't know," I said. "She was alive when the ambulance took her to the hospital, but I haven't checked on her."

"It's not your job to keep up with every junkie in town anyway," she said. "You have more important things to do, like catching the drug dealers."

"If I could catch the drug dealers, the drugs would be harder to find and maybe more people would quit using drugs."

"They'd just go somewhere else to buy the drugs," she said. "But, they might move out of town to get closer to the dealers."

"That would be a good thing," I said. "Less junkies would mean less crime."

"They do go hand in hand," she said.

"Yes they do."

"Let's go eat," she said, as she got up and started walking up the steps. "I'll let you mayonnaise the bread."

"Thanks, I always want to do my part," I said and laughed. I got up and followed her to the door.

"Kids, it's time to put your bikes up and come in to eat," she said and opened the door.

"They should be in about the time we finish making the sandwiches," I said and we walked in the house.

Chapter 8

I turned down Wilsonville Street and slowed when I saw the sign for the Millwood Fabric Warehouse. I pulled into the driveway and stopped at the fence that was blocking the entrance to wait for the guard to approach my Ford Bronco. As I waited, I noticed a panther black metallic Cadillac Escalade EXT parked beside the guard shack.

A man in his early sixties opened the door to the guard shack and hobbled toward my Bronco, using a cane for balance. He stopped once, to catch his breath, before continuing to the side of my truck.

When he reached my truck, he leaned against the door frame and began gasping for air.

"Are you alright?" I asked.

He hesitated for a second then closed his eyes to concentrate on his breathing.

"Do you need me to call for help?"

"I'll be fine in a minute," he forced out between breaths. Then he laid his head on my door frame and slowed his breathing.

I watch, as he tried to regain control of his breathing and didn't ask another question.

When he caught his breath, he raised up and took a step back.

"Are you alright?" I asked.

"I'm fine," he said. "The black lung has about got the best of me."

"Did you use to work in the coal mines?"

"I worked under ground for 25 years and then it got too hard for me to breathe," he said. "And my knees began the hurt from the cool temperature in the mine, so I had to stop working underground."

"It must of paid good," I said, as I looked at Escalade.

"Oh, that was a gift from my nephew," he said. "He bought it for me last year for my birthday."

"Who is your nephew?"

He quickly turned his head toward me but didn't say anything. He glared at me for a few seconds then smiled and asked, "Who are you and why are you here?"

"My name is Sam James," I said. "I'm the Police Chief for Thorton."

"Why are you not wearing a uniform?"

"I don't wear a uniform every day," I said. "That's one of the perks of being Police Chief."

"How can I help you?"

"I'm looking for Matt Curry."

"Well, you've found him," he said. "How can I help you."

"Do you know where Rodney Curry is staying?"

"Why are you looking for him?"

"He didn't show up for his court date and I need to talk to him about setting another one."

"That's a lie," he said accusingly. "You want to arrest him."

"I have to take him to the station to get another court date set."

He looked at the ground and kicked a stone off the driveway. "I don't know where he's staying," he said, with his eyes still looking at the ground.

"I heard he was staying in the warehouse."

"If he was in the warehouse, I would know it and I just said I didn't know where he was."

"Yes, that's what you said."

"What is that supposed to mean?"

"It means you may not want to turn your nephew in."

"Are you saying I'm lying?"

"I don't think you're telling me everything you know."

"I'm telling you everything I'm going to."

"Does it not bother you that he's selling drugs?"

"I've never seen him sell drugs," he said. "As far as I know, he could be selling anything."

"I'm sure the Escalade helps you not worry about what he sells."

"I think you need to leave," he said, as he raised his cane. "I need to go back to the monitors and do my job," and he took a step toward the guard shack.

"If you see him, tell him I'm looking for him," I said. "He can come to the station anytime he wants to and we can talk."

He stopped and looked at me for a few seconds. "I'll tell him," he said and smiled. "I'm sure he'll jump on that opportunity."

"If I find out you've been hiding him, I'm going to arrest you for obstruction of justice."

"Do what you have to do," he said. "But, I have a great lawyer and believe me

I'll sue you and the town of Thorton."

"We have great lawyers also," I said, as I looked him in the eyes and added, "And a great District Attorney who's really good at sending people to jail."

He opened his mouth and started to say something but then he turned and walked toward the guard shack. He paused when he reached the door, looked in my direction then stepped inside and closed the door.

I cranked my truck, backed out of the driveway and drove toward the police station.

When I passed Jack's Gas Station, I saw a blue onyx pearl Lexus ES 350 slowly pull out behind me and quickly increase speed until they were within a few feet of my bumper. I slowed to allow the car to pass but he slowed and followed. I turned right on 5th Street and increased my speed. The Lexus turned right and increased its speed to stay on my bumper.

When I slowed, it slowed. When I increased my speed it increased its speed. I turned left on 6th Avenue and stopped when I saw a black Cadillac Escalade with dark tinted windows blocking the street.

As I watched, I saw the window in the backseat began to lower and flashes of light erupt through the open space. I floored the gas and swerved to my right, as two bullets struck the hood of my Bronco. My truck jumped over the curb and I charged through a row of shrubs, like a fullback charging through the offensive line trying to score a touchdown.

Surging through the front yard of a two tone brick house I rounded the corner and skidded as I straightened my Bronco on 8th Avenue and floored it. I looked in my rearview mirror to see if I had lost them, but I could still see the Lexus quickly approaching.

I slammed on my brakes and skidded onto 7th street, then turned left on 10th Avenue and slowed as I turned into Ginger's Recycling and parked behind two stacks of compressed automobiles.

After reaching in my glove compartment and pulling out my 357 magnum, I jumped out of my truck and ran to the side farthest from the road to wait.

Within seconds, the blue Lexus speed past, followed by the black Cadillac Escalade.

I turned around, when I heard a door slam in the direction of the office. Ginger Mitchell, the owner of Ginger's Recycling, was standing at the door with her hands on her hips.

"What are you doing?" she yelled.

"Trying to get away from those two cars that just passed," I yelled. "They were shooting at me."

"You stopped here when you had people shooting at you," she said, as she got a little closer. "If my daddy was still alive, he'll be very unhappy that you put his daughter in danger," and she laughed.

"Your daddy was very protective of you but you know as well as I do that you can take care of yourself."

"That's right and don't you ever forget it," she said, as she gave me a hug.

"How have you been doing?" I asked, as I looked around the stack of cars.

"I've been fine," she said, as she looked at the hood of my truck and rubbed the scratches with her fingers. “Why would someone be shooting at you?”

“I think I might have asked too many questions about Rodney Curry,” I said. “I must be making them uncomfortable.”

I ducked down as I got a glimpse of a blue car turn down the street and began driving toward us. Ginger ducked down beside me and we hid behind my truck. I heard the car slow but continue down the street.

After it past, I looked at Ginger, who was holding a Beretta M9 in her right hand. “Where did you get that?” I asked, pointing to the gun.

“It was in my waist band,” she said.

“I didn’t know you carried a gun.”

“I have to protect myself,” she said lightheartedly. “I don’t have a strong man around to fight off these bums that try to come on to me.”

“I guess that’s a good way to say no.”

“They listen to it.”

“Listen to that,” I said, as I heard the engine of the Lexus turn back down the street. It slowed, turned into the driveway and sat with its engine running.

“Do you want me to ask them what they want?” Ginger asked.

“That might be a good idea if you were in your office, but I think it would look suspicious with you approaching from this stack of cars,” I said. “Let’s give them a few minutes to either get out of their car or leave.”

They sat with their engine running for about a minute then they backed up and drove away.

“I thought we were going to have a gun fight like they do in the movies,” Ginger said, as she pretended to shot her gun. “I even had another clip in my back pocket.”

“If I’m ever in a gun fight, I hope you’re beside me,” I said and smiled.

“I think they gave up,” she said, as she peaked around the stack of cars.

“Maybe for now,” I said. “But, I bet they’ll come after me again if I keep looking for Rodney.”

“Are you going to quit looking for him?”

“No, but next time I’ll have backup,” I said, as I stood up and walked around my Bronco.

“I thought I was backup,” she said and raised her eyebrows.

“You were, but next time I’ll have a police officer following me and ready for a fight.”

“I’m as good a shot as any of your officers and I‘m ready for a fight.”

“I’m sure you are, but I’d be more comfortable with someone getting paid to back me up, in case they were injured,” I said. “It wouldn’t look good if a civilian got hurt trying to protect me.”

“If you change your mind, let me know because a good fight sounds like fun,” she said and laughed. “I’ve been training with my gun for years and I’d like a chance to test my skills.”

“I’ll keep that in mind,” I said and smiled.

“Anytime,” she said and patted her gun.

“Thanks for your help,” I said, as I got in my Bronco and drove away.

Chapter 9

"Tony got a little carried away with your prisoner last night," Richard said, when I walked in the door.

"What are you talking about?"

"He has a new black eye."

"What happened?"

"Apparently Avery started yelling last night and threatening everyone," Richard said. "Tony took exception with the threats and went into the holding cell."

"Tony needs to learn not to react to these prisoners. He could end up in a lot of trouble," I said, as I rubbed my forehead with my hand and squeezed my eyes shut for a second. "Who swung first?"

"I'm sure it was Avery, but Tony may have encouraged him."

"Avery needs to understand that not everyone is afraid of him," I said and leaned up against the counter.

"If he spends much time in prison, I'm sure he'll learn that quickly."

"I need to get him transferred to the county jail this morning," I said, as I looked across the squad room which was empty except for Richard. "I guess I need to call Marty and see if he'll send someone to pick up Avery."

"Yes, we're a little short- handed with Johnny off sick."

"I know and we can't take him this morning."

"By the way, aren't you a little late this morning," Richard said, as he looked at the clock.

"I went by the Millwood Fabric Warehouse to talk to Matt Curry and apparently I ruffled some feathers," I said. "Someone in a blue Lexus ES 350 started following me and someone else in a black Cadillac Escalade shot at my truck."

"Did you get hurt?"

"No, but my hood got hit with a couple of bullets," I said. "I need to call Janice Walker and have someone from the CSI Unit come gather some evidence from my truck."

"You said it was a blue Lexus that followed you," Richard said. "I could run the car's description through the data base and see if I can match it with anyone in town."

"Yes, do that and if you get a hit, I'll call Marty Brees and get some backup from the Sheriff's department," I said. "We can give them a visit and let them know I didn't appreciate being chased."

"I should know something within the hour," Richard said, as he got up and walked to the master computer.

I watched Richard as he began putting information into the computer, then I went into my office and walked to the window. I looked across the parking lot to see if the black Escalade or blue Lexus were parked outside the station. Neither vehicle was in sight so I closed the shade.

I sat down in my chair, leaned back and called Janice Walker to ask her to send one of the CSI agents to the station to gather evidence from my truck. After much discussion and reassuring her that I was alright, she told me that someone would be at the station within the hour.

After I finished talking with Janice, I closed my eyes and took a few deep, slow breathes to try to regain my composure and settle my nerves from the car chase that occurred earlier.

As the adrenalin began to subside and my mind started to clear, I regained my focus on catching Rodney Curry. Intimidation may influence a lot of people but it's not going to change the way I perform my investigations.

A knock on my door startled me and I sat up straight in my chair with my hand going immediately to my gun inside my desk drawer. I took a deep breath, left my hand on the gun and said, "Come in."

"I found two blue Lexus ES 350 cars listed in Thorton," Richard said as he walked through the door. "One is registered to Dale West and the other is registered to a company called Morton Enterprises."

"Did you run a check on Dale West?" I asked. "Does he have a criminal record?"

"Nothing popped up when I ran his name, but that doesn't prove anything," Richard said, as he sat down in front of my desk. "His driver's registration listed him as living at Fair Green Apartments over by the city lake."

"What about Morton Enterprises?" I asked. "I've never heard of that company."

"I've never heard of them either, but I have an address," Richard said. "They're located at 1258 Vinemont Street."

"I'd like to drive by those places and look at the cars," I said. "But, I want some backup just in case they start shooting at me again."

"I'll go with you," Richard said and stood up.

"I appreciate the offer, but I was thinking about two or three people going with me," I said. "Go put your vest on and I'll call Marty to see if he can go with us."

"Sounds good," Richard said and he walked out the door.

I picked the phone up and called Marty.

He answered on the third ring and said, "Marty speaking, how can I help you?"

"This is Sam," I said. "Do you have time to go with me to talk to a suspect this morning?"

"Well let's see, I have a meeting this afternoon, but my calendar is open until three o'clock, so I guess I can," he said. "Where do you want to meet?"

"Come to the station and we'll leave from here," I said. "I'm waiting on someone to look at my truck, so I can't leave until they get here."

"I'll see you there."

"By the way, can you send some officers to take our prisoner to the county jail," I said. "I wouldn't ask, but Johnny's still out with the flu and I'm short-handed."

"That's no problem," he said. "They can follow me when I come."

"Thanks," I said and put the phone down on the receiver.

I pulled my vest out of the bottom drawer of my desk, put it on and walked into the squad room. I walked to the coffee pot, poured a cup of coffee and sat down beside Richard's desk.

"Did you get backup?" Richard asked, as he sat down at his desk.

"Marty's on his way," I said and turned toward the door, when I heard it open.

I put my hand on my gun as I stood up, but relaxed when I saw Daniel Young, from the CSI unit, walk through the door.

"What happened to your Bronco?" Daniel asked after the door closed. "I was told you had a couple bullet holes in the hood, but the grill has leaves and twigs sticking out in every direction like you went through a forest."

"I drove through a hedge row as I was running from the people that were shooting at me," I said. "I also drove through someone's yard."

"I feel a complaint coming on," Daniel said and laughed. "And I'm only thinking about what the mayor's going to say."

"I know," I said. "He's not going to be happy because we'll have to fix their yard."

"Did the car that was following you go through the shrub?"

"Yes, he stuck on my bumper like glue."

"Then I'll make a mode of the bullet holes and get a sample of the shrub in case we need to compare it to something you find."

"How did a Lexus drive over a shrub hedge?" Richard asked.

"I cleared the way with my Bronco," I said.

"If he went through the shrub, there should be some evidence left on the car and we can prove it was involved in the chase," Daniel said.

Marty and two of his deputies walked into the station.

Marty looked at Daniel, then at me and asked, "What happened to your Bronco?"

I told him what had happened earlier with the car chase and the reason I had asked him to come to the station.

"How many people are going to look at the car?" Marty asked.

"I thought three would be enough, as long as we are vigilant and anticipate the potential for violence," I said.

"Good, then my officers can get the prisoner loaded up and take him to jail while we're looking for this car," Marty said. "Do you have the transfer paperwork?"

"I have it ready," I said and handed it to him.

He glanced at it then handed it to one of his deputies.

"Where is the prisoner?" Marty asked.

"He's in the second cell, but I'll get him," Richard said and held his hand out. "Can I have a set of your cuffs?"

"Sure," one of the deputies said, as he took his handcuffs off his belt and handed them to Richard.

"I'll be back in a minute," Richard said and he walked to the back.

"I appreciate y'all coming to get him," I said. "I don't have enough manpower to guard him and watch Thorton too."

"We're glad we could help," Marty said.

Avery Moore walked into the squad room with his hands behind his back. Richard followed, pushing occasionally to keep him walking.

"Wow!" Marty exclaimed. "What happened to him?"

"He tried to kill me," I said.

"That wasn't such a good idea, was it Avery," Marty said and laughed.

"Shut up!" Avery yelled. "He caught me off guard!"

Marty looked at me and laughed.

"Take him away," I said.

Each deputy grabbed him by an arm and led him to the door.

"James, you'd better watch your back!" Avery yelled.

"You'd better watch your mouth," one of the deputies said, as he pushed him against the door.

"THAT HURT!" he exclaimed.

"You're such a wimp," one of the deputies said, as he opened the door and pushed him outside.

We watched as they walked him to the patrol car and put him in the back seat. They sat for a few seconds before driving out of the parking lot.

"How many cars do you want to take?" Marty asked after they had left.

"I think we should all drive separately and maybe even approach from opposite directions."

"That sounds good," Marty said. "We can follow each other until we're almost there, then I'll circle around the block and approach from the opposite direction."

"After I finish gathering evidence from your truck, I can go to the area where you went through the shrub to see if I can find any evidence left by the Lexus," Daniel said. "Where were you when you hit the shrub?"

"On 6th Avenue between 3rd and 4th Street," I said.

"I'll let you know what I find," Daniel said and he walked out the door.

We followed Daniel outside.

"Where do you want to go?" Richard asked.

"Let's start at Morton Enterprises," I said and looked at Marty and said, "It's at 1258 Vinemont Street."

"Let's go," he said and we all walked to different cars.

I lead the way, as we turned left at the end of the parking lot and drove toward

Morton Enterprises.

Chapter 10

When we got within a block of Vinemont Street, Marty turned and circled around to enter from the other end of the street.

I turned down Vinemont Street and began looking for a sign identifying the location of Morton Enterprises. I slowed as I neared a group of buildings and stopped when I saw 1258 posted on the wall of a little charcoal brick building that was squeezed between a pawn shop and a tattoo parlor.

When Marty to get close I turned into the parking lot and parked in front of the pawn shop. Richard parked on my right side and Marty parked on my left.

We got out at the same time and met at the front of my car. I looked around the parking lot which was relatively empty. A Chevrolet Tahoe LT was parked by the door to the pawn shop and a Ford Mustang GT was parked by the door to the tattoo parlor, but no one was parked by the charcoal building.

"Richard, you stay out here and watch our backs," I said, as I looked around the parking lot.

"Do you think anyone's there?" Richard asked.

"We'll soon find out," I said, as I started walking toward the building.

"I'll call you if the Lexus pulls into the parking lot," Richard said, as he leaned against the red brick wall of the pawn shop.

I took one last look around the parking lot then Marty and I walked inside the door with Morton Enterprises written across the top in black letters.

As we entered, we were immediately met by a lady in her early twenties, wearing a dark green sleeveless dress and knee high black boots. As she approached she asked, "Can I help you gentlemen?"

"Could we speak to the owner of this company?" I asked.

She half smiled, brushed her long blond hair back with her hand and said, "He's not here today, but I might be able to help you."

"I'm looking for a blue Lexus ES 350," I said. "I believe your company owns one."

She looked puzzled and looked at Marty, then turned to me and said, "We don't sell cars here."

"I'm not looking to buy the car," I said.

"Who are you?" she asked, as she cupped her hands together.

"My name is Sam James, I'm the Police Chief of Thorton and this is Marty Brees, he's the Sheriff of Walker County," I said and smiled, trying to reduce the tension.

"I'm afraid I can't help you gentlemen," she said reluctantly. "I'm the secretary at Morton Enterprises and anything to do with the business must go through management."

"Is anyone else here?" I asked. "I thought I heard someone in the back."

"Yes, Ben Lowe, one of the associates is in the back," she said. "I'll go get him," and she hurriedly walked to the back.

"I didn't see the car in the parking lot," Marty said, after she left. "We might need to look around the back of the building to see if we can find the car."

I put my hand on my gun when a large man, who looked to be about 6'6" and must have weighed over three hundred pounds, walked in the room. He looked at Marty and then at me and smirked.

"So, you're cops," he said and smiled. "What do you boy's want?" as the smiled went away.

"Does your company own a blue Lexus ES 350?" I asked.

"We own a lot of cars," he said. "Why?"

"What exactly does your company do?" I asked.

"We are in the security business," he said and looked at Marty. "Our clients don't think the police can do their jobs, so they call us to protect them and their families."

"Do you ever shoot at people to protect your clients?" Marty asked.

"We do whatever it takes to protect our clients, as long as it's within the law," he said.

"You didn't answer my question," I said, as I looked him in the eyes. "Do you have a blue Lexus ES 350?"

"I said, we have a lot of cars," he said. "We own over fifty different cars and trucks that we use to keep our clients secure. One of them might be a blue Lexus."

"Do you think it might be in the back of your building?" I asked.

"We have a garage in the back and it might be parked back there," he said. "I wouldn't know."

"Can I look?" I asked.

"Do you have a warrant?" he asked.

"No, that's why I asked if I could look instead of barging around the building and looking."

"I don't think I can let you look without a warrant," he said, as he looked at the lady that had moved up beside him.

My phone started ringing. I opened it and said, "What?"

"The blue Lexus just pulled into the parking lot and is parked beside my car," Richard said with excitement.

"Thanks for the information," I said and closed my phone. "Thanks for your help."

"I didn't help you," the man retorted.

"You told me I would need a warrant to look for the car," I said, as I opened the door.

"Are you getting a warrant?" he asked.

"I might," I said, as I walked out the door and came face to face, with a man in his early twenties, wearing a black tee shirt with the sleeves rolled up to his shoulders and a pair of black denim jeans.

His eyes widened when he saw me, then he turned his head. He stepped to the side, to allow Marty to pass then he walked through the door.

I walked to the front of the blue Lexus, which had recently been washed and still had water dripping from the underside and looked at the grill. There were visible scratches in the paint, with two small dents in the center of the bumper.

"Look," Marty said and he pointed at the headlight on the driver's side of the car. "There's a piece of shrub caught."

I leaned close to the light, but didn't touch anything.

"This is the car that was following me," I said. "I bet there's paint on the shrubs that will match the paint on this car."

I looked at the door of the charcoal brick building, but it remained closed. Then I looked at Richard, who was still leaning against the wall of the pawn shop with his eyes focused on the parking lot and the surrounding buildings.

"This car needs to be impounded so we can compare the evidence before it disappears," Marty advised.

"I know, but it will take a while to get a warrant to search the car," I said, as I walked to the back of my car and opened the trunk.

I pulled a boot out and was walking toward the Lexus, when I heard someone yell, "Hey, what are you doing."

I turned around and saw the man that I had met at the door walking toward me with Ben Lowe following and Richard not far behind.

"I'm putting a boot on this car," I said, then turned and continued walking to the back tire of the car.

"Why are you putting a boot on my car?" he asked.

"This car was involved in a high speed chase this morning and I believe there may be several outstanding tickets that haven't been paid," I said.

"I have no tickets," he said, as he stepped closer.

"What about the high speed chase?" I asked.

"I can't talk about what I did this morning," he said. "I'm not allowed to discuss business with anyone other than the client."

"Maybe you'll be able to talk when we arrest you," I said, then went to the back of the car and put the boot on his back tire.

"My job was to follow you and report your every move," he said.

"Stop!" Ben yelled. "You need to be quiet."

"I didn't do anything wrong," the man said, as he looked at Ben. "I was as surprised as he was when they started shooting at us."

"What is your name?" I asked, as I stood up.

"Jeff Bland," he said.

"Who did you report to?"

"I don't know," he said. "They gave me a prepaid cell phone with their number programmed in it."

"Who gave you the phone?"

"It was sent by Crown Carrier Service."

"So, you don't know who hired you to follow me."

"No, I don't know."

"Killing people's not part of your business?" I asked and looked at Ben who was glaring at Jeff as he spoke.

"Lord no, our job is to watch and report our findings to the people that pay us," he said defensively. "Our company has different branches that perform different tasks, but my division works with surveillance only, not violence."

"Then, why did you follow me through the hedge row," I asked.

"I was running from the bullets just like you and you made a path for me to go through," he said trying to justify his actions. "See, one of them scrapped the top of my hood," and he pointed to a scratched area on the hood of his car.

I looked at the scratch and rubbed my finger along the edges. "Why did you follow me after I got away from the shooter?" I asked, as I straightened up and looked him in the eyes."

He looked at his car, took a deep breath and slowly let it out. "I was trying to catch you to tell you I had nothing to do with the shooting," he said. "But you disappeared, so I left."

"And, you have no idea who hired you to follow me."

"No, but we have one of our other divisions looking into it and they should have an answer pretty soon."

"Does the name Rodney Curry sound familiar to you?"

"Not to me, but I don't remember names very well."

"Ben, what about you?" I asked. "Do you know Rodney Curry?"

He smirked.

"Well, do you?" Jeff asked, as he stepped back from him.

"I've heard the name, but I don't know him," he said.

"He's one of the biggest drug dealers in Thorton and I had just asked his uncle about his whereabouts before I was chased and shot at," I said. "Ben, do you know who had Jeff follow me?"

"No, I don't," he said. "I wouldn't put any of our men in that kind of danger."

"Are you going to take my car?" Jeff asked.

"Not since you cooperated with my questions and told me you were the driver of the car that followed me this morning," I said, as I walked to the back of the car and removed the boot from the back tire. "Did you see the driver of the black Escalade?"

"I just saw flashes of light coming from the back window and then I heard something hit the hood of my car," he said. "I didn't stay around to look for anything else."

"I didn't either," I said. "If you think of anything, give me a call," and I gave him my card.

"I'll do it," he said, as he took my card and put it in his pocket.

I stiffened as I saw a black Chevrolet Suburban slowly drive past the parking lot and turn right at the end of the street.

"Wow, my heart jumped when I saw that truck," Jeff said and he wiped his shirt sleeve across his forehead. "It brought back memories of this morning."

"It ran chills up my spine when I saw it too," I said. "I'll probably jump every time I see a black truck."

"Do you have any more questions?" Ben asked sarcastically. "We do have a business to run and I need to get back to work."

"That's it for now," I said and I started walking to my car.

"Then let's get back to work," Ben said and he started walking toward the door to Morton Enterprises.

Jeff followed without saying anything.

When Ben got to the door, he held it open for Jeff to walk through then he followed him inside.

"I'll follow you back to the station," Marty said, as he got in his car.

"Thanks, I'd appreciate it," I said, as I opened my door.

I got in my car and drove to the edge of the parking lot. Then I turned left and drove toward the police station with Marty and Richard following close behind.

Chapter 11

When I pulled into the parking lot, I saw Johnny Pew standing in front of my Bronco talking to Daniel. I pulled into the space beside them, rolled my window down and said, "I thought you were sick with the flu."

"The doctor said I could come back to work tomorrow," Johnny said. "I'm not contagious anymore."

"How do you feel?" I asked, as I got out of the car.

"I don't have any energy, but I think that will change if I start moving around some."

"Are you coming to work tomorrow?"

"I was planning on it, but I could start today if you need me."

"Tomorrow will be fine," I said. "You need some time for your nose to lose some of its redness."

"It's still running a lot, but I'm not having to blow it every five minutes like I was yesterday," Johnny said and rubbed the tip of his nose without thinking.

"It will be great having you back at work as long as you feel like being here," I said.

"What happened to your truck?" Johnny asked, as he pointed to the scratches on the hood.

"He got too nosey and someone didn't like it," Richard said and laughed, as he walked up.

"Daniel, do you know what kind of bullet was used?" I asked.

“It looks like a 9mm, but I won’t know until I run some tests,” he said. “I got a great mold of the bullet hole I found beside your windshield, so it shouldn’t be hard to match the bullet.”

“There’s a hole beside my windshield?” I asked, as I moved closer to my truck and peered at the hole. “I know it was an automatic weapon that fired the bullets, but I didn‘t realized they hit my truck more than twice.”

“Did you find the blue Lexus?” Daniel asked.

“Yes, we found it and according to the man that drove the car, he was as surprised as I was when the bullets erupted from the Escalade.”

“They used him as their eyes while they setup the ambush,” Richard said.

“I don’t know about you guys, but I got the feeling that Ben knew more than he was willing to tell us,” I said, as I looked at Marty and Richard.

“I got the same feeling,” Marty said. “And the way he reacted when you asked him if he knew Rodney Curry was very suspicious.”

“Yeah, I agree,” Richard said. “He knew more than he was saying,”

“Well guys, I need to go back to the office,” Daniel said. “If you need me again, just call,” then he got in his car and drove out of the parking lot.

“I need to get back home myself,” Johnny said. “I just went to get some Gatorade and thought I’d stop by to let you know I’d be back to work tomorrow.”

“Great, I’ll see you tomorrow,” I said.

Johnny looked at my truck one more time then he walked to his car and drove away.

I looked at the grill, which still had twigs and leafs imbedded in the radiator.

Then I rubbed my fingers across the scratched paint along my bumper and said, "I guess I need to call my insurance company."

"You may not be able to get it fixed now, but the insurance company will need to file a claim so they'll pay for getting it repaired when the investigation is over," Marty said. "Right now, I think you should leave it like it is."

"Yes, you're probably right," I said. "I'll call my insurance agent and get someone out today to file a claim."

"Listen guys, I need to get back to my office," Marty said, as he walked to his car. "If you need me, don't hesitate to call," then he got in his car and drove out of the parking lot.

We watched Marty leave then we walked into the police station.

I walked in my office, called my insurance agent and arranged for him to send an appraiser to look at my truck. Then I walked to the dispatcher's office and told Rachel to expect someone from my insurance company to come by and look at my truck.

"Are they going to tow it or just look at the damage?" Rachel asked.

"They're just going to look at it for now," I said. "I don't want it fixed in case we need to use it as evidence."

"Alright, I'll be expecting them."

"Just let them do what they need to do, but don't let my truck leave this parking lot."

"Does Richard know they're coming to look at your truck?"

"I told him I was going to call them, but I didn't tell him they were coming by this evening."

“I’ll let him know.”

“Great, because I’m going home,” I said and I walked out the door.

Chapter 12

It was a beautiful Sunday morning, with the sun shining bright, without a cloud in the sky. I got up and ran a mile to get my blood to flowing and to make sure no one was watching the house. When I got back from my run, everyone had gotten up. And they were excited about the prospect of getting to church early for a change.

Jenna was dressed in a light blue sleeveless dress that lay gently below her knees with a matching jacket. She also wore blue shoes with two inch heels that matched almost everything she owned.

Jenny was wearing a bright pink dress with white roses. Seth had his standard black dress pants and dark blue shirt that he wore almost every Sunday.

I was dressed in a pair of black dress pants, light blue shirt with a light blue and black checked tie. After slipping on my black dress coat I was ready to walk out the door.

I opened the door, looked around the street and said, "Alright, let's go," and we walked out the door.

When I pulled into the church parking lot, it was empty, so I backed into a space beside the road in case I needed to leave in a hurry.

"Are you expecting to have to leave," Jenna asked.

"No, but you never know and I don't want to be trapped," I said.

"You sure parked far enough away from the church," she said. "I guess a good walk won't hurt us though."

"That's the benefit of getting here early, I get to choose where I park," I said and I opened the door.

The kids got out of the car and ran to the front door of the church.

I opened the door for Jenna to get out and we began walking toward the church.

"The door's locked," Seth yelled, as he wiggled the knob.

"We may be the first ones here," I said. "Give me a minute and I'll open the door."

Seth stepped back from the door and sat down on the top step.

Jenny twirled around on the porch, then skipped down the steps and jumped back up, one step at a time.

When I reached the front door, I opened it and started turning the lights on. Then I unlocked the back door and sat down to wait for everyone to arrive.

By ten thirty, the church was almost full and singing had begun. We sang, Jesus Is Best of All, I Know Who Holds Tomorrow, The Lord Has Been So Good To Me and several more songs before preaching began.

At eleven o'clock, Elder Andrew Moss slowly started walking to the podium. He was wearing a pair of navy dress pants, bright yellow shirt, with a pull over tan cashmere sweater and a yellow and tan tie.

As he got behind the podium, he smiled and looked at the congregation. "It's good to see everyone here, especially with the beautiful weather and the temptations the devil puts in our way," he said. "I know a lot of you have had thoughts of staying home and enjoying the sunshine instead of coming to church, but you withstood the temptation and did what God would have wanted you to do."

"Amen," one of the Deacons said.

"It would be a great day to play golf or go fishing, but it's an even better day to worship God and give thanks for his grace and mercy he lovingly gives us every day," Elder Moss said.

I jumped as my phone started vibrating and took it out of my pocket. After looking to see who was calling, I opened it up and leaned over to Jenna and said, "I need to take this call," then I got up and walked out of the church.

"What going on?" I asked when I got outside.

"There's been an explosion at the Millwood Fabric Warehouse," Johnny said. "It looks like a Meth lab exploded."

"Are you at the warehouse?" I asked.

"Yes, I went there to help control traffic, but when the fire department got the fire under control, they discovered a mini drug factory inside," he said. "They said, it was more than a Meth lab."

"Did they find a body in the warehouse?" I asked.

"Yes, they found a charred body beside one of the tables."

"Have you been inside?"

"No, the fumes are too bad for me to enter the building without a mask."

"Has the County Hazardous Materials Unit been notified?"

"Yes, I called them," he said. "They're supposed to be bringing us some masks to use when we search the building."

"I'll be there as soon as I can, but I need to take my family home after church."

"Maybe we'll have some masks to wear when you get here."

"I'll see you then," I said and closed my phone.

I eased back into the church and sat down beside Jenna.

"What's going on?" she whispered, as she leaned close to my ear.

"Fire at Millwood Fabric Warehouse."

"Why did they call you?"

"They found a Meth lab inside and probably more drugs."

"When are you going?"

"After I take you and the kids home."

I looked up, as Elder Moss said, "If anyone missed this message and would like a CD, we'll have copies available in the back," then he looked at me and smiled.

I could feel my face redden, but I didn't look away.

After church was dismissed, I walked outside to wait for Jenna and the kids.

"Hey Sam, what was that about?" Rose Franks asked, as she stepped beside me.

"What are you talking about?" I asked.

"You normally don't get up and leave church during the service, so something must have happened," she said. "Can I help you with anything?"

"Alright, I think we're ready to leave," Jenna said, as she walked up.

"Why are you leaving so soon?" Rose asked. "The kids haven't had time to play with the other kids."

"Sam has some police business he needs to attend to," Jenna said.

"Then let him go and I'll take you home," Rose said. "I have plenty of room in my car for you and the kids."

"Are you sure?" Jenna asked.

"Of course, I'm sure," she said.

"You could get to the fire quicker, if you didn't have to take us home," Jenna said, as she looked at me. "But, do you have clothes to change into?"

"I have jeans and a tee shirt in the trunk of the car," I said. "Are you O.K. with going with Rose?"

"That's fine," she said. "That way I won't feel so rushed."

"I love you," I said as I kissed her. Then I turned to Rose and said, "Thanks for your help," and I ran to my car.

I got the plastic bag with my clothes out of the trunk of my car and ran inside the church to change.

After I had changed, I stuffed my suit into the bag and ran to my car. I got in and slowly drove out of the church parking lot toward Wilsonville Street.

Chapter 13

As I neared the Millwood Fabric Warehouse, I closed my windows and turned off the vents that provided air from outside the car. Dark black smoke was billowing out of the roof and the strong fumes, from the drug factory, was mixing in the air making my eyes burn with the toxins.

I turned onto Wilsonville Street, stopping immediately when a hazardous materials van passed me and stopped at the entrance of Millwood Fabric Warehouse, blocking the driveway.

I pulled to the side of the street and stopped.

Johnny ran to my car, with a handkerchief covering his nose and mouth. He opened the door and jumped inside. "If you get out, you'll need to protect yourself from the fumes," he said. "The smoke is really toxic."

"We need to get a mask from the haz mat unit," I said, as I pulled a handkerchief out of my back pocket. "Let's run to their van and see if they have one we can use," then I covered my nose and jumped out of the car.

I ran to the van, with Johnny following close behind.

"You guys need to leave," the man at the van said.

"I'm Sam James, the Police Chief and he is Officer Johnny Pew," I said. "We need a mask, so we can investigate this crime."

"I'm Chuck Jones, with the haz mat unit," he said, as he handed me and Johnny a mask. "You need to put coveralls on also because we don't know what type of chemicals are in the building and this stuff could be fatal."

"I need to go see what is inside," I said, as I put the mask on and took a deep breath of clean air.

"Let's go," Johnny said, as he put his mask on.

We both put on our orange coveralls and each put on chemo quality gloves to prevent absorption through the skin. Then we walked out of the haz mat van, past the guard shack into the fenced in area and stood beside the fire truck. I watched as the last of the water was sprayed on the roof to make sure the fire was completely out. The firemen started the task of hacking into the walls to make sure no hot spots remained.

"Is it safe to go inside?" I asked one of the firemen.

"It is as long as you keep your mask on," he said. "The fires out, but the fumes are deadly."

"Thanks," I said and we walked toward the large open area that used to be the door.

I walked through the opening into a large room with broken glass scattered everywhere. Partly burned tables were positioned every ten feet along the walls. Three tables, almost completely burnt, had been knocked over in the center of the room. The shattered remains of another piled in the middle. Burners and cooking pots had been tossed about by the force of the water from the fire hose.

"I bet the fire started here," I said, as I pointed to the area that was burnt the worst.

"It looks like the fire was focused on these tables, but the source was this table blown to pieces," Johnny said.

The flames had blackened the rafters and caused wide gaping holes in the roof, which let the sun penetrate into the building and illuminate a somewhat dreary room.

When I looked along the wall, I saw containers of drain cleaner and old batteries stacked in piles. I moved around a table and looked in one of the pots, which still had residue left from the cooking process.

"Do you know if anybody else was killed?" I asked, as I looked at Johnny. "It looks like someone was cooking when the fire started."

"I think the fire department is still looking for more bodies," Johnny said.

"We'll look while we're here," I said and began looking through some of the burnt rubble.

I walked to a table that had been blown away from the rest and looked over its side. "I've found the charred body you told me about," I said, as I looked at a badly burned and mangled body lying behind the table.

"Do you recognize the victim?" Johnny asked.

The flesh was burnt almost completely off the victim's face, with its arms crumpled underneath and one leg sticking out at a 90 degree angle.

"I can't even tell if it's a male or female," I said, as I looked at the body.

I took my phone out of my pocket and called Janice Walker, of the CSI Unit.

"Janice speaking," she said when she answered.

"I need you to come to the old Millwood Fabric Warehouse," I said.

"I'm here," she said. "Johnny called this morning and told us we would be needed at the fire."

"I'm sorry, I didn't know he had called you," I said, as I looked at Johnny. "But anyway, I'm standing beside the burnt body the fire department found."

"I'll be there as soon as I get my mask and coveralls on," she said and my phone went dead.

"Sorry, but I forgot to tell you I had called the CSI Unit," Johnny said.

"When did you call them?"

"I called them as soon as the fire department told me they found a body inside."

"Well, I'm glad you did, because the sooner they can start looking at the evidence, the sooner we can leave," I said and turned as Janice and two other CSI agents walked into the room wearing their trademark bright yellow coveralls.

"Where's the body?" Janice asked, as she got close.

"Behind the table," I said and point toward the charred remains lying on the floor.

"Victor, start photographing the scene and then we'll began gathering evidence," Janice said.

"We'll look for more victims, while y'all work here," I said and we walked to an area where boxes and metal buckets were stacked beside a three foot counter. I removed the lid of one of them. It was filled with small purple and white pills. I picked up a piece of paper that was lying on the pills and read, abortifacient in red writing.

"They were selling an abortion pill?" I asked to no one in particular.

"They wouldn't need a pill if they looked beyond the moment," Johnny said.

"They probably have these for the prostitutes in the area," I said. "They want to keep them working without kids getting in the way."

I moved to another stack of boxes and opened the one on top. It contained a mixture of yellow, black and red tablets.

"All I've seen so far is a bunch of pills," I said and I moved to another stack.

This time, the stack was wrapped in brown paper and tied together with twine. I opened the top, which revealed a white powdery substance that spilled out on the floor. "I may have found some cocaine this time," I said.

"Here are some bales of marijuana behind these boxes," Johnny said, as he pointed at a stack of boxes behind one of the tables."

We moved on around the partition and came upon a pile of broken bottles and empty drain cleaner containers. As we started to walk past, I saw a hand sticking out from under the pile of trash and stopped.

"Look at this," I said, as I pointed at the hand.

"We have another victim," Johnny said. "But I don't think this one was killed today."

"No, this person's been dead for a while," I said and I looked at Johnny. "You did, by chance, happen to call Diane Lynch."

"Yes, I called her right after I talked Janice," Johnny said. "She should be here any minute."

"Great," I said. "Let me go tell Janice about this victim," and I started walking toward her.

As I rounded the partition, I saw Diane Lynch, Walker County's Medical Examiner, wearing a mask and dressed in an orange pair of coveralls, standing beside Janice. They were looking at the remains as Victor finished taking photographs.

"We've found another victim," I said, as they looked at me. "But, I don't think this one was killed today."

"Was it burnt?" Janice asked.

"I don't think so, but all I've seen is a hand sticking out of a pile of trash," I said and stepped beside Diane. "I was about to call you."

"Why, didn't you think I was coming?" she asked.

"I just wanted to let you know that we had found two bodies," I said. "Are you in your van?"

"No, I was visiting family close by, so I'm not in my van, but I've call Samantha and asked her to go by my office to get it," Diane said. "She should be here in a few minutes."

"Victor, start photographing the other victim and we'll start gathering evidence from this area," Janice said and she turned to Daniel Young. "Try to get samples from the victim's clothing and burnt wood particles."

"No problem," Daniel said, as he eased toward the body.

"I'll show you where the other body is located," I said, as I walked away.

"Great," Victor said and he followed.

When we got near the body, Johnny stepped aside to allow Victor room to get past.

"Where's the body?" Victor asked.

"Under that pile of trash," I said.

"Oh, I see the victim's hand now," Victor said, as he stepped back and began taking pictures.

"We'll keep looking," I said and we walked away.

We finished searching behind the partition without finding another victim, so we moved to another part of the warehouse which contains offices.

I opened the door to the first office but it was empty. Not even a desk. So, I moved to the next room, which contained a row of filing cabinets and a large mahogany desk positioned in the center of the room.

Walking to the filing cabinet I opened the top drawer, but it was empty. So I moved down and continued opening drawers, without finding anything until I reached the bottom which was filled with loose papers stacked neatly in the back of the drawer.

I pulled a few sheets of paper out and thumbed through each one. It was documents from years past when the warehouse was functioning as a fabric warehouse, so I put the papers back inside and closed the drawer.

The desk was the next place I thought I would look so I moved over to it and opened the top drawer. A Romanian AK pistol, with two boxes of shells, was lying on top of a brown leather ledger. I took out the gun and laid it on top of the desk. Then took the shells out and placed them beside the gun.

After removing the ledger, I carefully opened it up and started reading. The first page was divided into three sections. The first section contained dates, the second had two digit numbers and the third had an amount of money.

I turned to the second page, which was setup in the same style.

"I think this is a record of drug sales," I said, as I looked at Johnny. "I understand the date and the money section, but I'm not sure about the other section."

"It must be some form of code," Johnny said.

I put the ledger by the gun and continued looking through the drawer, which contained a box of envelopes, a roll of stamps and two boxes of ball point pens. I closed the top drawer and opened the bottom.

"Wow," I exclaimed. "This one is full of money."

"Let me see," Johnny said eagerly, as he stepped beside me and looked over my shoulder.

"There must be over a hundred thousand dollars in here," I said, as I pulled a bundle of bills out and sat them on top of the desk.

"That would go a long way in the police department," Johnny said and laughed. "Too bad we can't keep it."

"It would be helpful with the budget, but right now it's evidence," I said.

"Have you guys found anything else," Daniel asked, as he walked in the room.

"We found everything on top of this desk in the top drawer and the bottom drawer is full of money," I said.

"No more bodies?"

"Not yet, but we're still looking."

"I'll collect this evidence and dust the room for prints," Daniel said and opened his evidence box.

He put the gun and shells in a plastic bag, then put it in his plastic evidence box. He dusted the ledger for prints, then put it in a large plastic bag and put it in the plastic box. Then he drug the plastic box around to the bottom drawer and carefully loaded the money in the box, making sure not to drop any.

"Now, I'll dust the room for prints," he said.

"While you're doing that, we'll look in the next room," I said and we walked out the door.

"There must be something valuable in this room," Johnny said, as he pointed to three large locks attached to the door.

"We need to see what's inside," I said and looked at Johnny.

"No problem," he said, as he grabbed a steal rod, that was leaning against the wall and snapped the top lock open with one quick pull. He opened the second and third lock, with the same ease and the door was hanging loosely by the hinges.

I opened the door, turned the light on and was standing in front of a mountain of cold medicine, which contained ephedrine, stacked to the ceiling. To my left were several cases of rock salt and to my right cases of ammonia, but the majority of the room was filled with cold medicine.

"This must be the most valuable ingredient in methamphetamine," I said.

"I've heard it was, but I thought the government controlled the sale of these kinds of cold medicine," Johnny said.

"They do, but that only works on honest people," I said. "People willing to break the law can always find a way around it."

"That's true," Johnny said. "They probably stole this from some warehouse."

"Might have, but it's ours now," I said. "I want you to call Richard and get him to bring a trailer here to gather the drug making material, so we can destroy it."

"What about the drugs?" Johnny asked.

"I don't think we'll have enough room in the trailer for everything, so I might get Marty to bring a truck to help move this stuff out of here."

"They'll have a larger place to store the drugs."

"We're not going to have room to store the ammonia and rock salt either," I said. "I guess we need to send everything to the county storage facility."

Johnny took his phone out of his pocket and walked away while he talked to Richard. I call Marty and made arrangements for him and a couple of his men to help transport our findings to his storage building.

"Richard will be here as soon as he can get hooked up to the trailer," Johnny said, as he approached.

"Marty's renting a truck also and he's bringing two of his deputies to help load everything," I said. "I guess the money will go to the CSI Lab."

"They might be able to trace where the money came from," Johnny said.

"Maybe," I said. "Let's check on Janice and see if they've found anything," and we walked toward the last victim's body.

We walked around the partition in time to see Diane and Samantha rolling the victim's body away on her stretcher.

"Did you find another body?" Janice asked when she saw me.

"No, but Daniel is gathering evidence from an office around the corner," I said. "We also found a drawer full of money."

"Great, maybe we can trace the money," she said.

"Yes, maybe so," I said. "Did you find any evidence here?"

"We gathered a lot of evidence, but we won't know if it will help us, until we run some test," she said.

"I'll leave you to your work," I said. "I need to meet Marty at the front of the warehouse," and I walked around the corner.

Chapter 14

Ken Wilson was standing at one of the charred tables, dropping pieces of burnt material into small vials and mixing it with chemicals in an attempt at finding the cause of the fire.

"I hope we didn't interfere with your investigation by removing the bodies," I said.

"I told Diane it would be alright, as long as she and Janice left some of the burnt material," he said. "I'm confident the fire started at the table where the body was found, but I haven't determined what flammable material was used to start it."

"Was it the result of a meth lab explosion?" I asked.

"I think it was, but I haven't proven that yet," he said, as he dropped another piece of ash in one of the vials. "That's interesting."

"What's interesting?"

"The fire was started with gasoline."

"What does that mean?"

"The meth lab didn't cause the fire," he said. "As you can see, the burners use propane as a fuel source and not gasoline."

"Did they use gasoline as one of the ingredients when making meth?"

"Some use kerosene, but I'm not aware of anyone using gasoline as an ingredient."

"Then, what do you think happened?"

"I believe the fire was started with gasoline, which ignited the propane tank and caused the explosion," he said. "It's a good thing the tables weren't any closer together or the entire building would have been destroyed."

"So, you think this was arson."

"Yes, I believe it was, but I still have a few test to run before I can make my final decision."

"Will it interfere with your test if we start moving some of these drugs out of the building?"

"No, it won't bother me as long as you don't get around this table."

"We'll make sure we stay out of your way."

I looked at the entrance, as Marty and two of his deputies walked through the front door pushing hand trucks.

"Where should we start?" Marty yelled.

"Everything is toward the wall," I yelled and started walking in that direction.

"Was anyone killed?" Marty asked, as we looked at the stack of drugs.

"We found two bodies," I said. "One by the burnt table and the other in the back."

"What kind of drugs did you find?" Marty asked.

"We found some bales of marijuana, bags of cocaine and some pills, that I believe to be abortion pills," I said. "We also found some yellow and black pills that could be almost anything."

"We'll take care of this for you," Marty said, as he turned to his deputies and said, "You guys start rolling this stuff to the truck."

"We also found material in the back that's used when making meth," I said. "Can we store it at the county warehouse?"

"Sure, we have plenty of room and it's guarded 24 hours a day," he said, as he slid the hand trucks under a stack of boxes, lifted it up and started rolling them out the door.

I went back over to where Ken was working and watched as he mixed a couple more chemicals with the burnt ash then he closed his computer and put it in his case. He closed his chemicals, put them away and said, "It's definite, the fire was caused by gasoline and was the cause of the explosion."

"How long will it be before it's safe for us to come in this warehouse without wearing a mask?"

He looked at the tables scattered around the room, looked up at the rafters and shook his head. "I wouldn't feel safe in here for at least a week," he said. "But I like to be cautious."

"I'll go with you on that one," I said and smiled.

He picked his computer up, placed it on top of his chemical case and rolled them out the door.

"We have the drugs loaded and locked in the truck," Marty said, as he walked through the door. "Do you want us to help Johnny and Richard load their truck?"

"If you have time, then y'all can go to the warehouse together," I said.

"We have about five more loads," Richard yelled, as he rolled past.

"Follow him," Marty said to his deputies.

They followed Richard in the back.

"What did Ken say?" Marty asked, after the deputies left.

"He said it was arson."

"Were the victims dead before the fire?"

"I don't know," I said. "I haven't talked to Diane, but I believe they probably were."

"That sounds like murder."

"Yes, it does."

Janice and Victor walked around the corner carrying plastic containers filled with the evidence they had collected. Daniel followed, pushing a set of hand trucks with three plastic boxes strapped to its frame.

"I think we have all the evidence we need," Janice said, as she walked past.

"Thanks for your help," I said.

"I'll try to have some information for you tomorrow," she yelled and walked out the door.

Daniel and Victor followed her to the van.

Johnny and Richard came around the corner, followed by the two deputies, pushing the hand trucks. "This is the last of it," Johnny said, as he past.

"I'm going to follow them out and we'll get this to the warehouse," Marty said and he walked out the door behind them.

I looked around the burnt warehouse one more time then I walked to the Haz Mat van. "Do you need to decontaminate the building?" I asked.

"We've cleaned up all the dangerous chemicals inside," Chuck said. "The rest will just take time for the air to clear."

"I'll lock the gate when you leave to make sure no one gets inside," I said, as I took the mask and coveralls off and placed them in a biohazard bag.

"That's a good idea." Chuck said, as he took the bag and put it in a biohazard container and closed the lid.

After everyone got in the Haz Mat van, Chuck drove away.

After everyone left, I ran to my car and drove to the gate. When the gate was closed, I took a chain and lock out of my trunk and locked it. Then I posted a keep out sign and wrapped crime scene tape across the front of the gate several times.

I scanned the area for possible witnesses, but the street looked empty. The guard was gone as well as everyone else so I closed my trunk, got in my car and drove home.

Chapter 15

I walked into the Medical Examiner's office with two cups of coffee and a dozen glazed doughnuts.

"I brought you breakfast," I said, as I set a cup of coffee on the top of Diane's desk.

After taking a doughnut, I placed the box in the middle of her desk, so both of us could reach the box without straining our arms.

"You better bring me something, if you come by this early," Diane jokingly said, as she sat down at her desk. "But, you're killing my diet with these sweets," then she took a doughnut out of the box and took a bite.

"What did you think about the bodies found yesterday at the Millwood Fabric Warehouse fire?" I asked, as I took another doughnut.

"I haven't had a chance to do an autopsy on them yet," she said and smiled.

"It's hard to eat just one," I said and bit into the doughnut.

"That's why I try to stay away from doughnuts," she said and smiled.

"I know you haven't done the autopsy, but what was your impression of the victims."

"Alright, I believe the first victim I saw was killed yesterday, but it will be hard to tell, because of the depth it was burned," she said. "I have no idea when the second victim was killed, but I know it was more than a day ago."

"When are you going to do the autopsy?"

"I'll start as soon as I finish my breakfast," she said, as she stuck the last of her doughnut in her mouth and smiled.

"Ken Wilson said the fire was started with gasoline," I said. "He made it sound like it might have been started to cover up a murder."

"He did?" she asked, as she eyed the box of doughnuts. "I'll keep that in mind when I conduct my autopsy."

"It looked like a functioning meth lab," I said. "But after looking through the warehouse, I think it was also a distribution center for a multitude of drugs."

"That was a good cover for storing drugs, but didn't the guards know what was happening inside."

"I'm not sure the guards walked through the warehouse," I said. "I think they only looked at monitors."

"Couldn't they see what was going on with the monitor?"

"They may have been paid not to look."

"Not very good guards were they."

"One of the guards was Rodney Curry's uncle."

"How old is Rodney's uncle?"

"I'd say he's in his early seventies," I said. "Why?"

"You'd think someone that old would know better than aid someone in selling drugs," she said, as she took another doughnut and closed the top.

"Drug dealer's come in all ages."

"I know, but at that age they've seen the damage it causes people in their lives," she said and slid the box toward me. "Keep that box close to you and don't let me eat another."

“Alright,” I said and moved it in front of me. “I think the key to most drug dealer’s success is their inability to care about the people they are selling drugs to.”

“So, you’re saying, he don’t care what drugs are doing to the people of Thorton.”

“Yes, that’s what I’m saying,” I said. “It’s all about the money.”

“Speaking of money, I need to get to work and earn mine,” Diane said and stood up. “I’ll call you when I know something.”

“Call my cell phone,” I said, as I stood up and grabbed the box of doughnuts. “I might be out of the office looking for clues.”

“I should know something this afternoon,” she said and rolled her chair against her desk.

“Thanks for all your help,” I said, as I walked to the door.

“I’m always happy to help catch a criminal,” she said. “Especially a murderer and drug dealer.”

“I think I’ll go back to Millwood and make sure we didn’t miss anything,” I said and walked out the door.

Chapter 16

The Millwood Fabric Warehouse looked quiet and isolated when I pulled into the driveway. The crime scene tape was still stretched across the gate just like I had left it the day before.

I stopped in front of the gate, got out of my car, unlocked the gate and eased around the crime scene tape until I was inside.

As I neared the front of the building, I stopped at the large opening, where the front door used to be, and surveyed the fire damage. The top of the entranceway was darkened from the fire and smoke, but the structure still looked stable so I went inside.

The fumes were overpowering, so I took my handkerchief out of my back pocket and covered my nose. I walked past a pile of broken tables and a stack of burners lying in a corner, to a pile of plastic drain cleaner bottles. Using my right foot I slowly started moving the bottles apart, while I looked for anything that might be hidden underneath.

When I didn't find anything helpful, I looked where the stack of drugs had been stored and saw a small pile of white powder lying against the wall. I picked up a bottle of drain cleaner that still had a small amount in the bottom, walked to the pile of white powder and poured the cleaner onto the powder, which washed it against the base board.

Moving around the building I stopped at the partition where we had found the second body but I didn't see anything helpful, so I continued walking around the warehouse.

I passed the door which had contained supplies for making meth then I walked past the one which had the money stashed in the back and the empty room. As I rounded the corner to circle back around and go back to the front of the warehouse, I heard a muffled sound coming from inside the wall.

I eased toward the sound and carefully slid my hand along the wall to feel for a break in the wall structure. As my fingers felt the texture where two boards connected, I discovered a small break in the wall, which indicated an opening.

As I listened, I could still hear the muffled sound of music playing inside the wall, so I gripped the opening with my fingers and pulled with all the strength I could muster. When the door opened, I was staring at an open space, with a large couch and recliner surrounding a 52 inch wide screen television.

The music was coming from the television, which was tuned to a station that played music videos all day, but no one was in the room to watch. There were no windows in the room, just a door in the front and a door in the back.

I scanned the walls for any hidden compartments, but I couldn't find anything, so I opened the back door and looked to see where it led. When I looked out, I was staring at the back parking lot, so I closed the door and turned the television off.

As I looked around the room, I thought, this is probably where Rodney Curry was staying, but where did he sleep and why didn't he have a refrigerator. Did he have people bringing him food or did he have a camper or trailer setup outside this door? It really didn't matter now, because I don't think he'll be back. The fire has brought too much attention to this warehouse and the drug business that went on inside.

I took my phone out of my pocket and called the police station.

"Thorton Police Department," Rachel said. "How can I help you?"

"Rachel, this is Sam," I said. "Tell Richard and Johnny to come to the warehouse and bring a truck."

"Anything else?"

"Yes, tell them to come through the gate and pull around to the back parking lot," I said. "I'll be waiting with the back door open."

"I'll let them know," she said and then my phone went dead.

I closed my phone, put it back in my pocket and sat down on the bottom step, to wait for Johnny and Richard.

The sound of a pickup truck pulling around the building jolted me to action. I jumped up, put my hand on my gun and stood ready as I wait to see who was driving around the building.

I relaxed my hand, when I saw Richard wave as he stopped beside the open doorway.

"What are we doing?" Richard asked, as he got out of the truck and instantly put his hand over his nose and mouth. "That smell is still strong," he said, as he took his handkerchief out of his back pocket and tied it around his neck to cover his nose and mouth.

Johnny did the same.

"Confiscating materials found in a drug house," I said and laughed.

"What material?" Richard asked. "I thought we got everything yesterday."

"I found a hidden room in one of the walls."

"What did you find?" Johnny asked, as he walked around the truck and stood beside Richard.

"A 52 inch television, couch and recliner."

"That would go great in our new lounge we were hoping to build," Johnny said.

"If we move some of the tables around, it will fit just fine in the back room," I said.

"That sounds good too," Johnny said and laughed.

"Where's it at?" Richard asked.

"In here," I said and moved back to let them walk inside the room.

"Can we get it on the truck?" Richard asked.

"I think so, as long as we tie it tight," I said.

"Let's get started," Richard said, as he walked over to the couch and grabbed one end.

Johnny grabbed the other end of the couch and I held the door as they loaded the truck.

Within thirty minutes the truck was overflowing with furniture and a wide screen television. They tied everything in place with four tie downs stretched across the back of the truck in many different angles.

"Take it to the back of the police station," I said. "I'll meet you there after I close everything here."

"We'll start unloading when we get there," Richard said, as he got in the truck.

After Johnny got in the truck, Richard carefully pulled out of the parking lot and slowly drove toward the police station.

I closed the back door, walked through the warehouse and exited through the front door. I closed the gate and reapplied the crime scene tape and locks, just like it was before I arrived. Then I got in my car and drove to the police station.

Chapter 17

As I pulled into the parking lot, I saw Richard and Johnny struggling with the couch and Rachel attempting to help by holding the door open. The couch tilted to the right, then to the left, before they regained their balance and carried it through the door.

I parked beside the truck, got out and walked through the back door.

The couch was sitting in the hall with Richard and Johnny standing beside it.

"The door's not wide enough to fit the couch through," Richard said.

"Will it fit if you turn it on its side?" I asked.

"I think so, but it'll be hard to balance," Richard said.

"I'll help get it on its side," I said, as I started lifting the couch.

Richard and Johnny grabbed the other end and we lifted it up on its side and carried it through the door. They placed it in front of the television.

"I know now where I'll take my breaks," Richard said.

"We don't have cable run back here yet," Johnny complained. "The television's no go until we have cable."

"I know, but the couch is a great place to relax," Richard said and smiled.

"Sam, you have someone here to see you," Rachel called down the hall.

"I wonder who that could be," I said, as I looked at Richard.

"That's a good question," Richard said.

"Who is it," I asked, as I got close to Rachel.

"He wouldn't say," she said as we walked into the squad room.

As I entered the squad room, a man wearing a maroon dress shirt, with a red and blue checkerboard tie and a light tan cashmere sweater was standing behind the counter.

"What are you doing at my warehouse?" he asked, as he walked around the counter.

As he circled the counter, I noticed his light brown cowboy boots, with a gold colored scratch guard at the toe and heel of each boot. He also worn navy blue slacks, with a three inch gold skull belt buckle attached to an ostrich belt.

He had a slight limp as he walked toward me, but made a conscious effort not to let it show. He stopped about ten feet in front on me and stared.

"You didn't answer my question," he said, as he pointed at me.

"What warehouse are you talking about?" I asked, trying not to notice his aggressive behavior.

"The Millwood Fabric Warehouse," he said.

"Who are you?"

"Kevin Brown," he said. "I want to know what happened to my warehouse."

"You might want to ask the guards you hired to guard the building."

"I didn't hire any guards to watch my warehouse," he said. "I hired a security agency to protect my property, but they didn't do their job."

"A security agency," I said. "What was the name of the agency?"

He looked angry, but didn't say anything. He walked back to the counter and leaned against it.

"Morton Enterprises," he said beneath his breath.

"Who?"

"Morton Enterprises," he yelled.

"So, Morton Enterprises hired the guards that were supposed to protect your warehouse."

"Yes, they did," he said. "You still didn't answer my question, what happened to my warehouse?"

"Someone was using it to make and distribute drugs around central Alabama."

"Did someone try to burn my building down?"

"That's still under investigation," I said. "All I can say, is the warehouse caught fire and has severe damage."

"Was it the people making drugs that started the fire?"

"I don't know yet, but it's a good possibility it was drug related."

"Can I go inside my warehouse to look at the damage?"

"I would rather you wait until the investigation is over."

"How long will that take?"

"I'm expecting a phone call this afternoon with some information and then I can make my decision."

"Was it destroyed"

"There was a lot of damage from the fire, but it certainly could have been worse."

"I was in the process of leasing the warehouse to a grocery chain as a distribution center," he said. "I guess that's not going to happen."

"They would have wanted to remodel the warehouse anyway," I said. "This just gives you a reason for the remodeling."

"I can see you are a positive thinker," he said. "I could use you in my business."

"Negative thinking only slows progress," I said.

"Good slogan," he said and smiled. "Your attitude made me feel better about the warehouse."

"I should know something in a couple of days."

"Could you call me when you know something?" he asked, as he handed me his card.

"Sure, I'll try, but if I haven't called in a couple of days, feel free to call me," I said.

"Thanks for the information," he said and walked out the door.

"His attitude sure did change after you talked to him a bit," Rachel said, as she walked out of her office.

"He was upset and needed to vent," I said. "Sometimes it helps just to let your thoughts out."

"I'm glad you let him vent," she said.

"It didn't hurt me to listen and show a little compassion," I said.

"It's nice to see something good happening for a change," she said and went back inside her office.

I walked to the coffee pot and poured a cup of coffee. I smiled, as Richard and Johnny walked into the squad room rubbing their backs.

"Now I know why I'm not working in the moving industry," Richard said, as he continued rubbing the right side of his back.

"Me too, that's too much like work," Johnny said and laughed.

"You'll appreciate the couch and television when you take your breaks," I said.

"I'm sure we will, but right now all I can think about is the pain in my lower back," Johnny said.

"I told you to lift with your legs," Richard said.

"I know, but I forgot when we were moving the couch," Johnny said.

"After you have rested, you might want to patrol the area and make sure the citizens of Thorton are safe," I said. "And don't forget to write a few tickets if you see anyone speeding."

"I'm ready," Richard said, as he looked at Johnny. "I'll take the south side of town and you take the north side."

"That's fine with me," Johnny said, as he started walking toward the door.

"Remember to be vigilant while you're out there and call for backup if you see anyone that might be dangerous," I said.

"Yes Boss," Richard said, as they both walked out the door.

I looked around the empty squad room, then walked in my office and closed the door.

Chapter 18

I sat in my chair, leaned back and put my feet on my desk. I opened the daily newspaper and started scanning the headlines. As I read, my head started bobbing up and down. I shook my head and tried to refocus my attention on the newspaper I was attempting to read, but the lack of sleep over the last few weeks was finely catching up with me, so I folded the paper neatly up and laid it on top of my desk. I leaned back in my chair and closed my eyes.

As my mind cleared and every muscle in my body began to relax, I jolted upright when my chest began to vibrate and the star spangle banner began to play. I pulled my cell phone out of my pocket and yelled, "Sam speaking."

"Did I interrupt anything?" Diane asked.

"No, you didn't," I said, as I lowered my voice. "I was almost asleep when you called."

"I'm sorry, I didn't think about you taking a nap," she said and laughed.

"I didn't intend to, but I haven't slept much in the last few weeks," I said. "This case and me trying to fill in for Johnny while he was out with the flu has taken a lot out of me."

"Being Police Chief is not always fame and glory."

"No it's not."

"I've finished the autopsies on the bodies you found yesterday."

"Great," I said. "What did you find?"

"I'll start with the burnt body," Diane said and cleared her throat.

"Alright, I'm ready," I said, as I got my notepad out of my desk drawer.

"The first victim was a female in her early to late twenties," she said. "She had discoloration of her teeth and gum erosion which indicated long time crystal methamphetamine use."

"Was she on drugs at the time of her death?"

"I found traces of crystal methamphetamine and cocaine in her system."

"She would have meth in her system just from being in the building," I said. "How did she die?"

"She was killed by multiple stab wounds to the chest, then doused with gasoline and set on fire."

"Was she dead before being set on fire?"

"Yes, the stab wounds were directly to her heart," she said. "She was dead within seconds after being stabbed."

"Do you know who she was?"

"No, not yet," she said. "I wasn't able to get prints because they were burnt off her fingers."

"What about DNA or dental records?"

"Yes, I got dental e-rays, but we need to have an idea who she is and which dentist she used to make that helpful," she said. "As for DNA, I sent it over to the CSI lab so they could run it through their database, she would have to be involved in a violent crime for it to be on record."

"Anything else?"

"Yes," she said and paused.

"What is it?" I asked in anticipation.

"After examining her pelvic area, I'd say she had given birth one or two times."

"So, you're saying she might have children somewhere in Thorton."

"Yes and if she does they're probably under the age of five."

"So basically all we have to go on is missing persons that may have given birth in the last five years. That is not much to go on to find two small children that she probably left home alone."

"The CSI agents are working as fast as they can," she said. "It just takes time for everything to process."

"I know," I said. "I'm just picturing two small children frightened and hovering in a corner in their house."

"Janice or I will let you know as soon as we have any results."

"Thanks," I said. "What about the second victim?"

"Well, let's see," she said. "The second victim was a male in his early thirties."

"Do you know when he was killed?"

"With the amount of decomposition, I would say that he was killed about three days ago from a gunshot wound to the head," she said. "He was shot execution style with a 9mm bullet."

"Was he tortured?"

"I didn't see any signs of torture," she said. "The shot to the head was the only wound to his body."

"Were you able to identify the victim?"

"Daniel came over from the CSI lab and got some prints off the victim," she said.

"I don't know if he got a hit on the prints yet."

"Did he have any drugs in his system?"

"He had a trace of methamphetamine but nothing else."

"That could be from breathing the fumes from the warehouse," I said. "I probably have a trace in my blood from being at the warehouse earlier today."

"That's a possibility," she said. "That's all I have for you right now on the victims."

"Thanks for the information," I said. "I'll call Janice and see if she's got the identity of the victims," and I closed my phone.

I looked through my frequent contact list and found Janice's phone number. I hit the call button.

"Janice speaking," she said, as she answered the phone. "How can I help you?"

"This is Sam," I said. "Do you know the identity of the victims from the Millwood Fabric Warehouse?"

"Let's see," she said. "We got the results from the finger prints we sent through the data base."

I leaned back in my chair as I waited for Janice to tell me the victim's name.

"I know it's here somewhere," she said. "Daniel just brought the results in here and I put it beside my phone. Here it is. One of the victim's was Harvey Green."

"Did he have a record?"

"That's how we got the results so fast," Janice said and laughed. "He had a record a mile long."

"Did you see anything that could connect him to Rodney Curry?"

"I'll read you a portion of his record," she said. "At 19 he was arrested for possession of a controlled substance with intent to sell, at 20 he was arrested for assault with intent to kill, at 23 he was stopped at a routine traffic stop and they found 20 kilograms of cocaine in his trunk."

"It sounds like he was deeply involved into selling and transporting drugs," I said. "I wonder if he was working with Rodney or against him."

"Whatever the case may be, it ended up bad for him."

"It usually does when you're dealing with drugs."

"That is so true, but most people just see fast money and don't think of the consequences of their actions until it's too late."

"Did you get the results from the burned victim yet?"

"Not yet," she said. "I probably won't have anything until late tomorrow if I have it then."

"Did you find anything at the warehouse to help catch the killer?"

"We really didn't find much evidence at the warehouse," she said. "Anything that might have been available that wasn't destroyed by the fire, the water finished off. And the only evidence we have on the other victim is the bullet Diane pulled out of his head."

"This case might be hard to solve."

"At this point, it will be impossible to solve."

"Call me if you get the results from the first victim," I said, as I put my notepad back in my desk.

"I'll get it as fast as I can."

"Thanks for your help," I said and closed my phone.

I got up and walked out of my office. As I entered the squad room, I saw Richard standing by the coffee pot, waiting for the coffee to brew.

"Are you already through patrolling?" I asked, as I walked toward him.

"I drove around south side a few times, but the streets are empty," he said. "I guess everyone is at work at this time of day."

"It's good that you're back, because we need to go to Morton Enterprises and see if we can talk to the owner," I said, as I got close to Richard.

"Do you want to take a cup of coffee with you?" he asked.

"Sure," I said and got two travel mugs out of the cabinet.

After the coffee was brewed, we poured our coffee and walked to the door.

"Rachel, we'll be out for a while," I said, as I stuck my head into the dispatcher's office. "Call Johnny if you need anything."

"I'll be fine," Rachel said.

"I know," I said and we walked out the door.

Chapter 19

I pulled into the parking lot and parked in front of Morton Enterprises. As we got out of my patrol car, I scanned the area for the black Escalade then walked to the door.

Richard opened the door and held it as I walked inside. We stopped suddenly when we saw Ben Lowe standing at the counter glaring in our direction.

“What do you want now?” Ben demanded, as he stepped toward us.

“Are you working as the secretary now?” I asked mockingly and smiled.

“Don’t be smart,” he responded. “Our secretary had to leave early so I’m helping out.”

“Good, maybe you can help me with what I need,” I said.

“What do you need?”

“I need to talk to the owner.”

“We told you the last time you were here the owner’s not here.”

“That was yesterday.”

“Well he’s not here today either.”

“Could you tell me the owner’s name?”

“Yes, I could,” he said and smiled. “But, will I?”

“What will it hurt to tell me the owner’s name?” I asked. “I could go to the court house and look at who bought the business license.”

“That is true,” Ben said, as he scratched the side of his face while he was thinking about whether to tell me. Then he responded, “Roger Hamilton owns Morton Enterprises, but you won’t find him here, because he stays out of the state most of the time."

"Who is in charge of the business when he's not here?"

"It depends on what branch you're talking about," Ben said. "I'm in charge of security and monitoring."

"So, you were in charge of security for the Millwood Fabric Warehouse."

"Yes, we had the account, but after the fire the owner called and said he didn't need our services anymore."

"Do you blame him?" I asked and laughed. "Your security allowed someone to use the warehouse for making and distributing drugs."

"We hired people through an agency to guard the place," he said. "I didn't think it was a big deal since it was just an empty warehouse."

"Did you know one of your guards was the uncle to one of the biggest drug dealers in Thorton?"

"Like I said, I went through an agency," he said. "I didn't know who they hired."

"Which agency did you go through?"

"Braswell Temp Service."

"Where is that located?"

"Their office is in the Fairway Shopping Center on 4th Avenue and 16th Street," he said.

"Did you ever go to the warehouse and make sure they were doing their job?"

"I went by a couple of times, but like I said, it was an empty warehouse with nothing to steal," he said. "The guards monitored the warehouse from their guard shack."

"Did you walk through the warehouse?"

"No, I looked at the monitors and talked to the guard, but I didn't walk through the warehouse," he said. "Why did you ask that?"

"I think they had the monitors rigged to give the illusion of showing the entire warehouse, but it left out a good portion."

"I saw the main room in the warehouse," he responded with a questioning look on his face. Then he asked, "You think they were making drugs when I went by to check on the warehouse?"

"With nothing moving, it could have been a picture in front of the camera."

"That sounds like something you'd see in a movie," he said. "This is real life nobody does that sort of thing."

"It was just a theory," I said, as I walked toward the door. "What did you say the name of the agency was?"

"Braswell Temp Service," he said. "It's at the Fairway Shopping Center."

"Thanks for the information," I said and walked out the door.

"That was weird," Richard said, as we got outside.

"Yes it was," I said. "He seemed eager to talk once he started talking."

"Are we going to the Temp Service?"

"Yes, I'd like to hear their side of the story," I said, as we got in the car.

I pulled out of the parking lot, turned right and drove toward the Fairway Shopping Center.

I turned left on 16th Street and slowed as I neared 4th Avenue. I turned on 4th Avenue and made an immediate right into the parking lot of the Fairway Shopping Center.

I drove past Jim's Family Steakhouse, Fran's Footwear and Joe's Sporting Goods before I saw a sign for Braswell Temp Service. Circled around the parking lot then pulled into a parking space in the middle of the lot, so no one would know where we were going.

After we got out of the car we casually walked toward the sidewalk not indicating where building we were going to.

"Do you want me to stay out here while you talk to them," Richard asked, as we neared the door leading to the temp service.

"That might be a good idea, but stay close in case I need you," I said then I opened the door and walked inside.

As I stepped inside, I was met by a lady with short red hair wearing a bright yellow blouse, dark brown skirt and dark brown dress shoes. She held her hand out as she approached. "How may I help you?" she asked, as she took my hand.

"I need to speak to whoever places people on assignments," I said, as I shook her hand.

"I thought you were a customer," she said, as she pulled her hand back and took a step back. "Who are you?"

"I'm Sam James, the Chief of Police for Thorton," I said. "I need to talk to whoever's in charge."

"That would be Victor White," she said. "It might be a minute because I think he's with a client," and she walked to the back.

I sat in a dark red leather chair and tried to relax while I waited. I heard voices in the back then Gloria Curry walked up the hall toward the front door. She stopped when she saw me sitting in the waiting room, turned and started toward the back. Then she turned back around and went to the front desk.

"Sam, why are you here?" she whispered, as she picked up a file that was lying on top of the desk.

"I've come to talk to Victor White," I said, as I looked at the file in her hand. "I didn't know you worked here."

"You don't know much about me," she said and walked back down the hall.

After Gloria disappeared down the hall, the secretary walked back in the room, sat down at her desk without saying a word and began looking through her rolodex. After a few seconds, she glanced in my direction and said, "He'll be with you in a few minutes," then she turned back to the rolodex.

"Thanks," I said, as I picked up a magazine and started looking at hunting equipment.

According to the ads, I was looking at the best rifle scopes for the professional hunter, a new and improved bullet to travel faster and straighter toward the target and a rangefinder that could judge the distance of your target to within 6 inches.

I closed the magazine, when I heard someone walking down the hall and laid it on the end table. I looked up to see a man in his late forties to early fifties walking toward me. He was dress in a light brown pull over shirt with Braswell Temp Service written in red letters across the left side, a pair of factory faded blue jeans and snake skin cowboy boots.

I stood up, as he approached and tried my friendliest of smiles.

He didn't appear to notice. "Is there a problem?" he asked, as he got to within three feet of me.

"I need to ask you a few questions about the security at the Millwood Fabric Warehouse," I said.

He turned and looked at his secretary. "Let's go to my office," he said, as he turned back to me. "It's down this way," then he pointed down the hall and started walking in that direction.

I followed.

He quickly walked down the hall, turned into the last room on the left and held the door open as I walked inside.

"Have a seat," he said, as he closed the door.

The room was small, but efficiently designed. Every inch was used to maximize the space. The back wall was lined with shelves, which contained a multitude of books from various authors. The wall on the right was lined with filing cabinets from floor to ceiling and the wall to the left had his printer/coping machine along with a paper shredder.

I sat in one of the padded straight back chairs that was positioned in front of his desk and waited.

Victor walked behind his desk, which was a solid oak executive style desk with a dark cherry finish and pulled his dark brown leather chair back. As he looked at me, he smiled a forced smile then he sat down and leaned back a little.

"What do you want to ask about the warehouse?" he asked, as he readjusted his chair.

"Did you supply the guards for the warehouse?" I asked.

"We supply a lot of manpower around Thorton," he said. "But, I believe we supplied the guards to that business."

"Who decides which person works which job?"

"Our associates determine which employee work at a particular site."

"Can you tell me who made the decision about the guards at the Millwood Fabric Warehouse?"

"Is that the place that had that fire?" he asked, as he crossed his arms.

"Yes, it is."

"Oh, well then I'm sorry, but I can't talk about that," he said. "Our attorney advised us not to discuss anything about that business to anyone."

"So, you can't tell me who made the assignment?"

"At this point I can't tell you anything," he said, as he stood up. "This discussion is over," and he opened the door.

"When you are able to talk, please give me a call," I said, as I gave him my card and walked out the door.

As I walked down the hall, I noticed Gloria Curry sitting at her desk working on her computer. I stopped and stepped inside her office.

She stopped working the minute I entered the room and minimized her screen.

"What do you want?" she asked without looking in my direction.

"Did you assign the workers to the Millwood Fabric Warehouse?" I asked, as I stepped a little closer to her desk.

"Yes, I was in charge of the Warehouse," she said, as she stood up. "I might as well tell you now because I know you're going to find out eventually."

"You hired your brother-in-law to guard the warehouse," I said. "Wasn't that a conflict of interest?"

"He needed a job and he was qualified to guard an empty warehouse," she said and moved toward the door. "I didn't treat him any different than anyone else."

"Does your boss know that he was your brother-in-law?"

"Yes he knew," she said and looked out the door. "Now you need to leave so I can get to work."

"Do you know where Matt is now?"

"I haven't seen him since the fire," she said. "Now go," then she walked back to her desk and sat down.

"Thanks," I said and walked out the door.

As I walked past the secretary, I stopped and laid my card on her desk.

"What's that for?" she asked with a puzzled look on her face.

"Call me if you think of anything that might be helpful about the Millwood Fabric Warehouse," I said.

"I think I'll let my boss talk to you about those matters," she said, as she took my card and slipped it in the top drawer of her desk. "But you never know, I might need you for something else," and she smiled.

My face reddened.

"Thanks anyway," I said. "I'd better get home to my wife and kids," and I walked out the door.

Richard met me as I got outside and we walked toward my car.

"Did you find out anything?" he asked.

"Glory Curry works there and hired Matt Curry to guard the warehouse," I said. "No one else would talk because of legal issues."

"Are they being sued?"

"They didn't say for sure, but I think that's what is happening."

"If I was Kevin Brown, I'd sue Morton Enterprises as well as this place."

"I don't think Mr. Brown will have to sue them, because his insurance company will do it for him," I said, as we walked to my car.

I cranked the car as Richard closed his door and drove through the parking lot. I turned left and drove toward the police station.

As I drove to the station, I kept looking in my rearview mirror for any vehicle that might be following.

"What are you doing?" Richard asked, as he looked behind us. "Are we being followed?"

"I was just making sure that we weren't being followed," I said. "I guess I'm still a little shaken from being shot at."

"Anybody would be," he said and glanced in the side mirror. "I think they were just trying to send you a message to back off from the warehouse."

"I think you might be right," I said, as I turned into the station parking lot.

I pulled beside the front door and stopped.

"Are you going home?" Richard asked, as he got out of the car.

"Yes, I'll see you in the morning," I said and drove away.

Chapter 20

I woke up early Tuesday morning, slipped on a pair of gray jogging shorts, bright red tee shirt and eased down the steps to the living room. I got the coffee to brewing and went out the door.

As I got to the road I turned left and slowly started jogging around the neighborhood. I quickly increased my speed, as my muscles got warm, until I was running at full speed by the time I got to the end of the block. I ran in a two block radius, so I could stay close to my house.

As I rounded the corner for the first time and was heading for my house, I looked across the street to look for a black Escalade or blue Lexus that might be parked across the street watching my house. I relaxed a little when I was certain no one was watching, but still remained vigilant as I ran. I slowed, as I neared my front door, then increased my speed and was again at full speed as I rounded the corner.

On my fourth round I was beginning to sweat heavily so I slowed my pace and began walking the last half of the final round. When I reached my front steps, I mindfully slowed my breathing and began stretching my legs to decrease the likelihood of cramping up.

After I had finished cooling down, I quietly walked inside my house and poured a cup of coffee. I stood by the counter sipping my coffee and watching the clock. After a few minutes, I sat the cup of the counter and went upstairs to shower and get ready for the day.

I showered and dressed in my freshly pressed uniform. Then I quietly eased through my bedroom without turning the lights on and walked out the door. I walked down the stairs to the counter and refreshed my coffee.

Then I sat down at the table and focused my attention on the clock. Today, I have to go to Avery Moore's bail hearing at 9 o'clock, so I didn't plan on leaving the house until 7:30 and going directly to the courthouse.

As the minute hand neared 7:25, I got up, poured my coffee in a travel mug and walked out the door.

The courthouse parking lot was almost full at 8:15 in the morning but I was able to find a parking space at the edge of the lot. As I got out of the car, I looked across the front of the courthouse building where two 100 year old oak trees stood towering over everything in the center of the yard and beds of yellow and white daffodils spotted the grounds every six to eight feet.

As I walked toward the courthouse I saw a mockingbird scampered across the sidewalk toward a small piece of abandoned bread that lay underneath one of the two wooden benches that sit under the trees.

At the base of the steps Sherry Howard the county DA was looking in my direction and waiting for me to approach.

"Are you ready for today?" she asked, as I reached the top steps.

"I guess," I said. "But I don't like this part of the job."

"Don't worry, this will be quick and easy," she said. "He'll either get bail or denied bail."

"Do you know who the judge is today?"

"Joyce Martin," she said. "She's usually fast but fair."

"Do you think he'll get bail?" I asked, as I opened the door.

"He might," she said. "They're trying to decrease the prisoner load in the jails," and she walked inside the courthouse.

We took the elevator to the third floor and sat down on a bench to wait for our turn in court.

At 9:15 the bailiff stood and said, "The city of Thorton VS Moore."

"Well, it's our turn," Sherry said, as she stood up.

"Let's get this over with," I said, as I got up and walked with her to stand behind the table reserved for the prosecution.

Judge Joyce Martin looked around the courtroom, then said, "The city of Thorton has charged Avery Moore with one count of attempted murder, one count of carrying a concealed weapon and one count of resisting arrest," and she looked at Sherry and asked, "Is that correct?"

"Yes, your honor," she said.

"I also see you broke your probation by carrying a weapon," Judge Joyce Martin said, as she looked at Avery Moore.

"My client was just carrying a pocket knife," Phillip Mays said.

"The record shows it was a switchblade," she said.

"He thought it was a simple pocket knife," he said. "He had never used the knife and didn't know how it worked."

"No one can be that idiotic," she said. "Every man that I've ever known has tested his knife blade before he has put it in his pocket."

Phillip Mays dropped his head and didn't say another word.

"Who did he try to kill?" Judge Martin asked, as she looked at me.

"Me, your honor," I said.

"So, he broke his probation and tried to kill a police officer all in the same day," she said.

"He's not a flight risk, because he has no family anywhere except in Thorton," Phillip said.

"That doesn't mean he will not run," she said and looked back down at the report. "Would council please come to the bench?"

Phillip walked to the bench and waited for Sherry to join him. They both leaned close to listen to Judge Martin as she spoke in a low voice.

"The jail is filled to almost capacity and I've been instructed to give bail to as many people as possible," she whispered, as she looked at Sherry. "I have made my decision and I don't want any outburst from anyone. Do you understand?"

"I do," Sherry said.

"I do," Phillip said.

"Alright let's proceed," she said.

They walked back to their respective tables to stand and wait on the verdict.

Judge Martin cleared her throat and looked across the courtroom.

"I have looked over the charges and believe them to be grave in nature," she said, as she looked at Avery Moore. "After much consideration, I set bail at one million dollars," and she turned to the bailiff and said, "Take him away."

The bailiff walked over to Avery as he stood and escorted him over to two county deputies that were standing on either side of the door leading to the holding cells.

One of the deputies handcuffed Avery's arms behind his back. Then they lead him out of the courtroom.

"Do you think he'll get out?" I asked, as I stood and turned to Sherry.

"It depends on who supplied him with his lawyer," she said. "If they can afford him, they can afford to pay the bail."

"Well, we did the best we could," I said and walked toward the exit.

"Yes we did," she said, as she sat down on a bench when we walked outside the door of the courtroom. "I have another case in about an hour, so I might as well stay here."

"Thanks for your help," I said and walked out the door.

I walked down the steps, dodging pigeons as I went and walked to my car. I got in and drove toward the police station.

Chapter 21

As I neared Thorton city limits, my phone started ringing. I took it out of my pocket and flipped it open. "This is Sam," I said.

"Ginger Mitchell just called and said she found the body of a man at her recycling business," Johnny said.

"When did she call?"

"About a minute ago," he said. "I just got off the phone with her."

"Call Diane and Janice," I said. "Have them meet us there."

"Anything else?"

"I'll meet you there," I said, as I closed my phone and put it back in my pocket.

I turned left and drove toward Ginger's Recycling.

I slowed as I neared Ginger's Recycling and turned into the driveway. I pulled up near the front door of the office and parked.

As I got out of my car, I looked at the office and saw Ginger looking out the window.

She hesitantly smiled and waved.

I walked toward the office and started up the steps when the door opened.

"Why are you so dressed up today?" Ginger asked, as she walked out of the office and closed the door. "You look like you went to a funeral."

"I had to go to court this morning," I said.

"I didn't think you usually wore that for a uniform," she said.

"It's my formal uniform," I said. "I only wear it when I have to go to court."

"I knew I'd never seen it before."

"Did you find a body?" I asked.

"Yes, I was looking through a new shipment of junk cars," she said and took a deep breath. "When I opened the trunk of that white Chevrolet Impala, I found the body," and she pointed to a white Impala parked at the edge of her lot.

"Where did you get the cars?" I asked, as I started walking toward the car.

"John's Body Shop," she said, as she followed. "I bought them from the Starlight Insurance Agency."

"When did the cars arrive?"

"Last night about 5 o'clock."

"Could the body have been put in the trunk last night?"

"I don't think so because I locked them behind my fence last night."

"Did you touch the car?"

"Only the trunk," she said. "I might have opened the front door also."

As we reached the car, I walked around the back to the trunk, took my handkerchief out of my back pocket and opened the trunk. I looked at the twisted up body of a man with graying hair lying on his right side facing the spare tire.

I leaned in the trunk and looked for wounds along his chest and abdomen, but none were visible. So, I moved up from his body and examined the back of his head. Then I moved a plastic bag away from his face to look for a wound, but stopped instantly as I recognized the victim.

"What's wrong?" Ginger asked.

"I know the victim," I said and backed away from the car.

I looked at the street when I heard a vehicle coming. I watched, as Janice turned into the driveway, with Diane following. She pulled her van beside where we were standing and parked. Diane pulled around Janice and backed her van toward the Impala.

"Where's the body?" Janice asked, as she got out of her van.

"In the trunk of the Impala," I said.

Victor Hayes got his camera out of its case and was walking toward the car.

Diane pulled a stretcher out of her van and slowly pushed it toward the trunk of the car. She stopped beside where I was standing to wait for the CSI unit to finish gathering evidence.

We watched, as Janice and Daniel walked past with their evidence boxes in hand.

"Did you see the victim?" Diane asked.

"Yes, I looked at him," I said.

"Sam knows him," Ginger said.

"Really," Diane exclaimed with surprise in her voice. "Who is he?"

"His name is Matt Curry," I said. "I met him when I was looking for his nephew."

"Did you see any wounds when you looked at him?" she asked.

"No, I didn't, but I didn't move the body to look," I said. "I didn't want to disturb any evidence that might be present."

I watched, as Victor finished taking pictures of the car and Daniel stepped up to dust the trunk for prints.

Johnny pulled into the driveway and parked beside my car. He got out and slowly walked toward where we were standing.

"Where have you been?" I asked, as he got close.

"After I called Diane and Janice, everything went wrong," he said with a frown on his face. "Gloria Curry came to the police station to complain about you going to her work place and threatening her job."

"I didn't know she worked there at the time," I said. "And I didn't say anything that would cause her to lose her job."

"She said you were harassing her and her family and if you didn't stop she was going to file a formal complaint," he said with a grin.

"That whole family has been a thorn in my side," I said and looked at the white Impala. "I wonder what she'll say when I tell her that her brother-in-law is dead."

"I'm sure she won't be happy."

"I think I'll wait until I get a little more information about the cause of dead before I tell anyone."

Daniel stepped back and helped Diane position the stretcher beside the trunk of the car. He then grabbed Matt's upper body and Diane grabbed his legs. They lifted the body over the edge of the trunk and carefully moved it onto the stretcher.

After closing the body bag, Diane strapped his body to the stretcher and she slowly rolled it toward her van.

"Could you tell how he died?" I asked, as she got near.

"I didn't see an obvious wound but I didn't examine the entire body," she said. "I'll know more after I get him back to the lab," and she rolled the stretcher to the back of her van and slid it inside.

I looked back at the car where Janice and Daniel were still gathering evidence, then turned to Johnny and said, “I need to go to John’s Body Shop.”

“Do you want me to go with you?” he asked.

“No, stay here until they’re through,” I said. “Then make sure this car is sealed tightly.”

“I can tow it behind my shop to keep anyone from seeing it,” Ginger said.

“That might be a good idea, but I still want the trunk sealed before you do that.”

“I’ll make sure it’s sealed,” Johnny said.

I watched as Diane drove past where we were standing and stopped at the edge of the road. She waited while two cars passed, then she slowly eased into the road and drove toward her lab.

“Johnny, make sure the car is sealed before you leave,” I said, as I watched Diane drive away.

“Sam, I said I’d make sure the car was sealed,” Johnny said.

“I’m sorry, I heard what you said, but I got distracted,” I said. “I’ll see you at the station,” and I walked to my car.

I turned left at the end of her driveway and drove toward John’s Body Shop.

Chapter 22

John's Body Shop was nothing more than an old barn that was converted into a paint and body shop. He had a small fenced in area connected to the side of the building that he used to store the cars he was working on, but everything else was parked in an open field behind the building.

I pulled into the driveway and parked beside the office door. As I got out, I looked inside the office window, but no one was inside, so I walked around the building into the shop area.

A man in dark blue coveralls was diligently buffing the hood of a Lincoln Town car and not paying any attention to my arrival. I saw another man standing in the back, with a grinder in his hand, looking at a door that was leaning against the side of a table. He turned toward me and looked surprised when he saw me standing at the door. He laid the grinder on the table then slowly started walking toward me.

"You're not supposed to be back here," he said, as he got close.

"I know, but there wasn't anyone in the office," I said and I took another step closer to the door. "I need to talk to the owner."

"You're talking to him," he said. "What do you need?"

"Did you sell some cars to Ginger Mitchell?" I asked.

"I might have," he said. "Why?"

"Did you deliver some cars to her yesterday?" I asked, as I looked over to the man that had stopped buffing the car and was slowly walking toward us.

"John is anything wrong?" the man asked as he approached.

"Seth, did you take some cars to Ginger Mitchell's place yesterday?" John asked.

"She bought those cars that was totaled by Starlight," he said. "You didn't want to keep them, did you."

"No, I didn't need them," John said, as he looked at Seth. "They were just in the way."

"I thought it would be alright," Seth said then he went back to the Lincoln and started buffing the hood.

"You heard the man," John said. "We took some cars that she bought from the Starlight Insurance Agency."

"Where did you keep the cars?"

"See that field where the other cars are stored," he said. "They were parked beside that last row of junk cars."

"How long were they parked there?"

"Less than a week," he said. "I'm not a junk yard and it makes my place look bad to have a bunch of junk cars parked around it."

"So, anyone could have gotten around those cars before you delivered them," I said.

"Yes, I suppose so," he said. "What's this all about?"

"There was a dead body in one of the cars," I said.

"Wait a minute," he exclaimed. "I don't know nothing about a dead body."

"I didn't say you did," I said. "Did you happen to see anyone hanging around the cars?"

"Occasionally I've seen people walking around the cars, but I don't sell parts, so I make them leave."

"Anyone in particular in the last week?"

"No, not really," he said and then turned to Seth and asked, "Have you seen anyone hanging around the junk cars around back?"

"What?" Seth yelled, as he put the buffer down and walked toward us.

"Have you seen anyone hanging around the junk cars in the back in the last few days?"

He looked at John, then turned to me and said, "I don't remember anybody being back there in the last week."

"Did Ginger go back there to look at the cars?" I asked.

"I don't think she looked at the cars," John said. "She dealt directly with the insurance company."

"She bought the cars without looking at them," I said.

"She bought the cars cheap and only wanted them for their parts," he said. "In fact, I sometimes buy parts from Ginger and I might need to get a part from one of those cars she bought."

"Why didn't you keep the cars?"

"Like I said before, I'm not a junk yard and I don't want a bunch of junk cars around my building."

"What about those other cars parked in the field?"

"They've been parked there for a few months," he said. "I haven't been about to find anyone to buy them."

"You own those cars?"

“I guess,” he said. “They were brought here by people who didn’t have insurance and they refused to pay to get them towed away.”

“Couldn’t you sell them?”

“I’m giving them six months and then I’m going to sell them for scrap metal.”

“Ginger might buy them from you.”

“She might.”

“You wouldn’t happen to have a security camera anywhere around here?” I asked, as I looked up at the ceiling.

“I can’t afford security,” he said.

“If you or Seth think of anything, please call,” I said, as I handed him my card.

“I’ll keep that in mind,” he said and put my card in his shirt pocket.

“Thanks for your time,” I said, then turned and walked to my car.

I got in and drove toward the police station.

Chapter 23

I pulled into the police station parking lot and parked in the space designated for me. I reached behind the passenger's seat, grabbed my bag of clothes and got out.

When I walked through the door, I saw Johnny sitting at his desk working on the computer.

"Did you get any information from John?" he asked, as he looked up from his computer screen.

"Nothing useful," I said, as I walked around the counter. "Did you get the car sealed?"

"It's sealed and parked in the back," he announced. "I've done my job," and smiled.

"I knew you would," I said and walked to the back to change clothes.

After I had changed into more comfortable clothes, I went to the coffee pot, poured a cup of coffee and started rummaging through the cabinets for something to eat.

Within seconds, I found a small pack of chocolate covered doughnuts and a pack of powder sugar doughnuts. I chose the pack of powder sugar doughnuts, picked up my cup of coffee and went to my office.

As I entered, I closed the door with my foot and turned the light on with my right elbow. I sat my coffee down on my desk, pulled my chair out and sat down. Then I opened my top drawer, took my notepad out and settled back to make a list of what I knew, which wasn't very much.

When clues are hard to find, I like to make a list which makes me feel like I'm doing something and not just wasting time. It also helps me to sort through the evidence I have.

I separated my page into three sections.

Above one column I wrote drugs, the middle column I wrote connection and above the third column I wrote death. Under the drugs column, I wrote Rodney Curry, Millwood Fabric Warehouse fire, Danielle Watts, Kim Black and Avery Moore.

Under the death column, I wrote Harvey Green and Matt Curry. Then in the connection column, I wrote Rodney Curry, Matt Curry and the Millwood Fabric Warehouse fire.

I sat back and studied the list.

Then I moved to the bottom of the page and wrote, could Morton Enterprises be involved with the drug business? Where is Butch Frost? Who is behind the death of Matt Curry and is his death related to the drug trade? I underlined each question then laid my notepad on top of my desk.

I bowed my head and prayed, "Dear Lord, please give me the wisdom to sort through the information I have in front of me, give me the guidance to choose the right path to follow and the right words to use when questioning the suspects. In Jesus name I pray. Amen."

As I picked my notepad up to look over the list, my phone started ringing.

"Sam speaking," I said after I opened my phone.

"I have the identity of the burnt victim from the Millwood Fabric Warehouse fire," Janice said. "I was going to tell you at the crime scene this morning, but I didn't have an opportunity."

"What's the name of the victim?" I asked with anticipation.

"Kim Black," she said. "We had her DNA on file from a previous situation when she was in prison."

"When was she in prison?"

"She went to prison when she was eighteen for stabbing her boyfriend," she said. "She spent three years at Montgomery's Women's Facility before she got out on parole."

"Well that eases my mind about the kids, because she was living on the street with Danielle Watts and they didn't have any kids with them," I said. "Does the report mention any kids?"

"DHR took them away three years ago and gave them to her mom and dad," she said. "She could visit them whenever she wanted as long as they were supervised."

"Where does her parents live?" I asked.

"In Winston County close to Double Springs," she said. "I'll e-mail you the address."

"I think I might go up there and let them know in person that she was killed," I said.

"That would be nice," she said.

"Did Kim kill the man she stabbed?"

"No, she didn't kill him," she said. "He's still around this area."

"What's his name?"

"Avery Moore."

"That's very interesting," I said. "How long ago has it been since she stabbed him?"

"Let's see, it's been eight or nine years."

"Do you think he had anything to do with her death?"

"It's hard to say," she said. "I wouldn't put anything past these guys."

"Me either," I said. "Not meaning to change the subject, but do you know if Diane found Matt Curry's cause of death?"

"She said he died from a drug overdose."

"Drug overdose," I said. "What type of drugs?"

"He had methamphetamine, heroin and cocaine in his system," she said. "They were all at doses high enough to kill someone."

"Did Diane think it was murder?"

"He had no track marks to indicate he was a drug abuser," she said. "And the puncture wound was along the back of his arm."

"That would be a hard place to stick yourself."

"After several tests where Daniel and Victor tried to stick themselves in the back of the arm with a blunted needle, we determined that it was impossible to insert a needle at the angle to which Matt Curry was injected."

"Someone else shot him up."

"Yes, someone else gave him the drug," she said.

"So, it was murder," I said.

"I would declare it as murder," she said. "Whether accidentally or on purpose, he was still killed by someone else."

"Did you find any evidence that might help us determine who killed him?"

"We didn't find any evidence that we could link to the murderer," she said.

"There were no fingerprints, except for Ginger Mitchell's, on the car, no blood stains or any other body fluid to connect the killer to the victim."

"Is there anything else?"

"That's all we have for now."

"Thanks for the information," I said and closed my phone.

I pulled the notepad close to me and wrote, Kim Black under the death column and also under the connection column alongside Matt Curry. Then I studied my list for a few seconds before putting it in my top drawer and closing it tight.

Then I glanced at the clock, realizing it was almost five o'clock, so I got up and walked to the dispatcher's office.

Rachel looked up and smiled, when I walked in the door.

"Lisa Jones, from the county courthouse, just called to let me know that Avery Moore just got out on bail," Rachel said.

"Did she tell you who paid the bail?"

"Phillip Mays," Rachel said. "His lawyer paid his bail and then picked him up from the jail."

"I wonder who gave Phillip Mays the money for bail."

"It's hard to tell," she said.

"I bet it had drugs behind it," I said. "Did she say when he left?"

"About twenty minutes ago," she said and then she placed her hand on my right arm. "You need to be careful, because he might try to get even."

"He's not the first criminal that's made threats against me," I said, as I took her hand and held it. "But, I will be careful."

"Please do," she said. "I'd hate for you to get hurt."

"Me too," I said and smiled.

"Are you about to leave," she asked.

"Oh yes, that was why I stepped in here," I said. "I'm going home to have dinner with my family."

"You're beginning to understand the importance of family," she said and squeezed my hand.

"I've always understood it, but now I'm learning to appreciate it," I said, as I let go of her hand. "I'll see you tomorrow," and I walked out the door.

Chapter 24

The disgruntled drug dealer sat across the parking lot watching the activity of a group of small time pushers, as they stood on the street corner selling drugs to people who pulled to the side of the street. The pushers used to sell for him, but now they work for one of the newer suppliers who promised a much higher return for their trouble.

He grimaced as Daisy Mayfield, one of his best customers, approached one of the dealers and bought a small bag of drugs. Then an old Ford Ranger pulled to the side of the street and waited for one of the pushers to approach his window.

With hatred he wrapped his hand around the handle of his Ruger LCP semiautomatic handgun and tightened his grip as he watched his former employees selling in his territory.

He thought, these small town punks don't know who their dealing with. I'll show them what happens to people who refuse my employment and then disrespect me by trying to take my customers away.

He watched as a woman in a white Dodge Caravan filled with small kids pulled to the side of the street, bought a bag of drugs and then drove away. A man in a blue Hyundai Sonata followed close behind the van and stopped beside the pusher as she pulled away.

Traffic remained steady for several hours with one car pulling up after another. They pulled to the side of the street, got their drugs and then drove away.

As the traffic slowed, he cranked his black Mazda RX-8 Sport and slowly drove toward the street corner.

When he got close, he slowed and pulled to the side of the street. As one of the pushers approached, he lowered his window, stuck the Ruger out and snapped four quick shots into the chest of his competition.

The pusher's chest exploded from the impact of the bullets and his body collapsed instantly to the ground.

He then turned to the other pusher, who was running away from his car and fired five shots in his direction. After the third shot, the pusher fell to the ground and didn't move. He put his car in reverse and backed alongside the body. Then he fire two more shots in the body lying on the ground.

After he was satisfied with his work, he looked for any potential witnesses and when he didn't see anyone, he drove away as fast as he could.

As he drove, he became more excited because he had vindicated his honor and sent a message to his competitors, not to cross over into his territory.

He thought, I'll send one more message to the community, so he circled the block and drove to the corner where the local prostitutes wait for business.

As he turned the corner, he saw his target standing beside a young girl with dark red hair trying to adjust her dress. He stopped about twenty feet away from the ladies and changed the clip in his Ruger.

Then he slowly pulled to the side of the street in front of the ladies, rolled his window down and fired three shots into each one. He watched as they fell, then he slowly drove away.

He turned left at the stop sign and drove away as fast as he could without drawing attention to his car.

As he drove, he looked in his rearview mirror several times, but relaxed when no one seemed to care about the gunfire. He smiled as he drove and thought, the smack master is back.

Chapter 25

Jenna and I were cleaning up the kitchen after supper. I put the dishes in the dish washer while Jenna washed the big pot that wouldn't fit.

After we finished, we stood at the counter and looked at the calendar in hopes of planning a mini vacation.

"If you could just take off on a Friday, we could be back by Sunday afternoon," Jenna said.

"It would be nice to get away for a few days," I said and pointed at Easter weekend. "What about this weekend?"

"I really don't want to go Easter," Jenna said. "Let's try to go the week after."

"That's fine," I said. "I'll see what I can do."

"Johnny can handle everything while you're gone," she said.

"I know," I said, as my phone started ringing.

I looked at Jenna who had started cleaning the table.

I opened my phone and said, "Sam speaking."

"I have two dead bodies on 15th Street and 5th Avenue," Franklin said.

"What happened?" I asked, as I leaned against the counter.

"Two guys were shot down on the side of the street," he said. "It looks like a drug killing."

"What do you mean?"

"Both victims had drugs lying beside their bodies," he said.

"Great, all we need is a drug war," I said, as I glanced at Jenna.

"Each person was shot several times," he said. "Whoever shot them meant for them to be dead."

"I'll be there as soon as I can," I said, as I closed my phone.

"What happened?" Jenna asked.

"There has been a shooting on 15th Street," I said, as I turned to her. "I guess I'll be out late tonight."

"At least you got to eat before you had to leave," she said and smiled.

"That's true," I said, as I opened my phone and started punching in the number to the CSI Unit.

After the second ring a lady answered the phone and said, "CSI, how can I help you?"

"This is Sam James, Thorton's Police Chief." I said. "I need someone to come to 15th Street and 5th Avenue to help investigate a shooting."

"I'll send someone immediately," she said and then my phone went silence.

I closed my phone to break the connection then I called Diane.

The phone rang several times without being answered and then it went to voice mail. I closed my phone without leaving a message.

"Did you leave a message?" Jenna asked.

"No, I hate talking to a machine," I said. "I'll call her later."

"If you left a message she might call you back," she said.

"I know," I said and started to put my phone in my pocket when it started ringing. "Sam speaking," I answered.

"This is Diane," she said in a winded voice. "I'm sorry I missed your call, but I got to the phone as fast as I could."

"That's alright," I said. "I know you can't stay by the phone all the time."

"Did you need something?"

"Unfortunately I do," I said. "I have two dead bodies at 15th Street and 5th Avenue."

"I'll call Samantha and get her to meet me at the office," she said. "Then we'll be there as soon as we can."

"I'll see you there," I said, as I closed my phone.

"Be careful," Jenna said, as she kissed me.

"I will," I said and started walking to the door.

As I reached for the door knob, my phone started ringing. I looked at Jenna as I took my phone out of my pocket. I took a deep breath before I opened my phone and said, "Sam speaking."

"Sam, this is Tony," he said and hesitated.

"What is it Tony?" I asked.

"I have two dead bodies at 18th Street and 7th Avenue," he said.

"Are you talking about the one's Franklin just called about?" I asked. "I thought they were on 15th Street and 5th Avenue?"

"No, this is a different set of bodies." he said.

"Could you tell what happened?"

"It looks like two hookers were shot while they were standing on the side of the street," he said.

"Are they both dead?"

"Yes, they're both dead," he said. "They were shot three times, each at close range."

"Great, now we have two murder scenes at the same time." I said with frustration. "Just keep the area secure and I'll be there as soon as I can."

"I'll start roping the crime scene off."

"Are you sure it's safe?"

"It looks safe to me."

"Alright then, I'm going by 15th Street first and then I'll be there," I said. "Do you need help right now?"

"No," he said. "There's no one here except me."

"On second thought, stay in your car until someone gets there," I said. "I'll have someone there as fast as I can get them there."

"Are you sure?" he asked.

"Yes," I said and I closed my phone.

Then I opened my phone again and called Johnny.

After the second ring, he answered and asked, "What's up Sam?"

"How did you know it was me?" I asked.

"I have your number programmed into my phone."

"Oh," I said and laughed.

"Is something wrong?" he asked.

"We've had two separate murder scenes happening at the same time," I said. "I need someone to go the 18th Street and 7th Avenue to make sure the area is safe while Tony ropes off the crime scene."

"It'll take me a few minutes to get dressed, but I'll be there as fast as I can," he said and then my phone went dead.

"We have two separate murder scenes," I said, after I closed my phone and looked toward Jenna.

I looked at my cell phone to check the battery then I slipped it in my shirt pocket.

"Do you think they're related?" Jenna asked.

"I won't know until I see the evidence," I said, as I reached for the door knob. "I need to go," and I walked out the door.

Chapter 26

I turned down 15th Street and slowed as I reached 5th Avenue. Then turned right on 5th Avenue and pulled to the side of the street.

As I turned my engine off, I saw Franklin getting out of his car. When he closed his door, he looked toward me and slowly began walking in my direction.

"Who reported the shooting?" I asked, as Franklin walked up beside me.

"They wouldn't give their name," he said. "But it was a lady's voice."

"Has anyone else been here since you called?"

"There was a lot of cars slow down like they are going to turn down 5th Avenue, but when they saw my car, they sped up and drove away," he said.

"Have you seen the bodies?" I asked, as I started walking toward the body that was closest to the street.

"I checked to make sure they were dead," I said. "That's when I saw the drugs lying beside their bodies. Then I went back to my car to wait for backup."

I stopped when I reached the first victim, bent down and looked at his chest wounds. "I can count a least three shots that went in his heart," I said then I stood up and started walking toward the other victim. "Did you see any shell casings lying on the ground?"

"To tell you the truth, I didn't look," he said. "I was concerned with seeing if they were alive and after I determined they were dead, I wanted to get out of the open just in case the shooter decided to come back."

I slowed my step when I got close to the second victim and carefully approached his body. The victim was lying face down with two large blood stains in the center of his back and another one below his right scapula.

"He was shot while he running away from the shooter," I said. "They may have been selling drugs in someone else's territory," and I pointed at three small packs of white powder lying beside the victim.

"I didn't touch the drugs," Franklin said. "I didn't want to tamper with any potential evidence."

"That's a good idea," I said and stepped back from the body. "Let's look for shell casings while we wait for Janice and Diane to arrive," and I started walking toward the street.

I slowly began walking along the side of the street with my head down and my attention focused on any potential shell casing that might be lying along the side of the pavement. I walked back and forth, scanning a three foot radius as I moved closer to the victim in an attempt to cover the entire area.

"Here's one," I said, as I stepped up on the sidewalk.

"How are we going to mark the shells," Franklin asked.

"Do you have any crime scene tape in your trunk?" I asked.

"I think I have yellow crime scene tape and orange caution tape," he said. "Which one do you think would be the best to use?" he asked as he started walking toward his car.

"Let's go with the orange," I said.

Franklin opened his trunk, took a small roll of orange tape out and started walking toward where I was standing. As he got close, he took his pocket knife out and cut about a foot of tape off the roll.

"This will make it easier to see the evidence," he said, as he handed me the piece of tape.

I took the tape and laid it beside the shell casing.

"Let me have another piece in case I find another shell," I said, as I held my hand out. "That way you can go look near the other body."

Franklin cut another foot of tape off the roll and handed it to me. Then he walked toward the victim lying beside the street and began looking for shell casings.

"I have two casings here," he said, as he stepped off the sidewalk into the street.

He stuck a piece of caution tape beside the shells and continued looking along the street.

"This victim was shot at least three times, so we should have at least three shell casings over here," I said, as I looked.

"I should have more casings over here than I'm finding," Franklin said.

"If they were shot from a car, some of the shell casings might have fallen inside," I said, and I looked down the street as I heard a car turning down 5th Avenue.

I watched as Janice pulled the CSI van to the side of the street and parked behind my car. I looked at the victim I was standing next to, then turned and slowly started walking toward Janice.

"What do we have Sam," she asked, as she opened her door.

I didn't say anything, but continued walking toward her.

She got out and closed her door.

"We have two victims here and two more on 18th Street and 7th Avenue," I said in a low voice.

"You've had two shootings?" she asked with surprise.

"Yes, Johnny and Tony are watching the other victims while we work here," I said. "I plan on going over there once you get started gathering evidence."

"Alright, what do you have here?"

"Two male victims," I said. "The one closest to the street was shot at least three times in the chest at close range and the one lying in the grass was shot at least three times in the back."

"Did you see any shell casings?"

"See that orange tape lying on the ground," I said, as I pointed at the tape I had placed on the ground.

"Yes."

"That's where I marked a shell casing," I said. "Franklin marked two by the other victim."

"Great," she said and turned to Victor and said, "Let's get started."

He took his camera out of its case and walked around the van. He snapped a shot of the shell casings lying in the street, then moved closer to the victim and began photographing the victim and the environment surrounding the body.

After he finished photographing the first victim, he moved to the second victim. He started at the shell casing, then moved toward the body and photographed the victim and the surrounding environment.

As he finished he walked back to the van.

Daniel slowly approached the first victim. He stopped at the shell casings and carefully slipped them in a plastic bag, then labeled it with the time, date and location where the casings were found.

He then moved to the victim and bent down beside him. He took a cotton tipped applicator out of his case, swabbed one of the bullet wounds, then put it in a glass vial and screwed the top in place.

"Sam, if you want to check on the other victims, we've got it here," Janice said.

"I think I will go over there," I said. "If you need anything, Franklin will be here."

"We'll be fine," she said. "Could you give Victor a ride so he can start photographing the crime scene."

"Sure," I said. "That will be no problem."

"Victor, go with Sam and we'll meet you over there when we're through here," Janice said, as she looked at Victor.

"Thanks for the ride," Victor said, as he grabbed his camera and hurriedly walked to my car.

I got in my car and waited for Victor to get settled. Then I cranked up and pulled out in the street. When I stopped at the stop sign at the end of the street, I looked in my rearview mirror and saw Diane slowly backing her van toward the sidewalk.

"Diane's here now," I said. "I hope she brought enough stretchers."

"Does she know there's four bodies?" Victor asked.

"I forgot to call and tell her we have more victims," I said and rubbed my fingers through my hair.

"She probably will have enough," he said. "I think she keeps three or four stretchers in her van at all times."

"I hope it's four," I said and then I turned left on 16th Street and drove toward 7th Avenue.

I went three blocks, then turned right on 7th Avenue and drove two blocks to 18th Street. I pulled to the side of the street as soon as I turned onto 18th Street and stopped.

Johnny and Tony were leaning against Johnny's red Ford Mustang looking across the street at the lifeless bodies lying on the ground. They turned when we got out of the car. After a few seconds, they slowly started walking toward the bodies. When they got to within ten feet of the bodies, they stopped to wait for us to join them.

"Could you tell what happened?" I ask when I got close to them.

"I think they approached a car together and the driver shot them," Johnny said and we began walking toward the bodies. "They were both shot at close range."

"Did you recognize the victims?" I asked.

"I didn't recognize them, but I'm not in this area very often," he said.

"Wait here and I'll photograph the crime scene," Victor said, as he stepped in front of the victims and started taking pictures.

He backed up a few feet and photographed the street leading up to the bodies. He then moved closer and photographed the sidewalk where the victims were lying. Then he stood over the victims and photographed their face and upper bodies. He continued moving to different angles and snapping off three to four pictures at every angle until he was satisfied that he had covered the entire crime scene.

"Alright, I'm finished," he said, as backed away from the bodies.

I stepped upon the sidewalk and cautiously walked toward the victims. I stopped about two feet away and looked at their upper bodies which was blood drenched from the gunshot wounds.

"How could you tell how many times they were shot?" I asked, as I continued looking at the wounds.

"I counted the holes in their blouses," Johnny said. "I still might have missed one or two wounds."

"It looks like they were both shot in the heart," I said. "That could explain the pool of blood they are lying in."

"Do you recognize the victims?" Johnny asked, as he stepped a little closer.

I moved around the bodies so I could get a good look at their faces. "Her hair is a little different, but I think the one with red hair is Ruby Marks," I said, as I leaned in close to her face. "I don't recognize the other one."

I stepped back as I heard the CSI van turning down 7th Avenue. Janice slowed as she pulled to the side of the street and parked behind Johnny's Ford Mustang.

"Now that's a police car," Janice said, as she got out of the van and walked beside Johnny's car. "Sam, I thought you had a small budget," and she laughed.

"Hey, I bought that car used," Johnny said in defense. "I couldn't afford a new one on my salary."

"It looks great," she said. "You must take real good care of it."

"He does," I said and laughed. "He treats it like it's his baby."

Janice's expression changed as she looked at the victims from across the street.

"Alright, what do we have here?" Janice asked, as she walked toward the bodies.

"Two women shot at close range to the chest," I said.

"It appears they were working women," she said. "I'm sure they weren't hanging on the street corner watching traffic."

"The red head was Ruby Marks," I said. "She was addicted to drugs and she worked the street to pay for her habit."

"So, she could have been killed by a disgruntled customer or a drug dealer," Janice said.

"That's a possibility," I said, as I watched Daniel open his evidence case.

"I think I see a small trace of gun powder around her collar," Daniel said, as he took a cotton tipped swab, rubbed it along the edge of her collar and placed it in a glass vial and covered it with a black screw top.

He carefully put it in his evidence bag then he swabbed the wounds and placed the sample in the same type of container.

Janice bent over the victim that I had identified as Ruby Marks and began looking for evidence. She swabbed the wound, placed the swab in a glass vial and sealed it tight with a black screw top. She placed it in her evidence bag then she began looking around the body for potential shell casings.

"Did anyone find a shell casing?" she asked, as she looked toward me.

"We looked along the street and around the bodies but we didn't see anything," Johnny said. "We didn't touch the bodies or look underneath them."

I turned and looked at 18th Street as Diane turned onto 7th Avenue. She slowly drove past our cars then backed her van toward the victims.

"I thought there were only two victims," she said, as she opened her door.

"I'm sorry, I was told about these two victims after I had called you and I forgot to call you back to let you know," I said. "I hope you have enough stretchers to get them."

"I always have four stretchers in my van," she said and she opened the back door.

"Thank God you're prepared," I exclaimed.

"The problem might be lifting the bodies up and placing them inside the van," she said, as she lowered a metal plate from each side which formed a platform above the other victims.

"Johnny and I can help lift the victims into the van once you have them secured to the stretcher," I said, as I stepped to the side to let Samantha get to the back door.

She reached inside the van and released two straps that were holding a stretcher to the right side of the van. Then she lifted it off the hooks that supported it and let it slid down the side of the van onto the platform.

I grabbed the stretcher and helped Samantha set it on the ground.

Diane took the stretcher and rolled it toward the victims.

I watched as she and Samantha loaded Ruby Marks' body onto the stretcher and rolled it toward the van.

"Let's get the other stretcher down before we put the body inside," Diane said, as she reached inside the van and released the straps.

She eased the stretcher off the hooks and lowered it onto the platform. Then she pulled it to the edge.

I grabbed the stretcher and helped lower it to the ground.

Samantha rolled the stretcher away from the van toward the other victim's body.

Then Johnny and I grabbed Ruby's body and lifted it onto the platform.

"Hold the stretcher there while I lock it in place," Diane said, as she grabbed a clamp from the platform and hooked it to the right wheel of the stretcher.

After she hooked the left wheel, she went inside the van and secured the front of the stretcher to the platform.

"The stretcher won't go anywhere now," she said, as she got out of the van.

Then she walked to the other victim to help Samantha lift her on the stretcher. Within minutes the other victim was strapped to the stretcher and ready to be loaded inside the van.

"Janice, here is a shell casing," Diane said and stopped to wait for Janice to approach.

"Where is it?" Janice asked, as she approached.

"It was caught in her hair," Diane said and pointed to a shell casing that was twisted in her hair.

Janice took a pair of scissors out of her bag and clipped the ball of hair that had entombed the shell casing and placed it inside a plastic bag.

As she maneuvered the shell casing around in the bag, she pushed it through an opening in the hair until she was able to get a good view of the casing.

"The same shooter shot these victims that shot the others," Janice said, as she turned to me. "This is an exact match to the shell casings we found at the other crime scene."

"So, we're looking for one shooter instead of two," I said. "I guess that's a good thing."

"It depends on how you look at it," Janice said and smiled.

"Sam, I need you to help load the victim," Diane said, as she rolled the stretcher beside me and continued toward the van.

I followed Diane to her van where Johnny was waiting to help lift the stretcher.

Samantha had gotten inside the van to be ready to hook the stretcher in place when we loaded it inside.

I took one side and Johnny took the other and we lifted the stretcher onto the platform and pushed it completely inside.

"Hold it while I connect the clamps to the wheels," Diane said, as she reached inside and clamped the left wheel. She then clamped the right.

I watched as Samantha clamped both the front wheels while Diane was clamping the back.

Diane grabbed the stretcher and shook it from side to side. She took the other stretcher and shook it also.

"They're not going anywhere," she said, as she closed the back door to the van.

"Are you going to need help unloading the stretchers when you get to your lab?" I asked.

"No, we'll be alright when we get there," Diane said. "We have a ramp that we can attach to the platform and slide the stretchers down to the floor."

Samantha slid into the passenger's seat to wait for Diane to get inside so they could leave.

"I'll come by in the morning and check on your progress," I said.

"Don't bring doughnuts," she said, as she opened the door and got inside. "I can't lose weight if I'm eating doughnuts."

"I'll just bring you a cup of coffee," I said.

"That will be fine," she said, as she cranked her van. "I'll see you in the morning," and she drove away.

"So, you've been bringing Diane gifts when you come to see her," Janice said with a smile. "I don't remember seeing any doughnuts when you've been by the CSI lab."

"I didn't think I was allowed to bring anything into the lab area," I said. "Your guard watches everything I do when I come by."

"He would probably let a dozen doughnuts go by if you gave him one or two," she said and laughed.

"I'll have to try that some time," I said and laughed.

"Alright let's go," Janice said, as she got inside the CSI van.

Daniel got into the passenger's side and closed the door. Victor got in the backseat through the side door and closed it.

"I'll talk to you tomorrow," Janice said and drove away.

"Johnny thanks for helping me out," I said, as we watched Janice drive out of sight.

"I wasn't doing anything anyway," he said, as he opened his car door and got inside. "I'll see you tomorrow," and he drove away.

"Tony, are you going to need help filling out the paperwork?" I asked.

"Franklin can help me," he said. "We can do our paperwork together."

"If you get stuck on anything, just leave it and I'll help you when I get there in the morning," I said. "I'll try to be in early tomorrow."

"Thanks, I'll remember that," he said, as he got in his car.

I watched as he drove away, then I got in my car and drove to 15th Street and 5th Avenue to make sure everything was cleared away from the murder scene.

The street was vacant, with no evidence of any violence except for a large blood stain on the sidewalk and a dark red spot on the grass where the other victim was lying.

Franklin had already gone back to the police station to file his report, so I turned right at the end of the street and drove home.

Chapter 27

I walked into the police station at 6 o'clock in the morning to find Franklin and Tony still sitting at the computer working on the reports from last night's murders.

"Have you had any problems with the paperwork?" I asked, as I looked over Franklin's shoulder.

"No, we haven't had a problem," Franklin said. "I'm just going over the report again to reinforce the need to fill out every sheet."

"So, you're through with the reports."

"Yes, we're through."

"Great, because I need to spend this morning filling out some paperwork to justify calling Johnny in to help with the crime scene," I said and then I walked in my office.

I turned my computer on and went to get a cup of coffee while it booted up.

When I got back, my screen was up and ready for me to sign in. I punched in my password and then pulled up the reports I needed to fill out.

Within twenty minutes, I had fully justified the overtime we would be paying Johnny for coming in on his time off. I saved the reports on my hard drive then I hit the print button and printed a hard copy to be sent to the Mayor's office.

As I pulled the papers off the printer, I realized the Mayor hadn't contacted me about the damage I had caused to the man's shrubs and yard when I was escaping the gun fire. In fact, I didn't get a complaint from anyone about the damage I had caused. Oh well, I'm sure I'll hear about it when they want to get the yard repaired.

I slid the report in a manila envelope and laid it on top of my desk.

I pulled up my monthly budget, filled in the necessary numbers and then printed the report. After the printer stopped shooting out pieces of paper, I pulled the report off the printer and put it in another manila envelope.

Then I sealed it up and laid it on top of the other envelope. I sat for a few seconds trying to decide if I wanted to take the paperwork over to the mayor's office this morning or wait until I was ready to go home.

After debating the issue with myself, I decided I needed the cash for my payroll, so I stood up, picked up the envelopes and walked out of my office.

"I'm going to drop these off at the mayor's office," I said, as I walked past the dispatcher's office. "I'll be back as soon as I can," I announced and I walked out the door.

The mayor's office was only a few hundred feet from the police station, so it only took a few minutes to walk the envelopes over and drop them off.

As I slid the envelopes in the mayor's mailbox, I heard the door rattle and then open. I turned to see the mayor standing with a concerned look on his face.

"Sam, can I speak to you a second?" he asked.

"I didn't expect to see you this early," I said and smiled.

"I needed to come by the office before I went to work," he said. "I heard you had some people trying to kill you the other day."

"I think I might have been a little too close to Rodney Curry and they were trying to get me to back off."

"Well, did you back off?"

"No, I just made sure I had enough backup when I was questioning people about

Rodney."

"Good idea."

"Did anyone complain about me damaging their yard when I drove through it?"

"You drove through someone's yard," he said and smiled.

"Yes, I did when I was running from the gunfire."

"I've already approved to have the yard repaired," he said. "After someone tried to kill you, I thought it was the least I could do."

"We had four people killed last night," I said. "Two looked like drug dealers and the other two looked like prostitutes."

"Bad things happen when you're doing bad things," he responded. "Were they connected?"

"I think so," I said. "I should get a report later from the CSI Unit."

"I trust that you will catch the killer," he said, as he closed his door and locked it.

"With God's help, I'll catch him," I said.

"I'll talk to you later," he said. "I need to get to work," and he walked to his car.

I turned and walked to the police station.

When I reached the door, I turned toward the parking lot as I heard Johnny pull into his parking space. I waited for Johnny to get to the door then I opened it and we walked inside.

Franklin and Tony were still sitting in front of the computer when we walked in, but this time they were looking at the weather report from a local television station.

"It should be a good day to sleep," Franklin said, as he stood up. "The sky's supposed to be overcast all day."

"Did they mention rain?" I asked.

"No, they just said it would be cloudy," he said and he started walking toward the door. He stopped before he got to the door, then turned to Tony and asked, "Are you going home?"

"I thought I might need to wait for Richard to get here," Tony said. "I didn't want to leave without coverage."

"That's fine, you can go home Tony," I said. "I need you to go home and get some sleep so you can come back tonight."

"Alright," he said, as he stood up. "I'll see you tonight," and he walked to the door.

Franklin opened the door and walked outside.

Tony followed.

"They seem to work good together," Johnny said after they walked out the door.

"Franklin likes to teach and Tony is willing to learn," I said. "They make a good team."

I walked to the coffee pot, poured two cups of coffee and handed Johnny a cup.

"Thank you," he said, as he took the cup. "I did need some coffee this morning."

"Me too," I said. "I didn't get much sleep last night."

"I didn't either," he said. "I was so wired when I got home that it took me a long time to calm down enough to go to bed."

"Listen, I want to thank you again for helping us last night," I said. "I'll make sure you get paid for your time."

"No problem," he said and then he took a sip of coffee. "I guess I need to patrol around town to remind people they need to obey the law."

"What's going on?" Richard asked, as he walked through the door.

"I was about to patrol around town," Johnny said.

"Wait a minute and I'll go with you," he said, as he laid his jacket across the back of his chair. "I can patrol the north side of town while you patrol the south side."

"Richard before you go I want to let you know that we had two shootings last night and four people were killed," I said. "So you need to be very careful while you're patrolling."

"Who was killed?" he asked.

"I believe one of them was Ruby Marks," I said. "I don't know the identity of the other victims."

"Ruby Marks?" he said and rubbed the side of his chin. "Isn't that the hooker that Avery Moore hit?"

"She was one of the ladies on the street corner," I said. "I don't remember which one he hit."

"Do you think he killed her?"

"At this point, I really don't know."

"Let's go," Johnny said, as he walked to the door.

"Let me get a cup of coffee," he said, as he ran to the coffee pot, poured a cup of coffee in a travel mug and ran out the door.

Johnny followed and closed the door.

I looked at Rachel when she walked out of the dispatcher's office and went to the fax machine. She looked at the papers she had in her hand, then turned them face down on the machine and punched in the number to the place she was sending the fax. Within a minute, the fax machine printed a paper confirming that her fax had been sent and received by the other party.

Rachel took the papers off the fax machine then went to the coffee pot. She poured a cup of coffee, put two creams and four sugars in her coffee and slowly started stirring the mixture together.

"So, you have another murder to solve," she said, as she walked toward me.

"Yes I do," I said. "As Thorton has grown the crime has really increased."

"A lot of people have moved here from our neighboring counties," she said. "They seem to have brought their criminal habits with them."

"People don't respect the law like they used to," I said.

"They don't have to stay in jail like they used to," she said. "They're not afraid of getting caught."

"I agree," I said and started walking toward the door. "I need to go to Diane's office and see what she's found out about our victims," and I put my hand on the doorknob.

"Be careful," she said.

"I will," I said and then I walked out the door.

Chapter 28

I stopped at Joe's Cup of Joe on my way to Diane's office and bought two extra-large cups of his specialty coffee. I parked in a space reserved for visitors because it was close to the door. I opened the door, got out, grabbing both cups of coffee as I went and closed the door with my foot.

As I walked toward the front door, I was trying to decide the best way to hold the coffee while I opened the door. My problem was solved when I walked up the steps because Diane opened the door and held it while I walked inside.

"Thanks for holding the door," I said, as I walked past her.

"You looked like you were struggling with the cups," she said and laughed.

"I didn't want to drop one and they were too hot to hold close to my chest," I said, as I walked inside her office and sat both cups on her desk.

"They have sleeves to go around the cups to protect your hands from the heat," she said. "Why don't you have sleeves on those cups?"

"I went through the drive thru and they didn't give them to me."

"You got ripped off," she said and laughed.

Then she picked up the cup closest to her and took a sip of coffee.

"It's good coffee even if you didn't get a sleeve for the cup," she said, as she sat the cup down. "I'll have to wait for it to cool a little before I can drink it."

"Have you performed an autopsy on any of the victims from last night?"

"Yes, I've performed an autopsy on the two male victims," she said, as she moved a sheet of paper in front of her.

"My goodness, you're fast," I remarked.

"I've been here since 4 o'clock this morning," she said and smiled. "That's why I was waiting at the door for the coffee," and she laughed.

"What did you find?" I asked, as I sat back in my chair.

"The first victim was shot four times in the chest at close range," she said. "Three of the four bullets went directly in his heart."

"That explains the blood loss."

"He was probably killed with the first bullet."

"Could you determine the type of gun that was used?"

"It looked like a 9mm but I'm not sure," she said. "I sent the bullets to the CSI lab along with the victim's clothes and the drugs that was inside their pockets."

"Drugs?"

"Both victims have their pockets filled with small packets of drugs."

"So, they were dealing."

"It appears they were," she said. "I thought you knew that already."

"I did, but I didn't really have the evidence to prove it."

"You do now."

"Could you identify the victim?"

"Daniel came over early this morning and got finger prints from the victims," she said. "He wanted to get a head start at identifying the victims."

"What about the second victim?"

"He was shot three times in the back and two times in the left side," she said. "One bullet struck his left kidney, one struck his spinal column, one struck his left scapula and the two that entered his side struck his left lung."

"Which one killed him?"

"It probably was a combination of all the shots, but the one that struck his spine paralyzed him so he didn't feel the other shots."

"When are you going to start on the women?"

"As soon as I finish my coffee," she said and smiled. "Do you want to watch?"

"I think I'll go to the CSI building and talk to Daniel, but I might come back and watch after I'm finished talking to him," I said, as I got up and walked to the door. "I hope to have a name for the victims when I get back," and I walked out the door.

I walked across the street and entered through the front door of the CSI building. I stopped suddenly as a lady wearing the CSI uniform stepped forward and looked at me without saying a word.

I was speechless as I looked at the mammoth size of the lady. She was at least 6'4" and weighed over 300 pounds with arms the size of any well-built linebacker and a trunk that could place her on the offensive line of any football team.

"Can I help you?" she asked in a deep voice.

I looked at her face which was smooth, slowly moved my eyes to her chest which indicated she was a woman then I looked away.

"Can I help you," she asked with a little irritation in her voice. "This is private property."

"I'm sorry, my name is Sam James," I said. "I need to speak to Daniel."

"You do," she said in a sarcastic way. "Why do you need to speak to Daniel?"

"Police business," I said and showed her my badge.

"Just a minute," she said, as she picked up the phone and punched in a couple numbers.

"I should have showed you my badge when I first got here," I said.

She looked at me for a second then she turned around and started whispering in the phone.

"He'll be here in a minute," she said, as she turned back around. "Just have a seat over there," and she pointed to a metal chair that was setup against the wall.

I moved to the chair and sat down.

She went back behind the counter and pretended I wasn't around.

I sat in my corner for a few minutes before I heard movement behind the guard.

"Where is he," Daniel asked, as he looked over the counter.

"I'm over here," I said, as I stood up and started walking toward the counter.

"Let's go to the back," he said, as he held the door open and allowed me to walk behind the counter.

I followed Daniel down the hall. He opened the door and we walked into the back.

"What happened to the other guard?" I asked after we were away from the guard.

"He's on vacation," Daniel said and smiled. "She usually works nights."

"I knew I hadn't seen her before," I said. "She would put any man to shame."

"Yes, she would," he said and laughed as he walked to a table where several small boxes were lined in the middle. "This is what we found in the male victim's pockets," and he pointed to the boxes. "The first three boxes were on the first victim and the second three boxes were on the second victim."

“Why do you have them separated in different boxes?” I asked, as I moved closer to the boxes.

“This box contains what the dope heads call crank,” he said, as he pulled out several small packages with clear powder in each and laid them on the table. “Dope heads melt this down and shoot it in their veins. They like this because it’s relatively cheap compared to other drugs and they get an instant high,” and he started putting the packages back inside the box.

He closed the lid and then opened the other box.

“This box contains what is call ice or glass on the street,” he said. “The dope heads smoke this to get their high,” and he put the lid back on.

He moved to the third box and opened the lid. He pulled out a hand full of packages with white powder in each and laid them on the table.

“This is the most expensive of their stock,” he said. “This is a refined version of cocaine,” he said and handed me a pack. “I tested a package when I got here this morning to determine the purity of the drug and I believe this to be about 50% less pure than the cocaine you’d buy off the streets.”

“What did they add to the cocaine?”

“See those off white specks mixed in the powder,” he said, as he handed me a package.

“Yes, I see it,” I said. “What is it?”

“It’s one of the active ingredients used in bathroom cleaners to remove mold and mildew,” he said.

“Why would they put something like that in the cocaine?”

"It increases the profit."

"That can't be good for someone to inhale," I said, as I handed the package back to Daniel.

"I don't think the dealers care," he said, as he put the package back in the box and closed the lid.

"What about the other boxes?" I asked, as I looked toward them.

"They contain the same drugs," he said. "I just put them in different containers because they come off another victim."

I walked around the table and looked at the shell casings that were lying beside the boxes. I picked up one of the casings and rolled it between my fingers.

"Were you able to determine what type of gun he used?" I asked, as I laid the shell casing back on the table.

"He used a Ruger LCP semiautomatic," Daniel said. "That's why the wounds were so close together," and he leaned his hands on the table.

"Were all the victims killed with the same gun?"

"I haven't got bullets from the other two victims, but the men that were killed on 7th Avenue were killed with the same gun," Daniel said, as he picked up a shell casing and laid it back down.

"Did you run their prints?"

"I ran all four victim's prints early this morning and got a hit on all of them almost instantly," Daniel said and smiled. "It seems they all had a criminal record."

"What a surprise," I said and smiled. "Drugs and criminal records seem to go hand in hand."

"Yes, they do," he said, as he picked up a sheet of paper and began looking at it. "Let's see, the victim that was closest to the road was Chuck Henson, the other male victim was Rocky Curry, one of the female victims was Ruby Marks and the other was Angel Marks."

"Rocky Curry," I said with surprise. "I think that's Rodney Curry's brother."

"The Curry family didn't seem to be doing very well in the drug business," Daniel said and laughed.

"It's only a matter of time before the drug business turns against you," I responded. "Did you say both women had the last name Marks?"

"Yes, I did," he said. "I think they were sisters."

"Sisters caught in the same addiction," I said. "What a tragedy."

"I did find a trace of gun powder in the samples I got from the victims," he said. "The women were both shot at close range as well as was Chuck Henson."

"Rocky Curry probably would have been if he hadn't ran," I said and stepped back from the table.

"The shooter's objective was to kill all the victims and he succeeded."

"Can I have a copy of those names?" I asked.

"Sure," he said, as he walked to a copier. "Here you go," and he handed me a copy of the list.

"Thanks for your help," I said, as I walked to the door.

"I'll call you if I find anything different on the other victims."

"Alright," I said and walked out the door.

I walked past the steroid induced guard without saying a word and went through the outer door.

I went across the street to see if Diane had finished with the other autopsies.

When I opened the door to the autopsy room, I could see Diane still leaning over one of the victims, digging inside her chest.

"Still hard at work," I said, as I approached the table.

"I've found something peculiar," Diane said, as she looked up. "Both women had transposition of great vessels when they were infants and they both had the Mustard procedure to correct the impairment."

"What is that?" I asked.

"It's a congenital heart defect where the great arteries are reversed," she said. "The aorta leaves the right ventricle and the pulmonary artery leaves the left ventricle which means the circulatory system doesn't communicate with each other and the heart pushes unoxygenated blood through the body."

"Is it common to see two people with the same heart defeat?"

"Only if they're related."

"I think our two female victims were sisters."

"That would explain it."

Then she got a pair of forceps off her work table, reached inside the woman's chest and pulled out a blood covered bullet. She dropped it in a tray and reached inside the victim's chest for another.

"I can see one more," she said, as she pulled a bullet out and dropped it inside the tray. "All the bullets were clustered together," and she dropped the third bullet in the tray.

"Did you determine the cause of death?" I asked.

"I'd say massive blood loss from a bullet hole to the heart," Diane said, as she reached inside the victim's chest with a scalpel and then pulled her heart out.

She put it on the scales then she laid it on her work tray.

"Were both ladies killed by the same gun?"

"Yes, they were killed by the same type of bullet," she said. "I'd say the same person killed both women."

"That's what I needed to know," I said and started walking toward the door.

"Are you sure you don't want to watch the autopsy?" Diane asked and smiled.

"I need to get back to the police station," I said and I walked out the door.

I parked in my parking space, got out and walked to the dispatcher's office. When I entered I saw Rachel working on the daily log where calls were recorded.

"Rachel, I had a long night and to this point it's been a long day, so I think I need to go home and get some rest," I said. "Tell Richard to hold the fort down."

"I'll tell him," she said.

"Thanks," I said. "I'll see you tomorrow," and I walked out the door.

Chapter 29

I pulled into the station parking lot at 6:55 in the morning and parked in my parking space. When I got out of my car, I noticed a car that normally wasn't in the lot at this time of morning. In fact, I'd never seen this car before.

I checked my Glock G17, then opened the door and walked into the squad room.

"Give me my son's body!" Gloria Curry demanded, as I walked in the door.

"I can't release the body right now because we're still investigating his murder," I said and looked over at Franklin.

"She's been pacing around the squad room for the past hour waiting for you to get here," he said and rolled his eyes. "I told her you were working on her son's case this morning, but she still demanded to talk to you."

I walked a couple steps toward her and stopped. "By the way, how did you know he was dead?" I asked when I looked her in her eyes.

"That's none of your business," she retorted. "I can't trust you to tell me anything, so I have to find out things for myself."

"What are you talking about?"

"You've had Matt's body for a couple of days and you haven't told me he's dead," she said and glared at me. "You should at least tell me when you find one of my relatives dead."

"We're still investigating his death also."

"Is that why you didn't tell me he's dead?"

"Sometimes during an investigation its best to keep the facts quiet," I said. "That might mean that I can't tell the family of their loved ones' death, because they'll want the body and I can't give it to them until I've gathered everything I need to investigate the murder."

"You can keep Matt's body," she said with irritation in her voice. "I don't want anything to do with him."

"Would you like a cup of coffee?" I asked, as I lowered my voice to try to calm her down.

"Lord no, I'd never get to sleep tonight," she said, as she took a handkerchief out of her purse and wiped her forehead. "But thanks for the offer," and she forced a smile.

"Would you like to go to my office and sit down while we talk?"

"That would be nice," she said, as she took a deep breath and slowly let it out through her mouth.

"This way," I said and pointed toward my office door.

I stepped in front and opened the door. "Please sit in one of those chairs," I said, as I turned the lights on.

"Thanks," she said, as she walked to the front of my desk and sat down.

I closed the door, then pulled my chair out and sat down. I studied her face for a few seconds without saying anything.

"Did the person that told you about Rocky's death give you any details?" I asked, as I leaned forward with my elbows on my desk.

"No, all they said was that he was dead," she said.

I sat back in my chair and asked, "Who told you about his death?"

"I don't know who told me," she said after a long pause. "Someone called me and told me he was killed."

"They wouldn't give their name?"

"They didn't give me a chance to ask," she said. "As soon as they finished telling me of his death, they hung up."

I watched Gloria as she talked and believed she was sincere with her answers. Then I asked, "Was it a man or women that called?"

"I'm not sure," she said. "I think it was a man, but some women have deep voices from years of smoking."

"When did they call you?"

"This morning about five o'clock," she said, as she opened her purse. "I came as soon as I could get ready," then she pulled a tube of chapstick out of her purse and began rubbing it on her lips.

"Gloria, we'll release his body to you as soon as we can," I said in a gentle voice. "But right now, we need to keep it."

"I know," she said, as she lowered her head and began to cry.

It started as a low pitched sound and increased in intensity until she was screaming in a high pitch voice.

"Who killed my baby?" she screamed. "Who killed my sweet baby?" and she lowered her head and cried.

I waited while she cried.

After a few minutes of hard crying, she swallowed a couple of times to regain her control. Then she wiped her eyes with a tissue she had taken from her purse, sat up straight and asked, "Are you going to catch this madman that killed my baby?"

"That's what we're working on right now," I said, as I leaned toward her and spoke in a gentle voice. "We intend on finding the killer."

"Please don't let his death be in vain," she said, as she sniffed. "When do you think I can bury my son?" she asked as she stood up.

"We should have everything we need in a couple of days," I said. "I'll call you as soon as I can release the body," and I got up and opened the door.

"I'm sorry I made a scene," she said, as she forced a smile. "I'm very upset."

"That's understandable at this time in your grief," I said and I escorted her into the squad room. "Why don't you go home and spend time with your family."

"I don't have any more family," she said, as a tear rolled down her face. "Rodney's the only one left and he's disappeared."

"It might be a good time to be with friends and church members."

"I can always count on my church family," she said and smiled. "I'll call Sister Karen and have some of the ladies in my church come by to spend time with me."

"I'm sorry for your loss," I said and I gave her a hug. "I'll do the best I can to catch the killer."

She wrapped her arms around me and said, "That's all I ask." Then she backed up a step and looked me in the face. "I'll help you anyway I can to catch this killer," she said and she walked out the door.

"I still haven't told Kim Black's family that she's dead," I said, as I walked to my desk and got the copy of Janice's e-mail with the address. "I'll be back in a couple of hours," I announced and I walked out the door.

Chapter 30

I turned right on Highway 195 and drove toward Double Springs. As I drove, I called to verify the directions and also make sure it would be a good time to visit. When I got near Double Springs, I turned onto Grady Franks Road and drove approximately a half a mile then turned onto Highway 32. I drove another mile before I saw the landmark I was looking for. A large metal bull, with horns three feet long, was standing beside the driveway like it was daring anyone to trespass on their property.

I slowed down and carefully turned into the narrow gravel driveway that would lead me to the parents of Kim Black. I eased up the long steep hill until I reached my destination which was a small white house with bright red shudders.

As I got out of my car, I saw a man in his early sixties sitting on the porch rocking in a wood rocking chair.

"Come on up and have a seat," he said when I approached the steps.

"Thank you," I said. "I believe I'll do that," and I started walking up the steps.

"Mr. James, you're here," a lady said, as she stepped out the door.

She was wearing a plain powder blue cotton dress with small yellow rose bud print. Her dark black hair was a product of self-coloring and the local discount store. I watched as she slowly walked to the rocking chair beside her husband and sat down.

"My name is Harvey Black and my wife is Emily," the man said, as he stopped rocking and asked, "Now why are you here?"

"Harvey," Emily exclaimed, as her face reddened.

"That's alright," I said. "I came here to talk to you about Kim."

"If she's gotten herself into trouble she'll have to get herself out," he responded. "We have nothing to do with Kim and her business."

"Those children of hers is a gift from God and we wouldn't take anything for them, but we didn't see ourselves raising another family when we got old," Emily said, as she tried to make up for her husband's gruffness.

"Those aren't her kids anymore, they are ours," Harvey demanded. "It takes more than giving birth to be a mother."

"She's still their blood mother," Emily said without raising her voice.

"Anybody that can run off and leave her kids ain't much of a mother to me," he said. "No matter how much blood kin they are."

"Are the kids around?" I asked, as I looked at the front door.

"They're in the back playing," Emily said. "Keith goes to day care and when he gets home he has to get some energy out."

"We sent him there so he can learn him his letters and numbers," Harvey said. "He'll start school next year and we want him to be right up there with the rest of the kids."

"Did you come to see the kids?" Emily asked. "I thought you wanted to talk to us."

"I'm sorry, I did come to talk to you" I said. "I just wanted to know where they were because I didn't want them to overhear what I have to say."

"They won't hear unless you yell," Harvey said, as he leaned forward in his rocking chair. "Now what do you have to say," he demanded.

"When was the last time you saw Kim?" I asked, as I looked at Emily.

"She can here with some cockamamie story about being on the street and needing money to pay for a place to stay," Harvey said and he started rocking as he talked. "She always had some reason to try to get money from us."

"Don't get us wrong," Emily said. "We gave her money on several occasions to try to help her, but she always took it and bought drugs."

"There comes a time to stop falling for her stories," Harvey said.

I didn't think it was a good time to tell them that her story was true about her being on the street, so I didn't say anything. It wouldn't bring her back. It would only make them feel worse.

"Why are you here?" Harvey asked again, as he stopped rocking and slid to the edge of his chair.

"This is hard for me to say," I said and then I took a deep breath.

"Just say it," Harvey demanded.

"Alright, Kim was murdered a couple days ago," I said.

Emily turned white and leaned back in her chair.

"Did one of her dope head boyfriends kill her?" Harvey asked, as he looked away.

"We're still investigating the crime," I said.

"Did she suffer?" Emily asked, as the color began to come back to her face.

"No, I don't think she did," I said. "The autopsy showed that she died instantly."

"I'm glad she didn't suffer," Harvey said. "But I won't miss her trying to interfere with the kids."

"What did she do?" I asked.

"We would make arrangements for her to come by and then she wouldn't show,"

Harvey said. "That would devastate the kids."

"After that, they would misbehave for a few days until we put our foot down and corrected them," Emily said. "Then things would go back to normal."

"When do we get her body?" Harvey asked. "I guess we need to bury her," and he looked at Emily.

"There's something I didn't tell you," I said, as I looked at Emily. "Her body was burned after she was killed, so it would have to be a closed casket."

"Oh, my God," Emily exclaimed, as she covered her mouth with her hand. "They set her on fire," and she started crying.

"Emily, we lost our daughter years ago when she got hooked on those drugs," Harvey said, as he took her hand and gently squeezed it.

"I know, but it's still hard," she said. "I want to bury her at the church."

"We will," he said. "We will."

"Call this number to make arrangements to get her body," I said, as I handed Harvey the number to Diane's office. "I think her body's ready to be released."

"Thanks," he said, as he took the piece of paper and put it in his shirt pocket.

"Please catch the people that killed my baby," Emily said.

"With God's grace and guidance, I will," I said, as I stood up and started down the steps.

I walked to my car and got inside. As I cranked my car, I looked on the porch and saw Harvey with his arms wrapped around Emily while she cried with her head on his shoulder. After a few deep breaths to fight back the tears, I backed the car up and slowly drove toward the police station.

I called Diane as soon as I got to the road and told her to expect a phone call from the Black family. I wanted her to have time to check with Janice and make sure they were ready to release the body before she had to give them an answer.

When I got to Highway 195, I turned left and slowly drove toward town. As I drove, I contemplated the gifts that God has given me with two healthy children and a loving wife. Then my eyes began to tear up as I thought, with everything I have, I truly am blessed of God.

Chapter 31

As I neared town, I saw smoke coming from behind the Community Science of God church. I turned left on 7th Street and drove toward the smoke.

When I got close to the Community Science of God church, I realized the smoke wasn't coming from the church, so I drove past the church and continued chasing the smoke.

I slowed when I saw the source of the smoke and stopped before I got close to the fire trucks that were parked in front of a small green house with flames shooting out of the top of its shingled roof.

As I opened my door to get out of my car, I smelled the unique smell of a meth lab that was being consumed with fire. I took my handkerchief out of my back pocket, covered my nose and slowly started walking toward one of the fire trucks.

"Is anybody in the house?" I ask when I saw the fire chief standing beside his truck.

"We're still searching, but I don't think anybody's inside," he said and looked toward the burning house. "It's been too hot for us to really do a thorough search."

I watched, as one fireman stood in front of the house spraying water onto the roof, while another sprayed water through an open window into the living room. As the fire decreased in intensity, they advanced toward the house.

"Do you want a mask?" Jeff Watson, our new Fire Chief asked, as he handed me a mask. "Those fumes will go through that handkerchief."

"I know, but it's better than breathing the air without a filter," I said, as I took the mask and slipped it over my head. "Oh, that's much better," I said, as I took a few deep breaths.

"Another meth lab goes up in flames," Jeff said, as he looked at the house. "The flames seem to be under control now."

I turned as the front door was kicked down and a fireman stuck a water hose inside. He turned the lever which allowed a large stream of water to erupt into the open doorway.

"Let's see if we have a victim inside," Jeff said, as he started walking toward the house. "I'll let you go in with me as long as the structure is safe."

"Sounds good to me," I said and followed.

We stopped at the door and waited for the fire to be extinguished by the water then we walked inside.

A blackened, saturated couch and chair was lying in the middle of the room. We walked past the furniture on our way to the kitchen.

"This is the source of the fire," Jeff said, as he pointed to the stove top. "Someone left a pan of grease on the eye."

I looked up at the ceiling, which had a large gaping hole in the center and was black from smoke.

"If the fire started over there, then why is there a hole in the center of the ceiling?" I asked, as I pointed at the hole.

"That's an old fire," he said. "See the chipped area around the opening," and he pointed at a chip on one of the boards. "The wood would still be black if it was burned in this fire."

"So, you're saying this isn't a meth fire," I said and looked at Jeff.

"This fire wasn't caused by a meth lab, but that don't mean the people in this house wasn't cooking meth," he said. "The fumes are caused by the chemicals used when making methamphetamines."

"I know," I said. "I recognize the smell."

We looked around the kitchen for potential victims. Next we looked in a bedroom and closet then moved to a bathroom without finding anyone. When we walked back to the kitchen, we met another fireman who had searched the other bedroom.

"I didn't find anyone," he said, as he walked past us and went out the door to get an ax to use to find potential hot spots.

"This house should be condemned," I said. "If it was a car, it would be totaled."

"I guess it all depends on the owner," Jeff said, as he looked around the house. "If he had insurance he might build it back."

"I wonder if the owner lived here or if it was being rented," I said.

"I don't believe we'll see the people that were living here again," he said. "Especially with the meth making material inside."

"If we do, I know where they will go," I said. "I have a cell with their name written all over it," and I laughed.

"That's why I don't think you'll see them," he said and we walked out of the house leaving the firemen to do their job of making sure the fire was out.

"I'll rope the place off," I said, as I walked to my car and got the police tape out of the trunk.

I started wrapping the tape around the house, leaving the front open for the firemen to work. Then I went to the front of the house and stood beside Jeff to wait for the firemen to finish. After the last firemen exited the house and announced that the fire was out, I wrapped the police tape around the front of the house to completely enclose it in police tape. Then I walked back over to Jeff who was standing in front of his truck watching me secure the house.

"Jeff thanks for the mask," I said, as I handed it back to him.

"No problem," Jeff said. "You didn't need to breathe the toxic fumes in the air."

"That's for sure," I said, as I turned and walked to my car, got in and drove away.

Chapter 32

As I pulled into the parking lot, I saw a dark blue Ford Ranger parked in my parking space, so I circled the lot and parked on the second row in front of the door.

"Who parked in my space?" I asked, as I walked in the door.

"Oh, I'm sorry," a man said, as he stood up and started walking toward me. "I didn't know that was your space."

"It has my name on a plaque at the front of the parking space," I said. "But that doesn't matter because I don't care where I park as long as it's not raining."

"I didn't notice the plaque."

"It's alright," I said and looked at Richard who was sitting at his desk.

"He wants to talk to you," Richard said and smiled.

"Can I help you with something?" I asked, as I turned back to the man.

"My name is Walter Davis," he said and looked down at the floor. "I want to file a complaint."

"What type of complaint do you want to file?"

"The people that were renting my house just burnt it down."

"Where is your house?"

"A couple blocks from the Community Science of God church," he said. "It burned this afternoon."

"I just came from the fire," I said. "How did you find out it burned so quick?"

"I drove past it when I heard the fire trucks," he said. "This is not the first time it's caught on fire."

"I know," I said. "Do you know what they were doing in the house?"

"I try not to get involved in what my renters do as long as they don't damage my property."

"They were cooking meth in your house," I said and looked him in the eyes. "You're still responsible for your property."

"That explains the fire," he said and looked away. "I guess I need to inspect all my properties."

"Yes, you do, before something happens," I said. "Did you have insurance?"

"Yes, I have insurance on all my properties," he said.

"Well this house will probably be condemned," I said. "It will take a lot of work to make it safe."

"How do I file a complaint?"

"Who did you have renting your house?"

"Cliff and Gus Brown," he said. "Why?"

"They're probably gone by now," I said. "If I were them I'd have left as soon as it caught on fire."

"They didn't the last time," he responded.

"Did they have materials in their house to make meth the last time?"

"That's a good question."

"You wouldn't happen to know where they work, would you," I asked and leaned against the counter.

"I think they both work at Frank's Lube and Tube on 8th Street."

"Richard, take this man's information and fill out a complaint," I said, as I looked at Richard and smiled. "Then go to Frank's Lube and Tube and see if our guys are at work."

"Come over here and take a seat," Richard said, as he pulled a chair over to his computer. "I'd be happy to take the information."

Walter went to the chair and sat down.

After Richard started filling out the report, I turned and went into my office.

I closed the door and sat down at my desk. I took my list out of the top drawer and wrote Ruby Marks, Angel Marks, Rocky Curry and Chuck Henson's name in the death column.

I looked at the names, then I wrote Rocky Curry in the connection column beside Matt Curry and in the drugs column I wrote Rocky Curry and Chuck Henson.

As I looked at the list, I wondered what connection everyone had together. The logical answer was staring me in the face, but I didn't have any evidence to connect it.

Every name on my list had a connection to drugs. Some were drug dealers, some were addicted to drugs and some were related to drugs dealers if not drug dealers themselves.

No matter how long I stared at my list, I still didn't have any physical evidence to find the killer, so I put the list back in my desk drawer and closed it.

I got up and walked in the squad room, but Richard was gone. So, I went in the dispatcher's office.

"Do you know where Richard went?" I asked when Rachel noticed me standing at the door.

"He went to someplace called Frank's Lube and Tube," she said and smiled.

"That's right, I ask him to go there," I said.

"You're beginning to look tired," she said. "Are you going home?"

"Yes, I've done all I can do today," I said and I looked back across the squad room. "I'll see you tomorrow," and I walked out the door.

Chapter 33

"I should just blow your brains out," the Smack Master growled between clenched teeth, as he pressed the barrel of his gun against his target's temple. "I told you I'd be back to defend my territory," and he walked to the other side of his target and slapped him across the face.

"You're not so bad now without your boys backing you up," and he hit his target again across the other side of his face.

The target started rocking back and forth in his chair. He tried to stand up, but something had him plastered to the back of the chair. He turned to his right and tried to look behind the chair at his arms to see how they were tied, but he couldn't. So, he twisted his wrist in an attempt at working his hands free from whatever had them bound and pulled hard against the chair.

"Pull and twist as much as you want, cause that's only making the tape tighter," he said, as he leaned in close to his face. "You're beginning to work up a sweat ain't you. I can see a little water drop slowly making its way down your face."

The target tried to rub his face against his left shoulder.

"I killed your dealers that betrayed me and sent a message to your customers that used to buy from me," the Smack Master said and laughed. "You have no more business in Thorton. I am back and you are no more," and he stuck the barrel of his gun under his target's chin. "In fact, you're dead," and he pretended to pull the trigger and yelled, "Bang!" and laughed.

The target jumped then he dropped his head.

"How does it feel to be helpless?" he asked, as he looked at the target. "Don't worry, this will be over in a few minutes," and he smiled.

The target looked up with eyes wide open with fear, but didn't attempt to say anything. He hoped, if he didn't respond his assailant might remove the tape that covered his mouth and he could yell for help.

"So, you're not talking to me now," the Smack Master said, as he stood in front of his target. "That's not very nice," and he punched him in the nose with the heel of his hand.

Blood gusted from the target's nose and ran down his face. It dripped off the tape that was covering his mouth and landed on the right side of the target's shirt.

"Don't worry, I have two pairs of latex gloves on to protect me from any blood disease you might have," he said and held his hands out toward the target.

Then he took a glove out of his pocket and slipped it over the bloody glove.

"I don't want to contaminate my handle," he said, as he raised his Ruger LCP and squeezed off two rounds in his target's forehead.

The target slumped over without making a sound.

The Smack Master looked at the clock, which indicated it was still too early for anyone to be out, so he tucked the gun in his waist band and walked out the back door.

Chapter 34

I was sitting at my desk working on some of the endless paperwork I find myself doing every week when Rachel opened my door and announced, "There has been a break in at Braswell Temp Service."

"What would anyone steal from there?" I asked, as I stood up and started walking toward the door.

"I don't know, but Victor White just called from his car," she said. "He said, his back door was open and something red was on the door knob that looked like blood."

"Let's go," I said, as I walked past Richard who was sitting at his desk working on some traffic reports. "We need to go to Braswell's and see what's going on," and I opened the door.

Richard turned his computer off, then got up and walked to the door.

"When you see Johnny, tell him that we'll be back after we're finished with this possible break in," I said and we walked out the door.

"Were those guys at Frank's Lube and Tube yesterday?" I asked Richard as we walked to the car.

"He said they had a family emergency about noon and they left," Richard said.

"That was probably when they found out about the fire," I said. "I bet they didn't show up at work today."

"I bet you're right," he said and stopped at the passenger's side door of the car.

We got in my car and drove in silence toward the Fairway Shopping Center. I turned onto 4th Avenue and drove toward 16th Street. I slowed, when I saw the large red sign announcing the businesses that were located inside the shopping center and turned into the parking lot.

As I entered the lot, I circled around to the back and pulled up beside a single car that was parked near the back door.

I looked over and saw Victor White sitting in his car with his hands firmly gripping the stirring wheel. He didn't look toward me. He continued looking straight ahead at the back door.

I got out of my car and walked over to his driver's side window.

He still didn't move.

I gently tapped his window with my knuckle.

He didn't respond.

This time I tapped it a little more forcefully.

He turned toward me and slowly rolled his window down.

"Did you go inside?" I asked.

He stared at me without saying a word and his face was as white as freshly fallen snow.

"Did you go inside?" I asked, as I shook his shoulder.

"What, oh," he said, as he looked at me. "No I didn't go inside I stopped when I saw that the door was open."

I put on my black leather tactical gloves with Kevlar lining, pulled my Glock G17 out of my holster and advanced toward the back door.

Richard followed close behind.

When we reached the door, Richard stepped to the side and stood ready to shoot.

I looked at the doorknob which had a blood like substance around the knob. There was no lock on the knob, but instead a large latch was attached to the door with a broken three inch padlock hanging loosely.

We remained close to the door and listened for a few seconds, but when we didn't hear anything, I pulled the door open and stepped inside with my gun drawn and ready to fire.

I motioned that I would look on the right side and for Richard to look on the left side as we searched through all the offices.

The first office I came to was the office of Victor White. His door was propped open with a door jam. As I entered, I carefully looked for an intruder that might still be in the office. When no one was in sight, I move to the next office.

The next office I came to was the office I saw Gloria Curry using earlier in the week. The door was closed so I turned the knob, but it was locked.

I looked at the other offices with their doors standing wide open and looked at Richard. "This is odd," I whispered when Richard moved close to me. "This is the only room with the door closed."

"I didn't see anything unusual in the other rooms," Richard whispered. "This may be where our perpetrator went."

I stepped a couple steps away from the door and motioned for Richard to move to the right. After he moved, I raised three fingers and lowered one at a time. After I lowered my last finger, I charged toward the door and planted my right foot beside the door knob, which caused the door to splinter away from the door frame and crash into the office. Then I charged in with my gun drawn and ready to fire.

Richard stayed at the door, with his gun ready, to make sure no one approached from the other rooms.

I stopped, when I saw a male body slumped over in the chair behind the desk. I scanned the room to make sure it was empty then I walked around the desk to get a closer look.

I felt for a pulse but there wasn't one. When I leaned close to check his breathing, I saw a large hole in the center of his forehead.

Then I took my cell phone out of my pocket and called Diane.

"Diane speaking," she said when she answered. "Sam, don't tell me you have another body."

"Unfortunately I have," I said. "This time it's at the Braswell Temp Service which is located at the Fairway Shopping Center."

"I'll be there as soon as I can," she said and hung up.

I then called Janice who answered on the second ring.

"CSI Unit," she said when she answered. "Sam, I don't think we have any new evidence to give you."

"That's not what I'm calling about," I said. "I have a body in the Braswell Temp Service building."

"Where's that located?" she asked.

"On 4th Avenue and 16th Street," I said. "It's at the Fairway Shopping Center."

"What happened?" she asked.

"Victor White, the owner, called this morning to report a break in at his office," I said. "When we went inside to investigate we found a male with a large bullet hole in his forehead."

"We'll be there within thirty minutes," she said and my phone went dead.

"What's going on?" Richard asked when he looked inside the room.

"This guy's been shot in the head," I said and lifted his head for Richard to see the hole.

"Did you recognize his face?"

"I really didn't look at his face," I said, as I looked a little closer. "It's hard to see his face with all that duct tape and thick blood all over his face."

"Step around the desk and look at him from the front," Richard said excitedly. "I think we might have found Rodney Curry."

"You've got to be kidding me," I said, as I moved around the desk and studied his facial features. "He's cut his hair and changed its color, but I think you're right. That is Rodney Curry."

I looked around the room at pictures of Rodney and his brother Rocky when they were young and playing on a community baseball team. A picture of Rodney with his mother sat on top of the filing cabinet which faced her desk.

"We need to make sure Gloria Curry doesn't come in here," I said, as I closed the door. "Put crime tape across the front door and I'll watch the back to make sure no one enters the building."

"I'm on it," Richard said, as he ran to the car, got a roll of crime scene tape out of the back seat and ran to the front of the building.

I closed the door when I came out of the building and slowly walked over to Victor White's car.

He was still sitting with his hand gripping the stirring wheel.

"You can't open for business today."

"Why?" he asked.

"There's a dead body in one of the offices."

"Which office?"

"It doesn't matter," I said. "What matters is we need full access to the building which eliminates the possibility of you doing business."

"It's too late to call my employees."

"Just tell them when they get here."

"Alright, I guess I have no choice," he said and looked at the back door.

"Did you ever see Rodney Curry around here?"

"Who's Rodney Curry?"

"Gloria Curry's oldest son."

"No, Gloria never allowed anyone to come see her at work," he said. "She liked to keep her family life separate from her work life."

"Did you know she hired Matt Curry to work at the Millwood Fabric Warehouse?"

"Yes, I did," he said. "That was the one exception."

"Did you approve it?"

"Gloria said he was down on his luck and almost homeless, so I approve the hire," he said. "She wouldn't have hired him if I hadn't said it was alright."

I looked up when I heard a car rounding the building. Janice slowly drove through the parking lot and stopped beside my car. As she opened the door to get out,

Diane pulled around the building and parked beside the back door.

Victor was the first to get out with his camera hanging from his neck.

"Where's the body?" he asked, as he stepped up beside me.

"Second door on your left," I said and pointed to the back door. "The door is unlocked."

Victor turned and started walking toward the building. He paused for a few seconds when he reached the door, then backed up and started photographing the door from different angles. After he finished photographing the door, he opened it and went inside.

Janice walked to the front of her van and waited for Daniel to get out then they walked to where I was standing.

Diane and Samantha jumped out of her van and quickly joined us beside Victor White's car.

"Let's walk toward the back door while we talk," I said, as I began walking toward the building. "I don't want him to hear everything."

"What did you find inside?" Janice asked after we were a few feet away from Victor.

"Our victim had his hands tied behind his back, his mouth was taped and he was shot in the forehead at close range."

"Was there any sign of torture?" she asked.

"I couldn't tell if he was beaten because his face was covered with blood from the gun shot," I said. "I didn't look anywhere else to see if he was tortured."

"Alright, I'm through," Victor said when he opened the door and walked out.

"Diane, let's go look at the body together and we'll try to let you have it as soon as we can," Janice said, as she looked at Diane.

"Samantha, get the stretcher out and bring it to the door," Diane said and then walked inside.

Samantha ran to the back of the van and pulled the stretcher out. She pushed it to the door and put the brakes on.

Diane and Janice walked down the hall side by side. They stopped at the door and looked at the victim.

"Try to leave as much intact as you can and I'll give it to you after I do my autopsy," Diane said and then she walked in the room.

Janice walked behind the desk and looked at the victim's arms.

"We'll have to cut the tape to get the body away from the chair," Janice said. "I think we can leave everything else in place."

Janice set her equipment case on the floor. She slowly started working at removing the tape from the victim's arms. After she got the tape loose, she put it in a container and placed it in her bag.

Diane walked outside and got the stretcher. She pushed it through the door and down the hall until she was outside the room where the victim was located.

"I'm ready for you to get the victim," Janice said when she saw Diane.

"We may have to move the desk away from the victim for us to get him onto the stretcher," Diane said.

"Could we move the chair back?" Janice asked.

"I think that would work," Diane said, as she moved to the head of the chair.

"Sam, do you think you and Richard can slide the chair away from the desk?" Diane asked when she saw me standing at the door.

"Sure, we'll try," I said and I walked inside the room.

Richard followed me inside and went to the left side of the chair. He put on a pair of latex gloves and stood ready.

After I put on some elastic gloves, I went to the right side of the chair.

Then Richard and I took the chair by the arm rest and slid it away from the desk.

"That's good enough," Diane said.

Richard and I moved to the front of the desk.

I watched as Diane moved the stretcher close to the chair and locked the wheels. She draped the body bag over the sides of the stretcher and attached it.

"Alright, if we can get him on the stretcher then I can wrap him up," she said, as she grabbed his shoulders.

Samantha grabbed his feet and they lifted his body onto the stretcher with one quick motion.

"We could have helped," I said.

"That's alright Sam we have a routine," Diane said, as she positioned the victim's body on the stretcher. "We do this every day and work well together."

Diane folded the body bag over the body and then zipped it closed. She tightened the straps around the body and rolled the stretcher out of the building.

"We need to take that chair as evidence," Janice said, as she turned to Daniel. "Can we get it in the van?"

"Sure, we may have to move a few things around but we can get it in the van,"

Daniel said.

"I'm going to leave you to your work," I said and I walked out of the building.

When I got outside, Victor White was standing beside a gray Ford Escort talking to a lady in her middle thirties.

As I walked toward them, she drove away.

"Who was that?" I asked when I got close to him.

"Just somebody that was driving by and noticed the cars," he said. "She wanted to know what happened."

"What did you tell her?"

"I told her that I didn't know anything."

"Good answer."

"Well, it's the truth."

"I need to talk to you a minute," I said, as I looked at him. "The CSI Unit is going to need to take some of your furniture as evidence."

"What will they need to take?" he asked.

"I think the only thing they need is a chair, but they're still looking at the room."

"I'll cooperate with anything they need."

"Good," I said.

"Do you still need me here?" he asked.

"No, you can go home."

"Thanks," he said and hurried to his car.

He cranked his car and slowly drove away.

"Do we need to stay here while they're looking for evidence?" Richard asked.

"After all, they might be here for hours."

"We need to stay here to make sure the place is closed up," I said, as the door opened.

I watched as Daniel and Victor came out carrying a large leather chair wrapped in plastic. They carried it to the back of their van and sat it on the pavement. Then they opened the door and slid the chair in the back.

"Diane already gone?" Daniel asked, as he closed the door.

"She was gone when I got back out here," I said.

"I think we're almost through," he said and turned toward the door as Janice stepped outside.

"You can lock things up," Janice said when she got close to me. "We've gathered everything we need."

I watched as they loaded everything in the van and drove away.

Then I went to the door and locked it with a new padlock I got from my car.

Richard and I got in my car and drove back to the police station.

Chapter 35

When Richard and I walked in the station, Rachel was standing at the door with a manila envelope in her hand.

"What's that?" I ask when she held it out toward me.

"It came by carrier this morning," she said. "It has your name on it," and handed it to me.

"I wonder what it could be," I said, as I took it from Rachel.

I felt along the sides of the envelope then I ran my hand across the middle.

"I can't feel anything inside," I said and then walked to my office.

I closed the door and laid the manila envelope on top of my desk. After I sat down, I put my Glock in my desk.

Then I picked the envelope up and looked at the opening that had been sealed with tape. I took the letter opener with the gold plated handle that Rachel had bought me for my last birthday the previous year and slipped it inside a small opening along the tape.

I held the manila envelope away from my face and carefully slid the opener along the tape, causing the seal to break. Then I turned it upside down to let the contents drop onto my desk.

Nothing came out of the envelope. Not even a dust particle.

So, I turned the envelope toward me and looked inside. There was a single piece of paper caught by the adhesive backing of the tape and sticking out at the edge of the envelope.

I took a pair of tweezers out of my desk, gently grabbed hold of the paper and pulled it out onto my desk.

The note was simply written with very few words. MEET ME AT JOHN'S SEA FOOD AT 10 O'CLOCK THIS MORNING. I HAVE SOMETHING TO TELL YOU. And it was signed JEFF BLAND.

I laid the note down and looked at the clock which indicated it was 5 minutes before he wanted to meet me. John's Sea Food was ten minutes away, so I would be late and anyway it shouldn't be open at this time of the morning, but maybe he wanted the meeting to be secret.

I took my gun out of my desk, slipped it in my holster and walked into the squad room.

"I'll be back as soon as I can," I said, as I walked to the door. "I have a meeting at John's Sea Food with Jeff Bland."

"Do you want me to go with you?" Richard asked.

"I'm afraid it might scare him off," I said.

"It's too dangerous for you to go alone," he said. "You need backup."

"Alright, let's go in separate vehicles," I said. "You can approach from the back side."

"That sounds like a good plan," Richard said, as he put his gun in his holster, then stood up and started walking to the door.

"Let's go," I said and walked out the door.

Chapter 36

John's Sea Food was located in a small blue metal building with a large green and gold glass fish protruding over the doorway. It sat in the middle of a large parking lot with parking spaces available on all sides.

It was located in the business area of town which made it one of the busiest restaurants during the lunch hour and a leading meeting place for after work drinks.

After I sat there a few minutes, I noticed two cars parked to the side of the building, so I slowly drove toward the cars and parking beside the car nearest the back door. I looked around to see if Jeff was in sight, but when I didn't see him I opened my door and got out.

After I closed my door, I stood at the front of my car trying to decide which direction to go. Then I heard the back door open and a voice whispering, "Sam, come here."

I looked at the opening of the door and saw Jeff waving for me to come.

I walked past the cars toward the door and stopped. "Who else is here?" I asked.

"The owner," Jeff said, as he backed away from the door. "I had to get someone to open this place."

"It's just you two," I asked, as I stepped inside.

"Yes, it's just the two of us," Jeff said. "He'll be in the kitchen getting ready for today's lunch crowd."

"The note said you had something to tell me," I said.

"Let's sit down first," he said, as he started walking away from the door. "Do you want some coffee?"

"Sure," I said, as I followed him.

We walked through the kitchen toward the dining room, but stopped when we reached the coffee pot. Jeff poured two cups of coffee and handed one to me.

"Do you put anything in your coffee?" he asked.

"No, I like it black," I said.

"Let's sit out here and talk," he said, as he walked through a set of double doors into the dining room. "This table should be fine," and he pointed to the first table we came to.

"How did you get him to let us come in here?" I asked and I looked toward the kitchen.

"Oh, John's my brother," he said. "And I own a small part of this business, so he didn't have a problem letting me use it."

"Why are you being so secretive?"

"Because I think something is going on at work and I don't want to lose my job."

"What do you think is going on?"

"I think Ben Lowe knew more about the people that shot at you than he said."

"Why do you say that?"

"Because I saw a black Escalade parked in the garage at work."

"Was it the one used by those people that shot at me?"

"I don't know," he said. "But it was defiantly a black Escalade."

"Anything else?"

"I saw Ben talking to some guys in the parking lot and when they noticed me they quickly stopped talking and drove away."

"Maybe they were through with their conversation."

"Could be," he said. "I might just be paranoid."

"Ben said that Morton Enterprises had many different services," I said. "Could one of those services be working with drug dealers?"

I looked around as the door to the kitchen opened.

"Would any one of you guys want a piece of pie?" John asked, as he approached the table carrying a plate with three different kinds of pie. "I have peach, apple and pecan."

"I'll take a piece of apple," Jeff said.

"Here you go," John said, as he sat the pie in front of Jeff.

"I'll take pecan," I said.

"Here's yours," John said, as he sat the pie in front of me.

"If you need anything else, let me know," John said and he walked back in the kitchen.

"We have divisions that will do whatever you pay them to do," Jeff said and then took a bite of pie.

"Who makes the decisions at Morton Enterprises?" I asked.

"For the most part, I believe Ben makes the decisions," Jeff said. "I think someone is behind him, but I don't know who that might be."

"Could it be one of the drug dealers?" I asked and took a bite of pecan pie.

"It could be almost anybody," he said. "Ben's the only person I see at work, but I know he answers to somebody."

"To your knowledge, have any laws been broken?" I asked.

"Not to my knowledge," he said. "But they don't let me know much about the business."

I finished the pecan pie and scooted the plate in the middle of the table. I drank the last of my coffee and sat my cup down.

"Keep your eyes open and call me if you see anything that I need to know," I said, as I gave him my card. "I'll try to run a background check on Morton Enterprises and see what I can find."

"Now, I'm not trying to close the company down," he said. "I just want everything to be within the law."

"If everything is within the law, everything will be alright," I said and stood up. "It's almost time for him to open, so I need to get out of here."

"I'll leave after you," Jeff said.

"Keep in touch," I said and I walked into the kitchen.

I opened the back door and walked out. When I got close to my car, I saw Richard standing beside his car looking across the parking lot.

"Did you have a good meeting?" he asked when I got close.

"Pretty good," I said. "I'll tell you about it later."

"See that car parked across the street."

"Where?"

"That black Toyota Avalon parked beside the gas station."

"Oh yes, I see it," I said. "What about it?"

"It's been parked there the whole time we were here," he said. "I'm not sure if they're watching the place or waiting on someone."

"Let's see what they're doing," I said and got in my car.

I backed up and drove to the edge of the parking lot. I turned right and drove around the block.

Richard followed me to the edge of the parking lot then he turned left and drove around the block.

I drove around the backside of the store and slowly pulled behind the car.

Richard pulled around the front of the store and approached the car from the side.

I sat behind the car for a few seconds running the tag number. There were no warrants or tickets out on the car, so I slowly got out of my car.

I carefully approached the car, keeping an eye on the driver as I went.

Richard got out of his car and stood at the door.

When I got near the window, I noticed it was a lady sitting in the car.

"Did I do something wrong?" she asked when I got near.

"Why are you sitting here at this gas station?" I asked.

"I'm waiting on my ex-husband to come get the kids," she said and motioned toward the back seat.

I looked in the back seat where a boy and two girls were sitting with their eyes wide with fear.

"Does the owner of the gas station know you're here?" I asked.

"No, I don't think so," she said. "Did he complain about me being here?"

"No," I said but then explained, "We have a law against loitering and I know for a fact that you've been here for more than thirty minutes."

"I'm sorry, but he was supposed to be here more than thirty minutes ago," she said. "I have a date tonight and he's supposed to watch the kids."

"It's still early in the morning," I said. "Do you think he's still at work?"

"He was supposed to call in today so he could get the kids," she said and laughed. "He probably went to work just to spite me."

"Let me get this straight," I said. "You wanted him to call in to work, so you could go on a date."

"You make it sound bad," she exclaimed.

"I think it's a wonderful thing for you to want him to spend time with his children, but he still has a responsibility to his employer," I said. "You could plan your date sometime when he doesn't have to work."

"You sound like my mom and dad," she said, as she rolled her eyes. "Always siding with him."

"I'm not siding with anybody, because it's nothing to me," I said and looked in the backseat again. "But, you do need to go somewhere else, because you've been here long enough."

"Would you make him leave if he was waiting on me?" she asked, as she glared at me.

"Yes, I would make him leave also," I said and looked at Richard. "If I see you here again, I'll have to give you a ticket."

"Then where can I meet him to drop off the kids?" she asked.

"That's between you and him," I said. "Wherever it is, you both need to be in agreement as to where and when you are supposed to meet."

"Thanks officer," she said sarcastically, as she cranked her car. "I'll keep that in mind," and she drove away.

"Broken families are hard on the kids," I said, as I turned to Richard.

"Especially when the parents still want to be single and act like they don't have any kids," he said and he got in his car.

I watched as her car turned right at the stop sign and then disappeared from my sight. Then I got in my car and drove toward the police station.

Richard pulled out behind me and followed closely as we drove to the station.

Chapter 37

I turned into the station parking lot and stopped when I saw a black Chevrolet Suburban parked beside my parking space.

When I realized it was a Suburban instead of a Escalade, I breathed a sigh of relief and then drove down to my parking space.

After I parked, I saw the driver's side door of the Suburban open and Charles Wallace from the ABI step out wearing dark black sunglasses. He straightened his suit to make sure the wrinkles were gone and then started walking toward me.

"I need to talk to you," he said, when I opened the door.

"Alright, let's go to my office," I said, as I got out of my car and started walking toward the door.

I stopped and waited for Richard to walk across the parking lot.

"Did I get your parking space?" Charles asked and smiled.

"Only the chief has a parking space marked for him," Richard said. "I park wherever I can find a space."

"Good, I didn't want to get your spot," Charles said.

"I'm sure it would have upset you to think you got my space," Richard said, as he walked past us and opened the door. "Gentlemen," and he held the door open for us to go inside.

"I want Richard with us when we talk," I said, as I looked at Charles.

"What happened to Johnny?" he asked and looked around the squad room.

"He's probably patrolling the neighborhood," I said. "I would want Johnny with me if he was here."

"Alright, let's talk," Charles said.

"Do you want a cup of coffee?" I asked.

"No, but a Dr. Pepper would be great," he said.

"I'll see if we have one," Richard said, as he walked to the refrigerator.

"Get one for me if there is another one," I said and I opened the door to my office. "Sit in either one of those chairs," and I pointed to the chairs in front of my desk.

"I'll take the one closest to the door," he said and sat down.

I waited while Richard got the Dr. Peppers and walked into the office. He placed two on the desk and kept one for himself. Then he went to the empty chair and sat down.

I closed the door and walked to my desk. I pulled my chair out, sat down.

"Thanks for the drink," I said, as I picked my Dr. Pepper up and opened it. "It is a little late for coffee," and I took a drink.

"I try to stop drinking coffee by noon," Charles said, as he picked up his drink. "Thanks Richard," and he opened it and took a sip.

"What did you need to talk to us about?" I asked, as I looked at Charles.

"Alright," he said. "We've been monitoring a drug ring that stretches across Walker, Jefferson and Winston County and possibly more. We've traced drug dealers from every corner of the state and we believe it all has originated from somewhere in Walker County."

"What has that got to do with me?" I asked.

"Let me finish," he responded.

"Alright, I'm sorry," I said. "Go on."

"We've watched a multitude of drug deals. Anything from cocaine, marijuana, ecstasy, heroin and methamphetamine being sold and transported to different areas in the state," he said and looked at Richard. "We were only days away from arresting the lead drug dealer when something damaging to our investigation occurred."

"What was that?" I asked.

"Our lead suspect was killed," he said and raised his hands up. "We took all this time gathering evidence and building a case for nothing."

"I still don't see where we fit in," I said. "We haven't killed anybody."

"I know and I'm not blaming you for the death," he said. "But, I want you to help me find the killer."

"I'm still not getting it," I said feeling a little confused. "Who was your chief suspect?"

He looked at me, then turned to Richard and hesitated.

"Rodney Curry," he said after a long pause.

"You knew where Rodney Curry was and you didn't help me arrest him," I yelled, as I sat straight up in my chair. "I thought we were all on the same side."

"I needed him out of jail to help me find the supplier," Charles responded in a defensive manner. "And we are on the same side."

"Sometimes I wonder," I retorted.

"What is that supposed to mean?" he demanded.

"I almost got shot while I was looking for Rodney Curry and you knew where he was, but you didn't tell me." I said.

"I've already told you why I didn't tell you," he said. "I couldn't jeopardize the case."

"But now you expect us to help you," I said.

"I'm asking you to help us," he said.

I took a sip of Dr. Pepper and slowly swallowed. Then I took a deep breath and let it out through my nose.

"What do you need?" I asked without taking my eyes off Charles.

"Do you know who killed Rodney?" he asked.

"No, not at the moment," I said.

"Do you have any evidence that could lead to the identity of the person that killed Rodney?"

"I haven't heard from the Medical Examiner or the CSI unit yet," I said and I looked at the clock. "I could call Diane and see if the autopsy has been done."

"It you don't mind, I'd appreciate the information," he said.

I opened my phone and punched in the number to the Medical Examiner's office. The phone rang four times without an answer, so I closed my phone.

"I'll try again in a minute," I said, as I laid my phone on the top of my desk.

"Do you think the CSI unit has had time to compile the evidence?" he asked.

"Let me try to call Diane again and then I'll call the CSI Unit," I said, as I opened my phone and called Diane's phone directly.

"Hey Sam," Diane said when she answer the phone. "I've just finished with the autopsy."

"Great," I said. "What did you find?"

"He was killed about three hours before his body was discovered," she said. "He was shot twice in the forehead, but either shot could have killed him."

"Was he tortured?" I asked.

"He had bruising to his face which indicated a small amount of torture, but nothing significant," she said. "His hands were bond with tape, which restricted the blood flow to his hands, but no damage was done."

"Did he have drugs in his system?"

"No, he was clean."

"Did you find anything else that I need to know?"

"That's all I have."

"Thanks for the information," I said and closed my phone.

"What did she say?" Charles asked with anticipation.

"She said he was beat up and then shot in the forehead," I said and smiled.

"She didn't find any evidence to link him to the killer?" he asked.

"No, she didn't find anything," I said, as I opened my phone and punched in the number to the CSI unit.

"CSI Unit," a male voice said when he answered the phone.

"This is Sam James," I said. "I need to talk to Janice."

"Hey Sam, this is Daniel," he said. "I'll transfer your call to her office," and I was put on hold.

The phone was picked up and someone started punching numbers.

"I'll transfer you now," Daniel said.

After a few seconds, Janice answered and said, "Sam, are you calling about the murder this morning?"

"I was wondering if you were able to go over the evidence that you gathered this morning," I said. "I hope I didn't call too early."

"We're still working on some of the evidence, but I can tell you what we have now," Janice said. "We found a shell casing under the desk that matched the shell casings that were found at the murders a few nights ago."

"So the same person that killed the four people the other night killed Rodney Curry."

"I don't know if it was the same person, but I'm sure it was the same gun," she said.

"Anything else?"

"The killer used standard two inch duct tape to hold the victim," she said. "He could have bought it at almost any store in Thorton."

"Did you find anything that could help to identify the killer?"

"There was very little evidence found at the murder scene," she said. "We found no finger prints, no blood except for the victims, no foot prints and no bodily fluids to get any DNA from."

"That's it," I said.

"That's all we have at this point," she said.

"Thanks for your help."

"I haven't done anything."

"Neither have I," I said and closed my phone.

"What did she say?" Charles asked.

"The same gun that killed Rodney Curry was used to kill four other people a few nights ago," I said. "She has no evidence to determine the identity of the killer."

"That's not much help," he said.

"That's all I have." I said.

"Thanks for the effort anyway," he said. "If I can help you in any way just let me know."

"As a matter of fact, there is something I would like you to do," I said.

"Really," he said. "What do you need?"

"I want you to run a background check on Morton Enterprises," I said. "I think they might be involved in something illegal."

"Morton Enterprises," he said and wrote the name on his notepad. "I can do that."

"I'll let you know if I get a lead on the killer," I said and I leaned back in my chair. "At least we got a major drug dealer off the street."

"That's true, but I wanted to get the supplier," he said.

"Let's be thankful for the blessings we have," I said.

"I am, but I still want more," he said and stood up.

"We'll keep trudging along with the investigation and maybe we'll catch the killer," I said. "We might even catch the supplier," and I got up.

"I wish I had your faith," he said, as he walked to the door.

"Pray and you might have it," I said, as I got up and walked to the door to open it.

"I'll call you when I find out something about Morton Enterprises," he said, then he walked through the squad room and went out the door.

I looked at Richard who was still sitting in the chair with his arms crossed.

"I think that went very well," Richard said and smiled.

“I think we both know where we stand,” I said. “Maybe we can help each other.”

“Whatever it takes to catch this guy,” Richard said, as he got up and walked into the squad room.

“I’ve had a long day,” I said and I walked to the door. “Richard, I’ll see you tomorrow,” then I walked to the door.

“Tomorrow’s Saturday,” he said. “I don’t work tomorrow.”

“Oh, that’s right,” I said. “Then I’ll see you Monday.”

“You’re not working tomorrow are you Sam?” he asked.

“I may have to come by for a minute, but I’m not staying very long,” I said.

“Well, I hope you have a good weekend,” Richard said.

“I plan on it,” I said and I walked out the door.

Chapter 38

I woke up at 7 o'clock and rolled over. I tried to stay in bed until at least 8 but by 7:30 my back was hurting, so I got up. After putting on a pair of shorts I walked down the stairs.

The warmth of the bright sunshine instantly engulfed me when I went outside. Trees were beginning to bud and flowers were blooming sporadically in the yard, which was a great indication that spring was near.

To get ready for my morning run I stretched my legs. Then I carefully bent over and touched my toes to stretch the muscles in my lower back and legs.

After five minutes of stretching, I slowly began jogging down the block. I started at a slow pace, gradually increasing my speed as I went until I was a full speed at the end of the first round.

I jogged the same route I normally did which was five rounds in a two block radius. I estimated the distance to be close to two miles, but I never officially measured it. Whatever the distance, it's enough to give my cardiovascular system a workout.

I slowed as I was finishing my last round and walked the last few feet. Then I stretched as I cooled down and went inside.

After I got the coffee to brewing, I went upstairs to shower.

Jenna rolled over when I walked in the bedroom.

"Is anything wrong?" she asked in a sleepy voice.

"Everything's fine sweetheart," I whispered. "I just have a few things to do this morning," then I kiss her on the cheek and went in the bathroom.

After showering I dressed in a pair of blue jeans, pull over tee shirt and my snake skin cowboy boots. Then I quietly eased through the bedroom and went down stairs.

The coffee was ready so I poured some in a travel mug and went outside.

After standing on the steps looking at the beauty God has given us, I walked to my car and drove away.

I only had one errand to run today, but it is probably the hardest part of my job which is to tell someone that their son has been murdered.

Gloria Curry's car was parked in her driveway so I pulled in beside it and turned the engine off. I looked around the neighborhood to make sure it was safe before I got out of the car.

After I got out, I slowly walked to the steps and stopped. I looked at the door, then went up the steps and knocked. I heard movement behind the door then it opened wide.

"What do you want?" Gloria demanded.

"I need to talk to you a minute," I said and looked at the gray cat that was wrapping its body around her leg.

"What could you possibly have to talk to me about?" she asked and frowned.

"We found Rodney's body yesterday," I said as gently as I could. "Someone murdered him."

"Oh God!" she wailed. "What have I done to deserve this?" and she collapsed in the doorway.

She suddenly stopped crying and glared at me. "I want you to catch this monster. He's taken all my children away from me and he deserves to die," she said in a growling voice. “If you can’t find him, I know some people who can,” and she stared off in the distance.

“Gloria, we’re doing the best we can,” I said, as I looked her in the eyes. “Don’t do anything that you’ll regret.”

“How will I cope with this loss?” she asked, as she looked toward the sky.

“Ask God to give you the strength,” I said. “God can help you through your time of sorrow.”

“How could God let this happen?”

“God didn’t cause this to happen,” I said. “Sin and our fleshly desires caused this to happen.”

“What are you saying?”

“Rodney was involved in some bad stuff because there was easy money to make and that bad stuff caught up with him.”

“I did the best I could,” Gloria said and dropped her head.

“That has nothing to do with it,” I said. “Everyone has temptation of the flesh and despite how we are brought up we all have to make a choice of whether to fall to that temptation. It’s sin that causes that temptation.”

“And he fell to that temptation,” she said and sniffed.

“Yes, he did,” I said.

“I still want revenge,” she said with anger in her voice.

“I’ll do my best to catch the killer,” I said. “Is there anything I can do for you?”

“I think I’m going to call my pastor and get some support from my church,” she said, as she stood up.

"That's a good start." I said. "If you need anything, just call," and I walked to my car.

I got in and drove back home.

Chapter 39

Jenna was waiting at the door when I walked in the house. She smiled and gave me a hug.

"Are you ready to take the kids to the park?" she asked.

"Sure," I said. "Just let me change shoes and I'll be ready," and I rushed to the bedroom.

After I changed into my tennis shoes, I ran down the stairs, going two steps at a time.

"Be careful," Jenna said. "We want to go to the park today and not the hospital," and she laughed.

I went to my Ford Bronco that had been repaired and attached the bike carrier to the bumper. Then I strapped our bikes in place.

"Is everybody ready to go," I asked, as I turned to the yard where Jenny and Seth were standing beside their mother.

"Yes!" they yelled in unison.

"Then, let's go," I said and smiled.

Seth and Jenny ran to the back seat and jumped inside my Bronco. Jenna walked to the passenger's side and waited for me to open the door.

"I'll make you a gentleman yet," she said and laughed.

"Just be patient," I said and laughed. "I'm a slow learner."

"We have a lifetime," she said and kissed me.

I opened the door and closed it after she got inside. Then I went to the driver's side, got in and drove to the park.

I parked beside the entrance to the bike trail and unloaded our bikes. Then I gathered everyone together and said, "Everyone must stay where I can see them at all times. That means you can go in front of us but you must stop if you get too far ahead, if you can't see me, then I can't see you."

"We will," Seth enthusiastically said.

"I promise," Jenny said.

Within seconds we were maneuvering along the dirt and rock surface of the bike trial that encircled the entire parameter of the city park.

Seth took the lead, followed by Jenna then Jenny and I stayed in the rear. It was a slow process, but the kids really enjoyed themselves and Jenna and I enjoyed watching them have fun.

We spent all afternoon at the park without interruption. My cell phone didn't ring which could have been in part because I didn't have a good signal, but for whatever reason, I enjoyed the day.

When everyone got tired, I loaded the bikes onto my Bronco while Jenna got the kids in the back seat.

As I walked to the driver's side, I took my cell phone out of my pocket and checked the signal. Three bars lit up, so I checked to see if I had any missed calls.

"Is everything alright?" Jenna asked when I got in the truck.

"Everything is fine," I said, as I got in and drove home.

Chapter 40

The next morning, I pulled into the church parking lot. I saw two cars parked close to the door, but the rest of the lot was empty. I drove close to the door and stopped to let everyone out. Then I went up the middle aisle and parked next to the road.

When I walked in the door, Elder Andrew Moss was standing at the entrance to the sanctuary greeting people as they entered. He smiled when I approached, stuck his hand out and said, “Good to see you this morning.”

“It’s good to be here,” I responded.

“I hope we can make it through the service today without any interruptions,” he said and smiled.

“Lord willing, we will,” I said, as my face reddened.

“Sam, I didn’t mean anything by it,” he said. “I just don’t want you to miss the message.”

“If the criminals cooperate I’ll be happen to stay and listen to the message,” I said.

“Maybe they will. We will pray for that,” he said and walked to the next person coming in the door.

I looked for the kids, but they were nowhere in sight. Then I looked around and saw Jenna who was standing in the middle of the sanctuary talking to Rose Franks and Danielle Watts.

I eased down the aisle, found the bench we always sat on and laid my bible down. Then I walked back to the aisle and greeted the members as they approached.

Susan Jones came in and said, "Good morning, Sam," and shook my hand.

"Good morning," I said and smiled, as she walked to another member.

"It's good to see you," Rose Franks said and shook my hand.

"It's good to see you too," I said and watched her move down the aisle.

"Good morning Sam," Danielle Watts said.

"Good morning," I said. "How are things going?"

"It's a struggle every day," she said and looked at her hands that had a slight tremor. "But I'm making it."

"You're looking good," I said.

"I feel a lot better," she said. "I've still got that craving for drugs, but I think I've made it through the hardest part."

We looked to the front when Greg Boone, one of the song leaders, said, "It's time to start. Please turn to page 146," then he looked across the congregation and waited for everyone to sit down.

We sang several songs, had prayer and then Elder Andrew Moss slowly walked upon the platform and stood behind the podium.

He laid his Bible down and opened it. Then he looked across the sanctuary without saying a word.

"I'm thankful to have everyone here today. I know it was hard getting up this morning and I know it was even harder coming to church when you saw the beautiful sunshine that God has blessed us with," he said and took a sip of water. "I'm sure the devil was putting thoughts in your mind like, they won't miss me today or I work all week and I deserve to go play golf or go fishing. But remember the sacrifice that Jesus made on that cross to save us from a miserable life of sin," he said, then looked at his bible.

He took a piece of paper out of his bible and laid it to the side. Then he turned a couple pages and looked back at the congregation.

"Dear friends, we are here to worship God. I pray that this message is from God and if it is not, I just need to close this book and go home. But I believe this is from God. Please pray that I will deliver it in a way that's pleasing to God and glorifies him," he said.

He cleared his throat and loosened his tie.

"If you have your bible, please turn to Psalm 127," he said and looked around to give everyone time to find it in their bibles.

" 'Except the Lord build the house, they labour in vain that build it: except the Lord keep the city, the watchman waketh but in vain.

It is vain for you to rise up early, to sit up late, to eat the bread of sorrows: for so he giveth his beloved sleep.' Psalm 127 verse 1 and 2," he said and looked up.

"We are to trust in the Lord to bless whatever we do. I know the town of Thorton has been having problems with crime lately, but everyone must trust in the Lord to give wisdom to the police officers, so they can catch the criminals and pray that God will protect us until they are caught," he said. "We are not to worry and lose sleep over things we can't control. Just be smart and vigilant when you're out in public."

I looked at Jenna and smiled.

"I hope they follow his advice and pray for us," I whispered. "We need God's help in finding this killer."

"We need God's help in everything we do," she responded.

"So true," I said and looked back at the preacher.

"In Hebrews 10 verse 31 we read, 'It is a fearful thing to fall into the hands of the living God'," Elder Moss said. "Whether these criminals succumb to the valiant efforts of the police department or are killed by other criminals, they are falling into the hands of the living God."

"Did he just say that criminals are doing God's work?" I whispered to Jenna.

"I don't think he meant it that way," she answered and then turned back to the preacher.

Elder Moss continued with his message until 12 o'clock then he closed his bible, leaned his arms across it and smiled.

"I don't want you to be afraid to leave your homes," he said. "Just remember to pray before you do and remember to pray for our police officers," and he stepped down.

We sang a song and were dismissed with prayer.

After service, I went outside to wait for Jenna and the kids to say their goodbyes. Occasionally I would shake someone's hand and tell them to have a good day, but for the most part, I watched people interact with each other and waited.

At 12:30 Jenna and the kids emerged through the front door and started walking toward the car.

I joined them as they got close and we walked to the car together.

"What do you want for lunch," Jenna asked after we got in the car.

"Hotdogs!" Seth yelled.

"Chicken!" Jenny yelled.

“What do you want?” I asked, as I looked at Jenna.

“I don’t care as long as I don’t have to cook,” she said.

“Alright, let’s go by Bud’s Burger Barn so we can get what everyone wants,” I said, as I drove out of the church parking lot.

I went through the drive thru, ordered everyone a meal of their choice and then drove home.

Chapter 41

I awoke to the alarm at 5:30 in the morning. I rolled over, hit the snooze button and went back to sleep. At 5:40 Jenna was punching me with her elbow. "Are you going to work today?" she asked in a sleepy voice. "If not at least turn the alarm off."

"I'm going," I said, as I rolled out of bed. "It's just hard to get up."

"What's wrong?" Jenna asked. "You're usually eager to go to work."

"I enjoyed being home with you and the kids this weekend," I said. "I guess I'm just not ready to go back to work."

"Unfortunately someone has to protect the citizens of Thorton," she said. "And, you asked to be that person."

"I know," I said, as I went in the bathroom and took a shower.

After I showered, I dressed in my standard navy blue uniform and went down stairs. I went to the coffee pot to make some coffee then I looked at the clock and saw it was 6:15 in the morning, so I abandoned the idea and went to work.

When I turned into the station parking lot, I was surprised to see only one car parked in the lot and that was Mary Henderson's, our night shift dispatcher, off white 2003 Toyota Camry.

I parked in my parking space and sat for a few minutes, surveying the area across the road in front of the police station. Then I got out and walked inside.

"Where is everyone?" I asked as soon as I stepped in the door. "The parking lot's empty."

"Day shift hasn't got here yet," Mary answered and then she walked out of her office. "I think Tim is still patrolling around the Millwood Fabric Warehouse," as she approached and stood beside me.

Tim Weeks is one of our part time employees who work's most weekends. He has a full time job at Framer's Manufacturing and works with the police department as a way of getting his foot in the door. He has, on many occasions, requested a position with the department when one is available and I have assured him that he would be my first choice if or when that occurred.

"Why is he patrolling in that area?" I asked and looked at the clock. "That's a bad area to be without backup."

"He said he wanted to drive through the area to let everyone know the police was still around," she said. "He was just going to drive through the streets."

"I need to talk to him about that. He still doesn't need to be in that area alone," I said, as I walked to the coffee pot and started making coffee.

Tim walked in a few minutes later and said, "The streets are quiet."

"I heard you were patrolling around the Millwood Warehouse. I don't want you in that area unless you have back up," I sternly said.

"I didn't feel like I was in danger," he responded.

"You were probably in more danger than you realized," I said, as I poured a cup of coffee and slowly walked toward him. "Anytime a police officer is in that area, they are in danger."

"What about the people that's in the area?"

"They're in danger too, but they choose to be there," I said. "Besides on the weekend I only have one officer on duty and I don't need you putting yourself in needless danger."

"Maybe you need more officers."

"I don't have the budget to have more," I said and turned toward the door when Johnny walked in.

"What's going on?" Johnny asked, as he walked toward us.

"Tim went in the Millwood Fabric Warehouse area to patrol last night," I said and looked at Tim.

"Not a good idea," Johnny said, as he looked at Tim and shook his head. "People get killed in that area just for stopping at a red light."

"Shouldn't we do something about that?" Tim asked. "We are supposed to protect everybody."

"With the resources we have, we need to pick our battles and a bunch of drug dealers fall low on my list when I have many good law abiding citizens that need protecting," I said.

"Alright, I understand," Tim conceded. "I won't put myself in that situation again."

"Please don't," I said. "I don't want to go to a funeral."

"Alright, I'm here to relieve you," Johnny said. "You can go home."

"I wish I could, but now I need to go to my other job," Tim said and walked out the door.

"If he doesn't get himself killed, he'll make a good police officer someday," Johnny said, after the door closed.

"He has good intentions," I said and took a sip of coffee. "I just made fresh coffee."

"Great, I think I'll get some and wait for Richard to get here before we go out to protect the citizens of Thorton," he said and walked to the coffee pot and poured himself a cup.

"What do you think is happening to Thorton?" he asked.

"With growth come challenges. With expansion come trials," I said. "Unfortunately growth and expansion lead to an increase in crime because there's always someone trying to get something for nothing."

"So what you're saying is we have an increase in crime because the town is growing and criminals are trying to take advantage of the people that are prospering from the growth," Johnny said.

"That's what I said," I said.

"I thought so," Johnny said and smiled.

"I need to get to work," I said, as I went in my office and closed the door.

Chapter 42

I pulled my chair back and sat down. Then I took my notepad out of the top drawer of my desk and slowly read over the names.

I thought most of the people on my list are dead, so I turned to a clean sheet of paper and wrote possible suspects at the top of the page then numbered the page from 1 to 10.

Beside the number one I wrote Ben Lowe then I dropped down to the number two and wrote Victor White. At the number three I wrote Avery Moore.

I dropped down to the middle of the page and wrote other names of interest in the center. Then I moved to the right hand corner and wrote Butch Frost and put a question mark beside his name. Below Butch Frost I wrote Roger Hamilton, Gloria Curry and Kevin Brown.

When I finished writing, I leaned back and studied the names.

As much as I tried I still have no evidence to connect any of these people to the murders, so I put my list back in my desk and closed the drawer.

I leaned back with my fingers cupped under my chin and looked out the window at the clear blue sky. As I looked, I thought this hasn't been a very productive morning, but maybe Charles has some information that can enlighten me with this investigation.

So, I picked my phone up and called Charles Wallace.

The phone rang four times without an answer, so I hung up and dialed the number again. "ABI office," a lady said when she answered the phone.

"I need to speak to Charles Wallace," I said.

"Who may I say is calling?" she asked.

"Sam James with the Thorton Police Department," I answered.

"Just a moment," she said and I was put on hold.

I don't mind being on hold as long as I have good music to listen to, but this time I was listening to silence. Not even elevator music. I found my mind wondering. I thought of the weekend and the fun Jenna and I had with the kids. I thought of the warm sunny day and wished I was out on the lake fishing.

To prevent my mind from drifting too far I closed my eyes and tried to refocus my attention on the task at hand. Then I opened my eyes and looked at my watch. I had only been on hold for a couple of minutes but it seemed like a long time.

I took a deep breath, leaned back in my chair and propped my feet on my desk. I was about to hang up when Charles picked up and said, "I'm sorry, but I was in a meeting. What can I do for you Sam?"

"Did you have a chance to check on Morton Enterprises?" I asked.

"Wait a minute, let me close my door," he said and I heard him lay the phone on his desk. "Alright, I think I can talk."

"Did you find anything?"

"You may have gotten yourself into a hornet's nest," he said. "I've only got a small portion of information pertaining to Morton Enterprises, but they seem to be involved in a wide range of activities, from simple security to possible gun running."

"Gun running?" I questioned. "In Thorton?"

"No, this company has many offices throughout the United States and even a few in Canada," he said. "I think the office in Thorton is used mainly for security."

"Do you think they're involved with drugs?" I asked.

"I wasn't able to see the full report on them, but I didn't see anything that would lead me to believe they were involved with drugs," he said. "A good portion of the report was sealed."

"Why was it sealed?"

"We have agents in the company that are working undercover and they have informants working for the ABI, so we have to keep files sealed to protect the agents," he said. "I would be worried about talking on the phone, but we have our phones checked for bugs once a week and my phone was checked this morning."

"Can you trust the person that checked your phone?"

"I think so, but I checked it myself after he left."

"That's the best way to make sure it's safe," I said. "Anything else?"

"I would be very careful around anyone working for Morton Enterprises," he said. "Take what they saw with a grain of salt, because they might be trying to get information out of you. Remember they specialize in getting information from people and using it against them."

"You think they might try to gain my trust in order to find out what I know."

"They might."

"Do you think they're selling guns in Thorton?"

"Not unless someone in Thorton is planning on going to war," he said. "They deal in large volume. Not in small number sales."

"Why haven't they been arrested for selling guns?"

"That's an issue for the FBI," he said. "That part of the file is sealed. I only know about the gun running because one of our agents mentioned it when I asked him about Morton Enterprises."

"Do you think he knew or was he speculating."

"I think he knew."

"Do you think they would kill someone?"

"I think they would do whatever they got paid to do," he said. "If someone paid them enough, they would kill."

"I think they may be involved with these murders but I have no proof."

"Just keep digging and something will come up," he said. "Just remember they are professionals and train very hard in whatever they do."

"That's what has me worried," I said.

"Even professionals make mistakes from time to time," he responded.

"That's true," I said. "Do you have anything else?"

"That's all I have for now," he said. "I have a few more people to talk to, but I'm not expecting much information from them."

"Thanks for the help," I said and hung up.

I pulled my list out of my drawer and wrote Morton Enterprises beside the number four under possible suspects. Still no evidence, so I put my list back in the drawer and closed it.

My stomach started growling so I looked at the clock. It was five minutes before eleven, so I got up and walked into the squad room.

"It's time for lunch," I said, as I looked at Richard and Johnny who were sitting at their computers processing the tickets they had written earlier.

"I'm ready," Richard said, as he closed the page he was working on.

"Me too," Johnny said, as he closed the page he was working on and stood up. "Where are we going?"

"Let's go somewhere that's in walking distance," I said.

"The deli down the street?" Richard asked.

"That's fine with me," Johnny said and he walked toward the door.

"Do you want me to bring you a sandwich?" I asked when I stuck my head in the dispatcher's office.

"No thanks, I brought something from home," Rachel said.

"If you change your mind, just call my cell phone," I said and we walked out the door.

Chapter 43

After lunch we slowly walked back to the police station to enjoy the brightness and warmth of the sunshine.

"Spring is here," Richard said, as we walked.

"This time of year really validates the wonderful grace of God," I said.

"Yes it does," Richard said, as he opened the door and held it open for us to go through.

When the door closed, I saw Rachel looking out her office door.

"Sam, come here," she whispered.

"What is it?" I asked when I got close.

"There's a hooker in the back room," she said.

"What?" I asked.

"A hooker came in here and said she was a friend of yours," she said. "She was frightened and was afraid of being seen in the squad room, so I put her in the backroom where the television is located."

"What have you been doing?" Johnny asked and laughed.

"Does Jenna know what you've been up to?" Richard added and laughed.

"She's in the back room?" I asked.

"Yeah," Rachel said. "I didn't think she should be in your office and she was too frightened to stay in the squad room, so I put her back there."

"What's her name?" I asked.

"I'm not sure," she said. "I think its Diane, Donna or Doris, no wait it's a flower.

It's Daisy. That's it, it was Daisy."

"Daisy," I said then asked, "Was it Daisy Mayfield?"

"Yes, that's what she said her name was."

"Did she say what she wanted?"

"No, she just said she needed to talk to you."

"Alright, I'll go see what she needs," I said, as I walked to the backroom.

When I got to the backroom, I stopped at the door and glanced inside. Daisy, who was wearing a bright red sleeveless dress that draped across her thighs, was sitting on the couch with her face in her hands.

"Daisy, did you want to see me," I asked when I walked through the door.

She raised her head and looked at me without saying a word.

I walked to the couch and sat down beside her.

"What's wrong?" I asked in a gentle voice.

"Ruby was killed the other night," she said sounding frightened.

"I know, I worked the case," I said. "Do you know who killed her?"

"No I don't know," she said. "I was hoping you had already caught him."

"Not yet," I said. "We're still investigating."

"I'm usually with Ruby when we're on the street," she said. "I could have been killed with her."

"Why were you not with her?"

"I bought some drugs and I was spaced out," she said. "I think my dealer used something different to cut what I bought cause I did the same amount I usually do, but I couldn't walk afterward."

"Who's your supplier?"

"Chuck Henson."

"He was killed the same night Ruby was killed."

"Yeah, I know," she said. "That's why I'm scared. These murders are just getting too close to me."

"What do you want me to do?"

"Word on the street is that you helped Danielle Watts get off drugs," she said and looked me in the eyes. "I want to stop using."

"I didn't help Danielle get off drugs," I said. "I introduced her to someone that helped her get off drugs."

"Can I meet this person?"

"She has a lot of rules to follow," I said. "Are you willing to follow the rules of the house?"

"Will I have a place to stay?"

"If she agrees to help you then you will be living in her house," I said. "You'll be required to go to church every Sunday."

"I don't have a dress for church," she said and looked down.

"That won't be a problem," I said. "She has a storeroom filled with clothing from jeans to church dresses."

"Can I meet her?" she asked with optimism. "I really want to stop using."

"Let me give her a call and I'll let you know what she says," I said, as I got my phone out of my pocket and walked to the door.

I went in the hall and punched in the number for Lighthouse Miracle Works.

After the second ring, a lady answered the phone and said, "Lighthouse Miracle Works, Danielle speaking."

"Hey Danielle, this is Sam," I said.

"Hey Sam, what's you want?" she asked.

"I need to talk to Rose," I said. "Is she close by?"

"Just a second," she said.

I heard Danielle yell in the background, "Sam wants to talk to you."

"Hello Sam, this is Rose," she said after a few seconds. "Can I help you with something?"

"I have a lady here at the police station that would like help getting off drugs," I said. "She asked for your help."

"My help," she said. "How did she know about me?"

"She didn't ask for you by name, but she knew I helped Danielle to get off drugs and she wanted the same help."

"Did you arrest her?" she asked. "Is she trying to stay out of jail?"

"No, I didn't arrest her," I said. "She's helped me get information from the streets and I guess she thinks it's my time to help her."

"Did you tell her I had rules?"

"Yes I did."

"And, she came to you."

"Yes, she came to me."

"Alright bring her here and I'll talk to her."

"When do you want her?"

"Right now will be fine."

"I'll see you as soon as I can get there," I said and closed my phone.

I walked back to the breakroom and smiled at Daisy. "She wants to meet you now," I said.

"What about my clothes?" she asked.

"You'll get different clothes there," I said. "Some of the clothes you wear won't be suitable to be worn at her house."

"I said I would follow the rules," she said. "And I'll do anything to be clean."

"Does that include praying?"

"Will he listen?"

"You won't know unless you try."

"Then I'll pray."

"Let's go meet Rose," I said and walked out the door. I walked down the hall and went into the squad room.

Daisy followed.

"I'm taking Daisy to Rose Franks' house," I whispered when I leaned close to Johnny. "I'll probably go home after I drop her off."

"No problem, we'll be fine," he said and smiled. "I do know your cell phone number if I need you."

"That is true," I said and laughed.

"We'll see you tomorrow," Johnny said.

"Are you ready to go?" I asked, as I looked at Daisy.

"I think so," she said. "I'm ready for a change."

"Alright let's go," I said, as I walked to the door and opened it.

Daisy hesitated for a few seconds then she walked out. I followed and closed the door.

After we got in my car, I slowly drove to the end of the parking lot. I turned left and drove toward Lighthouse Miracle Works.

Chapter 44

I pulled to the side of the street and parked in front of the small house that was known as the Lighthouse Miracle Works.

"Is this it?" Daisy asked when we stopped.

"It looks smaller from the outside," I said. "When you get inside you'll see that it's a good sized house."

"She said that she would help me?" she asked.

"No, she said that she would ask you some questions," I said as we got out of the car and walked toward the door. "It's how you answer those question that will determine if she'll help you or not."

"Now I'm really nervous."

"Don't be," I said. "They're easy questions."

"What does she want to know?"

"If you really want to stop using drugs."

"I do," she insisted.

"Well, just let her know that," I said and knocked on the door.

After a few seconds, the door was opened.

Danielle smiled when she saw me. "Come on in," she said and moved away from the door.

I stepped to the side and allowed Daisy to go first then I followed her inside.

Two ladies were sitting in front of the television watching some game show. They glanced in our direction, but didn't say anything.

"I'll go get Rose," Danielle said and then walked out of the room.

"Do you want to sit and wait or do you want to stand here?" I asked, as I looked at Daisy.

"I'm a little nervous, so, I think I'd better stand," she said.

I turned and looked toward the kitchen when the door opened and Rose walked out. She smiled as she approached, but didn't say anything.

"Hello Rose," I said when she got near.

"Hi Sam," she responded.

"This is Daisy," I said and looked at Daisy.

"Hi Daisy," she said.

"Hi," Daisy said.

"I have a few questions for you, so I need you to follow me to my office," Rose said and started walking across the living room.

Daisy looked at me then she followed.

I looked at the two ladies that were watching the game show then I sat down in the recliner closest to the door.

Danielle walked in and sat down at the end of the couch.

"How's thing been going?" I asked.

"Pretty good," Danielle said. "Rose keeps me very busy, so I don't have a lot of free time."

"Do you know Daisy?" I asked.

"I've seen her around, but I really didn't know her," she said. "She stayed on one street and I stayed on another."

"I'm glad you're doing well," I said. "Apparently word on the streets is that you have gotten off drugs, because that's what got Daisy here."

"What?"

"She came to the police station and asked me for help," I said. "She said she had heard that I had helped another person get off drugs and she wanted me to help her."

"Well you did," she said.

"All I did was introduced you to Rose," I said. "You and Rose did the rest."

"With help from God," she corrected me.

"Very true," I said.

I turned when I heard Rose and Daisy walk back in the room.

"She said I could stay," Daisy said and smiled.

"She didn't look surprised when I was telling her the rules," Rose said and smiled. "Did you screen her before you brought her here?"

"I just wanted her to know what she was getting herself into," I said.

"I think she'll make a good transition and be fine here," Rose said.

"Thanks for your help," I said. "I told her you could help her with clothes."

"No problem," she said and looked at Danielle. "Will you help her find some clothes to wear?"

"Sure," Danielle said, as she got up. "Follow me," and she walked toward the storage room.

"Thanks," Daisy said and she followed Danielle.

"What happened to the lady that usually opened the door?" I asked.

"Are you talking about Karen?" Rose asked.

"I don't know her name but she would open the door and stay by the television the whole time we were here."

"That was Karen," she said. "She got a job and moved into a apartment on the other side of town."

"Is she still clean?"

"Yes, as far as I know," she said, as she looked at the couch. "She was here for 6 months and I believe she had gotten to the point where she could withstand the temptation."

"I hope so," I said.

"We all have to have faith," she said.

"Yes we do," I said. "That's how we make it through each day."

Rose paused and looked at the room that Danielle and Daisy went into to look for clothes. She turned back and smiled.

"If you keep bringing people by, you're not going to have any drug addicts left to arrest," Rose said and grinned.

"Unfortunately as I'm bringing them to you, new ones are moving into town," I said.

"It's a never ending battle," she said. "No matter what you do about drugs people are still going to use."

"They think they can use without being hooked," I said as I got up and walked to the door. "It's that, I have control of my body mentality."

"They soon learn that the body is weak," she said. "Without the help of God, drugs will overpower us."

"I can do all things through Christ, which strengths me," I said and opened the door. "If you need me call," and I walked out the door.

I got in my car and drove home.

Chapter 45

When I pulled into the station parking lot on Tuesday morning, I saw Johnny coming out of the front door. He stood with his arms crossed and watched as I pulled into my parking space. When I stopped, he walked to my side of the truck and waited.

"We may have gotten a break," he said, when I opened my door.

"What are you talking about?" I asked.

"I just got a call from a man who reported an abandoned black Escalade parked at Franklin Lumber Company," he said.

"Do you know who reported it?" I asked with anticipation.

"No, he hung up as soon as he reported the Escalade," Johnny said. "He didn't give me time to ask his name."

"People are afraid to get involved," I said. "They think someone might kill them if they talk to the police."

"That's true," he said. "I wish people would get more involved with their community and help us fight the criminals that are trying to take it over."

"A lot of people would get involved if they thought we could protect them," I said. "Get in, so we can check out this black Escalade at Franklin's," and I closed my door.

Johnny walked around to the passenger side and got into my truck. I backed up and slowly drove out of the parking lot.

I saw the black Escalade that was reported, as soon as we pulled into the parking lot. It was parked at the side of one of the storage buildings, beside three large pallets with cement blocks stacked as high as they could safely be stacked.

"Do you see anybody around the Escalade?" I asked, as I pulled to the side of the parking lot and sat watching.

"Not on the outside," Johnny said. "With the windows tinted, I can't see if anybody's inside or not."

"Get your gun ready," I said, as I took my Glock out of my holster and laid it beside my thigh.

Johnny took his gun out of its holster and firmly gripped it in his right hand.

I reached behind Johnny and got my vest. Then I slipped it over my shirt and picked up my gun.

"Do you have your vest on?" I asked, as I looked at Johnny.

"I put it on earlier," he said.

I put my Bronco in gear and slowly drove toward the Escalade. When I got within fifteen feet, I stopped.

We sat watching the Escalade for a few minutes without seeing any movement inside or for that matter anywhere in the lumber yard.

"Are you ready?" I asked.

"Let's do it," he said and opened his door.

I got out and walked to the front of my Bronco.

Johnny met me there.

"You walk on the driver's side and I'll go to the passenger's side," I said and started walking toward the Escalade with my gun outstretched.

When I reached the passenger's side door, I slowly reached for the handle and tried to open the door, but it was locked.

Johnny opened the driver's side door and stepped back immediately, making a gagging sound.

"What's wrong?" I asked and started walking around the Escalade.

"We have a body and it looks like it's been closed inside this car for a few days," he said, as he covered his mouth and turned away.

"I can smell it already," I said, as I covered my mouth and continued walking toward Johnny. "The heat inside the Escalade has intensified the decomposition of the body."

As I looked in the driver's side door, I saw a man with dark black hair slumped over the steering wheel with his arms dangling lifelessly at his side. On his left ring finger was a yellow gold ring with a single diamond set in the center. He was wearing a black pull over tee shirt with the arms removed to reveal a blue and red dragon tattoo on his left bicep, black jeans and ankle high black military boots.

"The Escalade couldn't have been here no more than two days, because they were open Saturday and someone would have noticed a unusual vehicle parked in their lumber yard," Johnny said. "It's not like they tried to hide it."

"I'd say it was parked here right after they closed Saturday," I said and stepped close to the body. "At the moment I can't see how he died, but I don't want to touch the body until the CSI unit gets here and looks for evidence."

"I'm not sure I'd want to touch it then," Johnny said and stepped a little farther away from the body.

I closed the door and made another quick scan around the lumber yard for anyone that might be watching.

"I'll get the tag number and run it through the system," Johnny said, as he walked to the back of the Escalade.

"Thanks, I'll call the CSI unit while you're running the tag number," I said, and I walked to my Bronco. I leaned up against the hood and called Janice with the CSI unit.

She answered after the second ring and asked, "What's wrong Sam?"

"Why do you think something's wrong?" I asked.

"Because you only call when something's wrong," she said. "Most of the time it's because of a dead body."

As I listened, I watched Johnny write the tag number on a piece of paper. Then he walked back to my Bronco and got inside to call the tag number into the station to be run through the system.

After Johnny closed the door, I turned my attention back to Janice and the conversation we were having.

"Then I won't disappoint you," I said. "I have a dead body at Franklin Lumber Company I need you to see."

"I'm not sure I know where Franklin Lumber Company is located," she said.

"It's on 10th Avenue and 20th Street beside Wilber's Specialty Tire Store," I said. "There's a large red and white sign just before you get to the lumber yard."

"I should be able to find it without any trouble," she said confidently. "Hey Sam, I'll let Diane know about the body."

"Thanks," I said.

"Well, I need to talk to her for a few minutes about another case and then she can follow us to the lumber yard," she said. "The guys can be loading the van while I talk to Diane."

"We'll keep an eye on the crime scene and make sure no one disturbs it while we're waiting on you to arrive," I said. "At the moment Johnny and I are the only ones here."

"We'll be there as soon as we can," she said and my phone went dead.

I closed my phone, put it in my pocket and started walking to the side of my truck. As I reached my door, I heard a vehicle and turned to see it pulling around the side of the building.

A rust colored Ford Ranger slowed as it rounded the building, hesitated for a split second and then slowly drove to where we were parked. It stopped beside where I was standing and Brian Franklin, who owned and operated Franklin Lumber Company for the better part of twenty years, rolled his window down.

"Sam, what's going on here?" he demanded.

"Brian, this is a crime scene," I said. "I don't want anyone in this area until the CSI unit gets here and gathers what evidence there is to gather."

"Crime scene?" he asked. "What kind of crime scene?"

"At this point, I can't discuss that," I said.

"I've owned this business for 20 years," he said. "And that means that I'm responsible for anything that happens in and around this property."

"Are you responsible for that black Escalade being here?"

"It wasn't here when we went home Saturday."

"What time did you go home?"

"We close at noon on Saturdays, but it usually takes us a little while to get everything put away, so I'd say everyone was gone by one o'clock."

"Have you ever seen this car before?"

"No."

"You haven't seen it parked across the street or maybe around the block."

"No, I have never seen that car," he said with certainty. "What's going on with the Escalade?"

"There's a dead body inside and it appears to have been here since sometime Saturday afternoon," I said, as I looked toward the main building which sells building and hardware supplies. "You can open and do business as usual as long as no one comes down here."

"So I can't sell my treated lumber or the cement blocks," he said and looked at the pallets of blocks.

"Not this morning, but we should have all this cleared out in a couple of hours and then you can sell whatever you want," I said and turned toward the parking lot.

"Well if that's how it has to be, I'll let you do your job so you can finish up and we can do business as usual," Brian said, as he cranked his Ford Ranger and drove around to the other side of the building.

Brian wasn't gone ten minutes when Janice pulled the CSI van around the building and slowly drove to where we were parked. She stopped beside my Bronco and turned the engine off.

Diane followed the CSI van until it got close to my Bronco then she circled around and parked beside the black Escalade.

Victor was the first to get out. "Where is the victim," he asked, as he started walking toward the Escalade.

"Driver's side front seat," I responded.

He held his camera as he continued walking to keep it from bouncing with his steps. When he got within five feet of the crime scene he stopped and started snapping off pictures of the black Escalade and the surrounding area. He made a wide circle as he went around the Escalade, snapping a picture with each step.

Janice and Daniel got out of the van and walked over to where I was standing. Diane and Samantha quickly joined us and we all watched as Victor photographed the crime scene.

After he finished photographing the outer parameter of the crime scene, he opened the driver's side door and started photographing the victim and the inside of the Escalade. He unlocked the rest of the doors, then walked to the passenger's side and photographed from that angle. He opened the back door on the passenger's side and then went to the driver's side, opened the back door and photographed the seats and floor board.

He left the doors opened as he went to let the smell dissipate into the air. He walked to the back of the Escalade, opened the door and stepped back.

"You have another victim here," he yelled, then he started photographing the victim.

"Did you know about that victim?" Janice asked.

"No, we only opened the driver's side door because the other doors were locked and we didn't want to disturb any evidence," I said.

"Could you tell how the victim in the driver's seat died?" Diane asked.

"I didn't see any blood, but I didn't move him, so if he wasn't bleeding from his chest or abdomen I wouldn't have seen it," I said.

"Alright, I've done my part," Victor said, as he walked past on his way to the van. "It's your turn."

Janice and Daniel grabbed their evidence gathering equipment and walked to the Escalade. Daniel went to the back and Janice went to the victim in the front seat.

"We need to get two stretchers out," Diane said, as she looked at Samantha. "We can have them parked close to the victims."

"Sure," Samantha said and she walked to the Medical Examiner's van.

"I need to help her get the stretchers out and then we can talk," she said, as she walked to the back of her van.

"I'll help you," I said and followed.

Samantha had already opened the back door of the Medical Examiner's van and was pulling one of the stretchers out. She eased it to the ground and waited for Diane to grab the other end. They lifted the stretcher to waist high and Samantha rolled it toward the back of the Escalade.

I helped Diane with the other stretcher and she rolled it to the driver's side and left it a few feet from the victim. She walked back to the van and put on a pair of plastic coveralls.

We watched as Janice dusted the door, steering wheel, dashboard, and radio for finger prints. Then she took a small pair of tweezers out of her bag, pulled a tiny piece of fuzz off the victim's shirt and slipped it inside a sterile container and closed the lid.

"I can get the rest of the evidence after the body's gone," Janice said and she backed away from the body.

"Great, I'll take him to the lab and start the autopsy," Diane said, as she rolled the stretcher close to the door.

"Can I help you?" I asked.

"Yes, but first you need to put on these coveralls," she said, as she handed me a pair of plastic coveralls. "You don't know what fluids will come out of the body."

She waited while I put on the coveralls and a pair of gloves, then we lifted the victim from the seat and laid him on the stretcher. After she searched for wounds, she zipped the body bag closed and we rolled the stretcher to the back of the Medical Examiner's van.

When we moved the stretcher, Janice went back to gathering evidence.

"Did you see anything that you'd say was the cause of death?" I ask when we got to the van.

"I didn't see anything obvious," she said, as we lifted the body into the van and she strapped the stretcher to the floor.

I followed Diane as she went to the back of the Escalade. We stopped close enough to see the victim, but not be in the way while Daniel was gathering evidence.

"I think I can tell how this one died," I said, as I looked at a man in his late thirties with the left side of his face blown off.

"It would appear he died from a gunshot wound, but nothing is certain until I complete the autopsy," she said. "He might have been shot after he was killed."

"That's true," I said. "But if he wasn't dead, this would have killed him."

"Alright, you can get the body," Daniel said, as he stepped back.

Diane pushed the stretcher close to the victim. Samantha helped Diane pull the victim out of the Escalade and place him on the stretcher.

I stepped back with Daniel and watched as they closed the body bag.

"It appears he was shot in the back of the head with a large caliber gun," Diane said, as she strapped the body to the stretcher.

"Was it execution style?" I asked.

"It looked like it might be," she said. "I should be able to tell you more after the autopsy," and rolled the stretcher toward the Medical Examiner's van.

"Did you see anything on the victim that could tell us who he is?" I asked, as Daniel moved back up to the crime scene and started gathering evidence.

"I didn't go through his pockets," he said. "Diane will empty his pocket when she does the autopsy."

I watched, as Daniel took a sample of blood off the carpet and dropped it in a glass vial filled with a clear liquid. He closed the top and gingerly twirled the liquid around to mix it with the blood sample.

After placing the vial in his evidence bag, he took a pair of tweezers, carefully pulling something off the carpet that lined the inside of the Escalade, then dropped it in a plastic bag and closed it tight.

"What was that?" I asked.

"Hair fibers," he said. "It looked like human hair fibers."

"Do you think it's the killer's hair?"

"I don't know," he said. "It could be the victim's."

"Was it the same color as the victim's?"

"It looked similar to the victim's, but most people have different shades of color in their hair," he said, as he put the sample in his evidence bag. "At this point, I couldn't tell you if it was the victim's, the killer's or neither one of them."

"I'm finished with the front," Janice said, as she approached.

"I've got everything there is in the back," Daniel said, as he closed the door.

"What are you going to do with the Escalade?" I asked, as I turned to see a tow truck with CSI written in large black letters across the door pull into the driveway. "Never mind, I think I know."

"We need to tow it back to our garage so we can go over it more thoroughly," Janice said.

"So after it's gone I can tell Brian that he can go ahead and open this area of his business, right," I said and looked at Janice.

"Yes, as far as I'm concerned we have all the evidence that's here," Janice said.

I turned and watched Diane as she closed the back door of her van. "I'll get back so I can get started on these autopsies," she said while opening her front door.

She got in, waited for Samantha in get in the passenger's side and then drove out of the parking lot

We watched as the wrecker hooked up to the Escalade and towed it toward the CSI garage. Janice, Victor and Daniel loaded all their equipment in their van.

"I'll try to have something by late this afternoon," she said, as she got inside her van.

She cranked up and drove away.

"I need to let Brian know that he can sell this stuff down here now," I said, as I looked at Johnny who was leaning on my bumper.

"Let's stop by the front door as we drive by," Johnny said and he opened the door.

"Sounds good to me," I said and I got in my truck.

I stopped beside the front door and started to get out, but I saw Brian walking out the door. I rolled my window down when he approached.

"What's the word?" he asked.

"We're finished gathering evidence," I said. "Do business as usual."

"Do you know who did this?" he asked.

"Not yet," I said. "But they've just got the evidence and haven't had time to evaluate it yet."

"Thanks for letting me know that you're finished in the yard," he said, as he turned and went back inside his store.

"He didn't seem happy," Johnny said after Brian was inside.

"No, I don't think he was," I said. "He may have lost some business this morning."

"Wasn't our fault," Johnny said.

"I don't think he was mad at us, I think he was mad at the situation," I said, as I looked at the door that Brian had just walked through.

"I can understand that," he said and looked toward the lumber yard. "I'm sure they sell a lot of treated lumber."

"I would image they do," I said, as I cranked up.

"It's the best type of wood to keep the termites out," he said.

I looked at Johnny and asked, “Did you get anything on that tag number?”

“Yes,” he said, as he looked toward me. “It was registered to Morton Enterprises.”

“You’ve got to be kidding,” I exclaimed. “Everything seems to be pointing toward Morton Enterprises.”

“I wonder if these victims were the ones that tried to shoot you the other day,” Johnny said.

“It looked like the same Escalade, but I can’t tell the difference in one black Escalade from another,” I said.

“It will be interesting to hear what Ben Lowe has to say,” Johnny said and smiled.

“We need to pay him a visit later on today,” I said, as I put my Bronco in gear. “But, I’d like to wait until we know the identity of the victims before we go,” and I drove toward the police station.

Chapter 46

When we walked into the police station, I saw Rose Franks and Daisy Mayfield sitting in straight backed metal chairs beside my office door. They stood simultaneously when the door opened and slowly started walking toward me.

Rose smiled as she approached, but Daisy looked nervous and continued looking at the floor as she walked.

"Sam, can we speak to you a minute in your office?" Rose asked, as she stepped beside me.

I looked at Daisy, who was still looking at the floor.

"Do you mind if Johnny comes in the office with us and listens?" I asked.

"No, I don't mind," she said. "He might need to hear what we have to say."

"Then come on in and have a seat in the chairs in front of my desk," I said and started walking toward my office.

I opened the door and stood back to allow them to walked through the open doorway.

Rose sat in the chair closest to the window and Daisy sat in the one closest to the door. Johnny brought a chair in from the squad room and sat with his back to the filing cabinet.

After everyone was inside, I closed the door and sat down at my desk. I looked at Daisy for a few seconds then I turned to Rose and asked, "Alright, what do you need to talk about?"

"I think someone's been watching the house," she said and looked at Daisy.

Daisy looked up, but didn't say anything.

"Why do you say that?" I asked.

"I've seen a car parked across the street several times this week," she said.

"Did you recognize the person in the car?"

"I didn't, but I asked Daisy to look at the driver this morning and she believes its Avery Moore."

"Has he threatened anyone at the house?"

"No, he just sits and watches the house."

"I believe he's thinking about kidnapping me," Daisy said and laughed a nervous laugh.

"Does he show up about the same time every day?" Johnny asked.

"Yes, he's there about 7:30 every morning and he also comes back at around one o'clock in the afternoon," Rose said.

"What kind of car is he driving?" I asked.

"He was in a white Buick Terraza CX this morning," Daisy said.

"He was in the same car this morning that he always drives," Rose said.

"We may have to drive out that way this afternoon and talk to the driver of that car," I said, as I looked at Johnny.

"It would be interesting to find out why he parks there," Johnny said and smiled.

"I'm afraid for Daisy's safety," Rose explained. "If he's been known for having violent behavior, I don't want him coming into my house and trying to hurt anyone."

"Make sure you keep your doors locked until we come by this afternoon," I said.

"We keep the doors locked all the time anyway," Rose said. "We're trying to keep the bad influences out and the good influences in."

"Daisy, how have you been doing?" I asked.

She grinned and looked at Rose. "It's been tough, but with Rose's help, I'm making it through the hard times."

"With God's help she's making it through the hard times," Rose corrected her.

"I'm sorry, I meant with God's help," Daisy said. "I'm having a hard time giving God the credit He deserves."

"We all do that," I said. "We want to take credit for the good things and blame God for the bad."

"Which is the opposite of what we should be doing," Rose said.

"You're right," I said. "We should give God the credit for the good things and we should take credit for the bad."

"So, you're going to talk to the guy today," Rose said.

"Yes, we'll drive by your house about one o'clock and stay in the area until we're able to talk to him," I said. "Call me if you see him before one."

"Thanks," Rose said, as she stood up. "I'm just afraid he might do something to Daisy."

Daisy looked at Rose and stood up.

I got up and walked to the door.

"Be careful going home," I said and opened the door. "If you see the car on your way home, just circle back around and come back to the police station."

"We will," Rose said and they walked out of my office.

"Do you need me to follow you home?" Johnny ask when they reached the door.

“I think we’ll be fine,” Rose said. “We’ll do what Sam said and if we see the car we’ll come back here,” and she opened the door.

“Thanks for your help,” Daisy said and she walked out the door.

“I’ll let you know if I see the car before one o’clock,” Rose said and she followed Daisy out the door.

“What do you think Avery’s up to?” Johnny asked after they left.

“Probably trying to intimidate Daisy into going back to the streets,” I said.

“That should make her want to stay off the streets,” Johnny said.

“Yes, it should,” I said and walked to the coffee pot.

Johnny followed me and poured himself a cup of coffee. He then went to his desk to start filling out the paperwork related to the murders this morning.

I poured myself a cup of coffee and went to my office to start my paperwork for the day.

At 12:30 I laid my pen down and walked out of my office.

“Are you ready to go?” I asked, as I walked in the squad room.

“Yes, I’m ready,” Johnny said, as he stood up and started walking toward the door.

“Let’s see what this guy has to say,” I said and opened the door.

Johnny walked out and I followed closing the door behind us.

Chapter 47

When we got close to Lighthouse Miracle Works, I saw the white Buick Terraza CX, that Rose had reported, parked across the street partially hidden behind a lawn care service truck. I circled around the block to approach from the rear and slowly pulled in behind the car, parking close to its bumper to block any chance of him leaving.

I pulled my Glock G17 out of its holster and got out of my Bronco. Then I waited for Johnny to get out and we approached the car at the same time. Johnny walked to the passenger side and I walked to the driver's side.

When I got close, I quickly recognized Avery Moore sitting in the driver's seat.

He rolled his window down and looked toward me while shielding his eyes from the sun with his left hand.

"Are you planning on shooting me officer?" he asked, as he looked at my gun.

"I might," I said. "It depends on how you answer my questions."

"You can't shoot me," he exclaimed. "It's against the law."

"You're a fine one to be quoting the law," I said, as I put my gun back in my holster.

"Did you and your buddy come out here to harass me?" he asked, as he glanced toward Johnny.

"Why are you parked here?" I asked, as I leaned a little closer to the open window.

"I'm enjoying the beauty of nature," he said and laughed.

"If you want to enjoy the beauty of nature you need to go to the city park or to one of the national forests," I said. "This is a residential area and people are not allowed to park anywhere they decide."

"I'm not breaking any laws," he retorted.

"Yes, you are," I responded. "It's called loitering."

"Well, I can leave if it's a problem, officer," he smirked.

"Why were you watching that house?" I asked, as I pointed to Rose's house.

"I wasn't watching any house."

"The people that live there saw you parked here earlier this morning and yesterday," I said.

"They stole something from me and I want to get it back," he angrily responded, as he looked across the street.

"Why didn't you report it to the police?"

"It's a personal matter."

"What did they steal?" I asked, as I glanced at Johnny who was standing on the other side of the car.

"I said it's a personal matter," he said and his face reddened.

"I know the people that live in that house and I know the property you are talking about," I said and bent closer to his face. "If you don't want to be arrested, you won't show your face around here again."

"Is that a threat?" he asked.

"Just stating the facts," I declared.

"I can't leave because you parked too close to my car," he said, as he looked in his rear view mirror.

"I'll move so you can go but just keep what I said in mind," I said and I walked to my vehicle.

I backed up about five feet to allow Avery plenty of room. Then I watched as he pulled away from the curb and drove away, slowing occasionally to an almost stop as he went down the street.

"Do you think he'll be back?" Johnny asked, as he opened the door to the Bronco.

"If he does come back, we'll need to take him to jail," I said, as I opened my door. "I need to talk to Rose for a minute before we leave," and closed my door.

Johnny closed his door also and we started walking across the street toward Rose's house.

When we got to the door, Johnny pressed the doorbell. After a few seconds, the door opened a few inches and a female voice said, "Just a second," and the door closed.

I heard a chain rattle and then the door opened completely.

"Did you see him?" Daisy asked with anticipation.

"Yes we talked to him and persuaded him to leave the area," I said and smiled.

"He'll be back," she said with confidence.

"If you see him, I want you to call the station, immediately," I advised.

"Did you see him?" Rose asked when she walked up.

"Yes, we saw him and told him to leave," I said and looked at Rose. "Like I was telling Daisy, if you see Avery parked across the street, call the station immediately."

"Do you think we're in danger?" Rose asked.

"I don't think so, but I'd rather be safe."

"Thanks Sam."

"No problem," I said and I walked out the door.

Johnny followed me outside and we walked back to my Bronco in silence.

After we got to my car Johnny said, "We probably need to patrol this area a little more in the next few days," as he opened the door and got in.

"Good idea," I said and opened my door.

After I got in the truck, I cranked up and drove toward the police station.

Chapter 48

When we walked into the police station I heard Rachel said, “I’ll tell him when he gets here,” and then she hung up.

“Who was that?” I asked, as I stepped inside her office.

“Oh Sam, I didn’t know you were here,” she exclaimed, as she turned around. “That was Diane trying to get in contact with you.”

“Well, why didn’t she call my cell phone?” I asked a little irritated.

“She said she’s been trying for the last hour, but it keeps going to voice mail,” Rachel answered and then asked, “Have you been talking on your phone?”

“No. I haven’t talked to anybody this afternoon,” I said, as I took my phone out of my pants pocket and looked at it. “It turned itself off again,” I said and turned it back on.

“Does it turn off often?” Rachel asked.

“It does when I put my phone in my pants’ pocket and this morning I forgot and slid it in the front pocket of my pants instead of my shirt pocket,” I said and looked at my phone. “I think my pants presses against my thigh when I walk and that pressure makes my phone cut off.”

“Maybe you need another phone,” she said.

“I’ll get one when my contract runs out,” I said. “Until then I’ll try to remember to put it in my shirt pocket.”

“Don’t forget to call Diane,” she reminded.

“I’ll do that right now,” I said, as I walked out the door into the squad room and went into my office.

I closed my office door and sat down at my desk. I pulled my notepad out of my desk drawer and punched in Diane's office phone number. Then I waited while it rang.

"Medical Examiner's office," Diane said when she answered. "How can I help you?"

"This is Sam," I said. "I'm returning your call."

"Oh yes, Sam, I want to give you the results of the autopsies on those victims from earlier this morning," she said.

"Alright, I'm ready," I said, as I picked up my pen and opened my notepad to a clean sheet of paper.

"The victim in the front seat overdosed on heroin," she said. "He had enough in his system to kill three men his size."

"Do you think it was murder?"

"Yes, it was murder," she said. "The puncture site was in the Trapezius muscle beside the scapula. The needle penetrated at a downward angle and to the left which indicated the killer was right handed. The killer was slightly taller than the victim or the victim was sitting down when he was injected."

"Could you tell if the victim was tortured?"

"I found some minor abrasions to the victim's wrist which could indicate that his arms were tied at one time, but there wasn't enough tissue damage to indicate that the victim fought the ropes for very long."

"He may have been drugged while he was tied."

"That might explain the high level on heroin in his blood," she said. "They may have accidentally overdosed him."

"Did he have more than one puncture site?" I asked.

"No, only the one."

"So, they probably gave him the entire dose at one time," I said, as I wrote murdered with heroin on my notepad and circled it.

"That's correct."

"They meant to kill him."

"Yes, they meant to kill him."

"Were you able to determine his identity?"

"I sent his prints to the CSI lab along with his clothes," she said.

"What about the other victim?"

"Let's see, the other victim was shot twice execution style in the back of the head. The bullets severed the mid cerebral artery and nicked the posterior cerebral artery which lead to him bleeding to death," she said.

"He didn't die from his brains being splattered everywhere?" I asked.

I moved down to the middle of my notepad and wrote gunshot wound to back of head and circled it.

"No, he bleed to death," she said with emphasis. "The injury to his brain wouldn't have killed him. He would have spent his entire life being feed through a tube and not knowing he was in the world, but he would have been alive."

"Did he have any drugs in his system?" I asked, as I laid my pen down and leaned back in my chair.

"He had a trace amount of cocaine in his blood which indicated he probably did some cocaine within the last twenty-four hours, but nothing that would contribute to his death."

"Did he have any other wounds?" I asked.

"No, he only had the gunshot wounds," she said.

"Could you tell what type of gun the killer used from the size of the wounds?"

"No, one of the bullets went straight through his brain and exited out the front of his face, but the other bullet lodged in his brain," she said. "I was able to extract it and send it to the CSI lab to be examined."

"So, they have all the evidence at the CSI lab," I said.

"Yes, I've sent them everything I have," she said. "I wish there was more I could tell you, but that's all I have."

"Thanks for your help," I said. "I'll call Janice and see if she has any information," and I laid my phone down on the receiver.

I picked the phone back up and punched in Janice Walker's phone number. After the second ring, Janice answered and said, "CSI unit. How can I help you?"

"This is Sam James," I said. "I was wondering if you had anything on that evidence you gathered this morning."

"We're still evaluating some of the evidence, but I can tell you what we have," Janice said, as she started shuffling papers around on her desk.

"Let's see, I'll start with the victim in the front seat," she said. "His name is Bart Watson. According to his record, he's been arrested twice for attempted murder, but the charges were dropped when the witnesses disappeared. He's an ex-marine and is associated with several mercenary groups that have ties to the Middle East. At present I think he was working for Morton Enterprises because he had several business cards with his name under their logo."

"Did the killer leave any evidence?" I asked, as I wrote Bart Watson at the top of my notepad.

"The front seat was clean," she said. "We thoroughly searched the front of the Escalade but we found nothing."

"Do you have the identity of the second victim?" I asked, as I moved my pen to the center of my notepad in anticipation of the victim's name.

"Yes, the second victim is George Winfield," she said. "His record reads a lot like Bart Watson's. He's an ex-marine with ties to the same mercenary groups as Bart, but he has no criminal record. He also had business cards with the Morton Enterprises logo in his wallet. As you could tell at the scene, he was shot in the back of the head execution style," and she paused. "Let's see, the victim had a .357 Magnum bullet lodged in his brain which Diane retrieved and we analyzed."

"Anything else?" I asked, as I wrote George Winfield in the middle of the page.

"Daniel found hair fibers beside the victim and he's still analyzing those," she said and hesitated. "I don't know if this means anything, but the victim had a breviary in his shirt pocket."

"What's a breviary?" I asked.

"A Roman Catholic book of prayers," she said.

"So, this mercenary was religious," I said. "I bet that didn't stop him from killing people."

"Maybe he was asking for forgiveness."

"Might have been," I said and I wrote religious under his name. "Did you find any guns in the Escalade?"

"No, not a single weapon."

"Now that seems odd," I said. "For mercenaries not to have guns."

"The killer may have taken them."

"I saw Daniel get a blood sample off the carpet," I said. "Did he analyze it?"

"Yes, it turned out to be the victim's blood."

"Was there anything that could lead us to the killer?" I asked.

"The killer left no evidence behind," she said.

"I need to find a way to make the killer make a mistake," I said.

"What do you have in mind?" she asked.

"Right now I don't have a plan, but I'll do whatever I need to do to catch the killer," I said.

"Just be careful," she said.

"I will," I said. "Call me if you have any more information," and I placed the phone on the receiver.

I wrote mercenary and Morton Enterprises under each of the victim's names. Then I got up and walked into the squad room.

Johnny was sitting at his computer filling out a report pertaining to the murders that had occurred earlier today. As I approached, he hit the print button and the printer came to life, shooting out page after page until the report was completely on hard copy and ready to be placed in a file.

He got up, pulled the sheets of paper off the printer and handed them to me.

"Here's the crime scene report," he said.

I took the report, walked in my office and laid it on top of my desk. "I'll read it later," I said then I walked back in the squad room. "Right now, we need to go to Morton Enterprises."

I slipped my bullet resistant vest on over my shirt and waited for Johnny to put his vest on. I stuck my head in the dispatcher's office and said, "We'll be back in a little while," and I walked out the door.

Johnny followed and closed the door.

As we walked to my Bronco, he asked, "What exactly are we doing at Morton Enterprises?"

"I'm hoping to get the killer to make a mistake," I said.

"That's why we're going to Morton Enterprises?" he asked.

"I also want to see their reaction when I tell them we found their black Escalade with their employees dead inside," I said and got in my Bronco.

After Johnny got in, I cranked up and drove out of the parking lot.

Chapter 50

I pulled into a parking space beside the front door to Morton Enterprises. As Johnny and I got out of my Bronco, we each looked around to see if there was any potential danger, then we walked to the front door.

Johnny opened the front door and held it as I walked inside. He followed and stood beside the door with his back to the wall.

When I walked toward the desk, I was met by a lady in her early thirties with long red hair and freckles. She was wearing black dress pants, a navy blue blouse with a bright red scarf tied around her neck and no shoes.

"Can I help you with something?" she asked.

"Where's the other secretary?" I asked.

"She had to take some time off," she said and giggled. "I'm filling in for her while she's off."

"My name is Sam James," I said. "I need to speak to Ben Lowe if he's around."

"My name is Robin Smith," she said and smiled. "I'll check and see if he's not too busy to talk to you," and she started walking down the hall.

I moved to one of the straight backed chairs and sat down.

In a couple of minutes she walked back to her desk without looking at me and sat down. She turned to her computer screen and started working.

"Did he say he was going to talk to me?" I asked, as I stood up.

"He said you were the police chief of Thorton," she said without looking away from the computer.

"Yes, I am the police chief," I said, as I moved closer to her. "Is that a problem?"

"No, I just don't like talking to cops," she said.

"Is he busy or not?" I asked with irritation.

"He said he'd be out in five minutes," she said and looked around as Ben walked up.

"Are you harassing my employees," Ben asked without smiling.

"Not yet," I responded.

"Robin said you needed to talk to me," Ben said. "What's it about?"

"Can we talk in private?" I asked, as I glanced at her.

"Come back to my office," he said a little exasperated and started walking toward his office.

I followed him to his office and sat in one of the chairs in front of his desk.

He closed the door and sat down behind his desk.

"What's this about?" he asked.

"We found a black Escalade this morning that was registered to Morton Enterprises," I said.

"So we have a black Escalade," he said. "I told you the other day that we have too many vehicles for me to keep up with."

"It was the same black Escalade used when I was being shot at," I said and leaned forward.

"I can assure you that I didn't order anyone to shoot at you," he said.

"Someone did," I retorted.

He sat glaring at me for a few seconds then he asked, "Is that what you came here to talk about?"

"No, I came here to tell you what we found in the black Escalade," I said.

"Is this some kind of a game with you?" he asked, as his voice got louder. "What did you find?"

"Two dead bodies."

His face turned pale as he sat up in his chair and asked. "Who did you find?"

"Do you know Bart Watson and George Winfield?"

"I know who they are, but they work in a different division, so I've not had much contact with them."

"Do you know why someone would want to kill them?"

"I have no idea," he said, as he rubbed his forehead with his shirt sleeve. "How were they killed?"

"I can't tell you right now because we're still investigating the murders," I said and jumped up when I heard a lot of noise coming from the front of the building.

I opened the door and ran up the hall.

When I got up front, I saw Johnny standing beside a large man who was leaning over the desk yelling at the secretary.

I looked at Robin who had rolled her chair back away from the man and was staring at him with her eyes wide with fear and her mouth open.

"You need to calm down," Johnny said, as he moved closer to the man.

The man looked at Johnny and asked, "And what is it to you?"

"You're not going to get anywhere yelling at someone," Johnny said.

"Well, its none of your business," the man said.

"What's going on," I asked.

"This man came in and just started yelling at her," Johnny said, as he pointed to Robin.

"Ben, I think you need to do something," the man said, as he looked at Ben.

Ben walked up behind me and said, "I think you both need to leave," to Johnny and me.

"Who is this guy?" I asked when I turned around and looked at Ben.

"A valued customer," Ben responded.

"He may be a valued customer, but he needs to learn how to talk to people," I said.

"Just leave," Ben said.

"I'll be around," Johnny said and walked out the door.

I followed him outside.

When we got in my Bronco I asked, "What was that about?"

"Apparently she didn't fill out some papers that she was supposed to," Johnny said.

"It sounds like he tried to make a big deal out of nothing," I said, as I cranked up and drove out of the parking lot.

When I pulled into the station parking lot, I circled around to the front door and stopped.

"It's been a long day," I said. "I'll see you tomorrow, because I'm going home."

"I'm off tomorrow," Johnny said. "So I'll see you Thursday."

"Who's working with Richard tomorrow," I asked.

“I’m not sure. I think it’s just Richard and you,” Johnny said, as he closed the door and walked toward the police station.

I watched as Johnny went inside, then I drove home.

Chapter 51

The disgruntled drug dealer pulled his black Mazda RX-8 Sport car to the side of the street and waited for his trusted employee to get inside then he slowly drove away.

When he stopped at a stop sign at the end of the street, he turned to his employee and asked, “Did you do the job?”

His employee’s eyes widen with fear because he knew his employer had a volatile temper, having seen the results himself.

“Well answer me!” the drug dealer demanded, as he turned left and slowly drove around the block.

“Yes I did the job,” he responded.

“Tell me how it went Hamburger,” the drug dealer said.

He gave his employee the nickname Hamburger because that was what he ate every day for lunch.

“Well I did what you told me to,” Hamburger said, as he shifted in his seat. “I arranged a meeting with the people you had hired to burn the Millwood Fabric Warehouse.”

“How did you get them to come?” he asked.

“I told them you had another job for them,” Hamburger said.

“Good idea,” he said. “Alright finish your story.”

“I got them to meet me at that old Hardwood Furniture plant on 20th Street,” Hamburger said. “I had Frankie and Lou hiding inside the plant and when we got inside they came out with their guns drawn.”

Hamburger glanced out the window and then added, "Bart and George thought it was a joke until I told them to hold their hands up in the air and I patted them down and took their guns."

"So they didn't see it coming," the disgruntled drug dealer said and chuckled.

"No, they were completely caught off guard," Hamburger said with pride. "After I took their guns, we tied them both to chairs and I had a little fun explaining to them what I was going to do."

"How did you kill them?" the drug dealer asked with impatience. "You keep dragging it out."

"I gave Bart a heavy dose of smack," Hamburger said and laughed. "It was enough to kill ten people."

"That's a lot of heroin," the drug dealer said. "Are you sure you gave him that much?"

"Well, maybe not ten people, but I'm sure it was enough to kill five," he said.

"If you lied about the dose of heroin, are you sure you gave enough to kill him," the drug dealer asked.

"Yes, I know he's dead," Hamburger said and he started sweating. "I shot him up myself."

"What about the other mercenary?"

"I shot him in the back of the head with my 357 magnum."

"And you're sure he's dead."

"I shot him twice at close range," Hamburger said. "It blew half his brain off."

"What did you do with the bodies?"

"Frankie and I, loaded them inside their black Escalade and parked it in the back of Franklin Lumber Company," Hamburger said and looked toward the drug dealer. "I thought I'd let their bodies cook a while in their closed up vehicle."

"Well that should take care of those loose ends," the drug dealer said. "They almost messed up when they didn't kill the police chief like I told them to."

"Maybe now he'll be satisfied since he found the black Escalade," Hamburger said.

"You didn't leave any evidence behind that could lead him to me?" the drug dealer asked. "Did you?" he asked and leaned toward him.

Hamburger started breathing heavily as he looked toward the Ruger LCP semiautomatic handgun lying beside the disgruntled, paranoid drug dealer's right leg.

"No, I'm sure everything's clean," he said and looked away.

"It had better be, because you know how I deal with people that make mistakes," he said and laughed.

"I sure do," he said and forced a laugh.

"Where are Frankie and Lou?"

"They're selling dope on 5th Street."

"Good," the drug dealer said, as he pulled to the side of the street. "Now get out," he demanded.

Hamburger opened the door and jumped out just as the drug dealer started driving away. He stumbled but regained his footing and began running down the block. Then he turned the corner and slowed down to a brisk walk.

As he caught his breathe he thought with a smile, someday I'll kill you for disrespecting me but he refused to turn back and look because he was afraid his boss might see him.

"The Smack Master is back," the disgruntled drug dealer said, as he smiled and drove out of town to arrange another big drug sale.

Chapter 52

Richard was standing by the coffee pot talking to Rachel with a cup of coffee and a doughnut in his hand when I walked in the door. Richard held a doughnut up and asked, "Sam, do you want a doughnut?"

"Richard brought the doughnuts and I just made a pot of coffee," Rachel added.

I walked to where they were standing and looked in the doughnut box. "Sounds like a good breakfast to me," I said, as I laughed and poured a cup of coffee.

Then I took a doughnut and asked, "Did anything happen last night?"

"No, it was quiet last night and so far it's been quiet this morning," Richard said, as he got another doughnut out of the box.

"Maybe it'll be quiet so I can work on some paperwork," I said wishfully.

"Speaking of paperwork, I need to finish filling out my log book," Rachel said and she walked to the dispatcher's office.

I refreshed my coffee, took another doughnut and walked to my office. After I closed my door, I turned my computer on and finished eating my doughnut while it booted up.

Then I started looking over the fuel consumption over the last two weeks and compared it to the remaining money we had in the budget. I thought, "At this rate we'll have to stop patrolling before the end of the month."

I then pulled up the record of tickets and looked at the area where most of them had been written. They seemed to be spread out evenly throughout the entire town except for a long stretch of highway along 10th Avenue.

After I finished looking over the budget, I got up and walked into the squad room. Richard was still sitting at his computer filling out reports from yesterday.

"We're going to have to stop patrolling as much and just park somewhere," I said when I walked up to Richard. "You'll need to be parked where people can see you," and I leaned up against his desk.

"What about the neighborhoods that need our protection?" he asked, as he pushed himself away from his computer.

"We'll go when they call, but we can't drive the streets," I said. "We need to save gas."

"Do you want me to patrol any today?" he asked.

"No, just stay here and if someone calls in something than you'll need to go to it," I said.

"Criminals might catch on to this," Richard responded.

"We won't do it every day," I said. "So they won't know when we'll be out patrolling or not."

Rachel stepped out of her office and yelled, "Sam, you have a phone call."

"Who is it?" I asked.

"Ben Lowe," she said and went back in her office.

"I wonder what he wants," I said, as I walked in my office and closed the door.

I pulled my chair back and sat down. Then I picked up the phone and asked, "How can I help you Ben?"

"You asked me to call if I had some information," he said. "So I called."

"Great, what have you got?" I asked.

“I talked to the guy that was over Bart Watson and George Winfield,” he said and paused. “He said that they hadn’t worked for Morton Enterprises for quiet a while.”

“What do you mean?” I asked. “They had business cards in their wallets with the Morton Enterprises logo along with their names.”

“They freelance their skills and only worked there occasionally,” he said. “Those were old cards,” he added.

“Do you know when they last worked there?” I asked.

“No, he didn’t tell me that,” Ben said. “He just said that they hadn’t worked for him in months.”

“You wouldn’t know who they were working for, would you?” I asked.

“I have no idea,” he said firmly.

“Thanks for the information,” I said.

“Just trying to clear the company,” he said.

“Thanks anyway,” I said and hung up the phone.

I leaned back and tried to soak in the information I had just learned which really didn’t affect me any, because I didn’t have any evidence against Morton Enterprises or anyone else.

I sat straight up when I heard a knock at the door.

“Come in,” I said.

Richard opened the door and asked, “What did he have to say?”

“He said Bart Watson and George Winfield weren’t working for Morton Enterprises,” I said. “He said they freelance.”

“So, they were guns for hire,” Richard responded.

"Pretty much," I said.

"I need to go to 4th Street," Richard said. "Rachel just got a call about a minor fender binder."

"Do you need any help?" I asked, as I started to get up.

"I can handle it," Richard said, as he stood up. "I'll call you if I need help," and he walked out the door, closing my office door as he went.

I leaned back in my chair and tried to think.

Over an hour went by while I sat in my chair trying to come up with a good suspect but no one came to mind. I looked at my notepad, but didn't have anything to add to it so I put it away.

Then I turned back to my computer and started working over the budget again.

I looked at the clock and realized it was 4 o'clock, so I turned my computer off and walked to the dispatcher's office.

"I'm making an early night of it," I said when Rachel looked up from her computer.

"Tell Jenna I said hi," she said.

"I will," I said and walked out the door.

Chapter 53

Thursday started off the way Wednesday ended which was very quiet. But around noon everything changed when Robert Wilson, the owner of the local Piggly Wiggly, stormed in the front door and demanded, “You’ve got to stop the drug dealer’s that’s congregating around my business.”

I was standing beside Richard looking at the accident report he had filled out the previous day when Robert entered the station.

I looked at Robert and asked, “What are you talking about?”

“There’s a group of drug dealers that started hanging around the store and I need you to make them leave because they’re scaring away the customers,” he said.

“Why haven’t you complained before?” I asked and walked toward him. “This is the first time I’ve heard anything about it.”

“They just started bothering my customers last week,” he said. “And I hoped they would go away.”

“What exactly are they doing?” I asked.

“They’re standing across the street watching for potential customers,” he said. “And when someone pulls into my parking lot, they run up to them and asked them if they want to buy drugs.”

“Do you know the drug dealers?” I asked.

“No, I don’t know who they are,” he said. “Last week was the first time I saw them.”

“Have you heard them try to sell drugs to your customers?” I asked.

"No, but I've had a couple of my best customers complain about being approached," he said. "I need it stopped," and he walked around the counter and said, "I'm losing business every day because of this."

"Well they sure won't come up to us as long as we're wearing our uniforms," I said and looked at Richard.

"I could change into some of the clothes we have in the closet," Richard said, as he looked in that direction. "And I guess I could drive that old Mazda MPV we use for stakeouts."

"Where's Johnny at this morning?" I asked and I looked at his desk which showed no sign of him being in this morning.

"He called around nine o'clock this morning and said that he would be in around noon today," Richard said. "He mentioned something about having his car in the shop and needing to get it out."

"He should be in any minute now," I said.

About that time, the door opened and Johnny walked in wearing blue jeans, a red pull over tee shirt and dark brown cowboy boots with his uniform folded over his left arm.

He had a look of aggravation on his face as he looked across the squad room. Then he walked around the counter, laid his uniform across the back of his chair and said, "I'll be dressed in a few minutes," and he then he sat down. "I need to catch my breath first," he added.

"Are you having trouble with your car?" I asked, as I watched him wipe the sweat off his forehead with his forearm.

"The engine light came on this morning so I took it by Matt's Auto Repair to have it checked out," he said, as he turned his chair around so he was facing me. "According to their machine, I need a new timing belt and one of my gaskets is leaking."

"Too bad that didn't happen yesterday on your day off," I said. "That way you could have gotten it fixed."

"Oh, I'm getting it fixed," Johnny said. "I left it with them."

"How did you get here?" Richard asked.

"They gave me a loaner," Johnny said and smiled. "I never thought I'd be driving a station wagon but today I am."

I looked at Richard and smiled.

He smiled back as he realized what I was thinking.

"Are you going to get rid of the drug dealers today?" Robert asked impatiently.

Johnny looked at Robert and asked, "What drug dealers?"

"Robert said some people have been trying to sell drugs in his parking lot and his customers are complaining," I said. "And yes, Robert, we're going to try to catch them today. I'm just trying to develop a plan."

"Well, I'll leave you to your planning," he said and he walked out the door.

"What's the plan?" Johnny asked. "I know you have one because I saw that smile you and Richard exchanged."

"Richard is going to change into some different clothes and go to the Piggly Wiggly to see if they will try to sell him some drugs," I said. "If they do, I'm going to arrest them."

"What's my part in the plan?" Johnny asked.

“I want you to go to the parking lot about five minutes after Richard does and see if they try to sell you drugs,” I said and smiled. “Do you think they’ll care if you drive the station wagon?”

Johnny smiled and said, “They told me to drive it like it was my own.”

“Great, Richard, go get dressed so we can get started,” I said, as I walked to my office and put my bullet resistant vest on.

“Now let me get this straight,” Richard said. “If they try to sell me drugs, am I going to arrest them there?”

“I’ll be in the back of the van waiting to grab him,” I said. “If all goes well, they’ll not know where he went and we can catch two of the dealers.”

“How many dealers did he say there were?” Johnny asked.

“I don’t think he knows, but it sounded like more than one,” I said.

“I’ll be ready in a minute,” Richard said, as he ran to the closet, grabbed some clothes and went to the back to change.

“How will I know when to drive into the parking lot?” Johnny asked.

“Park a couple of block away and I’ll call you when its time,” I said and I looked down the hall as I heard Richard coming back our way.

Richard walked in the squad room wearing blue jeans and a blue jean button front shirt.

“Let’s go,” I said and we walked out the door.

I got in the back of the MPV.

Richard got in the front seat, took his Glock out of its holster and laid it beside him. Then cranked the van and drove toward the Piggly wiggly.

Johnny followed us out of the parking lot.

Chapter 54

I saw the drug dealers Robert Wilson was talking about as soon as we pulled into the parking lot. Two kids that looked to be in their mid-teens were standing across the street watching for potential customers.

Richard circled through the parking lot as if he was looking for a space, wanting to make sure our prey noticed us. Then he pulled into a parking space at the edge of the lot away from the kids.

"Here one comes," Richard announced, as he looked in his rearview mirror and let his window down.

"Hey man, looks like you could use some smack," the kid said, as he approached the van.

"What've you got kid?" Richard asked calmly.

The kid looked around the parking lot a couple of times without saying anything, then he turned to Richard and said, "I have smack for $25, crystal for $30, a small bag of weed for $25 and if you want some ecstasy it's ten bucks a pill."

"Do you not have any ice, man?" Richard asked, as he waited for me to get in position to open the sliding door.

"Not on me, but I can get some in about an hour if that's what you need," he answered.

"You said the crystal was $30 right," Richard said.

"Yeah, that's right," he said.

"Alright, I'll take $30 worth of crystal," Richard said, as he handed the kid $30 with his left hand and grabbed his Glock with his right.

The kid took the money and counted it. Then he pulled a small plastic bag out of his front pocket and handed it through the open window toward Richard.

Richard smiled as he reached toward the bag with his left hand, grabbing the kid's wrist instead and pulling him against the van. Then Richard raised his Glock and pointed the barrel in the kid's face.

"Hey man, I gave you a fair price," the kid exclaimed.

"Don't say another word," Richard said with a calm voice.

Then I slid the door open, grabbed the kid and pulled him inside the van. I cupped my hand over his mouth to keep him from screaming and whispered, "You're under arrest for selling drugs," and pulled him to the middle of the van.

He started kicking wildly with his legs in an attempt to break free. When that didn't work, he pressed his right foot against the door and pushed as hard as he could to try to knock me over.

I pushed back to counterbalance my weight in order to keep from falling. Then I shoved him against the back of the driver's seat and held him until he calmed down.

Richard tore a four inch strip of duct tape off the roll and stretched it across the kid's mouth.

After pulling him down to the floor I handcuffed his arms behind his back and attaching them to the framework of the seat.

"I'm going to slip out the side door and wait for Johnny so we can catch this other guy," I said, as I slid the door open and jumped out, sliding the door closed quickly behind me.

"I'll take him to the station and get him locked up," Richard said and drove away.

I took my phone out of my pocket and called Johnny as I walked toward the Piggly Wiggly.

He answered after the first ring and asked, "Are you ready?"

"Yes, I'll be standing on the sidewalk and start walking toward you when you make the transaction," I said and closed my phone.

I saw Johnny when he turned into the parking lot. He drove by the front door, then circled around and parked close to the street.

The drug dealer slowly started walking toward Johnny. He kept looking across the parking lot for his buddy as he went, but continued with his quest to sell drugs.

Johnny rolled his window down when the kid approached his car.

"I've got some junk at a good price," the kid announced.

"Is that all you have?" Johnny asked.

"No man," the kid said. "I have a large supply of drugs to fix you up."

"Like what?" Johnny asked.

"I have Oxycontin, ecstasy and Lortabs, if you're into pills," he said as he turned around and looked across the parking lot. "If you want something else, I've got some brown sugar that will send you into outer space and crank that will get your heart to racing."

"I'll take a bag of crank," Johnny said and reached for his wallet.

"Wow, what are you doing!" the guy yelled and jumped back.

"I'm getting my money," Johnny said and showed him his wallet. "Man, you're jumpy," Johnny added.

"I can't find my partner," he said nervously.

"He's probably on the other side of the building selling," Johnny replied.

"You're probably right," he said and moved a little closer to the window.

"How much do I owe you?" Johnny asked.

"One bag of crank is $25," he said.

"Alright, here it is," Johnny said, as he pulled $25 out of his wallet and handed it toward the kid.

The kid grabbed the money, glanced at it and stuffed it in his pocket. He then took a small plastic bag out of his shirt pocket and handed it through the window.

I watched as Johnny handed the kid his money, then I quickly darted around cars as I approached the drug dealer from the backside.

Johnny grabbed the kid's wrist and pulled him through the window.

"What are you doing!" the kid yelled.

"I'm placing you under arrest," Johnny said, as he raised his Glock and pushed the barrel against the kid's chest.

"Don't shoot me," the kid pleaded.

"I've got him," I said, as I grabbed the kid's left arm and pinned him against the station wagon. Then I patted him down as I pushed him hard against the car.

After I was sure he had no weapon, I handcuffed his arms behind his back and shoved him in the back seat. Then I got in and sat beside him.

"You can't arrest me!" the drug dealer yelled. "I'm a minor!"

"That won't stop us from arresting you and sending you to jail," Johnny said firmly.

"My daddy's going to sue you," he threatened.

"It won't be the first time I've been sued," I said. "Now shut up before I put tape over your mouth."

The drug dealer opened his mouth as if he was going to say something, then closed it and turned toward the window.

"Now you're using your head," Johnny said, as he cranked the station wagon and drove to the edge of the parking lot. Then he turned left and drove toward the police station.

Chapter 55

Johnny pulled around to the back of the police station and parked beside the back door.

I held onto the prisoner's left arm while Johnny got out and unlocked the back door.

After the door was opened, he walked back to the station wagon and stood waiting to help escort the prisoner into the police station.

"Alright, it's time for you to get out," I said, as I opened the door and pushed the prisoner toward Johnny.

Johnny grabbed the prisoner's right arm and pulled him toward him.

"Stop pulling on me!" the prisoner yelled. "I can get out myself," and he jerked his arm away from Johnny.

"Just trying to keep you from falling," Johnny responded, as he pulled his hand back. "It's easier to help you with your balance now than to pick you up off the ground."

Johnny watched the prisoner as he struggled getting out of the car but he waited patiently and let him do it himself. Then he escorted him through the back door.

I got out on the other side of the station wagon and followed them inside the police station.

When we got to the first cell, Johnny opened the door and said, "Get inside," and he followed him inside.

"What are you going to do?" the prisoner asked.

"Empty your pockets and lay everything on the cot," Johnny instructed. "And then pull your clothes off and change into this," and he handed him a pair of orange coveralls.

The prisoner looked to the next cell where his buddy was sitting on his cot and noticed that he was wearing the same exact type of coveralls.

"Why do I have to empty my pockets if you're going to take my clothes anyway," he asked.

"Because that's the way we want you to do it," Johnny responded, as he moved closer to the cot.

The prisoner looked at me, then turned to Johnny and slowly pulled a small plastic bag out of his pocket and laid it on the cot. He then pulled a hand full of plastic bags out of his right front pocket and laid them on the cot.

After he finished empting his right pocket, he started pulling plastic bags out of his left. Before long he had a small stack of plastic bags in the center of his cot.

"That's all I have in my pockets," the kid said, as he pulled his pockets inside out.

"Let's see what we have," Johnny said, as he walked to the stack of drugs and picked one of the bags up. "I see some heroin," he said and moved it to the side.

He looked at each bag and separated them into small stacks.

"What did he have?" I asked when Johnny was finished.

Johnny counted each bag, then turned to me and said, "He had 8 bags of heroin, a bag with 12 Lortabs, a bag with 10 Oxycontin and it looks like 20 ecstasy tablets," and he picked the plastic bags up.

"I'll step outside while you change clothes," Johnny said and walked out the door.

When he got out of the cell, Johnny put the small bags of drugs in a discarded coffee creamer box and handed it to me.

I took the box and walked to my office. When I opened my door, I saw another small box sitting on my desk, so I picked it up and put both of them in my safe.

"That's what the kid had in his pockets," Richard said, as he walked in my office.

I locked my safe, then turned around and walked to my desk. "Richard, go get the kid that you brought in and bring him to my office," I said, as I pulled my chair back.

"You want to question him in here," Richard said.

"Yes, I'd rather have him separated from his friend when I talk to him," I said and sat down.

"I'll be back with him in a minute," Richard said and walked away.

After a few minutes, Richard escorted the prisoner inside my office and said, "Sit down in that chair," as he pointed to a chair in front of my desk and closed the door.

The prisoner went to the chair and sat down without saying anything.

"What's your name?" I asked, after he sat down.

He didn't respond for a few seconds, then he slowly raised his head and said, "Tommy Moore."

"How old are you Tommy?"

"Fifteen."

"Why aren't you in school?"

"I skipped school today."

"Who are you selling drugs for?" I asked, as I looked him in the eyes.

"I'm not selling anything," he responded, as he looked away.

"You had a pocket full of drugs and ask Richard if he wanted to buy some," I said, as I raised my voice up a notch. "Remember I was in the back of the van when you did it and I heard everything."

"I want a lawyer," he demanded. "I'm not saying another word until I have a lawyer."

I looked at Richard who was still standing by the window and motioned him to come in then said, "Take him back to his cell and lock him up."

"What about my lawyer," the prisoner screamed.

"After you put him in his cell, call his father and tell him to bring a lawyer," I said.

"What's your father's name?" Richard asked.

"Jim Moore," Tommy said defiantly.

"What's his phone number?"

"Give me a piece of paper and I'll write it down for you," he said. "I don't want to have to tell you more than once."

Richard gave Tommy a small piece of paper and pen.

Tommy quickly scribbled the phone number down and handed it to Richard.

After Richard took the piece of paper, he grabbed the kid by the right arm and said, "Get up so I can get you your lawyer," and he pulled him to his feet.

"Tell Johnny to bring the other kid in here when you take him back," I said, as they walked out the door.

Within minutes, Johnny brought the other kid into my office and had him sit in the chair in front of my desk.

After the kid sat down, he nervously looked around my office without saying a word.

I closed my office door and sat down at my desk.

Johnny leaned against the wall beside the filling cabinet.

We both looked at the kid and waited for him to speak.

After several minutes, he looked at Johnny and asked, “Why did you bring me in here?”

“He needs to ask you a few questions,” Johnny said.

“What kind of questions?” he asked, as he turned to me.

“What’s your name?” I asked.

“Ben Richie.”

“How old are you, Ben?”

“Fourteen.”

“Are you and Tommy in the same grade at school?”

“Yes.”

“Why aren’t you in school?”

“Tommy wanted to skip to make some money,” he said and looked away. “Tommy said he found a great way to make a lot of money fast but we had to do it today.”

“Did he tell you what you would be doing?”

“No, he just said we could make a lot of money.”

“So, it was Tommy’s idea,” I said and looked at Johnny.

“Yes, it was his idea.”

“You sure knew a lot about drugs when you were trying to sell them to me,”

Johnny said, as he walked closer to my desk.

"Tommy told me what to say," Ben replied.

"Who were you selling drugs for?" I asked.

"Tommy said we were selling for some guy named Frankie Lewis or Louie," he said, as he looked at his hands. "I'm really not sure about the last name."

"Could he have said Frankie and Lou?" I asked.

"That's it," he said with excitement. "It was Frankie and Lou."

I looked at Johnny and smiled.

Then I turned to Ben and said, "You've been very helpful and I appreciate it, but we need to call your father to let him know you're here."

"He's going to be mad," Ben said, as he looked at me.

"Yes he probably well be, but we have to tell him," I said, as I laid a sheet of paper and pen in front of Ben. "Write his name and phone number down for me."

After he finished writing, he slid the sheet of paper toward me and said, "Tell him I'm sorry when you talk to him," and he dropped his head.

"Take him back to his cell and then call his father," I said, as I looked at Johnny.

"Come on, let's go," Johnny said, as he picked up the piece of paper, walked to the door and opened it.

Ben slowly got up and walked out of my office without saying another word.

Johnny followed and escorted him back to his cell.

After they were gone, I got up and walked in the squad room.

Richard was sitting at his desk talking on the phone, so I went to the coffee pot and started brewing some coffee.

I looked at Johnny as he walked in the squad room. He hesitated a second when he saw me at the coffee pot, then he went to his desk and picked up his phone.

I watched as both men finished their phone calls and hung up. Then I poured three cups of coffee and carried each one a cup.

Johnny rolled his chair over to Richard's desk.

I pulled a chair over from the wall and sat down.

"What did they say?" I asked and I took a sip of coffee.

"Tommy Moore's father said he would be here in about an hour with a lawyer," Richard said.

"Ben Richie's father should be here about the same time," Johnny said.

"Alright, I guess we have an hour to wait," I said, as I got up and walked in my office.

Chapter 56

At ten minutes until four, Johnny opened my office door and announced, "One of the fathers is here."

I got up and followed him into the squad room.

A man was standing at the counter with his arms crossed.

I walked toward him and asked, "Can I help you?"

The man looked at me then looked around the squad room like he was looking for someone.

After he had scanned the squad room, he turned back to me and said, "My name is Dan Ritchie," and he leaned against the counter. "I got a call earlier from someone who said my son was here."

"What's your son's name?" I asked.

"Ben Ritchie."

"Yes, your son's here," I said, as I looked toward the door and asked," Did you not bring a lawyer?"

"I can't afford a lawyer," he responded. "I barely make enough money to pay the bills I have and put food on the table," and he looked down at his hands and added, "I'd have to get a loan to pay for a lawyer."

"My name is Sam James, I'm the chief of police for Thorton," I said. "Come to my office so we can talk," and I pointed toward my office door.

He walked around the counter and stopped. He was wearing faded blue jeans, a blue jean button down shirt and black work boots with a small amount of red mud adhered to the side.

"We can talk out here if you'd like but it'd be more private inside my office," I said, as I took a step toward my office.

"Inside your office will be fine," he said and he started walking toward the door.

I followed him inside and closed the door.

He sat in the first chair he came to and crossed his legs.

I went to my chair, pulled it out away from my desk and sat down. "Thank you for coming by," I said, as I leaned back in my chair.

He looked at me for few seconds then he asked, "What did my son do?"

"He was selling drugs," I said.

"That's impossible," he responded. "He knows the dangers of drugs and the consequences of being involved with drugs."

"His pockets were filled with drugs and he tried to sell my officer some drugs," I said. "We caught him in the act."

Dan Ritchie dropped his head and quietly mumbled something to himself. Then he raised his head and asked, "What do I need to do?"

"He's been very helpful," I said. "I think I can encourage the judge to be lenient on him."

"Can I see him," he asked.

"Sure," I said, as I got up and walked to the door.

I opened the door and said, "Johnny, I need to you bring Ben into my office."

"Sure," he said, as he walked toward the jail cells in the back.

I closed the door and sat back down.

My office door opened a couple of minutes later and Ben Ritchie walked through the door with Johnny following behind.

Dan glared at his son for a few seconds then looked away.

"I'm sorry," Ben blurted out. "I didn't mean to get in trouble."

Dan turned to his son and said, "I told you that you needed to be careful with the friends you hung around with. They can influence you whether you know it or not."

"I was just trying to make some money," he said trying to justify his actions.

"Selling drugs is no way to make money," Dan said and looked away.

"I'll never do it again," he promised.

"What do we do now?" Dan asked, as he looked at me.

"He'll go before the judge tomorrow or the next day and then we'll know," I said.

"When will I know which day?" Dan asked. "I'll need to take off work to be in court."

"I should know before five today and I'll call you," I said.

"Is there anything else you need to know from my son?" Dan asked. "I can assure you that he will cooperate with whatever you need."

"No, he's told me everything I asked of him," I said.

"Good, because we respect the law in my house and don't break it," Dan said and looked at Ben.

"Johnny, you can take him back to his cell," I said.

"Let's go," Johnny said, as he opened the door.

"I'm sorry," Ben said, as he turned and walked out the door.

"Call me when you know something and I'll be at the courthouse," Dan said, as he stood up.

"I will," I said and I followed him into the squad room.

"Thanks for calling me," he said and he walked out the door.

"Tommy Moore's father and his lawyer are here," Richard said. "I put them in the back room to wait until you were finished with the other prisoner's father."

"Thanks," I said. "You can go get them now and bring them to my office."

"You won't believe who his lawyer is," Richard said.

"Who?" I asked.

"Phillip Mays," he said.

"I can tell already that this is going to be a more difficult meeting," I said with a frown. "Thanks for letting me know," and I walked into my office.

I sat down at my desk and waited for Phillips Mays and his client to come into my office.

Within minutes, Richard stepped in my office and said, "Gentlemen, you can sit in those chairs in front of his desk," and he stepped aside to allow Phillip Mays and his client to walk through the door.

The man was wearing a navy blue three piece suit, with a powder blue dress shirt and a bright yellow with navy blue trim bow tie. He looked to be in his early forties with salt and pepper hair that ran down the sides of his head and a large bald spot in the center.

Phillip Mays sat down and waited on his client to get settled before saying, "I want you to release my client's son."

"Who's your client?" I asked, as I looked at the man sitting beside Phillip Mays.

"My name is Alton Moore," the man said without expression.

"You can tell Mr. Moore that his son was caught selling drugs and he refused to cooperate with the police," I said, as I looked at Phillip. "He'll have to stay in jail until his hearing."

"He don't have to tell me anything," Alton retorted. "I can hear you just fine."

"When is his hearing?" Phillip asked.

"I haven't heard yet," I said. "I hope to hear from the courthouse before five o'clock today."

"Who caught him selling drugs?" Phillip asked.

"I did," I said. "He tried to sell to Richard while I was in the back of the van listening to the whole deal."

"So, both of you can testify against him," Phillip said.

"We will testify against him," I responded.

"He's just fifteen," Alton interrupted.

"It's still against the law to sell drugs," I said.

"I've always told him not to talk to cops unless he had a lawyer present," Alton said, as he looked at Phillip Mays and said, "Now get my son out of jail."

Phillip didn't say anything. He just looked at me and smiled.

"So, you were preparing him in case he ever got arrested," I said when I turned back to Alton.

"I know how you cops try to twist things around to get a confession," he responded. "And it's his right to have a lawyer."

"He wouldn't need a lawyer if he wasn't breaking the law," I said.

I turned as the door opened and Johnny stuck his head in and said, "Sam you have a phone call on line two."

I looked at the two men sitting across my desk, then picked up the phone and said, "Sam speaking."

"The bail hearing for your two prisoners will be at nine o'clock in the morning," said the voice on the other end of the phone.

"Alright, we'll be there in the morning," I said and put the phone down on the receiver.

"What was that about?" Phillip asked.

"Your client's bail hearing is at nine o'clock in the morning," I said, as I pushed away from my desk and stood up.

"We have nothing else to do until in the morning," Phillip said and he stood up.

"What about my son?" Alton asked.

"He'll spend the night in jail and we'll try to get him out tomorrow," he said and started walking toward the door.

I looked at Alton Moore as he stood up, then asked, "Do you know Avery Moore?"

"He's my nephew," Alton said.

"That has nothing to do with this case," Phillip interrupted.

"Alton, where do you work?" I asked.

"I'm self-employed," he responded.

"What do you do?" I asked.

"I'm in the import and export business," he said. Then he turned to Phillip and said, "I feel like I'm being interrogated."

"I was just making conversation," I said, as I opened the door.

"We've said all we're saying today," Phillip said, as he walked into the squad room and opened the door.

"I need to know who he was selling drugs for," I said.

Alton looked at me for a second without saying a word then he walked out the door.

"We'll do our talking in the courtroom," Phillip said and he walked out the door.

I walked to the window and watched as they got in a dark blue Lexus ES 350 and drove away.

After they were gone, I called Dan Ritchie and told him to be at the courthouse at eight thirty in the morning for his son's bail hearing. Then I hung the phone up and looked at the clock which indicated it was fifteen minutes past five, so I looked at Johnny and said, "I'm going home," and I walked out the door.

Chapter 57

I walked into the police station at eleven thirty Friday morning to find Johnny and Richard sitting at their desk eating lunch.

"How did the hearing go?" Johnny asked after he swallowed.

"The judge let Ben Ritchie out in the care of his father without setting bail and he set Tommy Moore's bail at one hundred thousand dollars," I said.

"Why didn't the judge set a bail for Ben Ritchie?" Johnny asked, as he scooped a potato wedge through a mound of ketchup and tossed it in his mouth.

"It was his first offense and I testified on his behalf because he was helpful when I questioned him," I said.

"What about Tommy Moore?"

"This was his second offense for selling drugs," I said. "I also testified against him and told the judge that he was very uncooperative when I asked him questions."

"What was Tommy Moore's reaction?"

"He just looked at me and smiled."

"I'm sure he won't be in jail long."

"His bail was paid before I left the courthouse."

"Of course it was," Johnny said. "I'm sure the person who was paying his lawyer could afford to pay the bail."

"I think Alton Moore paid the bail," I said.

"He may be the one with the money," Johnny said.

"After you are through with lunch, we need to give Frankie and Lou a visit," I said and leaned up against the counter.

Frankie and Lou Overton is a couple of gangster wannabes that dropped out of school in the seventh grade to make their fortune in the world. They're identical twins and make a joke out of dressing alike and trying to confuse people by changing names. They'll do almost anything to make a dollar and are constantly in trouble with the law. Other than breaking minor laws and being annoying they seem to be really harmless.

"Are you going to wear that?" Johnny asked, as he looked at my dress uniform.

"No, I'll change into my regular clothes while you're eating," I said, as I walked into my office and closed the door.

After I changed into my regular uniform and put on my bullet resistant vest, I went back into the squad room.

Johnny and Richard had finished eating and were sitting at their desk waiting for me to return.

"Are you ready to go?" I asked when I got close.

"I think so," Johnny responded and he looked at Richard. "We have our protection on and I have an extra clip in my back pocket."

Richard said, "I have two clips in my back pocket," and smiled.

"Where do you think we'll find Frankie and Lou?" Johnny asked.

"They used to hang out at Greg's Pool and Billiard Parlor on 6th Avenue," I said and then added, "If they're not there, I'm sure Greg can tell us where to find them."

"How many cars do you want to take?" Richard asked.

"Let's take three vehicles," I said.

"What's the plan?" Richard asked.

"Richard, I want you to go around to the back of the building and go through the backdoor," I said then I looked at Johnny and said, "Johnny, I want you to stay out front and watch my back when I go inside."

"Are they violent?" Johnny asked.

"They could be," I said. "That's why I want to approach them from both directions," and I walked to the door.

I opened the door and waited for Johnny and Richard to go outside.

"It will be to our advantage if we catch them by surprise," Johnny said, as he walked out the door.

Richard followed without saying anything.

"Let's get this over with," I said, as I walked out and closed the door behind me.

I got in my Bronco and drove to the edge of the parking lot. When Richard and Johnny were lined up behind me, I turned right and slowly drove toward Greg's Pool and Billiard Parlor with my backup following close behind.

Chapter 58

As I neared 6th Avenue I saw a large billboard announcing Greg's Pool and Billiard Parlor located on the next street. I slowed as Richard drove past and turned down 7th Avenue to approach from the back of the building.

Then I turned down 6th Avenue and 10th Street and slowly drove until I saw a sign with Greg's Pool and Billiard Parlor written in bright red lettering in the window of a dark tinted storefront. I slowed and carefully pulled into the first parking space I saw which was between a jacked up black Chevrolet Silverado with monster wheels and a cherry red Jeep Cherokee.

I sat in my Bronco and watched as Johnny drove past me and parked in a parking space on the far side of the door. After Johnny parked, I looked around the area for any potential danger then I got out and walked to the front of my truck to wait for Johnny to join me.

When he got close, I walked toward the sidewalk and we went to the front door together.

"Now you want me to wait out here," Johnny said when we reached the front door.

"Yes, stay here and cover me," I said, as I opened the door and walked inside.

The room was dimly lit but I could make out the shapes of several people standing around pool tables looking toward the door. I stood without moving until my eyes adjusted to the light.

As my eyes adjusted, I was able to distinguish the men from the women for the most part. It was still hard to distinguish the people that were standing in the back of the room because of the dimness of the light.

At the table closest to me were a couple of elderly men playing nine ball. Beside them were two ladies playing eight ball and trying to ignore my presence.

As I looked across the room, I saw a large cloud of cigarette smoke circling overhead. I coughed as I breathed in some smoke then I held my breath until I stepped past it.

I then walked to the counter where a man in his early forties with long stringy brown hair with gray streaks intermingled throughout was standing with his arms resting on the countertop. He straightened up as I approached and asked, "Can I help you with anything, officer?"

"I'm looking for Frankie and Lou Overton," I said.

"They're at the last table on your right," he said. "But now look. I don't need no trouble in here."

"There won't be any trouble unless they make it," I said and walked toward the back of the room.

As I walked, I past a man leaning over a rack of eight ball getting ready to start the game. He stopped as I approached and waited for me to pass before breaking the balls.

As I got close to the back of the room, I saw Frankie and Lou playing eight ball. They were in deep conversation about the game and didn't notice me.

I looked at the back door where Richard was standing with his arms crossed leaning against the door frame.

Richard uncrossed his arms and joined me in the middle of the room and we slowly walked toward the table where Frankie and Lou were playing.

"Who's winning?" I ask when I got close.

They stopped talking immediately and looked toward us with a look of shock in their eyes.

They were dressed alike as they always were but I had come in contact with them enough to be able to tell them apart. Frankie was slightly larger and his hair was a little thinner than Lou's.

"I didn't hear you walk up," Frankie said, as he picked his pool stick up and laid it over his shoulder.

"You sure walked quietly," Lou said.

"You were too busy talking when we walk up," I responded.

Frankie took the pool stick and slowly began tapping it against the top of the table. Then he laid it down and leaned up against the side of the table.

"Sam, we ain't causing any trouble in here," Frankie said defensively. "We were just talking while we played."

"No one called about your behavior in here," I said. "I came here because I need to ask you some questions."

"What kind of questions?" Frankie asked, as he looked at Lou.

"I need you to come to the station so we can talk in private," I said.

"Are we under arrest?" he asked.

"Not at this time," I said.

"Then I'm not going," Frankie said, as he stepped a couple of steps back.

"You can come peacefully or I can handcuff you and force you to come," I responded.

"I ain't going nowhere with you!" Frankie yelled, as he picked up the pool stick and slammed it against the top of the table splintering it in the process.

The place went dead quiet. Everyone stopped playing pool and stood watching to see what would happen next.

Frankie began waving the stick back and forth as he moved further away from us.

"Frankie, you know I could shoot you for threatening an officer," I said in a calm voice. "But I'll give you time to come to your senses and put the stick down."

"You wouldn't shoot me," he said.

"Don't tempt me," I said, as I took me Glock out of my holster.

"You wouldn't shoot me in front of all these witnesses," he said, as a baseball struck him in the forehead and he collapsed on the floor dropping the pool stick as he fell.

I looked at the baseball that had rolled about twenty feet away, then I turned around and saw the man that was behind the counter looking at me with a smile on his face.

"Did you do that?" I asked.

"I told you I didn't want no trouble," he responded.

"That was a great throw," I said, as I looked back at Frankie who was still lying on the floor.

"I used to pitch in college," he said. "That is until I blew my shoulder out."

"Well, you just saved him a knee cap," I said, as I walked over to Frankie and handcuffed his hands behind his back.

I looked at Richard who had handcuffed Lou and was standing behind him.

"I'll put Lou in my car and take him to the station," Richard said and he walked out the back door.

"What happened?" Johnny asked, as he walked through the door. "I heard a lot of yelling so I thought you might need help."

"Frankie didn't want to go with us, but this guy persuaded him to go without a fight," I said, as I pointed to the guy that had thrown the baseball.

Johnny looked puzzled but didn't say anything else. He just walked over to Frankie, grabbed an arm and asked, "Do you want me to help you drag him to the car?"

"I think he's waking up," I said. "We may not have to drag him."

"What happened?" Frankie asked and he shook his head from side to side.

"You fell down and hit your head," I said. "Now get up so we can help you to the car," and we pulled him to his feet.

I took his right arm and Johnny took his left and we escorted him out the door. He staggered as he walked, but we kept him upright until we got him to Johnny's patrol car and we helped him into the backseat.

"I'll meet you at the station," I said, as I closed the door to Johnny's patrol car.

I watched as Johnny got in his car and drove toward the police station. Then I walked to my Bronco, got in and drove away.

Chapter 59

I pulled into the station parking lot right behind Johnny and parked in my space close to the front door. When I got out, I walked along the side of the building to the back door where we always unload prisoners.

I looked in the back of Richard's car and it was empty so I walked over to Johnny's car.

"You might want to leave him in there for a minute," Richard said when he walked out the back door.

"Why?" I asked.

Johnny got out of the car and walked up beside me to listen to what Richard had to say.

"Lou had some interesting things to say while I was driving to the police station," he said. "You might want to talk to him before Frankie has a chance to intimidate him."

"We can't just leave him in the car," I said, as I looked in the back seat.

"I didn't mean that we needed to leave him in the car for a long time," Richard said. "I just didn't want them to see each other."

I thought for a minute, then I said, "Richard go get Lou and take him to my office, then you and Johnny can get Frankie out of the car and carry him to the jail cell."

"That would probably be best," Richard said and he walked back inside the police station.

"I'll stay out here and wait on Richard," Johnny said.

"Thanks," I said, as I walked through the back door and went toward my office.

When I got to my office, I left the door open and sat down at my desk to wait for Richard to bring Lou. In less than a minute Richard escorted Lou through my office door and said, "Take a seat in the first chair," and he pointed to a straight backed chair in front of my desk.

Lou hesitated at the door for a few seconds but then walked to the chair and sat down.

"Richard, come back in here when you get through," I said.

"Alright," he said, as he turned and walked away.

"Wh-why did you bring me in here?" Lou asked after he sat down.

"I have a few questions to ask you and I thought you'd be more comfortable in here than in the jail cell," I answered.

"Where's Frankie?" he asked.

"He's being taken to his cell."

"Why don't you bring him in here so we can talk together?"

"Because I wanted to question each of you separately."

"Wh-why?"

"To compare your answers."

"Fr-Frankie won't like that."

"It doesn't matter what Frankie likes," I said, as I moved closer to Lou and added in a stern voice, "I'm in charge here."

He sat looking around the room without saying anything for about a minute, seeming to regain his confidence, then smiled and asked, "What questions were you going to ask me?"

"I'm waiting for Richard to return before I start questioning you," I said and leaned back in my chair. "So, just get comfortable."

He repositioned himself in the chair, crossed his legs and said, "This chair's not as comfortable as yours."

"It's all you have to sit in, so make the best of it," I said, as I pulled my notepad out of my drawer and laid it on top of my desk. I got my pen out of my pocket and laid it on top of my notepad.

"Alright, if this is the best you have than I guess I'll have to be satisfied," Lou said, as he uncrossed his legs.

I turned toward my office door as it opened and Richard and Johnny walked inside. Johnny walked to the window and leaned against the window seal. Richard closed the door and leaned against the door frame.

"Now can we start?" Lou asked.

"What did you tell Richard when you were coming to the police station?" I asked.

"I don't remember."

"I do," Richard said. "Do I need to refresh your memory?"

Lou glared at Richard for a few seconds then he said, "No, you don't have to refresh my memory."

"What did you tell Richard?" I asked.

"I had nothing to do with those murders," he blurted out. "It was Hamburger that killed them and Frankie helped put them in the Escalade."

I looked at Richard and smiled.

"What is Hamburger's real name?"

"I don't know his real name."

"Where would I find him?"

"I don't know," he said. "He calls when he needs us and tells us where to meet him."

"Do you sell drugs for him?"

"Sometimes."

"Did you ask some kids to sell drugs for you yesterday?"

"Frankie did," he said. "Some kid that Frankie knows sells drugs for him from time to time and he asked him to sell for him yesterday."

"Do you know the kid's name?"

"Frankie calls him Slick."

"Were you at the murder scene?"

"I was there but I didn't kill anybody."

"Can you describe what Hamburger looks like?"

"Let's see, he's about forty and has blond hair."

"How tall is he?"

"He's about my height."

"What are you about 5'9"?"

"Yes."

"What does he weigh?"

"About two hundred."

"Alright, he's about forty years old with blond hair, 5'9" and weighs about two hundred pounds," I said. "Does he have any tattoos?"

"I didn't see any."

"Alright, take him to his cell and bring Frankie in here."

"Please don't tell Frankie I said anything," Lou fearfully begged.

"I won't," I assured him.

"Let's go Lou," Richard said, as he opened the door.

Lou slowly got up and walked out of my office.

"How are you going to question Frankie without letting him know where you got the information?" Johnny asked.

"I'll make him think we had the information before we picked him up," I said.

When Frankie walked through the door, my eyes immediately went to the large budging knot protruding out of his forehead with the outline of the baseball prominently imbedded along its edges.

"Sit in that chair," Richard ordered.

Frankie walked to the chair and sat down without saying a word. He looked at Johnny, then turned to me and proclaimed, "I'm not saying anything."

"What's Hamburger's real name?" I asked trying to shock him into responding.

"How do you know about Hamburger?" Frankie asked with fear in his voice.

"I know you and him killed two men and put their bodies in an Escalade and parked it at Franklin Lumber Company."

"I didn't kill nobody."

"We found evidence to link you to the murders," I said, as I glanced at Johnny.

Johnny raised his eye brows but didn't say anything.

"Like I said, I didn't kill nobody."

"You may not have killed them, but you were there."

"I'm not talking!"

"So Frankie, you've started letting kids sell your drugs for you," I said, as I moved a little closer to his face. "What would Hamburger think with you letting kids do your job for you."

His eyes widened with fear but he didn't say anything.

"If you tell me who Hamburger is I can see if the judge will give you a break," I said.

"You don't have anything on me anyway, so I don't need a break," he retorted.

I looked at Richard and said, "Take him to his cell."

Richard opened the door and said, "Let's go."

Frankie got up, looked at me and smiled, then he walked out the door.

"I think he's smarter than his brother," Johnny said after he was gone.

"I'm not sure I would call him smart," I said.

"What are we going to do with them?" Johnny asked. "We really don't have enough evidence to charge them."

"You and Richard can take them back to Greg's Pool and Billiard Parlor," I said. "I think we've gotten all the information out of them that we're going to get."

"We'll drive around after we drop them off and see if we can see anyone that fits the description that Lou gave us," Johnny said and he walked out the door.

After Johnny left, I picked up my phone and called Charles Wallace with the ABI.

He answered on the second ring and said, "Charles speaking, how can I help you."

"This is Sam James," I said. "Have you heard of anybody in the drug business with the nickname Hamburger?"

"I haven't, but I can ask around and get back to you," he responded.

"That would be great," I said.

"Do you have a description?"

"Yes, he's about forty years old with blond hair, 5'9" and weighs about 200 pounds."

"Is that it?"

"That's all I have."

"I'll see what I can do," he said and my phone went dead.

I hung up the phone and walked in the squad room. I looked around the empty room, then went into the dispatcher's office and said, "If you don't need me, I'm going home."

"I should be fine," Rachel said. "I'll call you if I need you."

"Have a good weekend," I said, as I walked out the door and drove home.

Chapter 60

I slept late Saturday morning which for me was anything after seven o'clock. To be exact I got up at five minutes after seven, slipped on a pair of shorts and went for a jog around the block.

When I got back, I put on a pot of coffee and went upstairs to take a shower. I showered and dressed in a pair of blue jeans, black pull over pocket tee shirt and put on my new tennis shoes that I had bought the previous week while visiting a discount shoe store.

Then I quietly went downstairs, poured a cup of coffee and sat down on the couch to watch some television. After flipping through the channels, I realized there was nothing to watch on a Saturday morning. I turned the television off and tried to enjoy the quietness.

I finished my first cup of coffee and was pouring my second cup when my kids ran down the stairs and turned the television on the morning cartoons. Since my quiet time was over, I sat down at the table to finish my coffee.

Jenna came down stairs, poured a cup of coffee and sat down beside me at the table. She looked at me for a few minutes then she asked, "What is wrong?"

"I can't seem to solve these murders," I said.

"Have you prayed?" she asked.

"I have, but not recently," I said.

"Maybe that's your problem."

"It could be," I said. "I think I'll go upstairs and do just that, thanks honey," and I got up and went upstairs.

I went in the bedroom, closed the door and got on my knees. Then I closed my eyes and said, "Dear Lord, please forgive me for trying to do things myself and not asking for your guidance. Please give me the wisdom to solve these murders and catch the criminals that are infesting the streets of Thorton. Please guide me in my day to day activities and watch over me while I try to make Thorton a safer place for everyone to live. Thank you for the grace you've shown me and the many blessings you've given me throughout my life. In Jesus name I pray. Amen." and I got up and walked back down stairs.

"Do you feel better now?" Jenna asked when she saw me.

"Yes, I feel a weight lifted off my shoulders," I said.

"That's what happens when you give your troubles to God."

"I know but sometimes I try to do things myself,' I said. "And that's when I fail."

"Do you have to go to work today?" Jenna asked.

"I thought about going in for a few hours, but they can handle it without me," I said, as I put my arms around her. "I think I'll spend some time with you and the kids."

"That would be nice," she said, as she kissed me on the lips.

"Yuck," Seth exclaimed. "That's disgusting."

"That's how a married man and woman express their love for each other," Jenna said.

"Well, I'm never going to get married if I have to kiss a girl," he responded.

"I think you'll change your mind when you get a little older," I said, as I looked at Jenna and smiled.

“What happened?” Jenny asked.

“Momma and Daddy kissed,” Seth said.

“Oh, is that all,” she said. “They do that all the time.”

“Well I don’t want to see it,” he said and he turned back to the television.

We sat back and enjoyed our time together while we drank our coffee.

Chapter 61

Sunday morning was a warm and beautiful day. The sky was vivid blue with an occasional white cloud but for the most part the sun was illuminating the whole sky.

We hurriedly dressed in our Sunday clothes so we could get to church on time. I wore my dark blue dress slacks, light blue and white striped shirt, solid navy blue tie and topped it off with a navy blue dress coat.

Jenna wore a powder blue dress with matching shoes, Jenny wore a yellow dress with blue butterflies and white sandals and Seth wore a black pair of dress pants and a white shirt.

I pulled into the church parking lot to find it almost half full, so I didn't have my usual pick of parking spaces. I slowly drove through the parking lot and dropped everyone off at the door then I drove to the edge of the lot and parked close to the road in case I needed to leave in a hurry.

When I got to the door, Jenna was waiting and we walked inside the church house together. I carried the Bibles to our usual bench and laid them in the seat. Then I went to the aisle, greeting everyone as they entered the building.

At ten thirty singing began and at eleven o'clock sharp Elder Andrew Moss stepped up to the podium and began the day's message.

"It's good to see everyone here today," he said, as he looked around the congregation. "I'm sure your flesh and the devil tried to get you to miss church today but you withstood the desires of the flesh and came to worship God."

He then looked down at his Bible and started turning pages. "I trust you've been praying for the message today and I pray that God blesses it," he said. "The subject for today is wisdom."

I looked at Jenna and smiled. "This one's for me," I said and turned back to the preacher.

He said, "Let's turn to Proverbs 1:2," and he read, "TO KNOW WISDOM AND INSTRUCTION; TO PERCEIVE THE WORDS OF UNDERSTANDING; TO RECEIVE THE INSTRUCTION OF WISDOM, JUSTICE, AND JUDGEMENT, AND EQUITY; TO GIVE SUBTILITY TO THE SIMPLE, TO THE YOUNG MAN KNOWLEDGE AND DISCRETION."

He preached about thirty minutes on our need to turn to God for wisdom and guidance. He also stressed the importance of giving God the credit he deserves and not trying to take credit ourselves.

As he began his closing remarks he looked across the congregation and said, "Wisdom is a gift from God and if we find ourselves in need we should pray to God to bless us with whatever we need. I'm not saying he'll give you your fleshly desires but he will fill your need," and he turned a page and said, "Turn to James 1:5," and read, "IF ANY OF YOU LACK WISDOM, LET HIM ASK OF GOD, THAT GIVETH TO ALL MEN LIBERALLY, AND UPBRIADETH NOT; AND IT SHALL BE GIVEN HIM."

"Whenever you find yourself in need turn to the one that cares, and pray," he said, as he closed his Bible.

After church was over, I stood around talking to the church members for a while then I went home to spend the rest of the afternoon quietly relaxing with my wife and kids.

Chapter 62

I looked at Jenna as my phone started ringing and took it out of my pocket. I opened it up and said, “Sam speaking.”

“Sam, I hate to bother you today but we’ve got two dead bodies behind Fairway Shopping Center,” Tim Weeks said apologetically.

“Have you called Diane Lynch and Janice Walker?” I asked.

“No, I just called you when I found the bodies.”

“Are you at the crime scene right now?”

“Yes, I’m parked beside the bodies,” he said. “I checked to make sure they were dead then I got back in my car and called you for backup.”

“Good job,” I said. “I’ll be there as fast as I can,” and I closed my phone.

“More dead bodies?” Jenna asked.

“Yes, at the Fairway Shopping Center,” I said and I ran out the door.

I called Diane and Janice while I was driving to the crime scene and told them about the bodies. They both said that they would come as fast as they could which would probably be over an hour, because they were both at family functions.

I slowed down as I got close to the shopping center and turned into the parking lot. I slowly drove around the building looking for Tim’s car as I went. When I rounded the corner of the building, I spotted his car parked by the back door of Braswell Temp Service.

I pulled beside his car and got out.

He got out when he saw me and walked to the front of his car.

"Where's the bodies?" I asked.

"In the bushes by the back door," he said as he pointed toward the back door to Braswell Temp Service.

"How did you find them in there?" I asked.

"I got a phone call from somebody and they told me exactly where to find the bodies."

"Did they give you their name?"

"No, they just told me that I would find two dead men at this location."

"Was it a man or woman that called?"

"I think it was a man but it could have been a woman trying to disguise her voice."

"Did they say anything else?"

"No."

"Let's rope the area off while we're waiting for Diane and Janice to get here," I said, as I walked to my back seat and pulled a roll of caution tape out. "We need to be careful and not damage any potential evidence."

"We could rope it off from one end of the building to the other and not get close to the bodies," Tim suggested.

"That sounds like a good idea, but I'd like to look at the bodies before Diane and Janice get here," I said, as I stepped on the sidewalk and leaned over toward the bodies. "I think I know the victims," I announced, as I looked at what appeared to be two men lying beside each other wearing blue jeans with matching powder blue shirts and black with red trim New Balance running shoes.

"How can you tell?" Tim asked. "Their facing the building and it's impossible to see their faces."

"I won't know for sure until I see their faces," I said, as I moved to the edge of the sidewalk. "Where did you step when you checked the bodies to make sure they were dead?"

Tim stepped beside me and said, "Along the edge of the flower bed," as he pointed to a large oblong shaped flower bed that was filled with Impatiens, Cosmos, Daffodils, and Hyacinth of various colors and sizes.

"Where did you step?" I asked.

"On the bricks that surrounds the flower bed," he said.

I moved a little closer to the flower bed to get a better look.

As I got near the flowers, the aroma emitting from the Daffodils and Hyacinths were almost overpowering. I could hear the bees buzzing from one flower to another as they gathered nectar to carry back to the hive.

The bricks looked safe so I cautiously put my right foot on the one closest to me and stepped toward the bodies.

"I'm going to see if I can see their face," I said, as I took another step.

I carefully walked along the bricks until I was beside the bodies that were lying between the flower bed and a shrub row. Then I carefully leaned over the bodies until I could see their faces.

"Yes, it's who I thought it was," I said when I got a good look at their faces. "It's Frankie and Lou Overton."

"How did you know before you saw their face?" Tim asked.

"Because they're dressed alike," I said. "They always dressed alike."

I stayed balanced on the brick and slowly looked over their bodies to see if I could determine how they died. I looked for a gunshot wound along their back and head but I didn't see anything.

"I wish we could turn them over to see if they were shot in the chest," I said, as I lifted one of their arms up to see if I could roll him over to his side.

"I thought you weren't going to touch the body," Tim said.

"You're right, I need to wait and not disturb the evidence," I said, as I let go of the arm, then turned and slowly started walking back to the sidewalk. "I guess we'll have to wait on Diane and Janice to get a good look at their bodies."

"I couldn't determine how they were killed when I looked at their bodies either," Tim said.

I got to the sidewalk without disturbing the ground surrounding the bodies or the flower bed. Then Tim and I walked back to my Bronco and got inside to wait for Diane and Janice to arrive at the crime scene.

We sat watching the crime scene for about twenty minutes before Janice drove around the corner in her CSI van and parked beside my Bronco.

When I saw Janice drive around the corner, I got out and walked around to the front of my truck. I leaned against the hood to wait for Janice and her team to get out of the CSI van.

Victor Hayes was the first to get out with his camera dangling from around his neck. He stopped when he reached the sidewalk and asked, "Where's the bodies?"

"Between the flower bed and the shrub row," I answered.

“Thanks,” he said, as he walked toward the flower bed and located the bodies.

Then he took his camera and began snapping off photographs of the surrounding area. He started at the sidewalk and photographed until he reached the flower bed. Then he carefully walked toward the bodies, making sure that he didn’t disturb any evidence and photographed the victims from all angles.

Janice and Daniel got out of the van, grabbed their evidence gathering bags and walked over to where I was standing.

“What do we have?” Janice asked when she got close.

“Two male victims lying between the flower bed and shrub row,” I said.

“Could you tell how they were killed?” she asked.

“I didn’t see any wounds but I didn’t move the bodies,” I said and looked at Victor as he approached.

“I’m finished,” he said and he walked to the CSI van to put his camera away.

“Let’s see if we can find any evidence to help catch this killer,” Janice said, as she picked her bag up off the ground, draped it over her shoulder and walked toward the bodies.

Daniel followed.

They stopped on the sidewalk and looked at the ground leading up to the bodies.

“Did anybody step in this area?” Janice asked, as she looked toward us.

“No,” I said. “We stepped on the bricks along the flower bed.”

“This looks like a partial foot print,” Janice said and she pointed at the edge of the sidewalk. “It could have been left by anybody but it could be the killers.”

“I’ll make a cast mold of the foot print,” Daniel said, as he opened his evidence bag and started pulling out his casting material.

"I'll continue looking around the bodies," Janice said and she stepped closer to the victims.

She stopped a few feet from the bodies, stooped down and opened her evidence bag. Then she pulled a glass container and tweezers out of her bag. She bent closer to the ground and carefully picked up some cigarette butts and placed them inside the glass container.

I turned when I heard a vehicle driving around the building and watched as Diane's van turned the corner and drove toward where we were standing. She slowly drove past my Bronco and backed her van toward the sidewalk.

After she stopped, she got out and walked to the back of her van to start unloading the stretchers.

Samantha got out of the passenger side and went to help Diane with the stretchers.

When Diane opened the back door of her van, I turned back toward the bodies to watch Janice as she gathered evidence.

I watched as Janice put the glass container in her evidence bag then she moved closer to the bodies. She took a magnifying glass out of her bag and slowly looked over the bodies in hopes of finding something the killer might have left behind.

After twenty minutes of diligently searching, she raised up and said, "I need someone to help me turn the bodies over so I can look underneath them."

"I can load them on a stretcher," Diane said, as she pushed a stretcher on the sidewalk. "We'll put them on their back and you can examine them before I close the body bag."

I looked at Diane who had slipped on her bright yellow coveralls and neon purple rubber gloves while she was at the back of her van. Samantha stood next to her wearing the same color coveralls and gloves.

"That sounds like a good idea to me," Janice said.

"Will I contaminate any evidence if I roll the stretcher toward the bodies?" Diane asked.

"I'm through here," Daniel said, as he stood up.

"We've gathered everything we could find," Janice said, as she looked around the crime scene. "So you can put the stretcher anywhere you want to put it."

"Let's angle the stretcher beside the bodies so all we have to do is pick him up and flip him over in one quick motion," Diane said, as she pushed the stretcher toward the bodies.

"Can I help with anything?" I asked, as I moved toward the victims.

"You can hold the stretcher and make sure it doesn't roll away from us," Diane said and she walked to the first victim. "Samantha grab his feet and I'll get his shoulders," and she took hold of his shoulders.

I walked to the middle of the stretcher and braced myself against the side to make sure it didn't move.

"O.K. on three," Diane said, as she bent her knees and got close to the victim's body.

Samantha bent her knees and grabbed the victim's legs.

"One, two, three," Diane said, as they picked the victim up and turned him onto his back as they brought his body to the stretcher.

Janice moved close to the stretcher and looked at the victim's chest and abdomen. "I don't see an obvious wound anywhere," she said then she stepped back.

"I'll let you know how he died after I perform an autopsy on him," Diane said, as she closed the body bag.

Samantha rolled the other stretcher onto the sidewalk and locked the wheels.

After Diane secured the victim's body onto the stretcher, she rolled it to her van and loaded it inside.

As Diane was loading the victim's body in her van, Samantha moved the other stretcher alongside the other victim and waited for Diane to return.

I positioned myself beside the stretcher to keep it from moving and watched as Diane and Samantha moved the other victim onto the stretcher in one quick motion.

Janice stepped beside the stretcher and looked at the victim's chest and abdomen. "Diane I guess I'll have to wait on your report," Janice said, as she stepped back and walked to her van.

Daniel carried his and Janice's evidence bags to the back of the van and loaded them inside. Then he walked to the front door on the passenger's side and got inside.

Victor opened the side door and sat down in the back seat.

Janice opened the driver's side door and stopped. She turned and said, "Sam, I'll run test on what little evidence we've found and let you know something tomorrow," then she got inside her van and closed the door.

I watched as she cranked her van and drove away. Then I walked to Diane's Medical Examiner's van and watched as she slid the last victim inside the back door and locked the stretcher in place.

"I'll start on these victims as soon as I can," Diane said, as she slammed the van door.

"How do you think they died?" I asked.

"I have no idea," she said. "But I know they were not shot."

"I'm not medically trained but I knew that much," I said and smiled.

"Without obvious wounds, I can only tell how someone dies after doing an autopsy, so right now it would be unprofessional for me to guess on such a matter," Diane said.

"So, in other words, you don't have a clue," I said.

"Not at this time," she said. "I should know something tomorrow," and she walked to driver's side door and opened it.

Samantha had already gotten inside and was waited for Diane.

"Thanks for your help," I said.

"No problem," she said, as she got inside her van and closed the door. "I'll see you tomorrow," and she cranked up her van and slowly drove away.

After she left, I turned and walked back to my Bronco.

"Should I stay here and watch the crime scene?" Tim asked when I got close.

"No you don't have to stay, but let's keep it roped off." I said and I looked around the parking lot. "Maybe this will keep people away from this area."

"Alright then, I guess I'll head back to the police station," Tim said and he got inside his car. "I'll file the report when I get back to the station and leave it on your desk."

"Thanks, Tim," I said. "You did a good job."

"No problem," he said, as he cranked his car and drove away.

I walked to my Bronco and opened the door. As I started to get in the front seat, I saw movement out of the corner of my eye at the end of the building.

I didn't acknowledge that I saw anything. I just got inside my truck, cranked up and slowly drove around the parking lot.

As I got to the edge of the building, I pulled beside the sidewalk where I saw the movement and stopped. I got out and walked around the building.

As I rounded the corner of the building, I saw a figure trying to hide behind two thirty gallon garbage cans.

"Alright, come on out from behind there," I ordered.

The figure hesitated for a few seconds before slowly raising up from behind the garbage cans.

"I didn't do anything wrong," she announced, as she started walking toward me.

"Why were you hiding?" I asked.

"I was scared."

"You were watching us, weren't you?"

"I wanted to see what you were doing."

"Were you the one that called the police station about the bodies?"

"I might have."

"What's your name?"

"Sugar."

Sugar looked to be about 18 or 19 years old, but she could have been in her early twenties. She had natural blond hair that rested lightly on her shoulders with bangs that she brushed slightly to the left. She had high cheek bones which enhanced her beautiful face and a small well shaped nose to go along with her narrow lips.

As I looked at her I could tell that her face was not all together natural. She must have had several plastic surgeries to form the face that she wanted, but the way she was dressed indicated that she was on the street which made me wonder what had gone wrong. She was wearing an old raggedy dark green dress with frayed sleeves and a pair of worn tennis shoes.

"Alright, Sugar, did you see the person that dropped the bodies off by the back door of Braswell Temp Service.

"What will you give me if I answer your questions?" she asked and smiled.

I now knew how she ended up on the street when I saw her smile. Her teeth were dark brown and rotten. She had several of her front teeth missing and the rest were on the verge of breaking.

I looked back to her face and realized that she had a thick coat of natural colored makeup covering the scars on her cheeks.

"How long have you been using meth?" I asked.

She looked away without answering and slowly put her hand over her mouth. Then she whispered, "About a year," without looking toward me.

"Do you live on the street?"

"I live wherever I can."

"Do you want to get off meth?"

"It ain't that easy," she said, as she turned toward me.

"The first step in getting off drugs is to really want to get off them."

"I'm tired of being hungry and being on the street."

"You didn't answer my question," I said. "Do you want to stop using meth?"

"Yeah!" she screamed and started crying. "I want to get off this terrible drug."

"I know someone that can help get you off drugs, but I need you to answer my questions first," I said.

She took a few deep breaths and stopped crying. Then she looked in my eyes with determination and asked, "What do you want to know?"

"Did you call the police station?"

"Yes, I called."

"Did you see the person that dumped the bodies?"

"I saw him, but I didn't recognize him."

"Can you describe him?"

"He was an old man with blond hair."

"How old would you say he was?"

"I'd say he was in his forties."

"That's not really that old," I said, as I scratched the side of my face.

"Well, it's a lot older than I am," she responded.

"So, you'd say he was about the same age as me," I said and smiled.

"Oh, I didn't mean to call you old," she said. "I meant the man that dropped the bodies off looked old."

"Is there anything else you can remember about him?"

"He was probably under 6 feet and looked heavy."

It sounded similar to the description of Hamburger, but I continued asking questions to see if I could get a better idea of who the man was.

"Did he have any noticeable markings such as a tattoo or scar?"

"I didn't see anything but he had a shirt on and a cap pulled down over his face."

"How could you tell what color his hair was?"

"Cause his hair was sticking out from under the cap."

"Do you think you could you recognize him if I showed you his picture?"

"I think so."

"Now, it's time for me to hold up my end of the bargain," I said. "Are you sure you really want to get off drugs?"

"Yes I'm sure."

"Give me a minute while I make a phone call," I said, as I stepped a few feet away and took my phone out of my pocket.

I punched in the number for Lighthouse Miracle Works. A female answered on the second ring and said, "Lighthouse Miracle Works, how can I help you?"

"This is Sam James," I said. "I need to talk to Rose for a minute."

"Oh, hey Sam, this is Daisy," she said. "Let me go get her," and I heard her lay the phone down.

After a few minutes, Rose said, "This is Rose."

"Rose do you have room for another person?"

"Are you out recruiting for me?" Rose asked and laughed.

"No, but I promised this lady that if she would give my some information I'd help get her off drugs."

"What kind of drugs has she been taking?"

"Meth."

"That's a hard one to get off of," she said. "Will she follow the rules?"

"I don't know," I said. "I haven't told her the rules."

"Bring her by and we'll talk to her," Rose said and my phone went dead.

I closed my phone and put it back in my shirt pocket. Then I turned around and said, "She said to bring you by and she'd talk to you."

"What is that supposed to mean?"

"If you don't agree to follow her rules she won't help you."

"What rules?"

"That's what she's going to talk to you about."

"Let's go," I said, as I started walking toward my Bronco.

She followed without saying a word and got in the passenger side of my Bronco.

I got in the driver's side, cranked up and drove toward Lighthouse Miracle Works.

Chapter 63

I pulled to the side of the street in front of Lighthouse Miracle Works.

"Is this it?" Sugar asked.

"It doesn't look like much from the outside but the inside is where the miracles happen," I said and opened my door.

Sugar opened her door and followed me up the steps to the front of the house.

The door opened before we got up the steps. Daisy smiled and said, "Come on in," and she stepped to the side to allow us to walk past her.

Rose was standing in the living room when we entered the house.

She smiled and said, "Hi Sam."

"Rose, how are you doing," I said.

"Fine," she said, as she looked at the person that was standing beside me. "Who do you have with you?"

"She said her name was Sugar," I said and smiled because I knew that Rose would never let anyone in her house using a street name.

Rose looked at me and frowned. Then she stepped in front of Sugar, looked her in the eyes and asked, "What is your real name?"

"They call me Sugar," she responded.

"That is a street name and you'll not live here using that name," Rose said with persistence. "What did your Mother and Father call you?"

"Beth Ann Ford," she said, as she started crying.

"There's no need to cry, dear," Rose said with compassion. "We just need to know the truth."

"I haven't used that name in over a year," she said between sobs.

"Come to my office so we can talk," Rose said, as she took a step toward her office.

Beth looked at me without moving.

"She'll ask you some questions and if you agree to follow the rules then she'll probably let you stay," I said in a low voice.

"Are you coming with me?" Rose asked sternly.

"Yeah, I'm coming," Beth Ann said and she followed Rose out of the room.

I sat down on the couch and started watching television.

Daisy sat down beside me.

"How have you been doing?" I asked without looking at her.

"I'm staying busy which helps me not think too much about drugs," Daisy said.

"Have you seen Avery Moore around?"

"Not since you told him to stay away."

"Good."

"Thanks for bringing me here," Daisy said, as she turned toward me. "I think you saved my life," and a tear rolled down her face.

"Your determination and God's grace is what saved your life," I said. "I just introduced you to Rose. She helped you get through the hard times with God's help."

"Thanks for bringing me here," she said and turned as Rose and Beth Ann walked back into the room.

"Daisy, take Beth Ann to pick out some clothes," Rose said and smiled. "She'll be staying with us for a while."

Daisy got up and said, "Let's get you some clothes," and started walking across the room.

"Do you have my size?" Beth Ann asked, as she followed.

"We have many different sizes," Daisy said, as she looked back at Beth.

"Good," Beth Ann said, as she smiled and followed Daisy across the room.

"I think she'll be fine," Rose said, as she looked at me.

"I think she used to have money," I said.

"Drugs don't discriminate," Rose said. "Anyone can get addicted."

"That's why it's best not to try them," I said, as I got up and walked to the door.

"Is she in trouble?" Rose asked.

"She might be a witness for me in a murder case, but I'm not sure yet," I said.

"I'll keep her inside for a few weeks, just in case," Rose said.

"Thanks for your help," I said and walked out the door.

I got in my Bronco and drove home.

Chapter 64

I got up early Monday morning and drove to the Fairway Shopping Center to see if anyone had tampered with the crime scene. I circled the building, drove to the back and parked in front of the back door to Braswell Temp Service. The crime scene tape was still wrapped around the building just like we had left it the night before. There was no sign of anyone in the parking lot, so I circled around to the front of the building, turned left and drove toward the police station.

When I turned down 4th Avenue, I immediately noticed a dark blue and white Dodge Cargo van parked on the side of the street. The hood was raised and a man, wearing blue jeans and a maroon tee shirt, was leaning over the engine like he was working on something.

I pulled in behind the van, got out and slowly started walking toward the front of the van. When I got close to the driver's side door I asked, "Do you need help?"

The man continued working under the hood for a few seconds without saying anything. Then he raised his head, looked toward me and said, "No, I'm fine."

"If you need me to call a tow truck, I can," I said, as I stepped closer.

"That's alright," he said. "I have a cell phone if I need to call anyone," and he leaned further inside the van.

The first thing I noticed about the man was that he kept his hands hidden the entire time I talked to him. The second thing that I noticed was that he strongly resembled the description I had been given of the man that everyone called Hamburger.

"Well, good luck getting your van fixed," I said, as I slowly backed up toward my

Bronco, while keeping an eye on the man leaning under the hood.

He pretended not to notice me as I walked away, but I could see him peaking around the hood until I got in my truck.

As soon as I got inside, I wrote the tag number of the van on a note pad and called it in to the Dispatcher's office to be run through the system. I sat for a few seconds then I cranked up to wait for Rachel to get back to me with information on the van.

As I waited, I could see the man looking around the hood occasionally then disappearing from my sight. He seemed to be concerned with me sitting in my truck, so I took my gun out of my holster and laid it beside my right thigh.

After a couple of minutes, Rachel radioed back and said, "The van has not been reported stolen and it's registered to Travis Brooks. According to his registration, his address is 1548 South Lane Road in Thorton."

"Does he have a criminal record?" I asked.

"Nothing major," she said. "Some minor disturbing the peace charges from bar fights but that's all we have on record."

"Thanks," I said, as I closed my phone.

I put my Bronco in gear. I started to pull around his van, but stopped instantly when I saw the man step around the van with a gun in his right hand, pointing toward me. I slammed it in park, grabbed my Glock off the seat and jumped out of my driver's side door keeping my truck between me and the man.

When I hit the ground, I heard his gun fire. The bullet hit my hood and bounced across the street.

"I know why you're here," he yelled and he fired another shot which struck my windshield causing the glass to shatter.

"Put your gun down and hold your hands in the air," I yelled.

"You'll have to make me!" he yelled and he fired two more shots into the side of my Bronco.

I moved to the back and looked underneath to see if I could see the man's legs so I could get an idea where he was standing.

After I located his legs, I counted to three, raised up and yelled, "Drop your weapon!" as I raised my gun and leveled it toward his chest.

He fired a shot, in my direction, as he took a step toward me.

I ducked, then raised up and fired two quick shots toward the man.

The first shot missed him but the second struck him in the chest which propelled him backward until he fell to the ground.

I watched for a couple of minutes but the man didn't move. I looked for his gun which was lying a few feet away from him then I cautiously stepped around the back of my truck and slowly approached the body.

When I got close to his body, I notice his chest wasn't moving. I took a couple more steps toward him, with my gun aimed at his face, until I reached his gun. Then, I took my right foot and kicked it away from him.

When I bent down to feel for a pulse, he didn't have one.

I looked at his chest which had a gaping hole on the left side with blood pooling on the ground. His color was already changing to a pale ashen gray, but I took my cell phone out of my pocket and call for an ambulance anyway.

After I call the ambulance, I called Diane and Janice and asked them to come to the crime scene. Then I called the police station and ask Rachel to send Johnny to 4th Avenue and 11th Street to be with me until everyone arrived.

While I waited, I punched in the number for Charles Wallace to inform him of the situation.

He answered on the third ring and said, “Charles speaking.”

“Hey, Charles,” I said. “This is Sam James. Did you get any information about the person everyone calls Hamburger?”

“It’s early, Sam,” he responded sleepily. “Why are you calling me this early?”

“Because I had someone try to kill me and I think it was Hamburger,” I said.

“Did he get away?” Charles asked.

“I shot him,” I said.

“Did you get any information from him?”

“I couldn’t,” I said. “He’s dead.”

“Where are you now?”

“4th Avenue and 11th Street.”

“I have some information,” he said. “I’ll talk to you when I get there,” and my phone went dead.

I closed my phone and put it in my shirt pocket. I brushed glass out of my seat in the Bronco and sat to wait for Johnny to join me.

I heard the ambulance before I closed my door, so I left the door open and watched as the ambulance come to a stop alongside the body. Two EMT’s jumped out of the ambulance and ran to the body.

The driver bent down and felt for a pulse then he bent closer to listen for breathing. He placed a heart monitor on the man's chest then he looked toward me and announced, "He's dead."

"I know, but I thought I needed to call you just in case he had a little life left in him."

"He would not have survived with that wound in his heart," the EMT said. "I think he died minutes after he was shot."

"Do you need to take him to the hospital so they can pronounce him dead?" I asked, as I turned and watched Johnny pull in behind my Bronco. "Or can we wait for the Medical Examiner to get here to pronounce him dead?"

"When will she be here?" he asked.

"She should be here within the next twenty minutes," I said.

"Sure, we'll wait," he said and walked back to his ambulance. He went to the back door, took out a disposable sheet and covered the man's body. Then he got inside his ambulance and cranked up to wait for Diane to arrive.

"What happened?" Johnny asked when he walked up beside me.

"That guy tried to shoot me and I shot him in the chest," I said, as I started walking toward my Bronco. "Let's get inside while we wait for Janice and Diane to get here."

"Sounds good," Johnny said as he went to the passenger side to sit down. He stopped before he reached for the handle and said, "You have two bullet holes in the side of your truck."

"He shot at me five times," I said, and I pointed at the windshield. "One hit the hood, one hit the windshield and two hit the passenger side door."

"What happened to the other bullet?" Johnny asked, as he took the door handle and opened the door.

"I think it missed everything, but I'm not sure," I said and I sat down in the driver's side seat.

Johnny got inside and closed the door. He looked at the windshield and said, "You'll have to get that fixed before you can drive."

"I'll call a wrecker to tow it to a body shop after Janice is finished, that is unless she needs it at the CSI lab," I said, as I cranked up and turned the air conditioner on.

We sat silently while we waited for Diane and Janice to come investigate the scene.

Chapter 65

Diane was the first to arrive at the scene. She drove around my Bronco, then pulled to the side of the road and parked behind the ambulance.

I got out as soon as I saw her park and started walking toward her.

She opened her door and asked, “Sam, what happened?”

“I’ll tell you later but first I need you to pronounce this guy dead so these EMT’s can leave,” I said, as I pointed to the body that was covered with the disposable sheet.

“Alright,” she said and she walked to the victim, lifted the sheet and looked at the body for a few seconds. Then she bent down and felt for a pulse. She took her stethoscope out of her bag and listened to his chest for about a minute then she placed the sheet back over the body.

“He was dead seconds after he was shot,” Diane said, as she started walking toward me.

The EMT that was driving got out of the ambulance when Diane started walking to the body and had stood beside me while she examined it.

“So, you’ll pronounce him dead,” the EMT asked.

“Yes, I’ll pronounce him dead,” she said.

“Will you sign my sheet saying that he was dead when we arrived?”

“I wasn’t here when you arrived,” Diane said. “But I know he was dead seconds after he was shot, so I guess I can sign,” and she took his notebook and signed his ambulance form.

“Thanks,” he said. “Now we can get back to work,” and he went back to the ambulance, got in and drove away.

When he got to the end of the street, I saw Janice's CSI van turned the corner.

"I'll tell everyone what happened when Janice gets here. I don't want to have to keep repeating the information," I said and watched as the CSI van parked in the same spot the ambulance had just vacated.

"You're still going to have to tell Charles Wallace when he gets here," Johnny said.

"That's true but at least I'll only have to say it a couple more times instead of three times," I responded.

Janice was the first to get out, followed by Victor and Daniel. Victor went to get his equipment out of the van. Janice and Daniel walked to where we were standing without looking at the body that was lying beside the dark blue and white Dodge Cargo van.

"Are you alright?" Janice asked when she got close to me.

"Yes, I'm fine," I said. "He got the worse of it."

"I can see that," she said, as she looked at the lifeless form that was entombed under the sheet. "What happened?"

"I thought his van had broken down so I stopped to see if I could help him," I said and pointed to the van. "But, when I started to pull away he came around the front of the van with a gun, pointed it at me and tried to shoot me."

"Did you know him?" Janice asked.

"I'm not sure," I said. "I think he may have been a drug dealer I've been looking for, but I'm only going by a description I got."

"Sam, you got shot at?" Victor asked, as he looked at the hood of my truck.

"See that spot on my hood and my windshield?"

"He did that?"

"Yes and I have two bullet holes in the passenger's side door," I said.

"I'll get started," Victor said, as turned and walked toward the body. He stopped about three feet from the body and started taking pictures. Then he removed the sheet from the body and took photographs from every angle. After he finished, he went to my Bronco and took pictures of the bullet holes.

Daniel walked over to where the gun was lying, picked it up and placed it in a plastic bag. Then he started looking for shell casings. He looked around the body, picked up three shell casings and put them in a plastic bag.

"There's really not much for us to investigate because we know who shot him," Janice said, as she watched Daniel gathering evidence.

"Why's Charles here?" Diane asked when she saw Charles Wallace turn down 4th Avenue and pull in behind Johnny's car.

"I called him and ask him to come," I said.

Charles got out and walked up beside where we were standing. He looked at Diane then at Janice and said, "Ladies."

"I've found five shell casings," Daniel called out, as he continued looking around the body.

"That's all there is," I said. "He only shot five times."

"Only five times," Diane exclaimed. "It only takes one to kill you."

"I know, but God was watching over me and He protected me," I said.

“Thank God,” she exclaimed.

“Is this the guy?” Charles asked, as he handed me a photograph of the man I had shot.

“Yes, that’s him,” I said.

“His real name is Travis Brooks but most of the drug industry knows him as Hamburger,” Charles said.

“I had Rachel run his tag and she said he didn’t have much of a criminal record,” I said.

“Sam, I’m glad you’re not hurt but I need to get to work,” Diane said. “I’ll load the body up and do the autopsy as soon as I can,” and she walked to her van.

I watched as she got a stretcher out and rolled it toward the body. Then I turned back to Charles and asked, “What do you know about him?”

“We think he worked for a drug dealer that came from California, but we don’t have any evidence to tie them together.”

“What’s the drug dealer’s name?”

“I don’t know,” he said. “We haven’t been able to identify him.”

“Sorry to interrupt but, Sam, I need your gun,” Janice said, as she opened a plastic bag.

I took my Glock out of my holster and slipped it in the plastic bag without saying a word.

“I’ll give your gun back as soon as I’m through, but I need it to match the bullet that killed out victim,” Janice said.

“That’s fine,” I said. “Keep it as long as you need to.”

"Thanks," Janice said, as she sealed the bag and put it away.

"Do you need my truck?" I asked.

"No, Victor took pictures of everything and Daniel got what bullet fragments he could out of the side, so I think we have everything we need," Janice said.

"Can I get it towed to a body shop?" I asked.

"Sure, you can't drive it like it is," she said.

"I'm ready," Daniel said, as he walked to the CSI van.

"I'll get back with you as soon as I know something," Janice said then she turned and went to her van. She threw her bag in the back, then walked around to the driver's side and got in. She waited for Victor to get in the back then she cranked up and drove away.

As she drove away, I caught sight of Diane loading the body in the back of her Medical Examiner's van. After she secured the body, she closed the door and turned toward me.

"I'll call you this afternoon," she said.

"Thanks," I answered.

I watched as she walked to the front of the van and got inside. She sat for a few seconds then she drove away.

"He probably shot at you because he thought you knew who he was," Charles said after Diane was out of sight.

"I guess that's what it was," I said. "It still bothers me when I shoot someone."

"Better him than you," Johnny said, as he looked across the street and added, "you can't kick yourself for protecting yourself."

"I know," I said, as I took my holster off and folded it up in my hands.

"Do you need a gun?" Charles asked.

"No, I'll just have to use my 357 Magnum instead of my Glock."

"Well, I told you all I know," Charles said, as he started walking toward his car. "I need to get to work," he added, as he got in his car, closed the door and drove away.

As Charles was driving away, I took my cell phone out of my pocket and called Gene's Body Shop to arrange for a tow truck to get my Bronco and take it to their body shop.

Gene answered the phone and assured me that he could be on 4th Avenue in about ten minutes, so Johnny and I leaned up against my hood to wait on the tow truck.

It only took him nine minutes to get to where we were and ten more to load my battered vehicle onto his truck.

"Do you want me to start working on an estimate as soon as I can?" Gene asked.

"Yes, and I'll call my insurance agent as soon as I get to the station," I said.

"Sounds good," he said as he got in his truck and drove away.

After the tow truck was out of sight, I got in Johnny's car and he drove me to the police station.

Chapter 66

Rachel ran up to me and wrapped her arms around my neck as soon as I walked through the door. She gave me a quick hug then stepped back and looked at me with concern.

After clearing her throat and choking back tears, she asked, "Are you alright?"

"I'm fine," I said. "The other guy is the one that got the bad deal."

"Rachel, are you getting emotional on us?" Johnny asked and laughed.

"I've kind of gotten attached to you guys and I wouldn't want any one of you to get hurt, especially Sam," she said, as she looked away and took a deep breath.

"It's part of the job," I said.

"I know, but this is the second time in the last few months that someone has shot at you," she said. "That's never happened before."

"As our town has grown we've had some bad people move in that don't respect the law," I said. "And I'm going to do whatever it takes to take them down."

"Just be careful," she said and smiled.

"I'll be as careful as I can be," I said and gave her a hug.

"Well, I'm glad you're not hurt," Rachel said, as she turned around and went to the dispatcher's office and closed the door.

Johnny and I watched as Rachel walked away.

After she closed the door, I said, "It's nice to be loved."

"I'm glad you didn't get hurt either," Johnny said, as he went to his desk and sat down.

"I am too," I said, as I walked to the coffee pot and poured a cup of coffee. "If I had been shot it would have ruined my day."

"I can see that as a bad way to start the morning," Johnny said and laughed. Then he turned to his computer and booted it up.

I took a sip of coffee to make sure it was fresh enough for me to drink then I went in my office and closed the door.

After pulling my chair out I sat down and called Jenna.

She answered on the second ring and said, "Hey babe, what's going on?"

"I just called to tell you I love you," I said.

"I love you too," she said questioningly then asked, "Is anything wrong?"

"Why?" I asked.

"Because you're usually too busy this time of day to call me."

"Alright, I did want to tell you that somebody tried to shot me this morning."

"OH MY GOD!" she interrupted. "Are you alright?"

"I'm fine," I said calmly.

"I know you said you're alright but did you get shot."

"No I didn't get shot."

"Thank God," she exclaimed then she continued, "I love you so much I don't know what I would do if anything happened to you."

"I'm fine honey I just needed to hear your voice," I said, as I leaned forward and added, "I wanted to tell you myself so I could let you know that I wasn't hurt."

"Thank you for calling me."

"I needed the comfort that your voice gives me," I said. "I love you and I'll see you tonight," and I put the phone down on the receiver.

Then I opened the top drawer on my desk, took out the notepad that I had made my list on and laid it down.

Under the death column I wrote, Frankie Overton, Lou Overton and Travis Brooks. Then I wrote the same names under the drug column.

As I looked at the notepad, I thought about putting Tommy Moore and Ben Richie under the drug column, but I decided not to because of their age. I couldn't believe they were involved in the murders.

I continued looking at the list hoping that something would jump out at me and give me a lead toward finding the person behind these murders. The majority of my suspects were dead, so that ruled them out.

After several minutes without anything beneficial happening, I closed the notepad and put it back in my drawer. Then I picked up my phone and called my insurance agent. After a short conversation about the weather, I told him about my Bronco and asked him to send someone to Gene's Body Shop to look at the damage.

He assured me that someone would be out sometime tomorrow and hung up the phone.

I put my phone down, leaned back in my chair and closed my eyes, as I thought about everything that happened during the morning. I ran the scene through my mind several times trying to determine if there was anything I could have done differently to have prevented the shooting.

Every scenario I thought of lead to the same conclusion. Travis Brooks was determined to shoot me and there was nothing I could do to prevent it.

After I had come to the understanding that I hadn't caused the shooting, I was able to focus my attention on the suspects that I had on my list. For the most part, I had them memorized. Ben Lowe at Morton Enterprises was at the top of my list, but then where did Victor White and Braswell Temp Service fit in. Three bodies were found at that site. Avery Moore is a low life drug dealer and sits at the bottom of my list.

As I thought through the list, I decided to start at the top and give Ben Lowe a visit. I pulled my 357 Magnum out of my desk drawer, got up and walked into the squad room.

Johnny was still at his desk working at his computer.

"Johnny, are you at a point where you can stop?" I asked, as I walked to his desk.

"Sure, I can save it and finish it later," he said. "What do you have in mind?"

"I want to talk to Ben Lowe and I want you to come with me," I said, as I clipped my holster onto my belt.

"Alright," he said, as he hit the save button and closed the screen. "I'm ready to go."

"Let's see if he knows anything about this drug dealer from California," I said and walked toward the door.

I went into the dispatcher's office and said, "Johnny and I will be gone for a while."

"Alright," Rachel said. "I'll call your cell if I need you."

"Call Richard first, unless it's an emergency," I said.

"O.K," she said.

"Bye," I said, as I walked to the door and went outside.

Johnny followed.

We got in the patrol car closest to the door, cranked up and slowly drove to the end of the parking lot. Then I turned left and drove toward Morton Enterprises.

Chapter 67

When I turned into Morton Enterprises' parking lot, I saw Jeff Bland standing on the sidewalk talking to a man wearing a large cowboy hat. I pulled to the parking space in front of them and stopped.

Jeff immediately stopped talking and looked to see who was in the car. He hesitantly smiled when he recognized me and slowly walked toward the driver's side of the car.

"Sam is there a problem?" he asked when I opened the door.

"No, there's no problem," I said. "I just need to talk to Ben for a minute."

"He's not here today," said the man wearing the cowboy hat.

I looked at Jeff, then turned to the man and asked, "What is your name?"

He stuck his hand out and said, "Danny Mims."

I shook his hand and said, "I'm Sam James the Police Chief."

"It's good to meet you," he said.

"Do you work at Morton Enterprises?" I asked.

"Oh no, I own this complex," he said and laughed. "I was having some remodeling done on one of my units and I came to check it out."

"So, Morton Enterprises leases from you?" I asked.

"Yes they do," he responded. "I came to talk to Ben to make sure everything was alright with the building, but he was off today, so I was talking to Jeff instead."

I turned to Jeff and asked, "Are you in charge when Ben is off?"

"Not really, but I could let him know if we were having problems with the building or not," he said.

I looked at Danny, then turned to Jeff and said, "I need to talk to you a minute in private."

"That's alright," Danny said. "I need to go, anyway," and he got in his truck and drove away.

"What do you need to talk about?" Jeff asked, as soon as Danny drove out of the parking lot.

"Have you had anyone from California ask you to do security work for them?" I asked.

"Not that I'm aware of," he said. "But, Ben would know more about that than I would."

"Do you know when Ben will be back?"

"I think he'll be in tomorrow," Jeff said. "He had some kind of family emergency that he had to take care of this morning."

Johnny walked to the front door and looked inside. "It's dark," he said, as he turned and looked at Jeff. Then he asked, "Are you closed today?"

"Yes, I decided to close early," he said. "Ben handles the business end and since he's not here, there's no need to be open."

"Have you heard anything about a drug dealer from California being in the area?" I asked.

"Ah, that's what this is about," he responded. "You think we've been helping a drug dealer."

"I'm just asking questions." I said.

"I can assure you that I haven't been helping a drug dealer and if I had heard of anyone else helping one, I would have called you," he said. "Like I told you before, I don't break the law."

"What about Ben?"

"You'd have to ask him."

"I will."

"If that's all the questions, I need to go," he said.

"That's all I have," I said. "Thanks for your time."

"No problem," he said, as he walked to his car and drove away.

"Was that a waste of time?" Johnny asked, as he got in the car.

"I'm not sure," I said. "We should know in a day or two," and I drove to the end of the parking lot. I turned left and drove toward the police station.

Chapter 68

When we got back to the police station, I went into my office and called Diane at the medical examiner's office.

She answered on the second ring and said, "Medical Examiner's office," and then asked, "How may I help you?"

"This is Sam," I said, as I sat down in my chair and leaned back. "Have you got the cause of death on the two victims from Fairway Shopping Center?"

"Good afternoon to you, too," she said.

"I'm sorry," I said. "Good afternoon, Diane."

"Good afternoon, Sam," Diane said, laughing. "Now let's get to those victims."

As I listened, I heard paper being shuffled around and Diane mumbling, "Where are those reports? Where did I put them? Oh, there they are. Alright, the first victim's name was Lou Overton. He died from a drug overdose."

"What did he overdose on?" I asked.

"He had a large amount of Heroin in his system, as well as, Cocaine and Methamphetamine," she said.

"Do you think it was an accidental overdose?"

"He had enough drugs in his system to kill three men," she said. "So no, I don't think it was accidental."

"Anything else?" I asked.

"He has a small puncture wound along the Rhomboideus muscle in the back which was probably where the drug was administered."

"What does that mean?"

"He couldn't have given it to himself."

"What about the other victim?"

"His name was Frankie Overton," she said. "He had the same drugs in his system."

"Did he have a puncture wound like the other victim?"

"Yes, his was in his medial trapezius."

"Where's that?"

"A little higher than the other victims, but they were both stabbed in the back with a syringe filled with drugs."

"Both were murdered?"

"Yes, I'd say both were murdered."

"Have you done the autopsy on the victim this morning?"

"Yes, I just completed it," she said. "It was straight forward. He was shot in the chest and died from severe blood loss."

"That's what I thought," I said, and then paused.

"What is it?" she asked.

"Could I have saved his life?"

"He died almost instantly," she said. "There was nothing you could have done to save him."

"Alright."

"Are you alright?" she asked.

"It's difficult when you kill someone," I said.

"He was going to kill you," she said.

"I know, but it's still not easy," I said, as I raised up and leaned my elbows on my desk.

"Sam, you did nothing wrong," she affirmed.

"Thanks Diane," I said and I hung up the phone.

As I got up to walk out of my office, my phone started ringing. I reached over, picked it up and said, "Sam speaking."

"This is Janice," a female voice said. "You can come get your gun now."

"What?" I asked.

"We matched your gun with the bullet that was removed from Travis Brooks, so we don't need it anymore," she said. "You can come get it whenever you want to."

"I'll try to come get it in a day or two," I said.

"I have it locked up in my office," she said. "Make sure I'm there before you come."

"Alright, I will," I responded, as I leaned against my desk, then I asked, "did you find any evidence at the Fairway shopping Center?"

"I found a trace amount of DNA on one of the cigarette butts that I found at the crime scene," she said. "I've sent it through the system but I haven't gotten any results."

"Did you find any other evidence?" I asked.

"We have the mold Daniel made of the partial foot print but unless we have something to match it with, it's useless," she said.

"Where does that leave us?"

"The cigarette butts and partial foot print were all we found at the crime scene and

I wouldn't call the cigarette butts evidence because they probably belong to the people that work at Braswell Temp Service," she said and added, "but I gathered them just in case they belong to the killer."

"Janice thanks for calling me and letting me know that I can pick up my gun," I said.

"Sam, I'm glad you weren't hurt," she said.

"Me too," I said and I laid the phone down on the receiver.

Then I walked in the squad room, looked at Richard and Johnny who were sitting at their desk and said, "I'll see you tomorrow," and I walked out the door.

Chapter 69

As the Smack Master drove down 4th Avenue, he looked on every street corner to make sure his dealers were at their posts and selling his merchandise to each customer when they pulled to the side of the street.

They nervously watched when he drove past because they knew their life depended on selling his drugs. He fed their habit and gave them enough money to eat but it was also well known that he had killed people when they disappointed him.

He turned right on 25th Street, then turned right on 5th Avenue and slowly drove by each street corner to check on his dealers.

As he drove, he had his Ruger LCP semiautomatic handgun lying beside his right leg in anticipation of seeing a rival dealer.

After he was satisfied that only his dealers were in his area, he turned down 3rd Avenue to settle a debt that he felt was owned to him.

When he neared 28th Street, he cut his engine off and coasted to the side of the street.

His target lived on 2nd Avenue and 28th Street, so he grabbed his gun, got out of his car and quickly ran across the street. He stopped beside a large oak tree and looked around the area for anyone that might be outside to witness what he was about to do.

After he was sure there were no witnesses, he looked at the numbers on the houses to make sure he had the right house. He spotted the number he was looking for on a large charcoal brick house with crimson shudders. There were two large Azalea bushes at each corner of the house and a large row of Bayberry bushes lining the porch that ran across the front of the house.

He counted to three then he ran across the street and hid behind one of the large Azalea bushes that was at the corner of the house.

He checked his gun to make sure he had a bullet in the chamber. After he scanned the area one last time to make sure there were no witnesses, he skirted around the house to the back door.

When he reached the back door, he stopped and listened intently for a few seconds. When he didn't hear anyone, he quietly picked the lock and walked inside the house.

As he entered the house, he looked around the room where a large glass table sat. To his right were the refrigerator, stove and dishwasher. To his left was a wall of oak cabinets from floor to ceiling.

After he got inside, he could hear the distant sound of a television in one of the rooms. It sounded like it was upstairs but he cautiously moved to the next room with his gun drawn in case his target was sitting in the dark waiting for his arrival.

The first room he entered was dark but he could see well enough to make sure no one was in there. So he slowly walked out of the room and headed for the stairs.

When he reached the stairs, he paused and listened for a few seconds before stepping on the first step.

As he ascended the stairs, he stopped after each step and listen to make sure he hadn't been discovered.

When he reached the top of the stairs, he saw a light illuminating from under a door at the end of the hall. As he listened, he heard the sound of the television coming from the room.

He moved along the wall toward the room.

As he got close to the room, he noticed the door wasn't completely closed. He pushed the door opened about half an inch and spotted his target lying in bed watching television.

He tightened his grip on his gun, then pushed the door opened and fired three quick shots toward the target.

Blood splatter the wall when the first bullet struck the target's head and he slumped over in the bed. The second and third bullet struck the target in the back as he lay on the bed.

After making sure his target was dead, the Smack Master quickly eased out the back door, locking it as he went. Then he casually walked across the street, got in his car and drove away.

Chapter 70

I was awakened from a deep sleep by the sound of my cell phone ringing. As I reached for my phone, I knocked it off my bedside table onto the floor. It rang one more time and stopped.

After rolling out of the bed I got on my knees to look for my phone and ran my hand along the base of my bedside table but I couldn't find it. Then I reached under my bed and felt for my phone.

As I was about to get up and get a flashlight, it started ringing again.

I spotted my phone about a foot from where I was searching as the screen lit up announcing the identity of the person on the phone.

I grabbed the phone, opened it without looking at the screen and said, "This is Sam."

"I'm sorry to call you this early, Sam, but I just got a call of shots being fired at 2nd Avenue and 28th Street," a man said.

"Who is this?" I whispered, as I got up and quietly walked out of my bedroom and stood in the hall.

"Tony Ford," the man said. "I thought you had caller I.D."

"I do, but I didn't look before I opened the phone," I said. "I was in a deep sleep when you called."

"I'm sorry," he said apologetically.

I had talked long enough to begin to wake up and I realized that he had mentioned a shooting but didn't say anything about going to the scene, so I asked, "Did anyone go to the scene?"

"Franklin and I are both on our way to the scene," he said. "I left the police station about five minutes ago."

"When did you get the call?"

"We left as soon as we got the call."

I eased down the stairs while I was talking and went in the kitchen. I walked past the table, leaned close to the clock that was hanging on the wall to see what time it was. I had a hard time focusing my eyes on the clock, so I asked, "What time is it?"

He paused for a second before saying, "It's three thirty."

"Do you have your bullet resistant vest on?"

"Yes, I put it on before I left the station."

"Good," I said. "You and Franklin be careful and I'll be there as soon as I can," and I closed my phone.

I went to the utility room where I keep an extra set of clothes just for this occasion. I opened the closet, got an old pair of blue jeans and a gray button down work shirt. After I slipped them on, I grabbed a pair of tennis shoes off the floor, a pair of socks off the top shelf and walked back into the kitchen. I sat down at the table and put my socks and shoes on.

After I was completely dressed, I went back in the utility room and got my Baretta M9 off the top shelf and slipped it in the waist band of my jeans. I got the bullet resistant vest off the top shelf that I keep stored beside my gun and put it over my shirt. Then I did one last check to make sure I hadn't missed anything before walking out the door.

I got in the patrol car I was using while my Bronco was being worked on and drove toward 2nd Avenue and 28th Street as fast as I could.

Chapter 71

I turned down 2nd Avenue and drove toward 28th Street looking for one of my police officers. When I got close, I saw two Thorton Patrol cars parked at the side of the street with what appeared to be two police officers and a man in his housecoat standing behind the car closest to me.

They turned toward me and watched as I slowly pulled in behind the car they were standing behind and parked.

I got out of my car, walked toward them and asked, "What's going on here?"

"This is George Cain," Franklin said, as he pointed to the man in the housecoat. "He's the one who called and reported the gun shots."

"Have you looked for the shooter?" I asked, as I looked at Franklin.

"I canvassed the area around the house but I didn't see anything," Franklin said. "Then I came back here to wait for backup."

I turned to George Cain and asked, "Did you see anyone leave the house after you heard the shots?"

"Yes, I saw a man walk across the street to 3rd Avenue and get in a black Mazda RX-8 Sport," he said.

"It's dark out here," I said. "How could you tell it was a black car?"

"He parked under a street light," George said, as he smiled and lowered his head. "I also saw him pull up and I'm sort of a car buff, so I walked across the street to get a better look at the car while he was away."

"You didn't by chance get a tag number while you were looking at the car?" I asked.

"I didn't when I was looking at it, but I saw it when he pulled away," George said.

"Do you remember the numbers?"

"It didn't have numbers," he said. "He had one of those specialized tags."

"Do you remember what was on the tag?"

"Yes, it had Smack written in large black letters."

"Smack," I said. "Now that's original."

"I don't understand what is on most people's tags," George said. "I guess they do when they have it put on their tags."

I looked at Franklin and said, "We need to go in the house and see if anyone's inside." Then I turned to Tony and said, "Stay with George and watch our backs," and I started walking across the street.

Franklin followed without saying anything until we got close to the house and then he asked, "Where do you want me to go?"

"Go to the back of the house and I'll go in through the front door."

"I'll meet you inside," Franklin said and he ran to the back of the house and disappeared around the corner.

I took my Baretta M9 out of my waistband and cautiously ran to the side of the porch. Then I took my right hand, pushed back some shrub branches and looked at the front door and windows along the front of the house to see if I could see any movement inside the house.

I watched for several seconds without seeing anything then I eased around the shrubs, up the steps and stopped beside the front door.

After counting to three I reached for the doorknob to see if it was unlocked.

As I reached to turn the doorknob, the door opened and Franklin stuck his head out and announced, "The backdoor was locked but it wasn't closed."

I jumped back and pointed my gun in his direction. "Franklin, you almost got shot," I scolded in a low voice and lowered my gun. "You need to be more careful."

"I'm sorry, I just wanted to help you get inside the house," he said.

"I appreciate that but I could have shot you," I whispered, as I walked inside the house. "Have you seen anything?"

"There's no one down stairs," he said.

"Then, let's look upstairs," I said and I walked to the foot of the stairs.

I put a foot on the bottom step and tested it to make sure it wouldn't squeak with my weight. Then I stepped up and slowly made my way up the stairs with Franklin following close behind.

At the top of the steps, I could hear the sound of a television in a room at the end of a short hall.

I motioned for Franklin to stay at the stairs while I moved toward the sound. Then I slowly moved toward the open doorway and stopped before I got to the entrance of the room, took a couple deep breaths and then stormed through the door with my gun raised and ready to fire.

I stopped almost instantly when I saw the blood splatter on the wall beside the bed.

I quickly scanned the room to make sure it was empty, then I cautiously walked to the slumped over body lying in a pool of blood on top of the bed and felt for a pulse.

After I was certain he was dead, I walked back in the hall and said, "We have a victim in here," and I walked toward Franklin and added, "We need to search the rest of the rooms to make sure no one else is here."

Franklin looked to his left and said, "I'll start at this end," and he slowly walked toward a dark room at the corner of the stairs.

I started with the room next to the one our victim was in and worked my way toward the stairs.

Franklin and I entered the last room about the same time. We searched it together without finding anything.

After I was certain we had no other victims, I took my cell phone out of my pocket and called Diane and Janice. I informed them of the situation and gave them the address of our latest victim. Then Franklin and I went downstairs to wait.

When we got outside and were walking across the street Franklin asked, "Did you know the victim?"

I stopped in mid stride and said, "I didn't look at his face." Then I looked back at the house and added, "I felt for a pulse to make sure he was dead, but I didn't look to see if I recognized him."

"We needed to make sure the house was clear anyway," Franklin said.

"I probably wouldn't have recognized him if I had of looked," I said as I shook my head. "Because he was shot in the head and covered with blood."

Tony walked toward us as we started across the street and asked, "Was there anybody in the house?"

"Yes, we have one victim," I said.

I looked at the patrol car where George was standing with his back against the passenger's side door.

Then I turned back at Tony and asked, "Did he have anything to say while we were gone?" and I pointed toward George.

"No, he was really quiet while you were in the house," he said.

"Let's see if he has any more information," I said as I walked to the patrol car and stood beside him.

He looked at me for a few seconds before asking, "Was someone killed?"

"Do you know who lives in that house?" I asked, looking him in the eye.

"I've seen him from a distance but I didn't know his name," he responded.

"Was it just one person?"

"I only saw a man come and go from the house."

"So to your knowledge only one person lived in this house."

"Yes, as far as I know only a man lived here."

"And the person you saw leaving this house tonight drove away in a black Mazda RX-8 Sport."

"Yes, that's what I saw."

"He had a special tag with SMACK written on it."

"That's what I said earlier," he said with a little irritation in his voice. Then he asked, "Are you doubting what I said?"

"No, I'm just trying to make sure I have it right," I said.

We turned at the same time when we heard the sound of a vehicle driving down 2nd Avenue. I let out a deep breath and relaxed when I realized it was Diane in her

Medical Examiner's van.

She slowed down when she got close to where we were parked and carefully drove over the sidewalk onto the front yard. Then she circled around and backed up toward the front door.

I started walking across the street as Diane opened the door of her van and got out. She closed the door and slowly walked toward me.

"What do we have?" she asked when I got close.

"One male shot at least once up stairs," I said.

"Is CSI here yet?" she asked.

"No, you were the first to arrive," I said and I turned to watch Janice turn down 2nd Avenue and park beside my car, blocking the street as she did so.

"Since they're here I guess I can wait on them before I go upstairs," she said. "I wouldn't want to damage any evidence."

Victor was the first to get out and waited at the front of the van for everyone to join him and then they all walked across the street at the same time.

Victor had his camera dangling from his neck, Daniel had an evidence bag in his right hand and a hard case which held his finger printing material in his left. Janice walked along beside them with her evidence bag in her right hand and holding her cell phone in her left up against her ear.

She stopped about ten feet before she got to me and said, "Send Jack and David to the scene," then she paused and listened to whoever was talking on her cell phone.

After a few seconds, Janice said, "I know they're new but I have a case to work and I can't be at two places at the same time," as she closed her phone and put it in her pocket.

Victor and Daniel had continued walking and were standing beside me.

Janice took a deep breath and slowly let it out. Then she walked up beside me and asked, "What do we have?"

"One male body upstairs," I said and looked toward the house. "He's been shot at least once, maybe more."

"Who has been in the house?" Janice asked.

"Franklin and I went upstairs, but I'm the only one that went in the room where the victim is located," I said.

"Did you touch anything?"

"I only checked for a pulse," I said. "Then I left the room and called you guys."

She looked at Victor and said, "Let's get started."

"Alright," he said and walked toward the house.

He started taking pictures before he reached the porch, then he snapped off several shots of the front door and walked inside the house.

"Do you have another case?" I asked, as we watched Victor photographing the crime scene.

"Yes, a body was found at the edge of Winston County but it was in Walker County so we have to investigate it," Janice said.

"Too bad you couldn't drag the body over a few feet into Winston County," Franklin said and laughed.

Janice looked at Franklin, opened her mouth but closed it without saying anything. Then she took a deep breath and blew it out before asked, "Do we know where the killer entered the house?"

"I think he or she entered from the back door," Franklin said, as he stepped a little closer. "The door was locked but not closed."

"Our owner may have just forgotten to close it," she said.

"I didn't see any evidence at the front door to indicate that the killer entered through it," I said.

"Alright we'll treat the back door as our entry point," she said, as she looked at Daniel and added, "Go back there and start looking for evidence."

"Alright," Daniel said, as he took the flashlight out of his evidence bag and started walking around the house.

"Where is the victim?" Janice asked, as we watched Daniel as he disappeared around the house.

"Turn right when you get to the top of the stairs and he's in the room at the end of the hall," I said.

Janice looked at Diane and said, "Why don't we go upstairs and look at the victim," and she started walking toward the house.

"Sounds good to me," Diane said and she followed.

"I'll stay out here and keep the crowd down," I said, as I watched them walk into the house. Then I went to the steps and sat down on the first step leading to the porch.

Chapter 72

As they walked in the house, Diane stopped at the edge of the living room and pointed at a large chocolate brown leather sofa with two matching recliners that surrounded a 65 inch flat screen television and said, "The person that lived here must have had some money."

"There's some expensive looking art on the walls," Janice said, as they walked to the stairs.

They carefully walked up the stairs making sure not to touch anything as they went. When they got to the top, they both pulled a pair of gloves out of their pocket and put them on and then they walked toward the crime scene.

Janice started through the door first but stopped when she saw the blood splattered on the wall. Then she brought her hand up like it was a gun and said, "If he was lying back in the bed when he was shot, then I think he may have been shot from the doorway."

"It looks like the right angle," Diane added.

"Diane, why don't you look at the body while I look for evidence around the bed," Janice said, as she continued into the room and went to the side of the bed.

Janice looked at the bed for a few seconds then she went around to the other side and sat her evidence bag on the floor. She got a cotton tip applicator out of her bag, gathered a blood sample off the wall and placed it inside a glass tube. Then she sealed it with a black screw cap and placed it in her evidence bag.

She moved a little closer to the wall and examined the blood splatter. "I don't see any bullet fragments in the wall," she said, as she ran her hand along the wall to feel for any indention. "The bullets must still be in our victim."

Diane leaned close to the victim's head and announced, "I don't see an exist wound in his head," then she took her finger and stuck it in the bullet hole. As she was feeling for the bullet she added, "The wound is from a large caliber gun and the fragments must be lodged in his brain."

Then she moved to his back and looked at the wounds. "It looks like the bullets are still in his back also," she said, as she raised up.

Janice looked at the bowl of melted ice cream that had leaked on the bed and said, "He was shot while eating ice cream and watching television." Then she placed the bowl in a plastic bag, then scooped the melted ice cream in a plastic container and placed it in her evidence bag. "I'll test this for drugs when I get back to the lab," she said.

"Are you ready for me to get the body?" Diane asked.

"Sure," Janice said. "I don't see much evidence here," and she walked toward the door.

"I'll get the stretcher," Diane said, as she walked out the door.

"I'll see if Daniel found anything while you load the body," Janice said, as she followed Diane down the stairs.

I stood up when I heard the front door open.

Diane came out of the house and opened the back door of her van. She unclamped the stretcher from the side of her van and pulled it out, dropping the wheels to the ground.

"Do you need help loading the body?" Franklin asked when she approached the steps.

"Yes, I could use some help," she said and smiled.

I looked at Franklin, who was smiling from ear to ear, then back at Diane and said, "I'd go with you but I'd feel like a third wheel."

Diane stopped smiling and said, "Thanks Sam, but we can handle it," and she rolled the stretcher past me, up the steps and into the house.

Franklin looked at me and smiled then he followed Diane into the house.

I went in the house when I heard Janice in the living room talking to Daniel.

As I entered the house, I saw them standing at the doorway leading to the kitchen. I moved toward them and stopped to listen to what they were saying.

"I agree with Franklin," Daniel said. "The killer came through the back door."

"Did you find any evidence?" Janice asked.

"The lock on the back door was picked by someone with a little experience picking locks, but they left a few scratches so it defiantly wasn't a professional that picked it," Daniel said, as he turned toward the back door. "They also locked the door back but with their eagerness to leave the crime scene they didn't make sure it was closed which leads me to believe our killer may have heard something or possibly seen your witness outside and so he left in a hurry."

"So you're saying our witness may be in danger," I said.

"He could be," Daniel said.

"Did he see anything?" Janice asked.

"Oh yes," I said and smiled. "He saw the killer as he left the house, he saw his car and he even got the tag number off the car."

"You need to protect that man," she said.

I turned as Diane and Franklin rolled the victim's body down the stairs. They stopped when they got beside me and Diane said, "I'll let you know what I find in the morning," and then they rolled the body out the door.

I watched as they eased the stretcher off the porch and rolled it toward the Medical Examiner's van. Then I turned back to Janice. "I'll need to put him in a safe house until we catch the killer and send him to jail," I said. "I guess I need to call Charles Wallace and get him to find me a good hiding place for our witness."

"Yes, it's not every day you find a witness as good as him," Janice said.

"That's true," I said, as I looked around the living room. "Has anybody found anything to tell us who our victim was?" I asked and stepped over to a bookshelf where a stack of magazines were piled.

Janice and Daniel looked at each other.

"I've been looking for evidence to catch the killer," Daniel said.

"Me too," Janice said.

I took the top magazine off the pile and looked at the name that was on the front. Then I looked at the second and third magazine.

Janice walked to the coffee table that was in front of the sofa, picked up a envelope and looked at the person that it was addressed to, then she handed it to me.

I looked at it and said, "Everything is addressed to Ben Lowe," and then I laid the envelope back on the coffee table. "I know Ben Lowe."

"So, is our victim Ben Lowe?" Janice asked.

"I really didn't look at his face but I don't think I would've been able to tell because of the amount of blood he had on his face," I said.

"Well, whoever he was, he had a lot of money," Janice said.

"That's not doing him much good now," I said.

"No, it's not," she said and started walking toward the door. "We've got some evidence but not much so make sure you keep your witness safe," and she walked out the door.

Daniel and I followed.

Diane pulled away from the house as we stepped outside onto the porch. Then she turned left and drove away.

"Where is your witness?" Janice asked, as she looked across the yard.

I squinted my eyes trying to locate him in the darkness. Then I saw him standing with Victor and Tony at the edge of the street beside my patrol car.

"There he is," I said. "By my car," and I let out a sigh of relief.

Franklin walked up with a roll of crime scene tape and asked, "Do you want me to rope off the area?"

"Lock the door and then wrap it around the house a couple of times," I said, as I walked down the steps.

"No problem," Franklin said, as he walked up the steps, locked the door and attached to tape to the door handle. Then he slowly started rolling it around the house.

"We need to get to the lab," Janice said. "I'll run some test on what we have and let you know something tomorrow."

"Thanks," I said.

"I'll talk to you tomorrow," she said, as she went across the street to the CSI van.

Victor had the doors open by the time they got there. He helped them get everything inside then he closed the door.

After everyone was inside the van, Janice cranked up and drove away.

I took my cell phone out of my pocket and punched in Charles Wallace's cell phone number. It rang four times than went to voice mail. I closed my phone and dialed it again. This time he answered on the second ring and said in a sleepy voice, "This had better be good."

"Charles, this is Sam," I said. "I need a safe house tonight."

"At this time of morning?"

"Yes."

"This can't wait until in the morning?"

"I'd like to do this before daylight."

"I'll meet you in your office in an hour," he said after a sigh and my phone went dead.

I closed my phone, put in back in my shirt pocket and walked over to where Tony was standing with our witness.

I looked at George who was still in his housecoat and said, "You're going to have to go to a safe house tonight."

"What?" he asked.

"We think the killer might know you saw him and your life may be in danger," I said and I looked at Tony and added, "go with him to his house and let him get dressed and get some clothes packed."

"Where am I going?" George asked.

“I’m not sure yet,” I said. “We’re meeting someone at the station in an hour that will help keep you safe.”

“Let’s go,” Tony said, as he started toward the man’s house.

I leaned against the hood of my car to wait for them to get back.

Within minutes, Franklin walked up and asked, “Where’s Tony?”

I told him what the plan was and we both leaned against my car to wait.

I looked across the yard at the big empty house and thought material things are not important, it’s family and friends that’s important. Then I looked at Franklin and asked, “Why were you and Diane smiling so much tonight?”

“I don’t know,” he said. “Can’t we be happy and smile.”

“Is there anything going on between you two?” I asked.

“No, I was just being friendly,” he said.

“Alright, I was just wondering,” I said and turned when I heard someone walking in the darkness.

I reached for my gun, but relaxed when Tony and George came into sight about thirty feet from my car.

George was carrying a dark brown leather suitcase in his right hand and a small overnight case in his left. Tony opened the back door to his car and George loaded his luggage inside.

Then George turned to me and asked, “What now?”

“Let’s go to the police station,” I said.

Franklin got in his car, George got in the front seat with Tony and I got in my car. Franklin lead the way with Tony in the middle and me following in the rear as we slowly drove to the police station.

Chapter 73

We sat in my office waiting for Charles to come with the location of the safe house he had chosen. I sat leaned back in my chair with my feet resting on the top of my desk and watching the clock.

George sat in one of the straight backed chairs in front of my desk with his hands folded across his legs. He periodically tensed up as he shifted his position and looked toward the door but when the door remained closed he relaxed and turned back to me.

Franklin had entered the name on the tag in the system in order to get our suspect's name and address. Now he was standing by the window looking out across the parking lot to alert us when Charles arrived.

Tony was in the squad room working on tonight's murder report and watching the front door.

"Well, it's been exactly an hour and ten minutes since I called Charles," I said as I looked at the clock.

"I feel like I've been sitting here for that long," George said.

"It just takes time to get everything set up," I said.

Franklin turned and announced, "He just pulled into the parking lot with another vehicle following behind."

Within three minutes, my door opened and Charles walked in with a man wearing a black leather jacket and a frown on his face following behind.

Charles looked at George and asked, "Is this our witness?"

"Yes, this is George Cain," I said, as I looked toward him. "He heard gun shots and saw a man leave the murder scene."

"Alright, let's get this man somewhere safe," Charles said, as he went to the chair beside George and sat down.

The man in the black leather jacket stood by the door without saying anything.

Charles placed his briefcase on my desk and looked back at Franklin who was still standing by the window.

"The fewer people know about the safe house, the safer it will be," Charles said when he looked at me.

"Franklin, will you go check and see if the results are back from the license plate?" I asked.

"Sure," he said and he walked out the door.

After he was in the squad room, I looked at Charles then I looked at the man standing by the door. I looked back at Charles with a questioning look on my face.

He turned to the door with a faint smile on his face and said, "Pete, will you step out for a minute and close the door?"

"Sure," he said, as he stepped into the squad room and closed the door behind him.

After the door closed, Charles said, "He already knows where the house is located."

"That's fine but I didn't want Franklin to feel singled out," I said. "If he had to leave, I thought your guy should also."

George watched Charles as he opened his briefcase and pulled out a stack of papers and laid them on the desktop. "This is the information I told you I would get on

Ben Lowe," he said.

"It's a little late if he was our victim," I said. "But thanks anyway."

"They might help explain a little bit about what has been going on around here," he said.

"Thanks," I said.

"What about me?" George demanded.

"I have a safe house set up for you to stay for a few days until the killer is arrested and sent to prison," Charles said. "But first I must ask you a few questions."

"What?" he asked.

"Will you follow the rules of the house?" Charles asked. "I can't put my agents in danger."

"What rules?"

"No phone calls while you're at the house," he said. "That includes cell phones."

"Alright."

"You must stay in the house at all times," he said. "You can't go to the mailbox, movies, grocery shopping or anywhere else."

"What if I need food?"

"The house has been fully stocked with whatever you might need," Charles said. "If we missed something, I'll bring it the next time I come to the house."

"O.K."

"You will have two guards at the house most of the time," he said. "If they have to leave for some reason, you must stay inside with the shades closed."

"That's a lot of rules," George said.

"That's to keep everyone safe," he said and then asked, "Can you follow the rules?"

"I have no choice," George said, as he looked at his hands. "I'll follow the rules."

"Good," Charles said, as he turned to me and added, "I'll keep the identity of the safe house to myself, so no one will know where it is except me and the agents I have assigned to guard the witness."

"That's alright with me," I said. "The fewer people that know where he is the better."

"Well, the sun's up so we don't have the protection of darkness," Charles said grumbled, as he pulled a baseball cap out of his briefcase and handed it to George. "Put this on and pull it down over your eyes when we start out the door."

"Alright," George said and took the cap.

"Let's go," Charles said and stood up.

"Thanks for the help," I said, as I stood up and opened the door.

"We're on the same team," Charles said, as he walked to the door and went out in the squad room.

George followed with the baseball cap in his hand.

I followed them in the squad room and watched as they walked to the door.

The man that Charles had called Pete opened the door and looked outside for several seconds before saying, "It looks clear."

"Put the cap on," Charles said in a stern voice.

"Yes sir," George said, as he put the cap on and pulled it down over his eyes.

"I'll call you tomorrow and get an update on this case," Charles said and they went out the door.

After the door closed, I turned to Franklin and asked, "Do you have the name and address of our killer?"

"It just came through," he said, as he handed me a piece of paper.

I looked at the paper and read it twice. "I need to call for an arrest warrant and a warrant to search his house and car," I said, as I held the paper up.

"Do you think he'll put up a fight?" Franklin asked.

"Possibly," I said, as I walked toward my office door. Then I stopped and added, "I also need to get some backup from the Sheriff's department."

"Johnny and Richard should be here in about an hour," Franklin said.

"I know, but you and Tony need to go home and get some sleep so you can work tonight."

"So, you don't want us to be involved in the arrest?"

"I don't know when I'll get the arrest warrant and I need you here tonight."

"Alright, I understand."

"Please put on a fresh pot of coffee," I said, as I walked in my office and closed the door.

I sat down at my desk, picked up my phone and punched in our county DA's cell phone number.

She answered on the third ring and said, "Hello, Sherry Howard speaking."

"This is Sam James," I said. "I need an arrest warrant and a warrant to search our suspect's house and car."

"What evidence do you have?" she asked.

I told her about our witness and the information he had given.

After she had listened to everything I had to say, she asked, “Is he a reliable witness?”

“I think he is,” I said.

“Alright, I’ll call you back as soon as I have something,” she said and then my phone went dead.

I laid the phone down on the receiver then I picked it back up and called Marty Brees.

After the fourth ring, he answered and said, “This is Marty.”

“Marty, this is Sam,” I said. “I need some backup for an arrest this morning.”

“What time?” he asked.

“I’m not sure,” I said. “I haven’t gotten the warrant yet.”

“I’ll be in your office in about an hour,” he said and hung up.

As I placed my phone back on the receiver, Franklin opened my office door carrying a cup of fresh black coffee. He sat it on my desk and asked, “Is there anything I can do?”

“You just did what I needed,” I said. “Thanks, Franklin.”

“No problem,” he said and walked out the door.

I took a sip of coffee then picked up the stack of papers that Charles had laid on my desk and started reading over the report.

Chapter 74

I slowly leafed through the stack of papers while I watched the clock. As I read, I got a better understanding of why our killer had chosen the victims he had during his killing spree.

I finished reading page thirteen and was reaching for the next page when my phone started ringing. I grabbed the phone on the first ring and eagerly said, "This is Sam."

"I have your warrants," Sherry said. "I'm faxing them as we speak."

"Great," I said. "Who issued them?"

"Judge Powell," she said. "He wasn't happy being woken up, but he issued the warrants without much resistance."

"Thanks for your help," I said.

"No problem," she said and my phone went dead.

I placed my phone back on the receiver, pushed my chair away from my desk and got up. Then I opened the door and went to the fax machine to see if the fax had finished.

When I got close to the fax machine I saw a small stack of papers lying on top. I picked them up and slowly read over each page to make sure the warrants were written correctly to make the arrest stick. Then I went to the coffee pot and poured another cup of coffee.

As I turned to go back into the squad room, I saw Johnny and Richard sitting with their backs against their computers. Franklin and Tony were standing beside them talking.

I went where they were and stood listening to Franklin as he filled them in on what had happened throughout the night.

After he had finished, Johnny looked at me and asked, "Are we ready to make the arrest?"

"I'm waiting on Marty," I said.

"Be careful guys," Franklin said, as he walked to the door. "I'll see you tonight," and he went outside.

"See you tonight," Tony said, as he followed.

"Do you think he'll put up a fight?" Richard asked, as he got up and put his bullet resistant vest on over his shirt.

"With any luck, he'll think he can talk his way out of the arrest and not put up a fight," I said. "But everyone needs their bullet resistant vest on just in case."

"I'll put my vest on so I'll be ready when Marty gets here," Johnny said, as he got up and slipped his vest over his shirt.

I went in my office and put my vest on. Then I walked back in the squad room and said, "Now we're all ready to leave when Marty gets here."

"Where are we going?" Johnny asked.

I took a sip of coffee and started to answer when the door opened and Marty walked into the police station.

I watched him for a second then I asked, "Are you alone?"

"No, my guys are outside waiting for us," he answered, as he walked around and stood beside me.

I turned back to Johnny and said, "Alright, our suspect lives at 786 Willington

Heights."

"That's a pricey neighbor, isn't it," Johnny said.

"Yes, that's where the wealthy live," I said.

"They'll be shocked when we show up," Richard said.

"Let's try to be as quiet as possible because we might catch our suspect off guard," I said.

"What's the suspect's name?" Marty asked.

"According to his car registration, his name is Casey Frost," I said.

"Does he have a record?" Marty asked.

"Not that I'm aware of," I said, as I walked to the door, opened it and added, "Let's get him," and I held it open for everyone to walk out.

Marty was the first outside, than Richard and Johnny followed and stood beside my car.

Marty's deputies joined him at the front of my car and turned when I approached.

I moved to the center of everyone and said, "Let's be as quiet as we can, but most of all, let's be safe."

Marty looked at his deputies and said, "We're going to 786 Willington Heights," then he added, "I want y'all to stay in the rear and watch our backs."

"No problem," one of them said.

"I'll lead the way and everyone else just fall in place," I said, as I walked to the driver's side of my car and opened the door.

I watched as everyone got to their cars, then I got inside and closed the door. I cranked up, drove to the edge of the parking lot and waited for everyone to get behind me. After everyone was in line, I slowly turned left and drove toward the suspect’s house.

Chapter 75

I slowed as I neared the entrance to Willington Heights sub division and carefully turned through the giant iron bars that were used at night as a gate. I drove to the guard shack and stopped.

The guard stuck his head out the window with a questioning look on his face. He looked at my car, then looked at the others and asked, “What’s going on?”

“John, I didn’t know you were working here as a guard,” I said when I heard his voice and realized it was John Cox, a man I have known for years. “I heard that you retired from Franklin Lumber Company.”

“Yes, I retired a few months ago and realized quick that I needed a part time job to pay the bills,” he said and looked down for a second, then he added, “Sam, I couldn’t see myself as a store greeter so I came here to work.”

“This looks like a quiet place to work,” I said.

“It don’t pay much but it is quiet and these people tip very well,” he said, then he looked back at the row of police cars and asked, “Why are you here?”

“We have business to attend to,” I said.

“What kind of business?” he asked.

“Police business,” I said, as I looked down the street and asked, “Where is 786?”

“The residents here aren’t going to like me letting you in without calling them first to let them know that you’re here,” he said.

“I have a warrant to arrest a murder suspect and to search his house,” I said. “Are you going to interfere with me executing this warrant?”

"No Sam," he said as his eyes widened. "I'll help you whatever way I can."

"Good," I said. "Where is 786?"

"786," he said as he thought on which house that number was attached to and added, "take the first left, drive two block, turn right and it's the first house on your right."

"Thanks John," I said and I drove away.

I turned left, drove two blocks and stopped. I looked in my rearview mirror and watched as Marty pulled in behind me, followed by Johnny and Richard and then Marty's deputies. When I got out of the car, I could see the house we were looking for through the trees.

"That's our target," I said and pointed through the trees at a large white house with dark red shudders. There was a large porch that ran along the front of the house with four white columns that extended to the second floor balcony.

Marty looked where I was pointing and said, "Big house."

"Apparently you can make a lot of money selling drugs," I said.

"Until you get caught or killed," Marty added.

"Alright," I said. "Marty and I'll go to the front door. Johnny, you and Richard go to the back door and the rest of you stay out here and watch for any potential danger."

Marty looked at his deputies and said, "That's the plan so let's do it," and he started toward the house.

I hurried to catch up with him and we stopped at the edge of the street in front of the house.

Johnny and Richard ran to the house beside our targets and disappeared around the corner into the back yard.

After they disappeared, I ran across the street and hunkered behind a large Butterfly bush beside the mailbox at the end of the driveway.

Marty ran past me and stopped at the edge of the porch beside the front door.

I looked at the house for movement but didn't see anything so I ran to where Marty was hidden and stopped.

"Did you see anyone in the house?" Marty asked.

"No, I didn't see anyone," I said. "I think he's asleep."

I looked toward the front door one more time to see if anyone was in sight, then I eased up the steps trying not to make any noise and stopped beside the front door.

Marty followed and went to the other side of the door.

I took my gun out of my holster and used it to knock on the door.

After several seconds and no answer, I knocked again and yelled, "Police, open the door!"

"I think I hear someone," Marty said.

"Keep your pants on," came a voice from inside the house. "I'm opening the door," and I heard someone unlocking the door.

I stepped back with my gun drawn as the door opened and a man wearing a pair of shorts and a tee shirt asked, "Can I help you?"

"Are you Casey Frost?" I asked.

"I might be," he said. "What do you want?"

"I'm Sam James with the Thorton police department and you're under arrest for the murder of Ben Lowe."

"I didn't kill no body," he said, as he stepped out on the porch and closed the door.

"That's for a jury to decide," I said, as I cuffed his hands behind his back.

"I'll be out in a few hours," he said confidently.

"Marty, will you have your deputies drive their car up here and take this guy to jail while we search the house?" I asked.

"Sure," he said and he took his cell phone out of his shirt pocket and punched in some numbers.

"You can't search my house," he demanded. "You arrested me on my porch. You have no right to go inside my house."

"I have a warrant that states that I have the right to search your house and car for the weapon used to kill Ben Lowe," I said.

"You'll regret this," he growled and glared at me.

In less than a minute, I heard a car pull into the driveway.

Marty said, "They're here."

I watched as they got out of their car and began walking toward the porch, but stopped at the base of the steps when Johnny walked around the house.

He walked up the steps and said, "I see you got him."

"Yes, he stepped out on the porch without putting up a fight," I said, as I looked behind Johnny and asked, "Where's Richard."

"He stayed by the back door."

"Read our suspect his rights and then take him to the sheriff's car," I said. "They'll take him to the police station for us."

"Do you want me to follow them to the station?" Johnny asked.

"Yes, follow them and book him when you get there," I said.

"No problem," he said.

"Go with this officer," I said and I nudged the suspect toward Johnny.

"Hey, stop pushing me!" the suspect yelled.

"Come with me," Johnny said, as he started reading him his rights and lead him down the steps.

After Johnny was off the porch, Marty looked at me and said, "I have some things I have to do but I want to talk to you about something this afternoon."

"Come by my office when you're through and we'll talk," I said.

"I'll be there," Marty said and he walked down the steps and went to his car.

I opened the door and went inside the house. I looked around the living room for a few seconds then I went in the kitchen and unlocked the backdoor.

Richard jumped when the door opened and swung his gun around toward me.

"Be careful with that thing!" I yelled as I dodged behind the door frame.

"I'm sorry, you startled me," Richard said, as he lowered his gun and walked into the kitchen.

"We need to search for the weapon he used to kill Ben Lowe," I said.

"Where is everyone?" Richard asked, as he looked around the kitchen.

"Johnny went with sheriff's deputies and the prisoner to the station to book him," I said. "And Marty has some business to attend to."

"So, it's just us two looking for the gun?" he asked.

"For now," I said. "If we don't find it, I'll call for help."

"Alright," he said. "Where do you want me to start?"

"I'd say the most likely place for him to have hidden it is upstairs or in his car," I said. "Let's start upstairs," and I started walking toward the stairs.

Richard followed.

I slipped on a pair of gloves and went in the suspect's bedroom. When I got inside, I looked around and decided to start looking at his nightstand. I opened the top drawer which was mostly filled with papers and slowly began looking through the drawer. I glanced at a few of the papers as I lifted them out of the drawer then I laid them on the bed. After a while I just picked the whole stack up and put it on the bed.

I didn't find a gun in the top drawer, so I moved to the middle drawer. I spotted the black and silver handle of a hand gun protruding from under a magazine as soon as I opened the drawer. I looked around the room for something to put the gun in but when I didn't find anything, I went downstairs and got a zipped topped storage bag from the kitchen. Then I went upstairs and placed the gun in the bag. I held it up and examined the detail of the Romanian AK pistol as I zipped it tight. Then I laid the gun on the bed and continued looking through the nightstand.

After I finished with the nightstand, I looked under the bed where I found a Bushmaster Superlite rifle and a gym bag filled with hundred dollar bills. I laid them on the bed and moved to the closet.

The closet was a room to itself. Two walls were lined with shelves from floor to ceiling and the back wall had a rack of clothes hanging. I started with shelves to my right which was filled with shoes and baseball caps. He had a cap from every major league team with shoes to match each cap and on the shelves closest to his clothes he had dress shoes to match each suit.

After moving to the suits I separated them with my hands to look for anything that might be hidden. When I moved the suits, I instantly realized that there was another three feet of storage area behind the suits with boxes stacked about four feet high. I slid the suits over and wedged myself through the opening until I reached the boxes.

The first box I looked at was filled with small bags of white powder which resembled cocaine. I moved to the next box and found the same thing. The first two stacks were filled with the same white powder. The third, fourth and fifth stack had bricks of what looked like heroin and the last stack of boxes where filled with hundred dollar bills.

I eased to the middle of the closet, took my cell phone out of my pocket and called Charles Wallace. After he answered, I told him of my find and asked for his help. He said that he and some DEA agents would be at the house in less than an hour and hung up.

I put my phone back in my pocket and turned to the shelves that I hadn't looked through. There were only two boxes on one of the shelves and the rest was empty. I opened the first one and looked inside. It had a blender in it, so I moved to the other box.

At the opened the box I found a single piece of paper with a list of names written in dark black ink. When I picked the paper up, I found something wrapped in newspaper lying underneath. I glanced at the names which were mainly a list of the people that have been killed then I picked up the newspaper and un-wrapped a Ruger LCP semiautomatic handgun. We got a plastic bag and closed it up inside.

I continued searching the bedroom but I didn't find any more weapons. Then I went downstairs where Richard was waiting. I laid the guns at the base of the stairs when I got downstairs. Richard was holding a Beretta 92 FS 9mm handgun in his right hand.

I opened a plastic bag and said, "Put it in here," and I zipped it closed and laid it with the others.

"Looks like you found an arsenal," Richard said, as he pointed to the guns.

"That's not all I found," I said. "He had boxes filled with money and drugs in his bedroom."

"I guess you can't store that stuff just anywhere," he said.

"I guess not," I agreed.

I looked around as the door opened and Charles Wallace walked through the door with three large men.

"Where's the drugs?" one of the men asked.

"Upstairs in the back of his closet," I answered, as I looked at Charles.

Two of the men raced upstairs while the other one stayed beside Charles.

"I see you found some guns," Charles said and he pointed to the pile of guns lying on the floor.

"Yes, I hope one of them can help prove that he kill Ben Lowe," I said.

"Are you going to take them to the CSI lab?" Charles asked.

"Yes, I thought I would once we lock the house up," I said.

"You can leave now if you want to, because this house now belongs to the DEA," Charles said. "We would take the guns but since I know you're taking them to the CSI lab to help with your murder investigation I'll let you take them."

"Those belong to the DEA also," said the man beside Charles.

"I know but we know where they will be if we need them," Charles said. "and right now he needs them more than you do."

"Thanks," I said, as I picked up the guns and walked out the door.

I got in my car, drove to the CSI lab and dropped the guns off. Then I drove back to the police station to meet with Marty at two o'clock.

Chapter 76

I was in my office looking over the report on Ben Lowe when Marty opened the door and asked, "Are you busy?"

"Just looking over this report," I said. "Come on in Marty."

He walked in with a cup of coffee in each hand and sat them both on my desk. Then he sat down in one of the straight backed chairs and said, "You need to get better chairs in here."

"If I had the budget I would," I said and leaned back in my nice padded chair.

"What're you reading?" Marty asked.

"Charles brought in a file on Ben Lowe which helps me to understand why our killer killed the people he did," I said.

"Can you prove the guy we arrested this morning killed Ben Lowe?"

"Yes, I got a call from Janice at the CSI lab just before you got here and one of the guns we found in his house matched the bullet that killed Ben," I said. "It also matched the bullets that killed a lot of our other victims."

"So he can be linked to some of the other killings," Marty said.

"Yes, his gun was used to kill Rodney and Rocky Curry and Ruby and Angel Marks and probably more people that haven't been matched yet," I said.

"Why did he kill his victims?" Marty asked.

"The guy we arrested today calls himself Casey Frost but his real name is Butch Frost and according to the file he was shot and thought to be dead about a year ago. He was shot by Rodney Curry who wanted to take over the drug business in Thorton," I said.

"What part did Ben Lowe play in this?" Marty asked.

"Apparently he teamed up with Rodney Curry and helped plan the takeover. He was the brains behind building a meth lab and drug distribution center at the Millwood Fabric Warehouse and he also helped persuade Frost's drug dealers to change allegiance and to sell for Curry."

"So, this was revenge," Marty said.

"Yes, this was a drug revenge," I said. "And in the process we had one drug dealer killed and we have one behind bars."

"Someone will come and fill that opening," Marty said.

"I know because there's always a need for drugs on the street," I said and I laid the file down. "But we do our best to keep the streets safe."

"Yes we do," Marty agreed.

"And this one will be sent away to prison for a long time," I said. "And his house will be sold or used as a safe house."

"Speaking of a safe house, what about your witness?" Marty asked.

"I have enough evidence to convict Frost without a witness, so I don't think the DA will put him at risk by putting him on the witness stand," I said.

"Good," Marty said.

"What did you have to ask me?" I asked.

"I have an opening in the department for a detective and I want you to apply for the job," Marty said and smiled.

"What?" I asked questioning. "You want me to work for you?"

"I can give you a ten thousand dollar a year raise and you won't have to worry about your budget," he said hopefully.

"That's a surprise," I said. "I'll need to think about it and talk to Jenna before I make a decision."

"Just think about it and let me know in a couple of days," he said.

"I've worked here for 25 years," I said.

"Just think about it," he said and he walked out the door.

I sat for a few minutes in a daze then I got up and walked to the dispatcher's office. I stuck my head in and said, "I'm going home," and I walked out the door.

Made in the USA
Charleston, SC
05 November 2011